FALLOUT

Best wishes

Dave Norton

FALLOUT

DAVE NORTON

Matador
9 Priory Business Park,
Wistow Road, Kibworth Beauchamp,
Leicestershire. LE8 0RX
Tel: 0116 279 2299
Email: books@troubador.co.uk
Web: www.troubador.co.uk/matador
Twitter: @matadorbooks

ISBN 978 1785898 754

British Library Cataloguing in Publication Data.
A catalogue record for this book is available from the British Library.

Printed and bound in the UK by TJ International, Padstow, Cornwall
Typeset in 11pt Minion Pro by Troubador Publishing Ltd, Leicester, UK

Matador is an imprint of Troubador Publishing Ltd

MIX
Paper from
responsible sources
FSC® C013056

To Christine - as always
and Clare and Richard
who helped without knowing.

PROLOGUE

Wednesday 22nd February 2223

Mike Cannon, holdall bag in his right hand, walked through the doorway and out into the cool, bright early morning air. He had taken three steps down the drive when the door clicked shut behind him prompting him to drop his bag to the ground, raise his left hand and check the time by his watch.

It was 0858.

He smiled to himself, wryly.

His due release date had been set for the next day – Thursday at 0900. He had been given a remission of just 24 hours and two minutes. Just his luck that the amnesty granted to prisoners serving 21 years had only come into force that very morning.

Mike looked up towards the end of the drive. A light flashed briefly as the low rays of the winter sun reflected from the windscreen of a car as it turned carefully in from the road. He watched as the driver pulled over then reversed into one of the parking spaces reserved for visitors. Right on time. Brother Frank had arrived, just as arranged, to whisk him away to a new, unfamiliar civilian life. Retrieving his bag Mike walked briskly towards the car, heading for the nearside front door but it wasn't until he extended his hand to grasp the handle that he noticed Frank gesticulating pointedly toward the passenger door on the other side. He grinned, scuttled around the back of the car and after placing his bag on the back seat quickly stowed himself in the front; he had forgotten that during his long stay in HM Burton Green prison Britain had forsaken the tradition of driving on the left hand side of the road. First Ireland and then Great Britain had joined the rest of Europe in taking to the right.

'Welcome to the real world,' said Frank, pointedly, as he pressed the ignition, checked for traffic and pulled out onto the drive, then the road, putting distance between themselves and Mike's home of the past decade. Burton Green was the last of three prisons that had been responsible for Mike whilst serving his 21 year penance.

They travelled for the most part in silence rather like a hire car driver concentrating on the road with his passenger lost in his own thoughts. The morning's programme had been carefully planned and set out by Frank over the last few months during his fortnightly visits to his younger brother on the inside. Frank didn't like loose ends. He had taken every step to ensure that the first few hours of Mike's freedom would be trouble free. There was little left to discuss.

Like Frank, Mike concentrated on the road. At first tensing and gripping his seat as they approached roundabouts he gradually relaxed as his body grew accustomed to the changed road layouts but as they travelled to their pre-arranged destination there were other things that made him feel as though he had stumbled upon a foreign land. Motorways were no longer motorways; they had become Expressways. And the surface of each departing slip-road was coloured to indicate the class of road that the motorist was approaching: Blue for another expressway, green when joining any other major route and red-brown for moving onto a local or rural road. Frank, making a rare comment, explained that the colour reminded the driver of the speed restriction to be expected when joining the new road. The police often lay in wait at the foot of a slip road to catch the unwary motorist as Frank had found out to his cost on a couple of occasions. The sight of a police traffic control vehicle reminded Mike of another change. The police no longer seemed to routinely carry firearms and he had not spotted the expected camouflaged tank or armoured car at or near strategic road junctions. All signs of the civil conflict of two decades earlier had disappeared.

They followed the E45 expressway eastwards, skirting the southern edge of the city of Coventry until, soon after passing the Kenilworth road junction they took a slip-road, coloured green, to the right onto the main road heading south towards Banbury. That Oxfordshire town, though, was some way beyond their planned destination. Not far past a junction signed Leamington another right-hand spur, this time coloured red-brown, brought them to a local road and the settlement of Hunningham. This village, previously of little interest to any but its residents, had grown in recent years on the back of the prosperity that had been enjoyed by the West Midlands as a whole. Smart, self-contained commuter developments marked the edge of Hunningham with Coventry close at hand

and central Birmingham reached, on a good traffic day, within 30 minutes. But it was towards the village centre that Frank directed his car, reducing speed at first to comply with the urban speed limit and than to allow him to spot the turning into Heathway Court. Reaching the entrance between two buildings in the main street they turned left into a small housing development comprising three four-storey blocks on the left hand side of the access road. Frank drove into a parking area behind the third block and slowed to a halt squarely in a light-blue outlined space numbered 32. There were two such parking places; the other was empty as were two adjacent spaces each numbered 31 and most of the others on that Wednesday mid-morning.

They sat quietly for a few seconds before Frank turned and stretched round to the rear seat to retrieve two small packages. He passed them across to Mike who opened the first one and took out a set of keys - a keycard and several smaller deadlock keys linked by a tag marked with the number 32 on the fob - which he placed on the dashboard, neatly folding the empty envelope before slipping it into an outside jacket pocket. The second envelope contained a small wad of banknotes. He didn't count the cash but pushed the notes back into the envelope, refolding the flap before stowing it inside his jacket. Picking up the keys he transferred them to his left hand and offered the right to his brother.

They shook.

'Thanks,' he said. 'I owe you.'

Without replying Frank leaned across and embraced Mike then settled back into his driving position. Mike got out and rescued his holdall from the rear seat before walking to the front and rapping on the driver's window to indicate that he was ready. Frank lowered the window.

'Bye. That's me done. Next time you need help ask your sister.'

Without further comment he raised the window, put the car into reverse, backed out of the parking slot and turned towards the road. Pausing briefly to check for traffic he raised his hand as a sign of farewell and drove away. He had done as his younger brother had asked and that was that; he had no plans to see him again anytime soon.

Studying the keys in his hand Mike turned towards the front door of his new home. He placed the larger mortise key in the lock and turned it. There was a brief, sharp click. Entry was completed by swiping the keycard and pushing the door open. He dropped his holdall down in the hallway and took a cursory tour of the accommodation. It was just as he had requested. Downstairs comprised a lounge/dining area with, off to one side, a small kitchen with essential facilities. The stairs rising from the corner of the lounge accessed two bedrooms and a shower room on the first floor. There was a toilet behind the fourth door off the small landing and another downstairs behind a door that Mike had previously thought was a cupboard. Pleased with the layout and tired by his first hour of freedom he put water on to boil for a hot drink, tried the video unit on the wall by flicking through a few television channels and checked that the mobile PERC (personal communicator) lying on the lounge table was live and working. It was. Also awaiting his attention on the table was a file containing papers relating to the purchase and ownership of Unit 32, Heathway Court plus agreements for the supply of power and water together with receipts for the purchase of furniture and household items. Perused briefly the papers were stuffed back into their folder and pushed towards the rear of the table to be dealt with later.

The water boiled.

Back in the kitchen he took down a mug from a line of three occupying a shelf then turned to a wall cabinet that contained a good stock of food including the immediately needed coffee and biscuits. Further investigation identified a fridge/freezer. The main compartment revealed milk and other items but the freezer section was empty apart for an envelope addressed simply to 'Mike'. Coffee made he sat down at the table, took a sip of his drink, opened the envelope and took out a single handwritten sheet.

'OK. That's it then', he read. 'You're stocked up until you can find your way round to the local shops. Not that there are many. Utilities have been paid till the end of next month so from April it's down to you. I've done what I could but stocking the freezer would have been beyond the call of brotherly duty. All the best. F.'

The note ended with a PS.

'Don't try getting in touch - I've changed all my contact numbers and addresses.'

Mike knew the PS was a joke but the humour did not completely mask a serious meaning. He had been given an hour and a half of Frank's time that morning plus a few words and a brief note. It was probably more than he deserved. Oh, yes. And he'd purchased a house for him.

And furniture and food. A few tears formed in the corners of his eyes, misting his view. He wiped them away and sat for a long time, thinking and remembering.

When he next sipped at his coffee it had cooled to an unpleasant temperature and a glance at the time on the screen of his PERC mobile made Mike realise how long it had been since he had eaten breakfast - eaten in another place, a place now firmly rooted in his past. In just four hours Burton Green Prison had become as alien to him as the life prison itself had eclipsed 21 years earlier. Mike stood, stretched and walked around the table towards the kitchen with lunch preparation in his mind when he was stopped in his tracks by the tones of his PERC ringing behind him. He reached back, fumbled with the unfamiliar icons and eventually breathed a slightly flustered 'Hi' into the machine. But it was not a phone call. A message on the screen asked if he wanted to read a text. Disappointingly it was just a welcome message from the PERC operating company but a second message just a few minutes later raised his spirits. Rapidly becoming familiar with the system he scrolled through the new text, producing a smile while he did.

'Welcome 2 yr new home, Josh. I've done as U asked. Let me know when U R ready. Love Sis'.

Mike's sister Gayle was about the only person who regularly used his first forename - Joshua. She had little money of her own and couldn't have found him a house in a hundred years but she was always happy to manage small tasks and was always pleased to see him. Gayle was truly loyal; not once had she expressed a personal opinion on his way of life either in prison or before. He sent an immediate reply.

'Thanks. Will B in touch soon. Regards to Rupert. Love, Josh.'

Buoyed up by Gayle's message he grabbed his bag from the hall and forgetting lunch ran upstairs to the second bedroom. There was no bed, no wardrobe nor bedside table. But the room was furnished. Under the window was a work surface topped by a computer with a monitor wired into a universal media point. A remote-sensor controlled multi-function printer allowed him to operate all the other functions he needed - phone, scan, copy and of course print. The pedestal cabinet that supported the desk to the right of the chair space consisted of three drawers, all empty but a cupboard fitted on an adjacent wall opened up to reveal not the rails, drawers and shelves of a wardrobe as had been envisaged when it was built but just shelves supporting boxes of paper (plain and lined), pens, clips, reels of tape and other items of stationary. Everything was just as he had asked. Mike had nearly completed the mental inventory of his office equipment when an unfamiliar chime heralded a visitor at his door. Since as far as he knew only Frank and Gayle (and the prison authorities) knew where he was he thought it must be a chance caller. When he moved to the window and squinted through the blind he was unable to see who was standing at the door but he had a good idea as one of his two parking spaces was now occupied by a clearly marked police van.

Mike trotted down stairs but not quick enough to avoid a second round of the door chime. The opened door revealed a uniformed policewoman holding a thin, brightly coloured orange folder. Her request to come in, although phrased as a question, left Mike in no doubt that he had little choice but to welcome his visitor. The officer declined Mike's offer of a seat and, remaining standing, opened the folder and handed over all the papers needed to establish his identity as a civilian British citizen:

- Registration details for a National Identity Card to replace his current provisional issue. Application online.
- Registration details for inclusion on the local electoral roll. Application on-line or in person at the local District Office.
- Application for a GB Passport. Application online or in person at the Passport Office in Birmingham.

Mike signed a form to show that he had received the post-release visit, confirmed that he would report to Coventry Central police station within the next three days and saw the officer to the door. As she was about to leave the policewoman turned and reminded Mike that any breach of his release conditions could see him returned to jail immediately. But this comment was unnecessary as he had no intention of going back to prison; he had far better things to do with his life. A brief thought that twenty years earlier he would have found the slim, dark haired policewoman rather attractive and the awareness that in fact he still did was soon replaced by thoughts of returning to the unfinished investigation of the spare bedroom upstairs. And that thought was itself eclipsed almost immediately by the gnawing realisation that he had now not eaten for some time.

A meal, a shower, a change of clothes and he was soon back in his office. IT skills learnt at school and used during has career as a journalist had been updated whilst he had been locked away so he was soon able to master the fairly simple set up he had asked Frank to obtain for him. Satisfied that he could now press on with his project he sat back and relaxed, staring at the monitor for a couple of minutes whilst he assembled his thoughts. Suddenly he leant forward and tapped an icon on the screen. The bland default pattern that backed the icons on his monitor screen was one he decided he could not live with a moment longer. He flicked through the thumbnails of about two dozen available backdrops. Of course he could customise the design but that would be for later. At present he just wanted to have a home page that would be a welcome to him whenever he logged on. Making his choice he tapped the thumbnail he required and the screen was filled with backdrop 17 - a large white bird flying through a lightly clouded sky above a choppy active sea. He nodded to himself, tapped an OK box and rearranged the home page icons so that they stood out clearly against the light blue of the sky.

Now ready to start he tapped the icon for New Word and brought up a blank page. Not for Mike one of the popular dictation to computer programmes such as Dictacom; he wanted to feel the full impact of each word as he set it down. He needed to set the record straight; to see and feel the work as it progressed.

A brief tapping at the keyboard brought up a title at the head of the first page.

'Mike Cannon's Diary'

He considered it for a few moments; he wasn't convinced that it was the most suitable title. The main text of his story was in his mind, written and refined over many years in prison. Word perfect. The small matter of the title could wait a while.

Mike leant forward again and wrote a sentence. Mike Cannon had started to write his memoirs.

PART ONE

THE REPORTER

CHAPTER ONE
THE BEGINNING

Thursday 2nd March 2180

Thursday, 1828 hours. 3 Gateacre Street, Redditch, West Midlands.

The doorbell rang. Alana Buckhurst, newly 13 years old, ran to the front door to welcome the first guests to her birthday party. Just six minutes and three more rings on the doorbell later Alana and her five friends were settled in the lounge, plates of snackable food within reach on a set of low tables and a video film newly ordered ready to download and view on the large wall screen. But, food apart this was hardly a traditional teenager's birthday party. A house party without non-stop music, a good supply of the so-called '12+' slightly alcoholic drinks and at least thirty people would have been rated as 'odd' or 'cheap' and shunned by most of her classmates but Alana's guests had been selected with care – they were all fans of the latest cult video series entitled 'War Heroes.' The original highly popular screening had been televised about six years previously with the re-release some months ago bringing the drama to the attention of a new, younger audience. Episodes of this epic followed the military exploits of succeeding generations of the Elverson family starting with the Great War in Europe in 1914, encompassing other conflicts of the 20th and 21st centuries and ending in the early years of the current century. From the eleven dramas the assembled friends had chosen to start with episode three chronicling the actions of marine James Elverson in the Falkland's War of 1982. It was a story complicated by James' marriage three years earlier to an Argentinean girl.

Alana was not too concerned about the choice of episode since the main birthday present from her parents had been the gift of membership of the Masterview Online Video Club and War Heroes episode 3 was just one film from the vast library that she was now able to access using her new credit account. To her surprise, excitement and great pleasure the film was prefaced with a personal welcome to the online service, arranged by her parents, together with the promise that her first evening's requests could be viewed absolutely free. Her credit remained intact. The little group soon settled down and apart from the odd one-off comment and the sound of munching they sat back contentedly as the titles rolled away to reveal the opening scene – a panoramic view across the rugged terrain of the Falklands; the hostile environment in which James Elverson became a true war hero.

Thursday, 1850 hours. The Ipswich Hospital, Suffolk.

Mr and Mrs Cannon's baby son's first cry was chronicled at ten to two that Thursday afternoon. At that moment he had not yet been blessed with forenames and his hospital record was simply headed Baby Cannon –

male. But before long he had been visited by his four year old brother Frank and his sister Gayle, Frank's junior by a year and by the time Frank, Gayle and their father had left for home half an hour later the fifth member of the family had been awarded the forenames Joshua Michael. Frank was a little cool about the addition of a rival male sibling but Gayle was cock-a-hoop with excitement. Yes, she had reassured her father, she knew that Joshua was not something to be played with like a doll but all the same she knew her little brother would need looking after and she would be happy to play her part. At 1922 hours the visitors departed to their home in the village of Reydon, near Southwold on the Suffolk coast leaving baby Joshua Michael and his exhausted mother to sleep and be reunited as a family the following day.

Thursday, 1928 hours. The Corner House, near Denham, Buckinghamshire.

Stacy Kenton and his wife Tallin Green settled down to watch the television. They had chosen to leave the large video screen in the lounge to the children and use the small freestanding set in Stacy's office. By that time probably about a third of the adult population of Great Britain were to be found looking at a monitor or a screen or had just called up National Channel One on their personal phone. The upcoming political broadcast by the First Minister had been widely advertised and the media had spent the previous week speculating on its possible content. Normal dreary pre-election broadcasts naturally gained far less attention unless attended by some recent scandal or a political event that had split the nation but there had been a General Election just eight months earlier and with the government's good working majority their was little prospect of a repeat any time soon.

TV5 News channel had suggested that unspecified changes were afoot in Europe and The New Times newspaper had developed the theme in its online editions, citing a source in Strasbourg, reporting that there were plans to split the European Union into eastern and western economic blocks. In contrast the Daily Register and its sister television channel UK Update thought that First Minister Kym Boston would announce her resignation over rumours of a fatal drug-fuelled driving accident during her student days in Aberdeen. Channel Four television news as usual provided the definitive version of the event explaining that the RTA referred to by the Register had actually involved a Kim Boston, a male student at Aberystwyth University, and in any case the Kym Boston who was later to become First Minister was then, before her marriage to James Boston, known as Kym Blackwall. At the time of the incident she was a postgraduate student studying in America. The Daily Register was not known for checking details carefully but was more than capable of selling enough papers, both on and off line, to cover the cost of frequent forays into the courts to defend the type of reporting that kept its circulation buoyant.

Kym Boston, the First Minister, was Stacy Kenton's boss. Five years previously Stacy had been elected as the English Nationalist Member of Parliament for the South Chiltern constituency. A minority party at the time, the

Nationalists had subsequently risen to power on the back of a Conservative party scandal. The English Nationalists in coalition with their Welsh and Scottish equivalents became the government and to show that they stood for real change the Prime Minister now called herself First Minister and Parliament had became the National Council. The members of parliament were, however, still known as MPs – Members of Parliament. So Stacy was now the MP for South Chiltern and a member of the governing party.

The last advertisement faded prompting Tallin to zap up the sound. A temporarily blank screen was replaced by a formal title in white on a deep blue background. It read:

A broadcast by the
First Minister,
the Honourable Kym Boston, MP

Stacy considered momentarily that perhaps he should have been sitting in a Westminster bar, viewing the broadcast with some of his Nationalist colleagues but a quick glance across at Tallin and her subsequent smile confirmed in his mind that he preferred being at home even if staying in Westminster would have been a wiser career move. The clock ticked over to 1930 and the title faded to be replaced by a view of Ms Boston sitting behind a desk that supported only a glass of water with a plain beige-coloured wall forming the backdrop. It was the First Minister's office at Westminster. Stacy knew that over her plain white blouse, unadorned by jewellery, the smart, plain, dark blue suit would be a trouser suit and he suspected that, hidden by the desk she was wearing the comfortable trainer shoes she habitually wore when not addressing the Council. He also noted that some time had been spent by the make-up team in reducing but not completely obliterating an area of dark skin on her left jawline.

The Kentons watched and listened.

'Good evening. I have decided to take the unusual step of explaining a new policy to you all. The project I shall describe is just that: A project. It has not yet been examined by your National Council. It is my government's preferred policy but we feel it is so revolutionary that we need to hear your views before we commend it to parliament. An election on this matter, or a referendum, would be enormously expensive. We need you all, therefore, to consider the plan that I shall put before you and let your own Member of Parliament know your views. This is not strictly a party matter. The Council will decide on the basis of the views that you express.'

The FM paused and took a sip of water from the glass. Stacy knew it was a ploy to divide up her speech, rather like starting a new paragraph on the written page. Now for the serious part.

'The Nationalists were voted into office less than a year ago,' she continued, 'with a programme to improve key features of our national life – Health, Security and Housing as priorities and, in the longer term Employment and Education. A common feature of all these programmes is our care for the environment. A particular ongoing concern of your government has been the loss of land, transport links and communities to the erosive action of the sea; a loss that *has been made worse by the consequences of a prolonged period of global warming. We have listened to academic forecasts for the rate of coastal loss and the practicability of repulsing this attack on our land and we have come to the conclusion that the present rate of expenditure will allow us to do little to help any but the most vulnerable communities. We are struggling to keep control and would have to divert large sums of money from other projects were we to plan complete control of this problem. However doubling or even trebling the budget would do little to satisfactorily handle the projected rates of destruction.'*

Another pause, another sip of water.

This time the camera moved in to give a closer view of the First Minister.

'After much thought and with considerable regret we conclude that we must abandon extensive coastal areas to the sea and also allow a few inland areas to become flooded. We shall use the funds available to support economically sensitive coastal areas and where we are unable to provide such protection we shall support displaced communities and replace vital road and rail links. This is not the time to describe all the measures we would like to take. From tomorrow these details will be available on the government netsite. For the present I shall just list the main features of our proposed action. We would provide generous grants for relocation within Britain or emigration to a number of recommended nations abroad. We would also support the creation of new communities inland where local councils feel the action justifiable – money would be available for

businesses to relocate or individual workers to retrain and learn new skills. Remnant local populations would be supported by national rather than local funds and these areas would be categorised as Restricted Areas, localities to which the new legislation would apply. In the longer term it may be necessary to use military personnel to support the police, borderguards and local authorities in these areas. All such measures would be subject to the normal passage of an enabling bill through parliament.'

A slight pause but no drink.

'I commend these proposals to you. Thank you for listening. I wish you all a good night.'

Silence.

Momentarily there was a blank screen before the government netsite address appeared. This text faded to give a plain dark blue screen that was replaced after another few seconds by the usual heading for the National Channel One 1930 newscast. The time was 1933.

Thursday, 1934 hours.

Like millions of other viewers across the country Stacy Kenton stood up, reached for the remote control and zapped off the TV. The news they had just received was quite enough for the present and in any case would only be repeated as the main item on the now silenced evening news and other newscasts throughout the evening and on into the following morning.

* * * * *

Kym Boston stood up, smoothed down her jacket and walked across the room, past the assembled television crew and on towards a small group of her staff standing at the other end, just inside the door. A 'thumbs up' from her press secretary brought a smile to her face as she led the group to an adjacent room to face questions from a selected group of media people.

* * * * *

Alana Buckhurst leant forward and lifted up the plate carrying the last chocolate bar. She offered the food to her friends. Jake, Brandie and Anya politely turned down the offer but when the plate was offered to Kyle he happily devoured the last of the party food, even before the fifth guest, Carron, had been considered. Normally Alana would have made a caustic comment regarding Kyle's manners but today she was more concerned with her own thoughts. As the credits for War Heroes 3 rolled down the screen she decided on her future – a future in the armed forces. Her mind was made up. Alana Buckhurst had set her mind on becoming an officer in the British Army.

* * * * *

Young Joshua Michael Cannon lay in a cot beside his sleeping mother. He stretched an arm, gave a small grunt and settled back to sleep again just five hours and fifty four minutes into his independent life.

CHAPTER TWO
WHAT THE PAPERS SAY

Saturday 4th March 2180

Saturday, 0752 hours. The Corner House near Denham, Buckinghamshire

The New Times
London, Saturday 4th March 2180
FM appoints Minister for Coasts

'Yesterday the First Minister Kym Boston announced to the National Council that she had appointed the South Chiltern MP, Stacy Kenton, to the post of Junior Minister in the Environment Department. The new minister, aged 26, will be responsible for promoting her party's policy on coastal defence – the policy she had outlined in her recent television broadcast.

Since becoming a National Council Member Mr Kenton has proved to be hard-working and popular in his constituency and at Westminster. Of the 472 constituency MPs Mr Kenton had the fifth highest attendance in the House of Commons last session. His appointment has been generally well received. The opposition Environment spokesman, Ashley Portland, expressed the view that Mr Kenton was a fair-minded man who would be ready to listen to opposition concerns. Government whip, Magdalena High, ventured further to suggest that the new minister would bring a degree of flair and innovation to government activity. Some members feel that Stacy Kenton lacks parliamentary experience but in general MPs are happy to wait and see how he performs in his first government office before passing judgement.'

Tallin put down The Times, rifled through a pile of newspapers and leaflets and pulled out the Daily Register.

Daily Register
London, Saturday 4th March 2180
Turncoat Minister for Coasts

'Can we trust this man? Stacy Kenton – Nationalist Member of Parliament and now Junior Minister – was once a member of the Conservative Party. The Register can reveal exclusively that Mr Kenton entered politics as a Conservative on Wycombe District Council. When the time came to stand for re-election he changed sides to the Nationalists and following that poll control in Wycombe passed from the Conservatives to his new party, the Nationalists. It appears that Mr Kenton is prepared to change policies just to preserve his position in power.

We can also report that last week the new minister had talks with the Opposition leader. Was he thinking of reverting to his old party? Was yesterday's appointment just a bribe by the First Minister to keep him on board? Stacy Kenton's appointment does not fit well within a government that came to power with promises of honesty and transparency.

You can, however, rely on this newspaper. The Register promises to keep a close eye on the activities of the new Junior Minister for the Environment. If he steps out of line we'll let you – the British Public – know.'

'The Register is at it again,' complained Tallin between taking mouthfuls of toast at breakfast that morning. 'Can't you complain to the editor or the Press Bureau or someone?'

Stacy smiled.

'The problem is that the facts are correct. They just put unconnected items together to make a story. Yes, I was talking to Jason Temple and yes, he is the leader of the Opposition but as you know he is also MP for Chiltern North, a neighbouring constituency and as such we have many concerns in common. Last week we were talking about the proposed new village that, if constructed, would fall across the boundary of our two constituencies. Of course we talk. I'll leave it to The New Times or National Channel One TV to tell the public the full facts.'

Apparently unconcerned Stacy got up, gave Tallin a kiss, picked up his briefcase and set out for work on his first full day as a government minister.

CHAPTER THREE
REWARDS

Friday 13th November 2195

'The Reverend Gareth Shadwell stood at the head of the track leading from the road to St Lawrence church and stared in disbelief. Three finely carved stone gargoyles that had always adorned the buttresses on the south side of the knave had disappeared. Their former positions were marked by three rectangular patches on the stonework that stood out brighter and less weathered than the surrounding surfaces – stone facings that had for centuries suffered from the attention of rain, wind, frost and sun. Rev. Shadwell blinked, saw an unchanged scene and then jogged around to the north side of the church to find another three patches of newly exposed stonework marking the former resting place of three other gargoyles. He returned to the south side, looked up again and then searched through his pockets for his PERC phone. A theft on this scale needed to be reported immediately to the Bishop's office. A brief conversation with one of the secretaries and then he was left sitting on the bench outside the church tower waiting for the promised prompt reply.*

Gareth had been rector of nearby Great Thornhill for

thirty seven years. Fifteen years ago the parish of St Lawrence in Spredishall, a largely depopulated community reduced in area as the sea had eaten away at its eastern edge, had been amalgamated with Great Thornhill and it had become his habit to visit this outlying part of the combined parishes on the first Monday of each month. Leaving his car beside the road he had habitually walked the 300 metres to the church, unlocked the security gate to the porch and then the heavy oak door to the knave. He held a brief service at 1000 hours, rarely attended by any parishioners, then set about his housekeeping tasks giving a quick dust to the altar area and the first few pews. Outside he would cut the grass in summer to restore the path to the church door and show some semblance of care for the few headstones still standing at the western end of the churchyard.

The rector's phone rang. As he expected it was the Bishop's office returning his call. The local constabulary, the Dean said, had been bypassed in favour of the specialist Art Theft Unit from Norwich. Could the Rev. Shadwell stay until they arrived? It would probably be within the next two hours.

After signalling agreement and with the conversation over the rector walked back to his car, found the bag containing his lunch and returned to the low wooden bench that had been provided in memory of a former churchwarden who had died many years ago at a time when St Lawrence's would see a regular if not large congregation each Sunday. Gareth would sit here on most visits, eat his lunch and in summer, if the weather allowed, doze in the warm sunshine for a few minutes before going on to visit the few parishioners still remaining in Spredishall.

At the start of the century there had been over 400 people living in the village. Even Gareth could remember when there were about 50 populated houses but now there were only five families and a further six people living alone. As the sea nibbled at the coast and the river marshes were transformed into a wide estuary there had been a steady demise of outlying farms. When things became so bad that the coast road had been threatened with collapse the local council applied for government funding and the road was re-routed two miles inland abandoning Spredishall on the backwater of a very minor road that led nowhere in particular. First the shop and then the pub, abandoned by passing traffic, closed down. Pupil numbers at the village school dwindled and those remaining were soon bussed to Great Thornhill until the numbers fell so far that the bus was replaced by a taxi. Families left. The government's relocation fund paid for a number of village families to move away – some to protected coastal towns such as Ipswich or Lowestoft, others to new housing and jobs provided by the New Towns inland whilst yet others emigrated to South Africa or New Zealand. The community had been dispersed, now held together today only by the Spredishall Memorial Netsite.

Two police officers arrived. They inspected the expertly cut surfaces. Not hacked out. Not pure opportunist vandalism but a well planned operation.

'Planned,' stated the older officer. 'Stolen to order. It's unlikely you'll ever see them again. You might just as well have reported the theft of a garden gnome for all the effort that's likely to go into solving this case. However we'll pass our report on to our senior officer; probably search a few abandoned farms nearby.'

Smuggling goods in and out of remote Suffolk coastal locations had become a growth industry. At first organised as small scale operations by local inhabitants deprived of their livelihoods in farming or service industries, these operations were replaced by professional gangs involved in a lucrative international trade. With the depleted police force, cut to match the decimated population and the overstretched borderguard unable to cope, the more sophisticated smuggling groups operated almost at will.

The police left. Rev. Shadwell locked up, returned to his car and started a belated tour of the much shrunken village with its ageing population.'

Mike Cannon put down the paper he was reading and looked out of the bus window. They slowed and pulled into the central lane at the Henstead turn whilst the driver gauged the traffic on the other carriageway before turning onto the detour to that village before returning to the main A12 road again at Wrentham. They were half way home. Mike folded the paper and put it into his bag before pulling out another edition of the same paper, the *Carlton Reporter.* Of course the journal was published and distributed electronically but there were always paper prints for the college and town libraries and Mike usually had a few copies for his own records. For some time now he had been in the habit of printing draft copies so that his articles could be corrected easily. He found it more convenient and relaxing to lie on his bed and flick over sheets of print than sit hunched over a monitor or peering into an e-book.

Mike, aged 15, was not exactly a fan of the education

provided for him at Carlton College in Lowestoft; he would rather be out in the countryside around his home village of Reydon. Fishing, cycling and exploring were the activities he preferred greatly to the standard school fare offered by the National Curriculum. Apart from English. The one lesson that kept him at the top of the attendance lists was his daily exposure to the written word. Better still was the time spent working on the college's twice-termly publication, the *Carlton Reporter*. Dinner breaks and after lessons he could be found in the small room, little more than a cupboard, where the 'Reporter' was produced. He was neither editor nor chief reporter but it was Mike's work as a columnist that had earned the Carlton College journal a prized national award just a week earlier.

Starting twelve months before, literally as a column, Mike's contribution had blossomed into an article so that "Here today, gone tomorrow" now occupied a whole page and sometimes more. Chronicling the impact of coastal erosion and climate change in East Suffolk the six articles written during that academic year had attracted the attention of the judges of a national competition promoting school and college journalism. In particular the panel of experts engaged by *'Schools' Writing'* magazine, published to stimulate budding authors and journalists, had picked on the story about the Vicar of Spredishall.

An engraved plaque now graced the trophy cabinet in the college reception area, a draft for a useful amount had been paid into the Carlton Reporter's bank account (an account that had to be opened especially to receive the prize) and a certificate lay in the front pocket of Mike's school bag.

Mike slid his hand into the bag, picked out the certificate and re-read the wording.

Young Journalist Competition 2195
First Prize
Awarded to the
Carlton Reporter and Joshua Michael Cannon

for his article entitled
'The Vicar and the Gargoyles'

Mike smiled to himself and carefully replaced the certificate in his bag before sitting back, oblivious to the noisy antics of a group of younger travellers and the view outside and casting his mind back to his interview with the now retired vicar. Following the award of the prize his article had been picked up and republished online in the regional daily 'East Anglian Guardian'. Mike promised himself that this was just the start. One day his writing would be on display nationwide and perhaps even further afield; he would, he was certain, become a famous journalist!

The bus turned into Green Lane to begin its tour of the village of Reydon before heading off to its Southwold destination. Somebody rang the bell – an unnecessary precaution since the bus always stopped halfway down the Lane, at the head of Mike's road. Hastily stowing the paper back into his bag he hurried to the exit and when the door opened jumped down onto the small roadside refuge that marked the bus stop on that side of the road that wasn't provided with a pavement. He waited for the bus to pull away before carefully checking the road for traffic. The recent removal of every third (and sometimes every second) street lamp had made Mike cautious when out in the dark. Just as well. Headlights suddenly turned into view from his right and came speeding towards him as he withdrew his foot to safety. A convoy passed by him travelling rather faster than the advertised speed limit for that road. A police 4WD was closely followed by an army all-terrain vehicle (ATV) and an armoured personnel carrier. They slowed a few metres after passing him and turned left into a lane, the convoy heading for the nearby hamlet of Reydon Smear. The sight of an army vehicle was not unusual. For much of his life, it seemed to Mike, he had lived in a Restricted Area where the police could call upon the armed services for support. In fact it had only been 5 years since East Suffolk had been given that status following on from earlier legislation when the authorities in Cumbria, West Wales and East Lincolnshire had been given the support of the army. As the population had declined and illegal activities such as smuggling increased the police and borderguard had found the task of keeping law and order almost impossible and the cost of such operations outside the competence of local finances. The convoy he had just seen appeared to be on an operation rather than just showing the flag.

Darkness and quiet descended as the sound of the convoy was lost as it travelled up the high-hedged lane. Mike checked again for traffic, crossed and turned into his own road. He had almost reached his house when, with a sudden throbbing roar, a helicopter rose from behind the houses ahead of him like a giant black insect, the intrusion of the growing, pulsating noise compounded a few moments later by the unexpected dazzling illumination of an airborne spotlight. Now behind him, Mike turned to watch the swath of light progress towards the area previously targeted by the army convoy. Gunfire crackled, followed by a heavier explosion and then a couple of dull thuds. Mike instinctively ran for the cover of his house but the event was over before he had turned his key in the door. As the countryside to the north subsided into its habitual calm winter blackness he pushed the door open and was safely home.

'Did you hear that, Frank?' he called to his brother who he assumed was somewhere in the house. 'What do you reckon they're after?'

'Probably another load of travellers,' Frank replied disinterestedly from behind a fishing magazine he was reading in the lounge.

'A bit heavy handed for travellers,' added their mother, calling through from the kitchen. 'Make sure you take your shoes off before charging upstairs, Michael. It's wet out there.'

'Anyway,' said Frank when a little later Mike, stocking-footed, joined him in the lounge. 'I'm sure it'll be on the late news.'

And so it was.

A dangerous prisoner, the newscaster reported, had escaped from jail in Norwich two days previously and had been cornered in a wood near Reydon on the Suffolk Coast. There had been a gunfight after which the fugitive had been recaptured, suffering minor injuries, and airlifted away to be taken first to hospital and then returned to prison.

'Well there we are then. We were all wrong,' stated Frank, referring to the opinions expressed earlier by his mother and his brother. Neither his father nor his sister Gayle were the sort of person to venture an opinion without the support of the media and Gayle, at 17, probably had her mind elsewhere.

'Who do they think they're kidding? We may've all been wrong. I accept that. But the story on the telly doesn't make much sense either,' stated Mike.

'OK brainbox. How do you work that one out? You're probably going to tell us whether we want to know or not so come on ace reporter – what's your take on it?'

'Well,' continued Mike, never shy of an invitation to express his views, 'first, they didn't report the escape of the prisoner yesterday. Usually they tell you the name and age of the prisoner and what crime landed him in jail followed by a warning not to approach him if he is thought to be dangerous. And they didn't interview a police or prison officer like they often do. Thirdly, they wouldn't need that amount of firepower to capture one person. If you ask me that report was a load of old bollocks.'

Mike's mother would usually have complained about such tasteless language but, like the rest of the family, she was left admiring her son's assessment of the news. What Mike had said rang true and made the news report suddenly less believable. If it wasn't travellers and wasn't an escaped prisoner then what had the operation been for? Nobody said anything further on the subject and seemingly turned their attention back to the news but each family member apart from Gayle was considering whether recent rumours could actually be true. Small outlaw bands, some of them armed, had reliably been reported as being active in West Wales and Solway in areas largely abandoned by the local population and where government services had become ineffective. Other rumours, as yet unsubstantiated suggested similar groups were operating in Lincolnshire and it seemed quite feasible that the authorities had discovered a similar renegade group here in East Suffolk.

As the local news ended and advertisements heralded the national news at 2200 Mike, Gayle and their mother went up to bed. Frank, uncharacteristically, took care to check that his car was securely locked before walking up the road to spend an hour with his girlfriend, Shelly, leaving his father to view the news alone. Headlines reporting a small cut in the Bank of England interest rate and the latest attempt by protesters in Leicestershire to force the abandonment of the construction of a new toll road were less than riveting news and by the time Stacy Kenton's picture appeared on the screen Clive Cannon had fallen asleep. The television announced to no-one in particular that Stacy Kenton MP, now shadow spokesman for coastal affairs since the Nationalists defeat in the previous year's election, had been speaking at an environmental conference in Switzerland. He had warned that the Conservative government's neglect of most coastal areas in Britain would lead to the disaffection of costal communities and the possible breakdown of the rule of law in some of the more remote and deprived locations. As Stacy's picture faded Mr Cannon's head lolled dramatically to one side, he gave a loud snort of a snore and sat upright to be presented with the sight of a highly individually dressed, nationally known singer who had just been awarded a music prize that he had never heard of before.

'Same old news, different faces,' thought Clive Cannon and very deliberately zapped off the TV to produce a sudden silence. He stood, stretched and then, leaving the light on for Frank's return, made his way to bed.

Friday 13th November 2195. Bentwaters, Suffolk.

Alana read through her report. She deleted one sentence and replaced it with a revised version then checked a couple of spellings and read the whole thing through again. Satisfied, she consigned the final version electronically to Company records, with a copy to her own personal file, before producing a couple of prints to be submitted to the CO. It was late. She was the only person still at work in the Company Office and was about to leave the paper copies to be dealt with in the morning when, on a whim, she phoned through to Company HQ. Having rehearsed a phone-mail message in her mind she was taken aback to be greeted by her superior officer himself.

'Colonel Morden speaking.'

'Er, sorry sir. I was expecting to leave a message.'

'Quite. I'm not usually in my office at this time. It's Buckhurst isn't it?'

'Yes, sir.'

'Well, sergeant, what was that message?'

'I've completed my account of this evening's operation, sir. You asked for a prompt report.'

'OK, Buckhurst. Send it across now. Er, no. On second

thoughts bring it yourself. Shall we say about thirty minutes time?'

'Yes, sir.'

The phone clicked off and Alana responded by collecting the printed reports, making a quick security check around the office and putting on her uniform jacket and beret before leaving the over-heated room for the cool of the November evening outside; a coolness enhanced by the strong, blustery wind blowing across the flat, exposed site as she dived for the comfort of her 'base buggy'. Of course during training exercises or on operations she enjoyed driving the Panther ATVs – that was part of her reason for joining the army – but she was equally at home flitting around the base in her electric Courier base car, known universally as the 'base buggy'.

By nature Bentwaters was a maze of concrete pathways. They had originally formed the runways and taxiways of an airfield that had been built way back in the 1940s during a war against Germany. But with most modern aircraft, apart from the largest transports, having vertical or short take-off capabilities the original main runway, well over 3000 metres in length, had long been defunct. Over the years most of the old airfield site had been sold off or leased but the army had earmarked a small southern area bordering Rendlesham Forest as a backup base. Used, abandoned and then occupied again, Bentwaters had acted as a temporary training base, a vehicle repair workshop and a storage facility but this was the first time in living memory that it had been used as a centre for active operations. The Army had nine such sites, all former airfields, covering the whole country. The Royal Highlanders had two in Scotland and The Royal Welsh one. There were two under the control of the Northumbrian Regiment in the north of England and a further two used by the Wessex Regiment in the south. The remaining two, one being Bentwaters were operated by Alana's Mercian Regiment. The Welsh had made their base operational three years previously to help local police deal with armed bands of protestors in some coastal areas in the west of their country. The army's low key operations had managed to control but not eliminate the problem. Now eight of those nine bases were actively engaged in similar work either attempting to eliminate outlaw gangs or hoping their presence would deter further growth of anti-government protests. Legally the army only operated at the request of the police but in practice they only needed police approval to execute their own plans.

The HQ buildings at Bentwaters were less than five minutes from the Company Office when travelling direct by base buggy but Alana took a more circuitous route via her quarters. Leaving the operations area for the domestic zone she was waved through by a guard who recognised her number plate and three minutes after leaving the office she was home. The individual prefabricated house had only recently been erected. It was a basic but comfortable two storey detached unit and she had known far worse. It could easily have housed two, three or even four soldiers but with the base operating at far less than maximum capacity Alana had the luxury of having all that space to herself. First a shower and then a change of clothes. Despite being well on into the evening Alana put on clean underclothes; she felt the visit to HQ demanded some attempt to keep up standards even if no one else would notice the change. She checked herself in the mirror fixed to the inside of the now open wardrobe door. Looking at her figure she was unexpectedly reminded of a schooldays incident when a boyfriend had told her that he loved her and had God given her larger tits she would have been perfect. She had immediately dumped him much to the amusement of his friends and the amazement of hers. Alana smiled. She was satisfied with what she saw in the mirror and when topped off with a clean uniform she felt fully prepared for the visit to her commanding officer.

No-one was waved on past the guardhouse at the entrance to the headquarters complex. No-one except the CO himself, of course. The guard knew Alana – they had met socially on a few occasions – but he acted as though she were a complete stranger when she halted her buggy at the barrier.

'ID.'

Alana handed over her badge.

'Destination?'

'Colonel Morden's office.'

'Buggy key, please.'

Alana handed over her key card.

'Wait, please.'

The guard spoke to his partner inside the guardhouse. If Alana's visit had not been registered by the CO she would have been requested to step into the waiting area of the guardhouse whilst her vehicle was checked for suspect devices and the purpose of her visit verified. As it was her name had already been added to the list of authorised visitors and her ID card and key were promptly returned.

'Thank you, sergeant.'

A neat salute and then a wink from the guard and, with the barrier raised, she was directed to a parking bay where another member of the security unit collected Alana and escorted her through doors and down corridors to the COs outer office. The adjutant, a man in his 40s, indicated a chair for her use whilst her arrival was reported to Colonel Morden.

A short wait followed allowing her the chance for a cursory visual inspection of the office that resulted in confirming her current opinion that she had no wish to move into administration. This inclination would no doubt put a ceiling on her chances of promotion – a limit to the rank to which she could aspire. Captain would be fine, possibly even major but when admin tasks became so great that you needed an office and staff then that would be a step too far. For Alana the army was organised for action and this demanded that officers led from the front; they should not issue orders from the comfort of offices at the rear of the front line. Leaders should be out there in the thick of any operation.

The adjutant's phone rang. After a brief conversation he turned to Alana.

'Sergeant, please, Colonel Morden will see you now.'

Alana was ushered into the colonel's office. There were two other people present; they were introduced. The first was Major East whom she recognised from her time at the regiment's Litchfield HQ. Colonel Morden then gestured towards the tall grey-haired man in civilian clothes seated on his left.

'And this is Brigadier Hale of the Royal Welsh.'

Alana was not sure how to acknowledge a superior officer in civvies.

'Sir,' she said and stood to attention but refrained from giving a formal salute. Fortunately this seemed appropriate as the Welsh brigadier stood and offered his hand which she shook briefly before he regained his seat.

'Please sit, sergeant.'

Colonel Morden picked up the copies of the report Alana had placed on his desk. He counted two copies before returning them to the desk.

'Perhaps you could give us a brief summary of your report, starting with the origin of this operation.'

'Sir. Aerial observations by pilotless drones indicated occupation of an abandoned barn at Reydon Smear. This was verified by the local police who didn't recognise the individuals and who asked us to investigate. We sent out a two-man observation team who kept surveillance over a period of three days. The barn was occupied by two men and a woman plus two dogs. Each day they followed the same routine. In the morning two of them took the dogs down to the beach below Easton Cliffs. In the afternoon two of them – the woman and one of the men – drove out in their 4WD vehicle, returning after about an hour, each time with what appeared to be a few provisions.'

'Where did they go in their vehicle?' asked Colonel Morden.

'We don't know. We always maintained our observation on the person remaining in the barn. They had time to visit Southwold or one of the villages on the main Lowestoft road but certainly not one of the larger towns.'

'So what was the purpose of today's operation?'

'This morning the police paid them a visit to check identities. They all had British ID cards that checked out with Police Central Records and claimed to be tourist visitors. But within two hours, around 1130 hours the police reported that they were gone.'

'Where did they go?'

'We don't know. They headed towards the Lowestoft road but neither ourselves nor the police have the manpower to check on such movements. We are looking at satellite observations to try and locate their vehicle on its travels. This evening we checked on the barn and the surrounding area with the aid of our base helicopter. The gang had clearly left hurriedly as food, bedding and clothing were abandoned, most unlike the usual behaviour of tourists. The police will make a full investigation tomorrow; the items left behind should give us some means to verify their identities. We supplied the media with a cover story for our operation and provided the local population with a few sound effects to let them know we were doing our job to protect them.'

'Tell me, sergeant, could they have been smugglers or travellers?' asked the Brigadier, breaking his silence.

'We think not, sir. Smugglers seldom stay around to reveal their identities and travellers – whilst they may leave behind unsightly piles of rubbish – are most unlikely to abandon good clothing and food they had only recently purchased.'

'Do you have any known armed resistance groups in your area?' continued the Brigadier, leaning forward as though to emphasize the importance of his question.

'Not to our knowledge, sir. That is apart from some

individuals that the police suspect of smuggling. There is a group of locals based near Leiston who put pressure on the local authority to keep their services going. They're called the Aldringham Seven. They organise things like mail collection and transport for the elderly to doctors or hospital appointments. They seem genuine.'

'Beware,' warned the Brigadier. 'We have a group like that in West Wales. They really do provide local services but we now know they are also a front for a resistance movement who object to the army's involvement in local affairs. Their activities have been financed through smuggling and we believe they may have killed at least one person who somehow got in the way of their plans.'

'So,' summarised Colonel Morden, 'we observe those suspected of illegal activity, move them on and prevent them from settling anywhere. This is the scheme so far. Any comment on that, sergeant?'

'Reydon, sir, is the furthest north we have had to investigate so far. Apart from us there's only the detachment at Sizewell that protects the power station and keeps an eye on the coast for smugglers. It would help to have another detachment further north. At present we do not have the manpower or the organisation to pursue suspects who move around our area. It would also be of great help if we were able to work without being purely assistants to the police. We should be allowed to mount our own operations.'

'Our thoughts exactly, Buckhurst,' confirmed the Brigadier. 'But there is little we can do without the police unless the government changes the law. And believe me. We haven't been backward in letting them know our feelings on that matter. That Stacy Kenton who was the coasts minister under the Nationalists at least listened to us; this new chap in charge since the Conservatives got back into power seems to wish we weren't here at all.'

'Is that your report completed?' asked Colonel Morden.

'Yes, sir, except that tomorrow the police will make a final check on the Reydon Smear barn and the area around.'

'Thank you. What are your duties tomorrow, sergeant?'

'I'm off duty, sir.'

'We'd like you to come back here tomorrow afternoon. Fourteen hundred hours, please. You'll be given time off in compensation. That's all for now.'

'Sir!'

Alana stood, saluted, turned and left. A guard escorted her to the guardhouse where she was checked out and within minutes was heading home across the base, the strong wind having subsided and given way to a fine spattering of rain that misted her view.

From her bedroom window Alana stared almost sightlessly across the darkened flatness of the old airfield. The lines of slender posts topped by the bright lamps that marked the paths and roadways of the base barely registered in her mind as she thought about the unexpected events of the evening, just thirty minutes earlier. It figured that Colonel Morden had a task for her. It also figured that any increased responsibility would bring with it increased authority and in the army increased authority was usually marked by higher rank. Alana had always looked ahead towards her next step up the military ladder. When she had joined it was enough to complete two years training and become a professional soldier. She had done a tour of duty in Canada on standby should the political turmoil in the United States engulf its northern neighbour. It had not and eventually that time of easy living had been replaced by peacekeeping in Central Africa as part of a United Nations Task Force. The inhabitants of a huge refugee camp on the border between two previously friendly states had been disowned by the governments of both neighbouring nations. The army's task here was as difficult and exhausting as the stay in Canada had been easy and relaxing but keeping control of food queues and patrolling poverty-stricken streets to prevent looting was not the type of action that had attracted Alana to join up in the first place. Compensation arrived when her skills and dedication were recognised with a promotion to sergeant. And then came Bentwaters. Not an exotic foreign posting but for the first time Alana was in action – low key perhaps but still action – against an elusive enemy. Tomorrow perhaps she would be able to set her sights further ahead towards the next step in her career.

Alana brought the lights of the base back into focus. She stared out for a while then closed the blinds, turned towards the bed, removed her uniform and laid it out carefully before fetching hangers from the wardrobe. Having hung the neatly arranged clothes on the rail of an open-fronted cupboard she returned to the wardrobe to close the doors when, for the second time that day she paused to look at herself in the full length mirror. She hesitated briefly then pushed the door wide open before slipping out of her underclothes. Raising her hands she cupped her chin and stared contemplatively into her own eyes. Slowly and gently she ran the little finger of her right hand around her slightly opened lips and then, looking down, moved her hands lightly across her breasts before moving down and cupping them together beneath her stomach and lifting it slightly as she did. Again Alana paused and then with one hand caressed the slight dome she had created. Moving down she touched the soft, smooth skin between her legs before returning her hands to cup her stomach once more. But it was not her hands that she saw in her mind's eye. They were the hands of Colonel Morden. But then again perhaps not Colonel Morden in particular. The hands represented an unknown lover, perhaps of similar rank and physique, at some undefined time in the future. Alana's thoughts were driven by a second agenda, one that ran parallel to her wish to remain an active soldier, contributing fully to the work of the army. Alana wanted to have children. But to raise a family she would need to give up active service, at least for a time and as necessary as that would be she would dearly love to remain close to army life. The answer was, of course, to marry a serving army officer and become an army wife. There it was then. No more flirting with the lower ranks! The next day, she believed, would create a springboard that would be able to propel both of her dreams into the realms of reality.

Saturday 14th November 2195, Reydon

Early the next morning, Saturday, Frank and Mike loaded fishing gear into the back of Frank's ancient, battered truck. It had usually been their habit to load up the previous evening to ensure an early start but now it seemed that with the possibility of unknown prowlers in the area it was unwise to leave items unattended and unlocked over night. There had always been travellers – the traditional itinerant families who parked up on farmland, with permission, and worked the area looking for old vehicles, farm machinery, electronics, furniture and scrap metal. But unlike the pleasant, polite, usually fair-minded groups that had been around for years, and quite possibly generations, there were now additionally gangs that didn't pay for the goods they removed. Taking over empty houses or parking on abandoned gardens the new breed were parasites who cased the area by day and stole by night. The reduced constabulary were no match for their cunning and the recently arrived army back-up seemingly had better things to do.

Gear aboard, Frank gunned the engine into life and headed his truck down to the end of their road before turning left and heading north on the Old Lowestoft Road. To claim the truck as his was probably debateable since Frank had exchanged it for a tankard of beer just six months earlier and the number on the licence plate was not registered to him anyway. The Kew family had taken the government's relocation grant and were off to a new life in Australia. At the farewell party an inebriated Jason Kew had shaken hands on the deal and Frank, in exchange for a beer, had become the new owner of the vehicle including its personalised registration plate KEW744JN. Over the succeeding two weeks Frank had scoured the area around Reydon and begged or bought enough spares from derelict vehicles to keep his runabout on the road for the foreseeable future. The National Driving Authority (NADA) were still under the impression that the vehicle belonged to a Mr J N Kew and until someone came knocking Frank wasn't going to announce to the authorities that the vehicle had been moved three doors down the road.

Frank loved his pickup. If he had been asked to tell the truth he would probably have admitted that he rated it equally alongside his girlfriend Shelly. Shelly Kew, though, doted on Frank who was the main reason she had remained in Reydon when the rest of the family emigrated. As a general rule Frank was, ownership of his beloved truck apart, honest and law-abiding. Although neither mother nor father came from a religious background they had both impressed on their children the value of honesty and hard work and above all to avoid the sort of trouble that would bring the police knocking at their door. Frank being the eldest child had come under pressure to present a good, law-abiding example to Gayle and Mike. And by and large he had. Except, that was, when his siblings were not around. As he grew up Frank found pleasures away from home in the pubs and clubs of Ipswich so now KEW744JN would make its way there, down the A12 road, usually twice a week – once mid-week and once on Saturday or Sunday. On the southbound journey he was commonsense itself but on the return he would gun the engine up to reach the legal speed limit, motor steadily past Woodbridge and then push his foot down further to enjoy the thrills of fierce acceleration and raw speed along the lightly trafficked, gently curving dual-carriageway section past Wickham Market and up to Saxmundham.

To date Frank had been caught twice by the traffic police. On the first occasion he had paid an on-the-spot fine and knew all was well when the officer pocketed the money and failed to issue a receipt ticket. After all they had both attended school together. A couple of months later on a warm, dry summer evening Frank had again been speeding past Wickham Market when a cop-car, that he had failed to notice, pulled out onto the carriageway behind him and sped after him, lights flashing. Foolishly he had tried to outrun his pursuer but before he could turn off the main road he had run into traffic and been forced to pull into a lay-by. Following a study of his Driver's Licence and an external inspection of the truck the lady police officer asked to look under the tarpaulin that covered the rear. Satisfied that there was no contraband or illegal goods stashed away she handed him a copy of the Road-Code booklet and suggested he read pages 57 to 59.

'That's the section on speed,' she said. 'We've got better things to do than check up on people like you.'

When she was gone Frank, forgetting about Shelly for a moment, turned to page 57 hoping that the attractive officer had left her contact details on the piece of paper she had used as a marker. He was disappointed to find only a formal message telling him that next time he were caught he would receive rather more than just a formal warning. Twice lucky, he had reflected at the time. Frank decided there and then not to chance his luck again and upset the undermanned, overworked police force as fortunately on neither occasion had the officer thought to check the ownership of the mottled green, rather dirty Toyota pick-up.

Mike had been fishing with his older brother for as long as he could remember. Rivers, lakes, marshes, the sea. There was great variety in the fishing locations found within a few kilometres of their home but their favourite was the sea and today they were headed towards the nearby coast. The Old Lowestoft Road no longer reached the town to which it had originally been connected as, barely a kilometre north of Reydon, it ended at Potter's Bridge. Older village residents could remember a ford at that point, one that was frequently too deep to cross in winter but the two Cannon brothers had known nothing other than a substantial barrier across the road with a notice warning that there was no vehicle access ahead. Pedestrians however, ignoring a second notice inscribed 'DANGER', could follow a potholed ribbon of asphalt until it disappeared beneath the waters of Easton Broad just 300 metres further on.

The Broad, though, was not their destination on this occasion but rather it was Easton Cliffs and the narrow path leading to the beach. Despite being one of their most popular fishing sites, visited regularly by the brothers, they were never sure exactly how the landscape would look. The shingle beach ridges of one visit could be replaced by a narrow ribbon of beach backed by piles of slumped cliff debris just a few weeks later but even so they were not prepared for the view that greeted them when they turned down the lane that led coastward. Just 300 metres off the Old Lowestoft Road they were confronted by a newly erected bright orange barrier, the top bar supporting a notice annotated with the single word 'DANGER' and below that a second message reading 'No Access Ahead'.

Frank drew up to the barrier before reversing back to his left onto an area of flattened vegetation that appeared to be a parking spot created by previous visitors using exactly the same manoeuvre. They got out and stared ahead. Beyond the barrier the lane that they usually took to the cliff-head path was no more. In its place a deep, canyon-like gully left the end of the lane hanging precipitously over a steep descent towards a jumble of rock, earth, stones and clumps of vegetation below. To their left a rudimentary path had been made by earlier visitors marking their meandering route to the beach below avoiding obstacles and the steeper sections of the newly formed cliff face. True, there had been equinoctial gales but to Frank's mind they had been no worse than the usual wet and windy squalls of autumn. The changes spread out below them were rather more than they had expected.

Noting that they still had reasonable access to the beach Frank and Mike unloaded their gear and made their way cautiously down.

'You could write about this in your magazine.'

'Journal,' complained Mike.

'Sorry, journal. Well, you could.'

'Yes, I could. I've seen some changes. But, no. People prefer to read about people, not things so I'll wait till something else turns up. It always does.'

It turned out to be a good day. The weather was reasonable – some cloud, some sun, a gentle breeze – and the sea yielded a reasonable harvest of fish. With lunch taken early, about 11.30, they packed up before the afternoon was barely an hour old and returned up the cliff path. With the ascent rather more taxing than their downward journey they took a brief break just over half way up. Sitting on a large block of slumped rock, soil and grass they spent a few minutes in silence staring out across the sea. Frank, who cared little about the future and saw no need to dwell on the past happily took in the sight and sounds of the gently heaving water, the trawl of the waves back down the beach and the flight and call of the gracefully wheeling seabirds. Mike in contrast, his eyes looking sightlessly at the same scene, cast his mind over recent events and the conundrum of the army's seemingly inexplicable action the previous evening. It was not the seabirds that he saw in his mind's eye but the black bulk of the helicopter hanging over him with its Cyclops-like beam prying into the depths of the dark November night.

'Let's go home by the Smear.'

'What's so interesting about three houses and a farm?' asked Frank feigning ignorance of his brother's motive.

'Just intrigued about last night.'

Rested, they walked steadily back, packed their gear into the truck and turned back towards the road. Instead of turning left, straight back home, they went right and after about 500 metres, just short of the barrier, took a track to their left. Originally little more than a footpath to the Smear hamlet, vehicles with off-road capability, taking a short cut, had widened the route into a track. They reached the access road to the farm and turned right towards the hamlet.

'Slow here, Frank.'

Unusually parked vehicles meant that there was no room to stop on the narrow lane but pulling out to pass a police vehicle they saw a field entrance ahead sealed off by 'no entry' tape and an armed policeman standing to one side beside a gate. They were held up for a few seconds as a car passed them heading east giving Mike a brief time to see what was going on. Inside the field there were two other vehicles – an army 4WD and another police van and two or three police officers. The policeman by the gate waved them on so they then had no choice but to accelerate away down the road, turning left and left again back to their village.

'What do you reckon?' asked Mike.

'Looks as though you were right,' conceded Frank.

Mike smiled to himself. A smile of vindication as his opinions of the previous evening had been confirmed.

Soon after entering the village they found their path temporarily blocked again, this time by a large removal van backing into the driveway of the first house in their road. It occurred to Mike that removing people's belongings between homes or home and storage had become one of the few legal growth industries in their part of the country.

'That's the Camdens off then,' said Frank.

'Yep. Camdens today, Cannons tomorrow perhaps.'

'Not whilst Dad's got work in Southwold and I'm OK working around the farms. Perhaps it'll happen some day but I don't see it happening soon.'

They drove the last few metres in silence whilst Mike thought about the families who had left Reydon in recent years. His mind set on the dwindling numbers in his class whilst he had been at the local Primary School. First the Brooks. Jay Brook's dad had been transferred by the Fire Service to the New Town being built to expand the small Suffolk town of Eye. And then there were the Streets. Frankie Street and her family had gone to North Yorkshire and set up a Farm Holiday centre with their relocation allowance. Yet further afield were the Bow family – twins Brian and Carrie who were his best mates at the time. They videophoned now and then from the Cape in South Africa, evidently greatly enjoying their adopted homeland. De-population was a fact of life although a few families had moved in. They were usually relatives of local residents taking advantage of cheap house prices but after the notorious case of the Newburys who moved in, claimed a relocation allowance and within a few months had promptly exited to Australia, the local authority had clamped down on incomers. And now the Camdens were going. Mike smiled to himself for the second time during the journey; a smile edged with a little wistful sadness but a smile that marked a discovery. Mike Cannon, prize-winning reporter had decided on another human-interest story to provide the print for his next column.

Saturday 14th November 2195, Bentwaters

Alana's return journey to the HQ block had been a mirror of her visit seventeen hours earlier. Same guards, same procedures, same questions, same reactions. That was until she reached the adjutant's office. Here the carbon copy ended. She was ushered straight into Colonel Morden's office and on this occasion he alone was in attendance.

No ceremony this time.

'Sit down please, Buckhurst.'

He indicated a chair and when she was seated explained the reason for their meeting.

'I'm pleased with your operations here sergeant and with your understanding of the situation here in Suffolk. So you will be excluded from normal duties for the next five days during which I need you to prepare plans – plans suggesting how we should deal with any unlawful operations in opposition to the government. To put any such plans into operation we need you to organise a newly formed task force – you should plan for such a force and request the personnel you need to staff it. In particular we need to keep an eye on the Aldringham Seven and any other similar organisations. We need to know if their work is completely legal. You should plan to make contact, either openly or covertly, to determine their personnel, their purpose and their organisation.'

'Would that go as far as planting a mole?'

'Hopefully not but if that eventually proves to be the best way forward, so be it.'

'Do we act with or without police knowledge, sir?'

'At all times keep within the law. Active operations must have police agreement but observation – and I'll leave you to interpret exactly what that word means – is within our existing operational remit. The government is not much help at the present but if the Nationalists are returned at the next election matters could improve but that's over three years away.

Colonel Morden paused then looked straight at his sergeant.

'Are you happy with that lieutenant?

Lieutenant! It took a few seconds for her promotion to

register with Alana. She stood up and shook the Colonel's outstretched hand. She couldn't help the corners of her mouth turning up to form a smile.

'Yes! Sir!' she replied, saluted, turned smartly and returned to the adjutant's office.

The short wait for the adjutant to appear allowed Alana to come down from Cloud Nine and begin to understand the extent to which the last five minutes would alter her life.

'Sorry to keep you,' apologised the soon returning adjutant.

'Right,' replied Alana then, pausing to read his name badge added 'Ian' (now that she was of equal rank) and asked, 'Where do we go from here?'

'Follow me and I'll show you your office, the Officer's Mess and other facilities.'

A little under two hours later Alana had been introduced to the new life that came with her elevated rank. A cup of tea with adjutant Ian signalled the end of her visit and when she reached the exit she was excited to see her buggy parked outside. A guard opened the door for her and addressed her as 'Ma'am'. And the deference continued at the guardhouse. The barrier was raised, the gate open and she was waved straight through. No checks, no banter, nothing. The phrase 'treated like royalty' came into her mind but Alana thought that being head of state would have nothing on how she felt at that moment.

Homeward bound across the base Alana could hardly believe that the first part of her recently formulated plan had become reality so quickly. Her smile spread into a grin and then relaxed again. She was pleased. No, more than that. She was ecstatic, over the moon in fact but there was one small pang of regret. The guard. The one at the HQ guardhouse. In future would he still wink at her after his salute? She knew, wistfully, that he would not.

CHAPTER FOUR
A CLOUD ON THE HORIZON

Wednesday 28th August 2199

Stacy didn't like flying. If he had to travel by sitting inside a metal tube he preferred to take the train. He felt happier knowing that there was some form of contact with the ground below. Travelling abroad was, of course, one of the obligations carried with the post of government minister. Since the Nationalists return to power and his promotion to Minister for the Environment, now assisted by his own junior Minister for Coastal Affairs, flying had become a more frequent part of his duties. When travelling to a European destination most of his colleagues would fly direct from London or a major provincial airport. However just two months earlier when attending a ministerial conference in Rome he had taken the Crossrail train to Stratford and then the Europa high-speed express to his destination with only two stops – Paris and Milan. On the return journey he had taken a more leisurely route via Switzerland and the Rhine Valley, a route along which he could savour a series of varied, picturesque and sometimes stunningly beautiful landscapes. By air there were only clouds to be seen and then even more clouds.

Today, returning from America, the clouds beneath his aircraft were even more monotonous than usual, the low cloud base prevented visual contact with the ground until the plane descended sufficiently for Windsor Castle to be the first recognisable landmark on the approach to London's Heathrow airport. Stacy had left England in the rain with flooding widely forecast for the south of the country and on his return it was still raining. The fast approaching ground below appeared as though it were one vast lake until details appeared as the pilot lined up with Heathrow's northernmost west to east runway. Three large reservoirs were identified by their retaining walls with the land between them, a designated flood relief area, now fulfilling its purpose. Horton church, its tower pointing skyward like a giant water level indicator stood with the remains of its now long abandoned village, buried beneath the gently rippling, silver-grey surface. The M25 motorway could be seen, busy with traffic, gracefully curving along its embankment together with the buildings in the villages of Colnbrook and Stanwwell Moor, their lights punctuating the overcast gloom, saved from Horton's fate by the protecting embankments of their man-made polders. Stacy felt pleased that, three years earlier, despite the opposition of his own party, he had supported an increase in the budget for such environmental work by the water supply companies.

An almost unnoticeable bump and they were back on land. During the last few minutes Stacy's dislike of flying had been forgotten as he took in the unusual aspects of the well known scene below but the landing brought him back to reality and catapulted to the fore his dislike for the ritual of the airport terminal – travelators, baggage reclaim areas and the personal checks that even government ministers had to go through before they could return to the world outside.

'Hi, Tal. I'm back. Can you meet me?'

'Hold on Stacy. What about Hi Tal, how are you?' chided Tallin with just the right amount of lilt to her voice to let him know that the comment wasn't to be taken too seriously. 'Actually I'm fine and yes, I will meet you. Usual place? I'd even come all the way to the airport if you wish.'

Tallin always offered to meet Stacy at Heathrow but they both knew that their usual pick-up plan was far better. To access the arrivals area on the western side of the airport a vehicle had to drive to the arrivals car park, pay for the privilege of parking, have their registration plate read by a machine similar to those used for monitoring toll road users and then sit in an allotted space for about half an hour. When the car registration was flashed up on the screen the driver was allowed to exit the holding area and pick up the waiting passenger. In that time, had Stacy not bothered to wait, he could have taken a taxi and quite likely made the journey all the way home.

'No. Usual place is fine, thanks,' he replied. 'See you in about thirty minutes.

Stacy ended the call, slipped his phone into his jacket pocket and exited the automatic doors to the airport arrival area only to see a southbound number 606 route bus slipping quietly away from its appointed stopping bay. No matter. There would be another one along in about ten minutes leaving him with plenty of time to meet Tallin without keeping her waiting. After checking for traffic he ran across the wide, windswept road to the shelter of the local bus interchange. It had always been a matter of mild surprise to Stacy that he could leave his plane, pass through the arrivals building and reach the terminals airlock style exit only to find it impossible to continue to his bus connection without braving the extremes of the British weather. Once safely under cover again Stacy found a seat, placed his bag and coat beside him, cleared the rain from his glasses and unfolded the New Times newspaper he had purchased in the airport terminal. The New Times was one of only two daily papers (the other was the Daily Register) that currently published paper editions although rumour had it that other, unspecified titles could soon join them in re-establishing the use of a physical media. Journalists' copy and its associated advertising had long been distributed electronically following huge rises in the cost of producing paper but that situation had changed now that a cheap plastic media, still known as paper, was available. The Daily Register saw the potential, producing and distributing a free 'headline' edition. Advertisers welcomed this as an opportunity to further infiltrate the vast market of commuters, shoppers, students and the like who relished the Register's daily dose of revelations and trivia. The New Times, not to be outdone, followed the Register's lead with a more sober offering.

Stacy didn't have to look far through the paper to find the item in which he was interested. Not front page news but pretty close. The headline on page three read:

'Greenville Conference success.'

Yes. The Climate Change Conference (universally referred to as the 3Cs) that had been held in the Gore Centre in Greenville, South Carolina *had* been a success. Stacy was pleased, even proud that, as the representative of Great Britain he had helped to broker an agreement for action to limit some of the more harmful aspects of modern day industry, energy production and transportation over the coming ten years. In all 187 out of the 201 nations present had signed the protocol – considerably more than once seemed likely for the quinquennial meeting. And he had won his bet! After the last conference five years ago Tallin had wagered that 3Cs would never be held on American soil. She had a way of provoking people that made Stacy disagree with her on principle but at that time he thought he was probably onto a loser. But two years previously things had changed in America and here he was successfully back from across the Atlantic.

He did not read the article – that could wait – he only wanted to assess the impact the conference had made in this country. So, with no bus yet in view he turned to the weekly column entitled 'Yesterday's History.' He was pleased to see that the columnist, a previously unknown provincial reporter named Mike Cannon had taken the opportunity to be topical and outline the circumstances that had brought about not just American participation but their desire to host the conference. No sooner had he folded the paper to find the column and read its headline than his bus drew up beside the shelter. He boarded, paid by contactless card then, on gaining a seat, settled down to read.

'The run up to an American Presidential Poll is usually quite boring to us Brits. Long-winded and expensive, the system offers little of interest this side of the Atlantic. And so it was in 2196. The Republicans chose veteran Kyle Kilburn, the long serving senator from the NE state of Rhode Island whose nearest rival, the much younger Governor of Texas, Santos Perivale, was not far behind in delegates but had graciously conceded defeat two months before the party convention. The Democrats were nowhere. The result on polling day in November was a foregone conclusion. So in due course, President Kilburn was sworn in and moved into the White House. All was well. The USA was still a world power and nobody, least of all the namby-pamby climate change lobby at the United Nations would tell them what to do.

If the 2196 election was forgettable then the events of six months in 2197 were not. A media briefing in Dallas called by the Texan Governor Perivale sent headlines spinning around the world. Texas was threatening to leave the Union! Little known at that time, outside US political circles, was the feud that had developed between the two presidential contenders following the refusal of the Rhode Island senator to give the Governor of Texas a post of responsibility in his government. This apparently trivial nose-thumbing to tradition was the final straw that broke the camel's back. And the camel was the United States. This column is not the place to go into historical detail but we should record that by high summer that year a swath of predominantly Latino-American and traditional southern states, upset by the seemingly biased policies of the government in Washington, had promised to join Texas if that state actually acted on *its threat to secede. It was however California's decision to join Texas that turned threat into reality. On 10ᵗʰ August in Santa Fe, New Mexico, Texas and 12 other southern and south-western states signed the New Mexico agreement to secede on the 1ˢᵗ of September if the US federal government did not take steps to meet their concerns. President Kilburn refused to talk to "rebels" so on that date the Republic of New Mexico was founded. Ten days later the northern and eastern states of the USA made a slight alteration to their countries name. They became the <u>Union</u> States of America and the old USA was consigned to history.*

To mark the new nation's inauguration and his own elevation to its presidency, Santos Perivale outlined a number of policies with which he was at odds with those of the former USA. Foremost among these was the decision to back international climate change agreements – a decision that culminated in this weeks Greenville conference. The Union States were, of course, absent.'

Stacy closed and folded the paper. Why Greenville? he thought. Most of the delegates had flown into Atlanta, Georgia, so why not hold the conference there? That city had plenty of conference space and more than enough hotels to cater for the worldwide influx of statesmen, environmentalists and press. Perhaps it was Greenville's location close to the southern border of North Virginia, a Union State, that President Perivale hoped would rub salt into old wounds. Or perhaps it was the word 'green' in the host city's name, emphasising the new republic's environmental credentials. Stacy did not know but further reflection on the matter was halted by the movement of the bus as it negotiated the Stanwell roundabout prompting him to collect his bag and coat and signal to the driver his need to get off at the next stop.

He alighted, noted the rain had eased and as the bus pulled away from the lay-by Tallin's car pulled in, illegally, behind. Stacy stowed his luggage and took the passenger seat beside her.

'That's good timing. Thanks. But you really shouldn't pick me up in the bus bay.'

They kissed lightly. Tallin checked the mirror and pulled away before an express coach pulled in behind her with a warning blast on its horn. She didn't reply to Stacy's comment. It was a ritual complaint that did not bother her.

'You seem tired,' Tallin observed.

'Yes. It's been a busy session at Westminster since Easter and then there was the conference in Rome and this transatlantic jaunt on top. I'm glad we've arranged to take a break away next week. I was working things out on the plane.'

'What things?' asked Tallin as she indicated and then turned the car onto the slip road to the motorway.

'How much work I've done over the years. I've been a Council member for twenty-four years, a minister for fourteen and in the cabinet for ten. When I first became a junior minister some of the present cabinet weren't even backbenchers, not even MPs , and one of them was still at school!'

There was silence as Tallin concentrated on driving and eased onto the northbound carriageway of the M25 at junction 14. When she had settled into the flow of traffic in the first lane her thoughts returned to their conversation.

'So how long do you reckon you'll go on for, up at Parliament?'

'There's a very important piece of legislation coming up in the autumn. We're trying to undo the harm done by the Conservatives when they were in power. When that's done and dusted and bedded down I'll go to the back benches. Possibly three, maybe five more years. Then I'll call it a day.'

'Serious?'

'Yes, deadly serious.'

Silence again, each partner thinking about life without the pressures of cabinet office and then again, a little later, life in retirement.

Junction 16 and round the sharp left-hand connecting lane to the M40, heading towards London, and then, a couple of minutes later slipping away left to their local road through Denham and home. The thought of two days doing very little then a weekend doing even less before taking a planned longer holiday helped Stacy to relax but as they approached the Corner House the sight of a well known bottle-green saloon car on his driveway suggested that he may not be starting his summer break quite as soon as he had hoped. An added ingredient to cause him concern was the sight of the two people standing beside the car. He recognised the driver. It was John Goldhawk who was Stacy's political agent, friend and chairman of the South Chiltern English Nationalists. The other figure was a stranger who carried an air of authority – possibly a police officer, despite his civilian dress, but a police officer whose rank gave him considerable power to act on his own initiative. Stacy lowered the window as Tallin drew into the drive and stopped beside the two men. John Goldhawk stepped a pace forward and leaned down towards Stacy.

'Sorry to appear without warning and intrude when you've just arrived home but Mr Oakwood here (John Goldhawk half turned towards the visitor) needs to talk with you rather urgently.

Stacy got out and stepped over towards Mr Oakwood.

'Oakwood,' the gentleman announced formally but rather unnecessarily, adding, 'Anti-terrorist Unit.'

Tallin, recognising a situation where she was not needed, turned on the ignition and disappeared around the side of the house whilst Stacy walked to the front door and ushered his visitors into the hallway.

'John. Show Mr Oakwood into my study, please. You know where the drinks are. I'll just wash and tidy up – five minutes max.'

When the office door had closed behind them Stacy went up the stairs that led from the hall to the first floor. In the en-suite to his bedroom he washed his face and hands, arranged his hair and moved over to his wardrobe to select a crisp, smart, plain blue shirt and a pair of lightweight trousers to replace the crumpled suit that had clothed him across the Atlantic. He would have liked to have showered or at least washed his feet but Mr Oakwood didn't appear to be the sort of person who would appreciate waiting too long, even for a government minster. Two minutes. Change complete he walked over to his bedside table, picked up the landline receiver and tapped out a number from memory. As expected there were a number of clicks on the line but no ringing sound before an automated voice answered.

'Good afternoon, Mr Kenton. Please give me your security code.'

Stacy used the keypad to tap in a sequence of letters and digits.

'What can I check for you, sir?' the same voice asked.

'Is there an officer named Oakwood in the ATU and should he be visiting me today?'

A pause. Then gentle, low electronic music played to reassure Stacy that he was still connected until after about thirty seconds came another slight pause and then a reply. It was a different voice and this time it delivered a live message.

'Affirmative on both counts. Thank you for calling.'

A click and the line briefly went dead before the return of the normal dialling tone. He hung up. Stacy had no great worry about Mr Oakwood's authenticity but it was always wise to check such things. Four and a bit minutes. He walked briskly down the stairs, crossed the hall and entered his study. Seated by the window, John Goldhawk had taken an easy chair where he appeared to become part of the background, a minor player in a scene dominated by Mr Oakwood who occupied a straight-backed chair facing Stacy's large antique desk. Stacy lowered himself into a swivel chair, one that matched the desk, sat back with his hands clasped lightly on his lap and waited for the visitor to reveal the purpose of his visit.

'Look at these items, please, Mr Kenton.'

Although phrased as a request Stacy was in no doubt that it was an order. Mr Oakwood had not travelled to rural Buckinghamshire for fun. Stacy took the two A4 sized sheets and looked at them. They were in landscape format, one sheet an exact copy of the other apart from the text. One sheet had text in English, the other in a language Stacy thought could well be Welsh.

'Welsh,' confirmed the ATU officer, as if reading Stacy's mind.

The left hand half of each page depicted a closely cropped head and the shoulders of a man wearing an open-necked shirt or tunic with a cartoon style speech bubble, the English version announcing:

'This is the Penycraig Community Council. We demand protection for all coastal communities.'

The right hand picture showed the same man but this time sporting a beret with a badge on it and his shoulders dressed in a camouflaged jacket. He had a military or paramilitary appearance and the more sinister message contained in his speech bubble proclaimed:

'Publish this leaflet or we will remove a Member of Parliament from circulation.'

'Where did they want this published?' asked Stacy, wondering exactly how serious the threat was and in particular if there was any threat to himself.

'It was sent to the West Wales Advertiser who are based in the small town of Machynlleth. They received it a week ago, on the Wednesday, no doubt the authors hoping that it would appear in the next weekly edition on the Friday. Whoever is behind this even paid the correct advertising fee. But this was not their first attempt. Back in January similar items in Welsh and English were sent but on that occasion the threat for non-publication was simply termed as a non-specific 'punishment.''

'Did they publish?' asked Stacy.

'On police advice they did not and the punishment was simply to have obscenities in Welsh daubed on their building in full view of the street.'

'And then this higher powered threat followed?'

'No. A second attempt to force publication followed two months later. The item to be published was identical but the threat this time was for an act of violence but again no detail was specified. Again the police advised non-publication. The retribution came two weeks later. Despite police surveillance the Advertiser's computer equipment was damaged. Very clever action according to our experts. A Trojan. They targeted the staff records on the back of an incoming official government message. Fortunately everything was backed up and the studio and printer systems were left untouched.'

'Where is Penycraig?'

'We're not sure yet. There is no Penycraig community in West Wales. There is a Penygraig in the Lleyn peninsular but that is some way away and there's no evidence of underground activity in that area.'

'And this latest threat. Is it serious?'

'So far they have acted as they have promised but in a fairly low-key manner. We have no idea of their timescale. It could be a minor stunt for publicity or a major threat to make a point. We may not know the details but we are certainly prepared.'

Stacy did not ask for details of the ATU's preparedness as he knew Mr Oakwood would be unable to give a meaningful answer. For the first time John raised a question from his window seat.

'Who could be under threat then?'

'The First Minister, Mr Kenton here, the minister for Communications and Development – that's Simon Bromley and Mr Kenton's junior, Kay Holloway, who looks after coast,' said Mr Oakwood, addressing Stacy rather than his questioner, adding, 'The local constituency MP, Plaid Cymru's Gareth James is not thought to be under threat.'

'And protection for Mr Kenton?' continued John.

'To all intents and purposes it will appear low-key. We will have officers from this unit keeping an eye on all possible targets who could be in line for this promised retribution. We don't expect you to notice them. On official visits you will have the usual uniformed attendants but from now on they will be ATU officers. To any casual observer nothing will have changed. We suggest, sir, that you only make unannounced visits to Wales and that you and your family take precautions when travelling; entering or leaving the house should be done by car and your vehicles should be garaged and if at all possible never left unattended outside. One further point, Mr Kenton. Do you play sport?'

'These days only riding my horses. I usually keep to the neighbouring farm estate.'

'In that case I strongly urge that you only ride out in a group – a minimum of three – and that you never keep to a routine in either the time, the day or the route you take.'

They discussed a few practical details then Mr Oakwood left Stacy with ATU contact details and took his leave. Stacy and John talked a little longer about constituency matters and how this new situation would affect their work and then they parted leaving Stacy to sit and ponder matters for awhile before he left his study in search of Tallin and some lunch.

Thursday 29ᵗʰ August 2199

The editor and owner of the West Wales Advertiser looked over the page set-ups for this week's edition. On page two there was a statement from the Penycraig Community Council, in English and Welsh, demanding greater protection for coastal communities. It was a simple statement. No threats were printed to back up the demand. The editor had agreed with the police that he should print the more benign part of the insertion required by these Penycraig people. He hoped this partial publication would prevent further problems for his business but he wasn't entirely certain that would be the case.

Friday 30ᵗʰ August 2199

Having kept quiet about Mr Oakwood's visit for over 48 hours and stayed largely out of his wife's way, Stacy decided that the time had come to share his concerns with her. Tallin, for her part, knew that in God's good time she would learn what had gone on between Stacy, John and their visitor. The content of a meeting that was so important that her husband was not even allowed a few hours relaxation on his return from America was not going to be divulged immediately the visitor had left. In fact Tallin had not even been told who the gentleman represented. Her lack of overt curiosity came from years of experience of being married to a politician. One event in particular, many years before, had been a salutary lesson for her. She had pushed and goaded Stacy to divulge Cabinet information for which any media editor would have paid good money but Stacy's following put-down was immediate and effective. Tallin had never been one to give up on a battle but on that occasion she had gone too far and it was a lesson that had stood her in good stead – she now knew that she would learn about Stacy's political life as soon as it was possible for him to divulge information, sometimes even before the same details were released to broadcasters and newspapermen.

Tallin was working in the kitchen. Instead of busying about making a drink and getting in her way as usual Stacy just stood in the doorway. Sensing his gaze on her she turned with a questioning look on her face.

'Fancy lunch out? I'm thinking about "The Ferryman".'

Tallin's face briefly showed suspicion and caution – it was unusual for Stacy to suggest a lunchtime outing – but memories of earlier visits to the riverside inn brought a smile to her face.'

'We haven't been there for ages. Yes, it would be nice to relax a little before going on holiday next week,' she replied. 'Just give me fifteen minutes and I'll be ready.'

Forty minutes later the Kenton's car crept along the driveway, stopped at the road and then turned right towards the motorway. The Ferryman was a country pub and restaurant near the Thames-side town of Henley. Despite the promise of a speedier journey on the main road the Kentons avoided the motorway and took the old London Road to Beaconsfield before travelling south to cross the river Thames at Cookham. Returning to the northern side at Marlow they passed through the attractively wooded Buckinghamshire countryside soon reaching their lunch venue picturesquely situated between the road and the river.

The car park was fairly full. The chatter and clatter coming from the open doors to the restaurant, together with the well-occupied garden tables, indicated a good take-up for the lunchtime menu but as they stepped inside the bar area they were met by an air of relative calm enlivened only by the low voices and clink of glasses as a handful of customers ordered drinks from the two bar staff before carrying their well-laden trays out to the garden.

Tallin and Stacy sat at their favourite bay-window table. A welcome light breeze wafted through the opening which, now and then, moved the curtains lazily back and forth. When the group at the bar reduced to just one pair Stacy walked across to buy drinks and as he waited he looked around. Was he being watched? Had the ATU sent an officer to track his every move? At that moment a man, dressed in unusually formal attire for a warm summer lunchtime, entered from the car park. He stood for a few seconds, looked around and then selected a corner seat away from the bar before taking out his personal phone and composing a message. Could that be, Stacy wondered, his ATU tail?'

'Hello, Mr Kenton. Haven't seen you in here recently.'

'No. I've been rather busy recently. You may have heard about it.' Stacy smiled as he replied to the barman's greeting.

With a matching smile in return, the barman asked

Stacy for his order and with drinks requested and supplied Stacy looked over questioningly towards Tallin who jabbed at the menu and mouthed her request for food.

'Two cheese and ham ploughman's, brown bread, please and black coffees to follow. I'll pay for all that now please.'

They ate slowly, enjoying the view over the river and occasionally discussed minor details about their upcoming holiday, starting the following Monday. Then with plates, cutlery and glasses cleared away and coffees served promptly as requested, they subsided into silence. When Tallin had finished she placed her cup back on the saucer and looked across at Stacy questioningly. Their next move was not as Tallin expected a gentle walk along the river but, after tipping the attentive barman and stepping out into the bright light of the beer garden, they walked down to the waterside where Stacy directed her towards the boat hire compound. Using the touch pad menu at the entrance he selected his required craft and length of hire time, presented his cashcard for payment and took the receipt offered by the pay machine. The boat hire yard was busy but they didn't have to wait long before a two-seater craft became available for their use.

'Are you sure you can still do this?' asked Tallin. 'You haven't done this for years.'

Stacy replied wordlessly by pushing off from the bank, deftly avoiding a couple of returning craft and turning right into the broad meander of water that had brought the Thames across from the southern side of its flood plain. Stacy rowed steadily but also kept an eye on the banks and water for ATU followers. None of the other rowers however or any of the occasional walkers, cyclists and joggers who graced the banktop path seemed to have any interest in the middle aged couple gliding gently downstream towards Henley.

Tallin, in contrast, sat back, relaxed and remembered the first time she had let Stacy row her out onto these waters. The young businessman, co-owner of a café-cum-bookshop in Bourne End and the young single mother were then both councillors on Wycombe District Council – he a thoughtful Conservative, she a firebrand Socialist. They had clashed often until one day, as members of the Planning and Development Committee they had surprisingly ended up on the same side. A large new development had been welcomed by all parties but whereas the Socialists and Liberals supported a developer who was willing to include a good proportion of social housing the Conservatives favoured a rival bid that was promising to provide a business and retail park instead. Evenly balanced, the committee chairman, Stacy, had the casting vote and sided with the need for the housing. Needless to say when it came to the full council vote the committee's recommendation was ignored but from that moment she had formed a high regard for her opponent's integrity. A week or so later she had marched into Stacy's café-shop, 'Food for Thought' and invited him out to dinner and, with her daughter stowed safely overnight with her mother, the two councillors had eaten at 'The Ferryman' for the first time. After a hesitant start their friendship had soon grown into love and then marriage. On that first meeting they had taken a boat out on the river and she remembered with a smile that she had to teach him how to row.

Brought back to the present when a wave created by a passing cruiser rocked their boat Tallin realised that they had left the congestion of the laughing, oar splashing family boaters behind and apart from a few more serious rowers and idly drifting lovers they were well clear of the holiday bustle of a fine late summer's day at 'The Ferryman'. Soon Stacy angled their boat towards the southern bank, slid up against it with a small bump and held the craft firmly to the side so that Tallin could step out. He tied the boat to a mooring ring set in a post beside the towpath, reached into the boat to retrieve their bag and then set off, turning left along the path whilst holding his hand out for Tallin as he did so. She took his hand, squeezed it and then gently gave him a quick kiss before they settled into an easy pace at first following the curving waterside path for about ten minutes and then turning back on a straight track that cut across the wide meadow that occupied the inside of the river's bend. The river itself was soon lost to view, its presence marked only by the increasingly distant passing of craft powered by muscle, motor or the movement of the wind and as they roamed casually across the grass they soon seemed quite apart from the rest of the world.

'OK, councillor,' pronounced Tallin, mimicking their days of confrontation on the District Council, 'what's all this about then?'

He told her everything about Mr Oakwood's visit.

They continued in silence until they reached the river again and turned left along the waterfront towards their boat. Tallin held back briefly. Stacy turned.

'What does this mean for us?' she asked.

They sat for a while on the bank and discussed the

level of threat. They talked about the implications for their family. And they discussed the need for Stacy to resign as an MP and should he do so immediately. Eventually they came to a conclusion; a decision that could be altered if circumstances changed. Stacy would stay on as Environment Minister until two important Bills that were in the pipeline were passed into law – hopefully during the next six months. He would then resign his post, probably in the spring 2200 and return to the back benches. No longer a minister he should then not be under any threat for his life. Should Mr Oakwood advise otherwise he would resign immediately and quit parliament. At that moment resurrecting his old business 'Food for Thought' seemed to Stacy to be a very good plan for their future.

They rowed back in silence. Having left the boat available for the next pair in the queue they set out across the now less full car park stopping briefly to let a smart black saloon set off for the exit. Stacy recognised the driver through a half opened window. It was the formally dressed gentleman he had seen earlier in the bar. ATU? Probably not but the thought that one or more of Mr Oakwood's men were probably somewhere around brought him a welcome feeling of confidence that the plan they had formed earlier would be seen through to its end.

* * * * *

That week's West Wales Advertiser had been on sale for about eight hours but the Penycraig announcement had raised few concerns. So far there had been one phone call and three e-mails asking who these people were. Most of the Advertiser's readers seemed to have quickly passed over page 2, attracted by the centre page spread that gave a brief description and several large coloured photographs recording the bumper attendance at the previous weekend's Aberdovey Carnival.

CHAPTER FIVE
MARTIAL LAW

Wednesday 5th February 2200, National Council Chamber, Westminster

At 1100 hours Karyn Sloane, Chairwoman of the National Council, called the members to order. Although officially 'Chairwoman', Ms Sloane was usually referred to as the 'Speaker', an ancient term for her office, despite the fact that very few MPs understood the exact meaning or origin of the title.

When the hubbub of the chamber had subsided to a low hum Ms Sloane introduced the first speaker of the morning – Stacy Kenton. Stacy stood, half turned and surveyed the packed house whose members had lapsed into near silence. There was an unusually large turnout for a Wednesday morning, a session that was usually given over to routine matters. Word had circulated that the provisions of the 'Coasts (Amendment) Bill' would be fiercely attacked by the opposition. The advertised details for this Bill had turned out to be rather more than just a minor tinkering with the existing legislation.

'Ms Sloane, First Minister, Honourable Members,' Stacy started. 'For many years the Government's plans for coastal areas have kept a difficult situation under control.' Stacy paused to allow a few comments from the opposition benches to subside. 'A balance between defending some areas and abandoning others whilst assisting migration and maintaining services has been completed within strict financial limits. The change of governing party five years ago however brought new policies to bear on our coastal problems. Their promise of support for added assistance in certain marginal constituencies led in a large part to their election victory. Unfortunately in order to fulfil their promises they removed support from many other areas. Disenchantment with this change led to opposition and in some cases spawned local defence groups including, occasionally, armed outlaw bands, that ceased to recognise the authority of the police. These armed groups have popularly become known as 'Brigades'. Although small in membership and only active in a few areas they represent an intolerable defiance of law and order. Equally worrying is the copycat growth of urban groups, usually criminal gangs, in less affluent areas. This Bill presents your government's plan to return to the policies that previously worked well. Unfortunately there are now areas where our tried and tested policies cannot be applied until civil control has been completely restored.

To this end we are planning to create zones where the armed forces will be tasked with the work usually undertaken by the police. Each such zone will be known as a 'Military Restricted Area', to be referred to as MRAs for convenience. Each MRA will have to be approved by this Council. Therefore three supplementary Bills are added to the main Bill to give MRA status to West

Wales, Cumbria and the Lincolnshire coast. It may prove necessary to extend this provision to other areas. Requests from Holderness and East Suffolk, where smugglers are the main problem, have been deferred until we see the effectiveness of the first group of MRAs. In view of the urgent need to establishing these zones the timetable for passage of the Bill has been abbreviated. The first reading will take place tomorrow and, assuming it gains approval and the Upper House agrees, the final reading will take place one week later.'

The New Times
London, Thursday 13ᵗʰ February 2200
Good News for Coastal Communities

'*Yesterday the National Council passed into law the provisions of the Coasts (Amendments) Bill and the Upper House passed the provisions into law unopposed. 'This Act will provide additional support to people who live in coastal areas of the country,' stated Environment Minister Stacy Kenton, adding, 'In areas of depopulation the provision and cost of services will become the responsibility of central government rather than a burden on local taxpayers. Where law and order becomes difficult to maintain the local police may be assisted or supplemented by detachments from the armed services. These areas will be termed Military Restricted Areas. And to attain this status the National Council must approve an amendment to the main Act specifying the area to be covered.'*

Amendments approved with yesterday's legislation cover parts of West Wales, Cumbria and Lincolnshire. When asked whether any other areas would be added to this list in future the Minister said that several areas had lobbied for inclusion and were being looked at to see if they met the criteria for inclusion. A spokeswoman for the opposition said that after many years of political consensus over coastal matters the Conservatives had broken rank with the government over this new Act because the new law eroded local democracy and in however limited a rôle the armed forces should not be involved with civilian policing.'

Tallin pushed The Times away and picked up the Register. She expected something extreme from the paper but even she was amazed to read the huge headline that occupied the whole of the front page except for a small note at the foot to explain that details would be found on the inside pages.

Daily Register
London, Thursday 13th February 2200
Martial Law!

'Wales, Cumbria and Lincolnshire. The government announced yesterday that control of finances and services such as transport and education in these areas would pass from local to national government. But buried in the act there are other provisions that could destroy our democracy. The armed services are to be given the right to manage law and order in these areas and, if thought necessary, eventually extend their powers to any part of Britain. This in effect adds up to our nation being placed under MARTIAL LAW.'

'I reckon the opposition have their eye on the next election, don't you, Stacy?' asked Tallin, putting the Register down and pushing it across the table to her husband.

'Maybe. But any opposition worth its salt would take this chance to plant a seed of doubt in the voter's mind. Any erosion of democracy worries people and yields good results for the other parties.'

'But people will benefit from this new funding won't they?' continued Tallin.

'Yes. They will. But those who don't – the vast majority of voters who live inland – may think that the coasts are getting a bigger slice of the financial cake than they deserve. A low-key media campaign may be needed to redress the balance.'

'You mean pay a tame journalist.'

'Something like that.'

'What about the Register then?' asked Tallin.

'We wouldn't use them – you can't trust the Register to do what you ask!' replied Stacy, trying to keep a straight face.

'No! Silly. What I meant was, what about the Register's report this morning.'

'On the face of it there was nothing in the Bill for the Register to latch on to. Have you seen pages four and five? Bigamist councillors are much more in their line of expertise for selling newspapers. But that headline is a stroke of genius. It gives the opposition an undeserved peg to hang their campaign on.'

Tallin reached across and pulled the Register back towards her. She turned to page four and began to read.

After a while she gave an 'umm' of surprise and a little later a giggle of amusement. Perhaps the Register was right. Perhaps politicians weren't all the pillars of society her husband cracked them up to be. She put the paper down and looked up and across at Stacy. As she did so the expression on her face turned more serious.

'Now this Act has been passed, will you resign from the cabinet?'

Stacy thought for a moment than reached across the table and held her hand.

'Yes. I'll let things settle down for a week or so then it'll be the back benches. At the moment I mean to retire at the end of this session, in the summer.'

Tallin gently pulled her hand from beneath his, got up, walked around the table to stand behind him and then leant forward, pressing her breasts against his shoulders and gave him a kiss on the back of his head where recently thinning hair promised to be the start of a bald patch.

CHAPTER SIX
THE EAST SUFFOLK
ASSOCIATION

Thursday 10th July 2200.

Alana looked out at the broad expanse of azure sky and the gilded tops of the clouds below. It had been a long flight from New Zealand but now the little flight map on the screen fixed to the back of the seat in front indicated their position near the coast of Wales, only a short distance from landfall. The Airbus Trooper of the Army Logistics Division began its descent so that her view through the cabin window soon became obscured by unbroken grey cloud with lighter wisps occasionally passing her window and the odd raindrop splattering against the glass.

She turned to look at her companion in the next seat and smiled. Lieutenant Christian Carter Blake slept, head rather awkwardly set at an angle to one side, threatening to plummet onto Alana's shoulder at any moment. With the view outside failing to improve and her flight partner failing to offer much companionship her mind turned back to the trip now nearing its end. It was back in 2197 that she had left Bentwaters. It was March, she seemed to remember, certainly early spring, when she had been posted to a training unit at the Royal Mercian's Litchfield HQ. Then in spring 2200 a detachment from the training unit plus a unit from their base in Alford, Lincolnshire, had been sent on a Middle and Far East goodwill tour. First there had been joint exercises in Jordan – a useful lesson in desert warfare – then a training exercise in Malaysia and thirdly a two week 'Show the Flag' R and R break in Australia. It was there that Alana had fallen in love with Blakey. She had got to know him during operations in Jordan but it was not until they sat next to each other on the flight from Singapore to Brisbane that they realised they wished to spend the rest of their lives together. On their last free day in Australia he had taken her out to dinner and afterwards proposed marriage. They were unofficially engaged. There was, naturally, no ring, no meeting with parents and family and no formal announcement. There was also no immediate forward planning since at that time there service futures were unknown to them. They could look no further ahead than the final weeks of their tour that would see them working on exercises with New Zealand army and air force medics on evacuation procedures.

But whatever vague ideas they may have entertained were thrown into confusion when, after landing in Auckland on New Zealand's North Island, they were disembarked and bussed to the terminal whilst their baggage and equipment meanwhile remained undisturbed on the plane. After about 45 minutes an announcement had made. The detachment's commanding officer informed them that they had an hour to eat, drink and shop if they wished before returning to their aircraft for the return flight to Britain. New Zealand had been cancelled. He gave no explanation but a message filtered down through the ranks that unspecified changes in GB security needed them to head immediately for home. There was some disappointment, some relief and some excitement at their early return but Alana had her own particularly disturbing thought. Within 24 hours she could be separated from Christian by several hundred kilometres, neither of them knowing what the future held for themselves or their lover.

A metallic chime sounded.

The route map on the screen was replaced by an instruction to passengers to fasten their seatbelts. With one hand Alana squeezed Christian's hand and with the other gently shook his shoulder. He awoke and smiled.

'Seatbelt, Christian. We're home!'

Soon the huge troop transporter was transformed from being a free-flying bird into a lumbering land creature as it touched down on the Lakenheath Air Base runway. Whilst trundling along to the marshalling area, two thirds of the way along the runway, Alana looked over to the northern side of the airport, the part that housed the civilian flight terminal. Three Hi-Liners stood inert at that terminal. Two were arrivals; a Russian plane, probably from Irkutsk and a British flight, almost certainly from Sydney. American aircraft, American designed and built, the only hypersonic aircraft in existence, the Hi-Liners had for some years now graced the Panama corridor on flights between Britain or France and Australia, Japan, China and Siberia. As they trundled on down the runway the sun's rays, released by parting clouds, fitfully reflected from a third aircraft standing at a departure gate revealing it's operator to be Germany's Lufthansa. The Europeans – British, French, Germans and Russians – operated a pool system for their service with each nation unable to afford the astronomic cost of purchasing a full fleet of these planes on their own. To be economic these hypersonic aircraft had to fly very long distances between major centres of population. The former USA, producer of the aircraft, had been unable to take full advantage of their invention since a squabble developed between the manufacturers, now in the Union States and the airline now based in the New Mexican state of California.

Slowing to a stop at the marshalling point the giant troop carrier connected with its tug and moved on sedately along the runway to the southern section terminal – the HQ for Army Logistics. At last the aircraft halted next to a line of vehicles comprising three army transports and a civilian coach, the later signed as belonging to Forest Coaches of Brandon in Suffolk. Disembarkation followed. Not directly to the transports as was usual but, as in New Zealand, into the terminal building where an order for quiet brought a Major, unknown to Alana, to organise their onward travel. Two detachments of soldiers were despatched to Litchfield. At the end of each departure Alana relaxed as neither her name nor Christian's had been called. At the start of the third roll-call, for those destined to travel to Lincolnshire, Alana found herself again in a state of tension even to the extent of biting the nails of her left hand, a habit she thought she had abandoned in childhood. But yet again 45 men and women were sectioned off so that this time she knew that, whatever their destination she and Christian would be together. She looked across at him, crossed her fingers and smiled.

'Detachment Four. No slumming it in an army transport for you lucky people.'

The Major looked at his list.

'Lieutenant Buckhurst,' he called out.

Alana stepped forward.

'You're in charge, Lieutenant,' he instructed. 'You're headed for Bentwaters.'

'Sir!'

Despite all the remaining soldiers being on the list for the last transport the Major continued to read through his list to the very end. List completed Alana led her group out to the coach, smiling to herself as she did so. Another hour and she and Christian would be home. She already regarded Bentwaters as the nearest thing to a home that she could have in her peripatetic life and she was confident that before long her Blakey would feel the same way.

Just over an hour later the coach turned into the entrance at the Mercian's Bentwaters base. To Alana's eyes nothing much seemed to have changed. The guards were unknown to her but the buildings and routines appeared unaltered. The coach proceeded to the same parking area as always and the detachment disembarked outside the main assembly building. Alana stepped forward to be met by a lieutenant. They saluted.

'Welcome to Bentwaters. Please take your detachment to the assembly hall and the Base Commander will address you there.'

Whilst he was talking she noted his name badge –

Lieutenant Pinner – and she used that information in her reply. Then she turned, gave a slight nod to her troop and walked towards the building as requested. Christian, recognising her instruction, shepherded the group in behind her.

The Assembly Building was, externally, the same as Alana remembered but inside it was a different matter. In her memory she carried a picture of a building that had served as a mess for the lower ranks, a gymnasium and a meeting and briefing hall, a general-purpose facility with utility furnishings that lacked an air of permanence; seemingly waiting for imminent redevelopment. Today however she noted that the trestle tables and bench seats that had occupied one end of the large room had been replaced by circular or rectangular tables of varying sizes designed to service groups of between two and twelve soldiers in individual, upholstered chairs. A handful of men and women were finishing their meals. The large servery hatch in the adjacent wall was still there but the canteen facilities had been enhanced by the addition of a long, well appointed serving bar situated between the hatch and the tables. To one side a series of low occasional tables were the focus for comfortable chairs – some covered in leather, others in cloth. The larger part of the building was given over to an assembly facility with gently banked, permanently fixed rows of seating either side of a central aisle, facing a platform that was designed to be the focus of attention. Gone were the stacks of metal chairs lining the wall and gone was the gymnastic equipment. This new air of permanence suggested to Alana that in her absence the base had been set up to service a campaign that was clearly expected to last for some time.

She had several minutes to take in all of these changes before a Colonel, one of a group of three officers who had been standing on the platform, turned and walked up the aisle towards her. Colonel Morden, she decided, would not have left them waiting. He would have been at the door to meet them. The new station commander, Colonel Westbourne, had not presented her with the most favourable impression and her respect for him fell further when he gave her details of the detachments immediate programme. Alana would have expected him to welcome the newcomers, making contact with the men and women from the start. But perhaps he had more important things to do. For now she would give the Colonel the benefit of her doubts.

'OK,' she prefaced her report of the station commander's instructions. 'You have 45 minutes to eat and relax. The washrooms are through the doors to your left. Promptly at 1430 we assemble here for a briefing. Thank you. You are free to go.

By 1430 the detachment was settled towards the front of the seating area, facing the platform. It was not Colonel Westbourne who stepped up to address them but a major – James Arch – who Alana knew from her previous deployment at Bentwaters. She relaxed. They were in good hands, at least for the next twenty minutes or so.

'Welcome to Bentwaters. I hope Lieutenant Buckhurst has put in a good word for this base, your home for at least the next eighteen months, and the soldiers who staff the place. After this briefing you will be allocated your quarters. That task will be down to Lieutenant Blake. At 1700 hours we shall reconvene here and be given a tour of the base facilities. From 0900 hours tomorrow you will be granted leave for one week, reporting back to base by 1800 hours next Friday, the 18th July. Any questions?'

'Some of us are from Alford, sir. We have families and possessions up there. What arrangements are in place for relocation, sir?'

'My office is open until 2200 hours this evening and will be staffed again from 0800 hours tomorrow. Report there and Welfare will deal with each case individually, sergeant. Any further questions?'

There were none.

'So now it's down to business.'

A map appeared on the wall screen. It showed East Anglia.

'Next Wednesday, the 16th July it is expected that the National Council in London will pass a vote to add East Suffolk to the list of MRAs – that's Military Restricted Areas. The armed services will then be jointly responsible with the police for maintaining law and order in this area. The Mercians have been working in the existing MRA in Lincolnshire and it is that experience of operations that has led to your redeployment down here.'

Major Arch turned to the map that now had the proposed East Suffolk MRA added to the base map as a highlighted area.

'We have three main duties here that the police will be pleased for us to take over. The major task is to tackle smuggling. With the declining population and the long coastline punctuated with broads and estuaries it has become a growth industry in these parts. Secondly there are the travellers. On the whole the travelling population are known to the police but at times they will require additional manpower and we will aid them by keeping track on any bands that are hell-bent on flouting civilian laws. And thirdly there are illegal bands who oppose the government or the military or both. They are mainly locals who think they are getting a raw deal compared with the mass of the British population. Before the MRAs we had few such groups, mainly charities, some well-meaning but since the government handed us greater powers they appear to have become more belligerent. One of the local groups has reorganised itself along military lines with a headquarters that organises local activist groups based throughout the area. We are as yet not sure of this local group's aims but in other parts of the country, Wales for example, they have actively targeted military personnel. With the new powers we shall be able to expand our operations in order to contain or eliminate them as necessary.

Some of you will join the existing anti-smuggling operations that will now be under the control of Lieutenant Blake who has undertaken similar work in Lincolnshire. The remainder will join Lieutenant Buckhurst in a new intelligence unit monitoring local dissidents. From time to time small numbers may be withdrawn from these units to help with other operations'.

The Major continued to give further details of the planned developments and the equipment available at the base so that the newcomers were clear about their rôle in the forthcoming operations. He finished his task by reminding the assembly that Welfare was housed in D7 and this location would be made clear to them on their forthcoming tour of the base. Having completed his briefing Major Arch handed over to Alana who, he assured his audience, could deal with any problems that may arise.

Alana stood with her back to the platform, facing the assembly. She was clearly in command yet also one of them, in no way detached from her troops. Her first task was to read out the names of the soldiers allocated to the two units, those to be placed in her care and those entrusted to Christian. As the personnel were dismissed she became aware that underneath her outwardly calm persona she had an almost undetectable smile on her lips and a slightly raised heartbeat indicating a measure of excitement. She was back at Bentwaters, back in operations, back with an opportunity to gain promotion. Perfect, she thought. And Christian would be nearby. Just Perfect.

* * * * *

*Wednesday 30*th *July 2200*

Many of us, when travelling home after making a visit outside our local area, recognise a landmark that stands at the point where we feel we have reached home territory. It may be a river crossing or a public house, a signpost or just a bend in the road that when it comes into view lifts our spirits. It is the point where we think, 'Not long now!' and relax a little, raising a smile or perhaps beginning to hum or sing to ourselves. It means we're nearly home. For Mike Cannon it was the bridge over the River Alde carrying the

A12 road north-eastward through Suffolk. The village of Stratford St Andrew to the west of the river was in foreign territory yet Farnham, barely one hundred metres to the east, felt like home. At least that had certainly been the case up until a few weeks ago. Today, though, after two weeks away Mike didn't even reach the Alde crossing on his journey home; he turned off the main road at the northern end of the Wickham Market by-pass – just five kilometres short of the Alde crossing – and took the A1116 road heading to the north-west. Mike now had a new home. Of course a newly built township in mid-Suffolk could not compare for character with his recently discarded home village of Reydon but inevitably, if reluctantly, he had left the coastal familiarity of his childhood to pursue his career from a base in the rapidly growing New Town of Framlingham.

The crunch had come when Dad looked like loosing his job. As a long time employee he had been retained by Southwold Printmasters long after the economic decline in the town had seen others released. There was still work available in Southwold but those who delivered print supplies and those who serviced and repaired equipment had become reluctant to travel as far east as that coastal backwater or charged exorbitant rates to do so. Costs soared and the Printmasters had to choose between closure or relocation. The growing town of Framlingham beckoned. Well positioned to regain their status as a major regional business yet near enough to their old home to retain many of their existing customers, the firm had moved west. And Dad had followed.

Sister Gayle had married and moved away from the

area but Frank still lived in the family home with his partner Shelley who, on Mr and Mrs Cannon's departure had moved in from just three doors down the road. Unlike Gayle, who would never have considered living with a man unless they were married, Frank had never even considered formalising his relationship with his girlfriend. Mike could have stayed in Reydon with brother Frank but whilst a day or even perhaps a weekend back in Reydon was OK, living full-time with Frank and Shelley and their relaxed attitude to time would not have been comfortable. Reluctantly following Mum and Dad had become the better option.

The new Framlingham road followed the higher ground northwards as it by-passed the old road that connected the villages in the river Ore valley below. The journey was new enough to Mike for him to notice previously unseen things each time he travelled along the road. A change in the light or the weather or the traffic could bring to his attention something missed or blocked from view on a previous occasion. Today as the road turned towards the town and the view opened up he noticed a railcar, newly departed from Framlingham, travelling along the tramway towards the main line at Wickham Market. The half-hourly service operated by the battery-electric railcars followed the course of a long disused former rail line and as such was representative of major transport investments the government had made in the area.

The Cannon family had taken a comfortable modern house in Apsey Green – one of three new townships constructed around the old market town. Apsey Green together with Brabling Green and Cole's Green had followed tradition by taking their names from the former hamlets that had now been completely enveloped so that only the names and a few cottages were left to represent the once quiet rural locations. For Mike one advantage of living at home was the readily available meal service available courtesy of his mother. A late breakfast was in preparation when, at about 1000 hours he arrived at 27 Down Court. The meal served two purposes. For Mike it provided much needed sustenance following an early departure and a long road journey. It also gave his mother an opportunity to sit down opposite him, her hands nursing a mug of tea ready to quiz her son on his latest assignment before details were broadcast by whichever media concern had sponsored his latest project.

Mike had returned from a tour of the bases used by the army to house the troops who were assisting or replacing the police in the Restricted Areas. He had been an observer with helicopter patrols searching for smugglers in Lincolnshire and with foot patrols manning roadblocks near Inverness where itinerant bands were looting and burning abandoned properties. And he had sat around with soldiers in Cornwall who, at the time seemed to have very few commitments. But it was in West Wales that he had seen the most disturbing and exciting operations. It was clear that the local police were completely out of their depth in attempting to deal with small, mobile bands of armed outlaws who disrupted road and rail services and intimidated the remaining local population.

When Mum's curiosity had been satisfied Mike relaxed by watching TV for a while before taking a shower, changing his clothes and heading out to the pub for a drink and hopefully some companionship. Away from home, when he was working, he seldom had a drink but when at home he had developed a habit of visiting The Vine at Brabling Green. The Vine and Harvester to give the pub its full name was not Mike's local. Although each of Framlingham's new neighbourhoods had been provided with a public house along with a primary school and a health centre, the pubs had, within a couple of years, developed their own specialised trade. Closest to Mike's new home, in fact only 200 metres away, was The Beehive. A good restaurant and a children's playground marked it out as a family pub – one that Mike's Dad sometimes used and Mike had occasionally been along there with his parents. No one in the family had ever gone to The Holly Tree at Cole's Green. The very fact that it had recently been re-named Maddie's Bar was enough to warn most of the population older than about 21 to give the place a wide berth. Mike had no wish to be crammed in with a large group of just legal drinkers, assaulted by loud music and unable to carry on a reasonable conversation without shouting himself hoarse.

Since leaving Reydon Mike had linked up with a number of old friends. Some had moved to Framlingham from Reydon or Southwold whilst others he had known at college. Incomers of a similar age from other areas had naturally gravitated to this group so that it was common, even at lunchtime, to meet up with several familiar faces at The Vine. Today, though, for some unknown reason the place was barely occupied. Just inside the door a couple sat at a small table concentrating on their food to the extent of ignoring each other and Mike at the moment he entered. One other customer graced the strangely quiet pub. She was perched on a bar stool, back to Mike but was recognisable from the lengths of blond hair reaching half way down the back of her light blue sleeveless top.

Mike walked to the bar and stood beside her.

'Hi, Carly.'

She turned, smiled and put a hand on his shoulder.

'A pint of Greene King's isn't it?'

'Yes, please.'

Mike hoped the surprise he felt at Carly's welcome wasn't reflected in his reply. He knew Carly of course but only as a member of a larger gathering. He had often spoken to her but generally only in greeting and his contribution to conversations had consisted of little more than two or three unimportant comments in a group discussion. He would not have been able to say what Carly's usually liked to drink. Mike's beer arrived and Carly paid. Picking up her own half-empty glass she motioned towards a bay window and they moved there to sit facing each other across a small circular table.

'Not out gathering news today then?' she asked.

Mike was not at all surprised that Carly knew how he earned his living; it was commonly a topic of conversation when he was with a group of friends.

'Just taking a break. I've recently come back from a two week assignment.'

'Do you like travelling?' she asked. But before he could answer she added, 'Daft question really. You must do!'

'Yes. This last assignment took me all over the country.'

'When are we going to see this latest report in print?'

'It's a four part series for The New Times. First part should be out on Saturday, not this one coming but next week. I've been out with the army in the Restricted Areas.'

Carly's eyes widened and she moved her head closer, her folded arms resting on the table.

'That must have been scary, judging by TV reports about areas like Wales.'

'By and large it was just shadowing routine patrols, on foot and by helicopter but I did see a brief encounter with smugglers in Lincolnshire but that was from a safe distance.'

'How about the illegals? Have you had any contact with them?'

'No. My brief was to report on the work of the armed services. I didn't talk to any dissidents.'

For a couple of minutes they drank in silence until Carly finished hers and Mike bought a repeat order from the bar. After an initial sip Carly looked up and smiled.

'Do you reckon you'll do a follow up series on the dissidents?'

'It's possible. No one has asked me to do that yet but it's an interesting suggestion though it would be rather more difficult to contact such groups than walking into well-marked army bases.'

'Have you heard of ESA – the East Suffolk Association?'

'You mean the group who do things like taking people to hospital appointments because the local bus service has been stopped?'

Yes. That's them. Not exactly on a par with armed bands in Solway or Ceredigion but non-the-less critical of the government's response to their situation. Well, my cousin Carlos works with them. Collects and delivers mail and that sort of thing. If you would be interested in talking to him let me know. Next time he's around I'll introduce you.'

'Thanks. If I can get anyone to sponsor me it could well be the start of an interesting new investigation. I'll let you know.'

They talked further about Mike's work and then about people they knew in common. First one and then several more of Carly's friends arrived and crowded around the small table until Mike, no longer the centre of the conversation, felt that he should go home and file the rest of his report for The New Times. As he got up to go he caught Carly's eye. She smiled and gave him a wink that Mike took to mean 'Keep in touch.'

Friday 15th August 2200

It was another couple of weeks before Mike thought to visit The Vine again. Local matters – putting together reports about a series of suspicious fires in farm buildings around the market town of Bungay and the growing band of protesters camped on the course of a controversial new railway project near Peterborough – had kept him busy. He had also needed to take a trip to London to discuss a proposed new weekly column to be written for London Life. Whilst in the capital he had an informal meeting with Carl, his contact at The New Times.

'Just to keep in touch,' Mike explained as they sat down at a corner table in the Clipper Bar.

'Come off it, Mickey.' Carl was the only person who

regularly called him by this form of his name. 'You've never called me for a chat without there being some particular reason.'

'OK,' admitted Mike coming straight to the point. 'Any chance of a regular Saturday slot in the Magazine?'

'Greedy! Your Wednesday column is doing OK isn't it? It's not going to fold as far as I know. Everybody loves your work. Mind you that cantankerous old cow Simi Preston can love you one day and cut you off without a thought the next. So, then. What's the big idea that needs a glossy weekend spread rather than a midweek column? It had better be amazing if you want me to put in a good word for you.'

'Well. The Restricted Area articles are good.'

'Yes'

'So what about the view from the other side? The outlaw bands and other renegades.'

'Not so easy to set up as the military!'

'Point taken but I've already got one contact in the pipeline and there should be others who want to talk. After all, people with a grievance always want to air their views. And it's topical; a few weeks ago two new MRAs were sanctioned and there are rumours that there are at least another couple in the offing. It would take until the autumn to get the thing going but four monthly articles would be quite feasible.'

'Leave it with me. Draft up something for mid September and I'll see what can be done.'

Another pint, a brief account of Carl's rather stormy relationship with his partner, an even briefer chat about Mike's non-existent girlfriends (too busy, always moving around) and the meeting ended. On the underground ride back to Stratford station – he had left his car at Ipswich and come in by train – Mike decided that having made a start he now needed to firm up an arrangement with Carly and her cousin. So that evening there would have to be another visit to The Vine.

In contrast to his previous visit The Vine exuded its usual Friday, end of the working week, busy, buzzing atmosphere. Mike knew what to expect from the fact that he had to park along the road as the car park was full. Inside the door he stopped and looked around the throng. Two old college friends were propping up the near end of the bar and one of them saw him and beckoned him over. Mike smiled and waved back. Another evening of risqué jokes was looming ahead; Miles always needed an audience and at the end of each story laughed louder than those who were hearing it for the first time. As Mike pushed through the throng he looked for Carly. At first he didn't see her. She wasn't standing with the other members of her usual group. He scanned the room again and this time he saw her seated at the far end of the bar talking to a tall, well-built and frankly handsome man who Mike hadn't seen before. As if aware of his gaze on the back of her head Carly turned and with the slightest of smiles gave him a brief signs of recognition before returning to her conversation.

Absolutely in character, when Mike finally reached him Miles was standing with an empty glass in his hand.

'Just in time, Mike. I'll have another one of my usual, please.'

Miles looked upon a free evening's drinking as the

reward for his joke and story telling. Mike pushed through the throng gathered around the bar and waited for his turn to be served. He shuffled forward a little but turned when he felt a hand on his shoulder. It was Carley.

'I'm glad you're in tonight, Mike. Do you remember me talking about my cousin Carlos? He's here and he'd like to meet you. No hurry. We'll be here for at least another hour. When you're tired of Miles just pop over and say hello.'

Without waiting for a reply she was gone.

The evening dragged a little. Not unpleasant, not really boring but Miles was not at his best. A dearth of new material meant that he had to fill in with some old favourites. Mike was not exactly a captive audience but he stayed on. Miles had his uses. Miles took in everything, seeing and hearing and remembering things as he made his rounds as a salesman for a national wholesaler supplying village stores. Every now and then he had picked up on local gossip that, when passed on to Mike had been the basis of some good stories – one of them even making the national press. When Miles left the group to visit the toilets Mike took the opportunity to move across to where Carly and, he assumed Carlos, were seated still deep in conversation. As he approached Carly her companion stood, pulled across another bar stool and extended his hand to Mike. They shook and then Carly made the formal introductions.

'I work with ESA, Mike,' explained Carlos. 'You're welcome to come and spend a day with us. Meet some of the Association's Members. Ask questions; any questions. We'd be pleased to have you along.'

'Thanks. Where and when do you suggest?'

'Well, you could start at our Saxmundham HQ and then we could visit one of the bases from where our members operate. That should give you a start but you could always pay us another visit if you needed more information.'

Carlos leaned to one side, reached into a back trouser pocket, pulled out a wallet and extracted a business card that he passed over to Mike. Mike read the card.

East Suffolk Association
Saxmundham
Carlos 107 734 363 109

He looked up with a questioning expression, first facing Carlos and then at Carly.

'We tend not to use family names,' she explained in answer to Mike's unexpressed query. Mike passed a card of his own to Carlos. It was then that Mike realised that he only knew Carly by her forename and for all he knew that could have been made up or was perhaps a nickname or a variation of her real name. The same, he supposed, could apply to Carlos. Perhaps he was reading more into the situation than it required but he was certainly intrigued by Carlos and ESA.

'OK. I've raised the idea of writing about ESA and possibly some other groups with one news company who have already shown some interest. I'd like to make a visit. When's convenient for you?'

'I could show you around next Wednesday. It needn't be a formal arrangement. Either of us could phone and call it off if something more pressing arises. If I don't hear from you I'll pick you up from.......Down Court,' suggested Carlos, reading from Mike's card, 'at about 0940.'

Mike and Carlos shook hands.

'Thanks. I'll see you then.'

Mike stood up, smiled at Carly, turned and headed back towards the sounds of laughter coming from the other end of the bar. Miles seemed to have regained his touch.

Wednesday 20th August 2200

The mist that had dogged them since leaving Framlingham had begun to clear as Carlos turned his Peugeot Saloon off the A12 road at Benhall and headed down the road towards Saxmundham. Although the sun could not be seen there was now a brightness that suggested it was at work burning off the moisture. And so it was. A few minutes later as Carlos entered the Urban Traffic Area the sky lightened further and the sun's orange disk became visible to their right.

Carlos activated the sun visor and hit the edge of town travelling rather faster than the advertised speed limit. He braked steadily so that by the time the first houses were reached he was travelling legally.

'For twelve years I've travelled this route, almost daily, and I've never been caught for speeding.'

'What about the number plate recognition camera we passed back there?'

'Cameras! Don't make me laugh. That machine hasn't worked for years and even if it did no one would ever check it. The local traffic cops don't have the manpower.'

They drove on into the High Street. Soon Carlos pulled over to the right-hand kerb and parked in front of what appeared to be an un-signed double-fronted shop. They got out and as Carlos collected something from the boot of the car Mike studied the building. The two windows either side of a recessed central doorway were glazed with a bronze-tinted glass of the type that was opaque to the viewer standing outside on the pavement yet transparent to those inside the building. To the left the neighbouring unit was clearly marked 'Teleworld', the countries most widespread telecommunications retailer. To the other side the shoppers of Saxmundham were able to purchase 'locally produced fruit and vegetables' at J S Rahman's Foodstore. As they walked up to the door Mike noticed an A4 sized sheet of paper taped to the inside of the glass panel backed by a beige-coloured blind. The notice proclaimed that the building housed:

The East Suffolk Association (ESA)
Reg. Charity No: E7217735
All visitors welcome
0900 – 1630. Monday – Saturday

Carlos pushed the door open and they walked inside. A short central corridor housed doorways to left and right and led to a further room at the back. The door to the right was closed whilst the doorway opposite was just an archway leading into a reception area. To the front of this area the reception desk supported a phone consul and a monitor screen. The receptionist seated at the desk had a name badge identifying here as Dina who greeted Carlos and then Mike as they passed. Behind Dina another desk under the supervision of Beth was furnished with a further phone and monitor together with a printer and piles of books, files and papers. Beth looked up, smiled at Mike and returned to her work.

On reaching the room at the end of the corridor Mike saw that it was principally occupied by a large rectangular table surrounded by eight chairs. Some sort of meeting place, he thought. Two men and a woman, deep in conversation, stood at the end beside a window, near an open rear door. As Carlos led Mike into the room a tall man in a business suit peeled away from the group and walked towards them. He held out a hand in greeting.

'Welcome Mike. Please sit down. Carlos will get you a tea or a coffee. I shan't be long.'

Seated, Mike looked around. To his left a long table against the wall supported cups, saucers, glasses and trays of cutlery. The only other furniture in the room was a set of shelves attached to the same wall, further down near the window. Carlos walked through an archway in the wall to the right into a kitchen area where he set about making drinks. The conversation at the end of the room soon ended and a man in casual summer clothes and the woman dressed in camouflage jacket and trousers left through the rear door leaving the tall man free to move back and take a seat opposite Mike.

'My name is Kassim. I'm the ESA president'

Carlos returned, took orders for drinks, found some biscuits (He obviously knew his way around the kitchen) and set up items on a tray.

'We're glad you could come. We liked your articles about the armed forces work in the Restricted Areas but there's still some confusion about the activities of various groups that have set themselves up in opposition to the government's plans. At one extreme there are the self-styled *Brigades*. They grab most of the headlines because of their paramilitary activities and anti-government intent. At the other end of the spectrum there are charities such as ourselves who are intent on supporting the local population with services that the local authorities find themselves unable to provide. We in ESA act as a supplementary social, postal and transport service. Some similar organisations have tried to act as para-emergency services, particularly in the medical field but we do not have the expertise although we would provide assistance if called upon to help. Now, if it's OK with you I'll let Carlos take you to see one of our units. Ask as many questions as you like and write about anything you see – it may well help to bring in more supporters and sponsors for our work. Enjoy your day!'

Kassim stood and shook Mike's hand again. Clearly the meeting was over. If Mike had any questions they would have to wait until he reached the ESA unit. Everything seemed very open but Mike wondered if he was only being allowed to see what they wanted him to see.

Carlos waited until Mike had finished his drink then ushered him out by the rear exit. The door opened onto a yard where three vehicles were parked, one of them being the car that Carlos had driven from Saxmundham. But it was a Land Rover Terrier ATV, an all-terrain vehicle, they headed towards. Not exactly a recent model and not particularly clean but a classic from the much admired and ever reliable Land Rover stable. Seated and belted they backed down to a service road and turned onto the High Street to travel north, past Kelsale, to where they re-joined the A12 Lowestoft Road, again heading north.

'So, Kassim is the boss then,' stated Mike as an opener to the questions about the organisation of ESA that were forming in his head.

'Yes,' replied Carlos, succinctly, whilst concentrating his gaze on a slow-moving lorry convoy ahead.

Mike waited until the traffic thinned before continuing.

'Did he start it all, then?'

Carlos gave Mike a glance and smiled briefly.

'OK. Here's a brief history. Have you heard of the Aldringham Seven?'

'Yes. They're a group of retired old boys who provide services for local people in the Leiston area.'

'Wrong on two counts. They *were*, not *are* active and they had ladies as members as well. They formed about sixteen or seventeen years ago at a meeting in the local pub in Aldringham. Mostly newly retired they had time to run people to doctor's or hospital appointments, collect mail or collect prescriptions. All the things you can't do through a computer terminal. As the members became old, infirmed or died new people came in to replace them or enlarge the group. Kassim became interested in about 2193. He was adamant that the area should remain in civilian control; he hated the idea of the army, newly arrived in support of the police, having any influence at all.

'Why does Kassim dislike the support given by the army?'

'In part because the armed forces are controlled from London. He is a great believer in local control by local people. But perhaps even more telling was a tragedy the previous year. Kassim Wood, as he was known then, was married to Sarah West. They ran a small farm out at Knodishall. Sarah and their daughter Jane were returning from shopping in Saxmundham when their car was hit by an army vehicle – they were nudged over the parapet of a bridge and ended upside down in a stream. Sarah was killed immediately and Jane was injured. He took Sarah's family name of West in memory of his wife and is now known as Kassim Wood-West. Ever since then he's been on a mission. I don't think he hates the military; he just wants to do anything possible to limit the need for the army to be here. That's why he formed ESA – to expand the area originally worked by the old Aldringham Seven.'

'And what happened to Jane?' asked Mike.

'Grew up, married, moved away. Somewhere abroad I seem to remember but I don't really know. I never knew her.'

They had reached Yoxford. Mike, who knew the area well, was wondering where they were headed. Conversation over he kept his eyes on the road. They passed the turns signed Westleton and Darsham before Carlos slowed, indicated and turned eastwards along a minor road that carried no name or indication of their destination. At the end of the road they turned left. Mike was puzzled, even more so when they continued past the only side road of note, the turning that led to Dunwich. The way ahead led to Blythburgh and back to the A12. Why then the detour? He soon found out. Just a kilometre past the Dunwich turn Carlos indicated right and they turned onto a track that again headed east. A wooden sign to the left of the track may have once given the name of the property they were now crossing but any lettering had long since faded or fallen away to leave a mottled, dull grey weathered surface. They crossed open heath, skirted an area of woodland and then across another area of heath travelling for about four minutes before coming to a halt beside an open-ended barn like structure on their left. A large house was partly visible through a screen of trees a little further on. As Mike climbed down from the Land Rover he turned and looked across to the other side of the track where an area of water was backed by extensive woodland and fronted by a patchwork of tall reeds and low bushes together with a few small trees. It was not a place he had visited before but he knew enough about the area to guess that it was probably Westwood Broad, less likely Dingle Broad. It was definitely too far south to be Blythburgh Broad.

'Know where you are?' quizzed Carlos as he stepped down to join Mike.

'More or Less. Westwood Broad?'

'Very good! You'll need to know your way around here if you're going to keep up with us after today. We're at Westhead House.'

'Where now?' asked Mike, unable to see any sign of the ESA unit with which he was to spend the rest of the day. Carlos pulled a bag from the back of the Land Rover, locked the vehicle and led Mike, not to the adjacent house but across the track and down a grassy slope to where a small boat, previously hidden to view by the reeds, lay tethered to a bollard. It was a broad, almost rectangular vessel rather like a punt. It reminded Mike of similar boats used by the watermen who kept the broads and shallow rivers free from reeds, fallen trees and other obstacles to navigation such as discarded household items and shopping trolleys. Carlos motioned to Mike to get in, picked up a pole from the floor of the boat, flicked the mooring rope off the bollard and punted them through a narrow channel between the reedbeds and past mudbanks to reach the open water. At this point punting was abandoned and Carlos fired up a small outboard motor, steering the boat towards the opposite forested shore. To the west an area of forest dominated the reedbeds that marked the landward end of the broad. Turning his gaze to the east Mike narrowed his eyelids, squinting against the rays from the late morning sun until he could make out a low coastal bar rising above the water at the mouth of the broad and beyond that, through a small gap, a narrow band of speckled sunlit sea presenting an ever changing pattern as the angle of the waves reflected light towards him then away.

As they approached the shore ahead of them two things became clear. They were heading for a small shingle beach and standing, waiting for them was a figure in combat clothing. Soon the front of the boat ground on the pebbles and shuddered to a halt. The figure in the combats, a girl with her light brown hair tied neatly back, greeted Carlos and smiled at Mike. She was slim, tanned, a little shorter than Mike but probably a couple of years older. He logged her in his mind as the third member of ESA he had met, after Carlos and Kassim – the fourth if you counted Carly but her connection with ESA, if any at all, was unclear. Later he would need to add a name to his image of the girl and hopefully learn a little more about her. Mike had already formed an outline for his article about the members and the purpose of the East Suffolk Association.

The girl took the painter, tied it to a metal stake and then turned and led them towards the woodland. A dry earth track formed by regular use crossed the undergrowth towards a building located on a slight rise about 150 metres from the shore. At first partly obscured by the trees the cabin, occupying a small clearing, soon became completely visible. Mike smiled to himself. Far from being a complete surprise the building turned out to be similar to several hundred found throughout the eastern counties and as far as he knew equally common in many other parts of the country. It was known as a *Star-Cab* – the English name for a type of modular prefabricated cabin that had originated with the Danish STR company over half a century earlier. They had been widely used as accommodation or storage units for workers on projects as varied as road and rail construction, leisure complex development and forestry. Mike had first become acquainted with one that was used for storing sports equipment during his days at Carlton College and later he had seen various modules grouped to form a small village for workers when the East Suffolk rail line had been diverted inland to avoid regular flooding near Blaxhall between Wickham Market and Saxmundham. A shop, a recreation room, a first-aid centre, a gymnasium, an equipment store and accommodation had all been provided using a variety of combinations of the basic Star-

Cab. When work on a project had been completed some modules were moved on for further use but many were sold and left in-situ or abandoned unused where they stood. Mike guessed that this one may have been first used by the gangs who built up the coastal defences between Dunwich and Southwold after damage by the Great Winter Storm of January 2188. At that time, just seven years old, Mike had been mightily impressed by the power of nature as trees were uprooted, cliffs broken down and rivers and the sea flooded large areas of farmland. In part his memory of the event was sharpened by the need for unplanned school closures and the extension of the Christmas holidays by a whole week.

The cabin ahead of them took the form of a long single-storey metal building with a gently pitched roof. It appeared to comprise three units bolted together. The floor was raised above the ground by about a metre on stout concrete pillars, the space below being unused. Mike thought this space was probably to allow for the possibility of flooding. Some Star-Cabs had fascias of timber, metal or other material to conceal their having been cobbled together but not here. Cabins used by construction gangs were usually left unadorned apart from graffiti – some artistic, many less so. The grey metallic exterior of the cabin just exhibited a dullness gained through years of weathering and the staining of deposits from trees and birds.

To the left-hand end three broad, low-rise steps with a handrail gave access to the cabin. They climbed the steps and walked through the open doorway into a small, dully-lit lobby that, with the door closed behind them provided an airlock situation before opening the inner door to the right. The first section of the building contained a galley, a storage area and what appeared to be an eating area with bench seats along the wall plus two square tables with a number of free standing chairs and stools around them. Beyond lay a larger, more open section. A large rectangular table was placed in front of a bench seat fixed to one wall. It seemed to Mike that the three people sitting around the table had been forewarned of his arrival as they appeared to be unoccupied, just sitting and waiting. Carlos and the girl took their leave. A tall man with greying hair stood, walked over to meet him and shook his hand warmly leaving Mike little time for further examination of the surroundings.

'Welcome Mike! We're glad you could come. Please. Sit down.'

There was one remaining chair. He sat down, facing the window. At the left hand end sat a girl characterised by red hair and dressed in dark trousers and a green T-shirt top sporting an ESA logo across her chest. At the other end, in what appeared to be a position of authority, the tall man, dressed in combat trousers and shirt had regained his seat. Opposite, seated on the bench seat by the window sat an athletic looking lady dressed in combat jacket and trousers, probably about ten years older than himself and of a similar age to the girl on his left. She gave him a quick slight smile of welcome. Mike's eyes lingered on her face for a few seconds longer than was strictly necessary to acknowledge her greeting. She lacked the attracting red hair and fuller figure of her companion but there was a steeliness in her eyes that issued an indication of strength and self-reliance. She could, he thought be the same girl he had seen earlier at the ESA headquarters but he couldn't be certain. It seemed to Mike that combat gear was the uniform for the unit although the word *uniform* was a little inappropriate as the colours and style seemed to have been individually selected – probably from ex-armed forces stock.

'I'm Michael Warren, leader of ESA's Leiston unit. This,' he said extending a hand forward to indicate the girl in combats, 'is Heron, our second in command here and at the end is Cindy, one of our support staff. You've met Cassandra outside – she and Simon, who is not here at the moment, are our other full time members. Then there are also two part-time operations officers and our technology expert James who are not on duty today. I suggest you start by having a chat with me and after that Cindy can show you around and also provide you with lunch. In the afternoon Cassandra can take you back across the broad where you will meet Simon who should be back from his mail run. I hope that's OK.'

'Sounds good. Thank you.'

'Right then. Heron and Cindy have work to do so let's move over to the easy chairs. Would you like a drink?'

'No, thanks. I'm OK. I had coffee at Saxmundham on my way here.'

'Right then. Ask what you like and write what you like. We're not out to censure anything.'

Mike took out his note pad and pen. He could have audio-recorded their conversation or he could have typed straight into his e-pad but experience had told him that the act of handwriting left interviewees most at ease.

They spoke for about fifteen minutes by which time

Mike was satisfied with the notes appended to each heading on his pad. Whilst Michael excused himself to take a phone message Mike checked down the information he had recorded.

ESA/Leiston Unit. Interviews. 20.08.00

Name: Michael Warren
Age: 53
Joined ESA: 2195 (5 years service)
Background: Born Leiston. Solicitor/ family firm/ Warren & Hills. (no Hills for last 150 years!) Firm now run by older brother with his (Michael's) son. District Councillor for 19 years before joining ESA.
ESA History: Part time helper, Aldringham Seven 2194. Mainly hospital car service to Ipswich or Yarmouth. Now full time ESA – no financial need to work, no ESA salary. Knew Kassim from Aldringham Seven days and believed in his aim to keep local services going and under local control. No need for the armed forces to expand operations in the area. Kassim turned old A7 into efficient unit when he formed ESA. Expansion of work in 2199 led to formation of 3 separate units covering areas beyond the Saxmundham HQ. Rendlesham unit in south. Leiston unit-centre. Wrentham in north. Michael was given job of organising Leiston unit. Mainly works with communications. Heron plans and oversees operations for the unit.

Michael soon returned with Cindy. Mike thought that she was the sort of person that would have gone unnoticed in the street were it not for here shoulder length red hair.

'I'll leave you with Cindy. Any further questions come and see me later.'

Mike stood, they shook hands, Michael returned to his phone and Mike turned towards Cindy.

'I'll show you around my empire. Won't take long!' Cindy laughed and led him through the cabin to the door at the back. The third unit beyond was a bunkroom with two pairs of bunks and beyond that an open door revealed a shower and wash room and, as Cindy opened further doors, a heating unit, a linen cupboard and two toilets.

'So who sleeps here?' asked Mike, intrigued.

'No one regularly. We keep one bed made up for emergencies. I even got snowed in last winter, only been in the job a week. My partner wasn't too pleased. But that was freak weather wasn't it. Not seen snow like that since I was at first school. Heron sometimes sleeps over if it suits operations.'

They turned back to the 'day room' as Cindy called it and walked through to the galley where she made it quite clear that this was her domain and she didn't like people messing around in it.

'So Michael isn't in charge out here.'

'Certainly not!' confirmed Cindy followed by another infectious peel of laughter. 'And before you ask, they won't get me into combats either.'

Cindy prepared drinks and sandwiches to Mike's requirements and they sat at one of the small tables whilst she answered his questions or, to be more accurate,

without much prompting gave him a potted history of her
life.

> *Name:* Cindy Stratford
> *Age:* 33
> *Joined ESA:* this year
> *Background:* Born Reydon, moved to Southwold,
> now back in Reydon. Husband lorry owner/driver.
> Decline in haulage work and therefore income. So
> C had to find a job. Opportunity came up with
> ESA – appreciated their work, needed the money.
> *ESA History:* Been here half a year. Loves the job. No
> one tells her what to do, it's up to her. If it was nearer
> home she would have loved to work full time.

Mike turned the conversation to the others in the unit. Cindy
chatted easily but Mike didn't take notes. He wanted to be fair
and only use direct testimony. He was, however, intrigued by
Cindy's assessment of her colleagues. Simon Upton, who
Mike was scheduled to meet later was a lovely lad – a real
hard worker and always appreciative of her efforts. James, the
tech. man could sort out any piece of equipment. He was a
real genius but untidy. She didn't see much of him and they
usually contacted each other through messages stuck on her
notice board. His brother Reuben was rarely seen at the cabin
as he worked part-time from home in Walberswick. Similarly
Gianni Prince worked out of Wenhaston. He was the
opposite of Simon. You always knew when Gianni was about
as he was always either cheerfully loud or silently morose. He
loved practical jokes. She seldom saw him; perhaps he was
avoiding her and only turned up on her days off.

'And Heron?' asked Mike when Cindy paused.

'Heron. We're usually known by our first names or a nickname. She's unusual; only known by her family name. I think she was once married to a Mr Heron. A couple of phone callers have asked for her as Mrs Heron. Pleasant enough person and really enthusiastic, never stops still for long. I think she's the real driving force here.'

Meal finished, conversation exhausted, Mike returned to the day room to report to Michael who was still seated at his desk.

'How's it going?'

'Fine. I'm getting just what I need for my article.'

'OK. We'll find Cassandra and she can take you back across the broad.'

They left the cabin with Mike receiving a cheery 'Bye' from Cindy as he passed through her galley and found Cassandra beside the beached ferry boat.

'All the best Mike. I hope all goes well. Put in a good word for the Leiston unit in your article and come back and see us soon.'

The two men shook hands.

Cassandra turned, looked at Mike and smiled. A warm smile, not just with her mouth but with her eyes as well. Then she returned to attending to the boat and with the untied painter in one hand motioned for Mike to climb in. She pushed the boat out, climbed in and punted the craft out for a short distance until they had travelled far enough to start the motor. Cassandra concentrated on steering the boat towards the house on the opposite bank and they remained silent for a while as Mike wondered how best to develop a conversation. She wasn't shy, her smile told him that and she didn't appear reticent but she was perhaps a private person. He was used to talking to all sorts of people in his line of business but in this case he felt he couldn't just dive in with a direct question. Mike decided to use an old standby, a corny old icebreaker.

'So, Cassandra, what's a nice girl like you doing in a place like this?'

She looked at him directly and smiled again.

'I prefer 'Cassie'. Michael's the only one who calls me Cassandra. I'm here because I respect what ESA are doing. Also,' she paused briefly, 'they pay me.'

'You're local then?'

'Walberswick born and bred. I've moved around a bit but now back where I was born.'

Gradually, between bouts of concentrating on navigation she gave him an outline of her life. Mike didn't make notes but stored the information to record later.

Name: Cassandra Vale

Age: 22

Joined ESA: 2197 (3 years service)

Background: Lived Southwold. Parents lost job when brewery closed. Parents moved to Essex. Cassie (17) stayed to complete college course – lives with grandmother in Walberswick. Neighbour to ESA activists James and Reuben Court. Showed interest in ESA, offered job.

ESA History: Part-time fundraising 2197/2198. Full time 2198. Assists Cindy, operates ferry, works with Heron on operations (no detail given).

Their craft entered the reed passage and Cassie concentrated on punting up to the low grass bank where she lassoed the mooring bollard, pulled the boat in and jumped out.

'That's it, Mike,' she said as she secured the painter. 'Simon should be waiting for you up by the barn, just over the track.' She looked up and smiled. 'See you again soon.'

She turned, untied the boat, waved a farewell and was soon on her way back across the broad. Mike walked up the grassy bank to the track. He wished he had been given enough time to ask about ESA 'operations' but perhaps he would get that information from Simon. At least Cassie had called him Mike.

In front of the barn the Land Rover Terrier used by Carlos was parked exactly where it had been left that morning. Behind in the shade of the large barn stood three further vehicles – another Terrier, a saloon car of a make not instantly recognisable and a medium-sized white van. With its rear to the track and both rear doors open there was no way Mike could identify the vehicle but there was no doubt in Mike's mind that the person seated on the floor above the rear bumper would turn out to be Simon. Probably about Mike's height when standing he was well built, muscular with closely cropped hair behind a receding hairline.

'Hi. This way, Mike. Sit here,' the man said patting the van floor beside him. Again Mike sensed that as with the trio in the cabin Simon was another member of the ESA staff ready and waiting for him. He thought that Simon must have been warned of his imminent arrival. Communications seemed to be the key to ESA operations.

'I'm Simon.'

They shook hands. Mike had taken a liking to Simon even before they had really spoken.

'No combats?' he asked having studied Simon as he had walked towards him. He was dressed in dark blue shorts and a green ESA T-shirt complete with logo.

'No. No combats. That's one of Michael's pet ideas and useful if you're punting a boat or clearing someone's overgrown garden but generally not so good for most ops. I've got combat shirt, trousers and jacket back at home.'

'So what are these ops?'

Simon leant to one side, pulled a small, light notepad from a trouser pocket, unlocked it and passed it across.

'Here you are. My list for ops today. You can print out the list later if you wish but I'll talk you through it anyway. Normally on a Wednesday I'd do the school run but of course its holidays at present. Westleton has the only remaining First School in the area so we bring children in from Walberswick, Darsham, all over – any family that can't access the Southwold to Leiston bus route. I do Tuesdays to Thursdays, Gianni does Monday and Friday. You haven't met Gianni yet. Now there's a treat for you to look forward to!' Simon chuckled. 'Today I started by taking a couple of people to Saxmundham Clinic, collected mail from three pick-up points and delivered it to the Post Office then back to the clinic to take the couple home. Then there were a couple of packages from the Post Office to deliver plus some groceries from the Westleton village shop to go to old Mr Putney in Middleton. No-one delivers daily round here any more. With no return school run it was quite a light day really.'

'Who makes up the duty lists?'

'Heron does the rotas and lists for our unit. She gets info such as requests for hospital visits from Michael, adds in the routine trips such as school runs and sends the list to the operators by 0730 each day. Saturday and Sunday or National Holidays we have one person on standby for any emergency operation.'

Mike sensed an enthusiasm for the ESA cause. They talked about Simon himself, about ESA, about the government, about the army. After half an hour Mike had a good idea of how the organisation operated and his fourth interview filled out much of what else he needed for his article.

Name: Simon Upton

Age: 24

Joined ESA: 2196 (4 years service)

Background: Born Aldringham. Father supported Aldringham 7 through cash donations but not active. School, Leiston. Then taxi driver in town. Did occasional school runs for ESA in 2195. Offered full-time job about 9 months later. Moved to Westleton with his partner when ESA developed into three units – knew Michael Warren from Leiston days so pleased with new arrangements.

ESA History: Main work as driver using car and minibus. Also visits to elderly/ill/disabled plus gardener/handyman in school holidays. Not strongly against army supporting the police but understands ESA (= Kassim's) philosophy.

'Time to leave,' concluded Simon. 'I'll let Carlos know we've finished. The Land Rover's open so you can go and sit in if you like. See you soon.'

With a pat on Mike's shoulder Simon eased himself down to the ground, pulled out his PERC, scrolled down to a number and, phone to his ear raised his other hand in farewell and set off towards the adjacent house. Mike walked over to the Land Rover, opened the passenger door and climbed in. As he waited he wrote down the information he had gained from Cassie Vale. Before long he heard footsteps on the path leading from the house. He turned, expecting to see Carlos but even as he began to move he sensed the stride pattern described by the crunching of feet on the gravel path was that of a tall but lighter person moving with an easy grace. Kassim Wood-West appeared around the hedge that part-hid the house and half raised a hand in salute. He walked around the vehicle and climbed in beside Mike.

'Hello Mike. I thought it worth catching you before you left us. I hope the team looked after you. How has the day been?'

'Fine, thank you. Everyone has been helpful. I think I've collected enough material for the article I plan to write.'

'Do you mind if I look at your notes?'

Mike was a little taken aback following Kassim's earlier assurance that he could write what he liked but he had no real objection and handed across his notebook. Fortunately he had written in longhand using only obvious abbreviations and his hand was reasonably neat. Kassim scanned the summaries of the four interviews.

'Good. I like your approach. Between the four of them you seem to have a good coverage of our work and organisation. I was just concerned that some detail may have eluded you.'

'Would you like to see a draft before publication?'

'No. It's your reporting. I'm more than happy for you to go ahead. Good luck. I look forward to seeing our little organisation presented in print. You're welcome to come and visit us again. Just have a word with Carlos to arrange date and time.'

'There's just one thing,' added Mike. 'Carlos gave me a brief history of ESA and your involvement – you know, the Aldringham 7 and your wife's accident. I may like to use some of that if it's OK.'

Kassim did not hesitate.

'Anything Carlos has mentioned may be used. And if you need qualification contact me at HQ.'

Kassim leant across, handed over a business card and then shook Mike's hand.

'Here's Carlos. Have a good journey back.'

Carlos took Kassim's place. He gave a brief smile by way of greeting, started the engine and steered the Land Rover back onto the track, returning to the road along the way they had come earlier in the day. On reaching the Westleton Road they crossed over onto a minor road and made their way directly to the A12 then travelled south towards Saxmundham. Carlos asked Mike about his visit and commented liberally on the character of the ESA members Mike had met. Phrases such as *don't be taken in by that* and *you can't believe anything that one says* enlivened their conversation but shed little further light on the activities of Michael Warren and his unit. Mike did, however, feel that the Leiston unit were a cohesive group with the members sharing some sort of common aim and a good degree of friendship. Rather than enter the town Carlos took the by-pass around Saxmundham to reach and then turn on to a secondary road aiming for Framlingham. Unlike the new Framlingham road further south this route through Rendham had not been upgraded so Carlos needed to focus his attention on the sharp bends of the winding road. Their conversation lapsed and they travelled the last few kilometres with barely a comment.

Left to his own thoughts Mike reviewed his day. He was pleased with the information. He had enough to make a good article – one that would challenge the headlines that characterised all those opposed the army's activities as dangerous paramilitaries. When Cumbrian dissidents blew up new bridges or damaged construction sites or Welsh activists threatened to kill National Councillors it was front page news but the work of charities such as ESA was rarely reported. Mike planned to restore the balance with his forthcoming article.

He looked up when Carlos braked sharply and hooted another road user who had turned out of a side road just in front of him. Then back to his thoughts he became concerned that perhaps he had not seen everything with which ESA was involved. Three things were lodged in the part of his brain that stored anomalies. Firstly he had been told on four occasions, *Write whatever you like*. OK. Kassim, Michael and the others seemed open and helpful but had they laboured this point more than necessary? By concentrating on the stories of the four ESA members he had interviewed had he been programmed in a particular direction? Had he missed other aspects of ESA's work? Secondly everyone had said something like, *Hope to see you again* or *Come and see us again*. Was he being groomed for the role of tame reporter? Would he in future be fed propaganda that he would pass on via the media having previously been led to believe that ESA was an open book with nothing to hide? Mike didn't know. Perhaps he was over-reacting; being suspicious where no suspicion was justified. His third query was, though, less ambiguous. A charity that clearly operated in small towns and villages and along a network of rural roads and lanes clearly needed a headquarters that was easily accessible. The Saxmundham HQ fitted the bill but why then was the unit covering their central area located in a remote forest clearing reached by a small ferry boat after negotiating a rough track off the nearest road? Surely premises could be found in one of the larger villages such as Westleton or even in the town of Leiston itself. Mike's reporter's instinct, as he called it, was hard at work. He felt there was probably much more to know about the ESA people and their operations.

Slowing traffic, roundabouts, houses. They were back in Framlingham. Mike was brought back to the here and now as they turned onto the ring road that swung northwards around the castle and headed west and then south-west to Apsey Green so avoiding the stop/start traffic of the town centre. Mike was home.

That night Mike had difficulty in sleeping. This was unusual. It may not have been literally true that he always fell asleep the moment his head hit the pillow but minor adjustments to the bedding and a few turns to get comfortable were usually all that was needed to induce slumber. He had long ago taught himself to abandon all thoughts of the day's investigations and the last time he had lain awake for any length of time it had been the previous winter when a rare head cold had inflicted sleeplessness due to bouts of coughing. Prior to that he could only recall tossing and turning for ages before sleeping during the sudden onset of the intolerably hot summer of 2193.

This however was different. He could not let go the image of Cassie that had invaded his head. To some extent he was surprised. Cassie was not the type of girl who normally attracted his attention; she could have walked into The Vine and he wouldn't have given her a second look. At about one metre eighty she was just a little shorter than Mike, slim but not skinny and possessed a shapely but not over large bust. Mike had always claimed to be attracted to shorter girls with, as he put it, a bit of meat on them. Cassie was a brunette whereas in the past Mike's girlfriends had been red-headed or blonde. But the picture stored in Mike's mind scarcely featured any of these characteristics. The image that had caused his wakefulness was just a snapshot, almost his last view of her at the moment she had waved goodbye. It was the slight smile on her lips and the brightness in her eyes that kept him from sleep. She was speaking but there was no sound. It was just her lips and eyes and the wind off the broad gently blowing strands of hair across her face that had utterly captivated him.

CHAPTER SEVEN
ILLEGAL ACTIVITY

Friday 22nd August 2200, The Corner House, Denham, Buckinghamshire.

Even leaving to one side those living in Canada and Ireland the Green clan, Tallin's family and relations, were fairly well spread about. Yet despite these distances they had remained close. Her immediate family and a whole host of aunts, uncles and cousins related back to Grandad Green who had lived in Harefield, an urban village that had somehow escaped the outward flowing tide of London suburbanisation that had enveloped most of the former county of Middlesex two and a half centuries ago. Grandfather's 78 years had encompassed a large part of the previous century until his death in 2182 and he had produced a family with seven children – three with his first wife; two boys, the second being Tallin's father and a girl. The fourth child, a boy, came along with Grandad's second wife who had, like him, been widowed. They added two girls and a boy of their own to complete the family.

Harefield was the type of place where people were pleased to settle for life but their children, finding limited local opportunities for housing, employment and enjoyment, moved on. Thus it was that Tallin's mother, Sofia, lived not too far away in Wycombe but she had aunts, uncles and cousins in places as diverse as Swindon, London, Cambridgeshire, the Welsh borders, Dublin and a small village named St Croix in Canada. To add to this dispersion Tallin's younger sister, Paris, had left a lucrative interior design business in London she shared with a former college friend to marry upholsterer Joseph Gillespie, another college acquaintance, moving to her husband's birthplace of Wooler in Northumberland.

It had been Tallin's habit for almost as long as she and Stacey had been married to spend a week or two with one of her tribe each summer. A couple of years after their marriage it had been a trip to visit an unmarried aunt in the remote Welsh countryside near Brecon. Another year it had been Swindon and the plethora of relations scattered around Wiltshire and Gloucestershire. But this year it had been Northumberland. Despite the greater distance travelled from the Corner House the trip to stay with Paris and Joseph was Tallin and Stacy's favourite visit. Stacy got on well with Paris. She was so relaxed and lacked the intensity that her older sister brought to things and he enjoyed being with Joseph. Best of all the north-east offered opportunities for Stacy and Joseph to go horse riding. There were long unbroken stretches of sandy beach where his mount could be given its head or they could take to the country lanes at the edge of the uplands where on many days horses outnumbered vehicles so that a long trek could be taken at a leisurely pace. And then there were the Cheviot Hills themselves where wind and rain, normally regarded as a nuisance, added to the dramatic quality of the ride along open ridges and down wooded valleys. Having taken Mr Oakwood's advice Stacy had not ridden out at all at home in the days before his holiday but here with Tallin and Joseph and others he could indulge in his favourite pastime in a group and feel quite safe. In any case he had resigned from the cabinet at the beginning of the summer, resigned as a minister, rejected the opportunity to chair this committee or that investigation and had returned to the back benches. At one time he had thought to resign completely but he had been persuaded to remain until at least Christmas, just one more parliamentary session, to act as advisor to the new Minister for the Environment.

It had been Tallin and Stacy's habit, after they had relaxed at the home of the chosen relative, to spend a week or two later in the summer abroad in Europe or America but on this occasion they had opted for a further week taking a leisurely trip home staying overnight in locations connected with one of Stacy's favourite twentieth century authors. Some years previously, after a visit to Swindon, they had spent time touring Thomas Hardy's Wessex. This year it was D H Lawrence's Nottinghamshire. Whilst Tallin spent several hours happily shopping in the city Stacy had greatly enjoyed making a tour of villages around Nottingham that featured in the great man's novels and completed his pilgrimage with a visit to the Lawrence museum in Eastwood.

Their return to the Corner House that Friday left three weeks before Stacy need return to Westminster unless of course some political crisis was about to crash down on them and bring MPs scurrying back from their various holiday pursuits. It had been a relaxing holiday. Stacy, unburdened by ministerial concerns, had stretched his muscles, broadened his mind and temporarily forgotten about affairs of government. Of course the matter of Mr Oakwood, the ATU and Penycraig had entered his mind occasionally but since his return to the back benches such matters had not worried him and had taken on an almost surreal comic book character.

'Good holiday,' commented Tallin by way of conversation after a takeaway Indian meal had been eaten on the evening of their return home. It was a statement rather than a question and a way of leading into the topic of Stacy's plans for the next few weeks.

'Yes. I wish we had the variety of riding country round here. Perhaps we'll retire up that way.'

'Retire? I'm not expecting that yet. I don't want you under my feet all day so you'll need to get another job after leaving parliament. Anyway we need to stay here as long as the children need a base to come home to. I'm sure you could ride here again now you're no longer a minister. Get Matthew to go with you and as long as you keep to the well populated trails around the Water Sports Park you should be fine. If you're worried phone that Mr Oakapple or whatever his name is. Pity to waste the weeks before you're due back at Westminster. Anyway, what have you got planned for the next few weeks?'

'There's a little research, some writing and of course it's back to constituency surgeries on Wednesdays. Yes, I'll talk to Matthew, exercise the horses and perhaps sort out the garden.'

'Promises!' stated Tallin, doubtfully.

Monday 1ˢᵗ September 2200

Three phone calls to make. Stacy looked at the list scribbled on his notepad. Despite all the electronic devices available for recording information the paper pad and pen method for making lists still seemed to him to be the most convenient. Stacy's life needed organisation. At times he had notes fixed to his bedside table, the car dashboard, his desk of course, his locker at Westminster and even in the garden shed not to mention the stable. He had already been working for about two hours on the draft of a speech that the new Environment Minister had asked him to cast his eye over. She needed his comments as soon as possible. The drafting needed to be word perfect, the legal scrutiny painstaking and the behind the scenes bargaining carefully orchestrated. There was no point in carrying on and rushing the job. He needed a break but before leaving off for refreshment he decided to clear at least one call from his phone list.

Stacy looked at his watch. OK. Matthew first. Matthew Park was his neighbour at Oakend Grange and his oldest and most trusted friend. It was Matthew he had sat next to on his first day at the village school and it was Matthew who had joined him in starting their Café Shop business in Bourne End and importantly it was Matthew who pushed him towards a start in politics when he persuaded him to stand for election to Wycombe Council. He knew Matthew usually had a break about this time so he rang the landline to The Grange. He didn't want to try Matthew's mobile as it was possible that he could still have been busy on the farm.

'Hello, Stacy.'

'Matthew. Fancy a ride out later?'

They spent a little time making the arrangements, knowing there would be plenty of time for conversation when they met.

Stacy felt happy at the thought of his forthcoming ride and decided to make one further call, one that was less exciting but non the less important. From memory he called the number of the Anti-Terrorist Unit and when prompted tapped in the current security code.

'Good morning, Mr Kenton. What priority is this call?'

Stacy thought quickly. He hadn't found a bomb and he didn't suspect that a terrorist was lurking in the woodland fringe along Marsh Lane so he could hardly claim his call merited the urgency to be ranked as Priority One. If he downgraded to a mere request for information, a Priority Three he would be passed to an on-call duty agent who had probably never heard of his case. He needed to talk to Mr Oakwood in person so level two it had to be.

'Priority Two,' he replied

'Thank you Mr Kenton. Hold the line please.'

A brief pause and then he heard the instantly recognisable voice of Mr Oakwood.

'Good morning. How may I help you?'

'Penycraig,' Stacy stated. 'Any developments?'

'No, sir. It's been quiet for some time and although we have no plans to downgrade the threat there is no indication of any ongoing activity. We are now well in control of local anarchist brigades in Wales. Although you are no longer a government minister we will continue to provide you with the same level of protection as before.'

'Thank you. That's reassuring.'

Stacy rang off. There seemed little danger in riding out with Matthew and he needed the exercise anyway. He looked back at the list on his pad. John Goldhawk. A minor constituency matter. That, he decided, could wait.

Wednesday 10th and Thursday 11th September 2200, East Suffolk

Mike was pleased with the draft for his article about ESA. So far, written as a series of first hand comments by ESA members, it carried the stamp of authenticity yet, as such, it could have been regarded as pure propaganda. His account needed the finishing touch of independent verification. The article had been put together within 24 hours of his visit to Westwood Broad but it was another two days before he had decided how to add that final detail. Thus it was that after a phone call to Carlos, who had then had Mike's further visit OK'd by Kassim, he was on his way to shadow the daily operations of ESA's Leiston Unit.

Mike made his way to Saxmundham and just as before Carlos took him on to Westwood Broad. As they drew to a halt outside Westhead House, almost exactly on the dot of seven thirty, Simon Upton was there to meet them. Dressed in blue trousers and an ESA green T-shirt – this time emblazoned with the phrase *ESA cares* – Simon opened the passenger door and reached up to shake Mike's hand.

'Hi! I hope you're not too disappointed that it's me and not Cassie! Anyway come in for a bite and a drink and I'll fill you in about the day ahead.'

Simon led Mike around the adjacent hedge and up a path that led them beside the wall of Westhead House and around the back to the right where a large back extension faced onto a well-kept garden. Entering the back of the house Mike found himself in a large kitchen already occupied by a tall slim girl, older than him by some years he guessed, who was seated at a small corner table with a mug of drink, reading some papers. She half turned, saw it was Mike and return to her reading without making any greeting or comment.

'Not speaking today then Vandra?'

'I've said *Good morning* to you once today. I think that's enough,' she replied.

'Well, how about saying *Hello* to Mike?'

Vandra put the papers down, looked up and turned around.

'Mike as in Mike the famous journalist?'

'Yes. The very same.'

'Or is it,' continued Vandra turning her gaze to Mike, 'Mike the spy, Mike the government lackey or Mike who writes glowing reports about the army? Whatever it is I don't need to speak to anyone who has chosen to spend time at Bentwaters.'

She drained her mug, picked up her papers and stood up.

'I'm out of here,' she explained rather unnecessarily as she crossed the room and walked out.

'That's Vandra Mornington. Charming lady when you get to know her,' stated Simon waving Mike towards a stall beside the kitchen's large rectangular central bar. 'She's one of the Rendlesham Unit, up here on cover. You'll get used to her.'

Simon busied himself preparing refreshment.

'Coffee? Black, white?' he asked. 'There's a couple of currant buns if that's OK.'

'Fine. Black, please.'

Simon pulled his notepad from his back trouser pocket, found the entry he needed and slid it across the table to Mike.'

'Here's today's programme. Heron wired it across just before you came. Much of it's about as routine as usual.'

The brightly lit screen was headed with the day's date and the time: 0637. Below that the programme header read *Operator 4. Simon* and a list of times set out the school runs and other duties. Mike read the list and had just finished when the click of the kettle switch, a smell of burning and a mild curse from Simon indicated that the meal was almost ready. Simon passed a mug and a plate across and occupied a second stool. For a short while they ate and drank in silence.

'Who owns this house then?'

'Karen Ravenscourt and her husband.'

'As in Ravenscourt's Electronics Company in Southwold?'

'Yup. That's them. He's retired now and sold the business and did pretty well out of it. Mind you she was the brains behind it; without her he'd still be working from a market stall to earn his pension. They really are great ESA supporters. They've given us this facility free of charge.'

Coffee drunk, crockery stacked in the washer, Simon led Mike back around to the barn garage where they climbed aboard a 22 seater coach. Before settling in the driving seat he pulled a box down from an overhead locker, picked out a T-shirt similar to his own and lobbed it across to Mike.

'Here you are. It should fit. You're one of us for the day.'

He climbed into the driving seat, motioned Mike to take the courier's seat at the front and set out coastward along Lodge Lane. When they reached a junction they turned right onto the spine road that ran along the higher ground towards the coastal village of Walberswick. On reaching the landward end of the village Simon guided the bus into a lay-by where a group of children, many with attendant adults, stood under a roadside shelter. The canopy of the shelter was adorned by a faded sticker with curling edges that marked it as a stop for the 783 bus route – a service long since withdrawn. Route 783's original daily timings, now remembered only by the older residents of the village, had been reduced to a Fridays and Saturdays only service with one bus each way ferrying passengers to Westleton, Darsham Rail Station and Saxmundham in the morning and home in the afternoon. But even that limited service had ceased about seven or eight years previously. These days the Southwold Community Bus collected college students daily to connect with the Lowestoft bus service and gave shoppers a chance to visit Saxmundham on a Tuesday and Southwold on a Thursday. Apart from that there was only the ESA school run or a four and a half kilometre hike to the main road. Mike knew Walberswick well. Until quite recently the community of boatmen, artists and writers had shared the village with well-off retired folk and second-homers but the general run down in services had prompted most of these outsiders to move elsewhere. Their recently built homes had fallen in value and been snapped up by local people who had turned their attention to the short-stay holiday market. There were now several bed and breakfast guest houses and, where expensive cars had once adorned driveways, caravans and motorhomes now stood – some of them to let and others belonging to visitors. The community of artists and writers who preferred to be remote from urban life had remained, though considerably reduced in recent years and appeared now to be a stable and contented section of the local population.

Simon knew all the children by name. He greeted them individually as they climbed aboard the bus, spoke briefly with mothers and fathers (and grandparents) and determined why Arthur Becton (high temperature) was not on board this morning. He then checked that seat belts had been fastened before edging around the turning circle and heading back inland with his first seven passengers. A request for music led Simon to oblige with a rendition of a recently popular song until a chorus of protest led to a cassette being played, music filling the bus and the boys and girls relaxing back into their seats. Mike guessed that this was probably a daily ritual when Simon was in charge. He considered that things would be rather different if Vandra happened to be on duty.

At the next village, Blythburgh, a similar pick-up occurred except that a circular tour of the village collected each of the five pupils at or near their front door. Since the main A12 road had been diverted inland to cross Blyth Broad at a narrow section the village had become isolated and would today probably have been little more than a hamlet had the Blyth Fishing and Farming Cooperative not established a fish farm between the village and the new A12 causeway. This provision of jobs had preserved a village large enough to support a pub and a shop but not a school. Then Simon turned southwards to the Westleton Road before turning off to the right to zigzag through country lanes picking up more scholars at hamlets, isolated farms and cottages.

By 0830 they had a full compliment, less the poorly Arthur Becton, but with the addition of a large parcel from one of the farms destined, as Simon informed Mike, for Saxmundham Mail Office later in the morning. On reaching Westleton School each passenger disembarked to a cheery smile, a word or a helping hand from Simon and was ushered into the care of the duty teacher. Bus empty and suddenly quiet Simon and Mike locked and left the vehicle to walk a short distance along the Yoxford Road to where a small close of eight dwellings lay on their left. Turning into the close Simon walked towards the door of the first small semi-detached house.

'This is where I live,' stated Simon, 'and where you'll be my guest overnight.'

They walked around the side where he pushed opened the door and they walked into the kitchen.

'We'll take a coffee break now before the mail run. Marissa's at work now but you'll meet her this evening.'

'And who's Marissa?'

Simon laughed. 'Sorry! She's Mrs Upton. You didn't think that this underclothing belonged to me did you?' he joked, pointing at a neat pile of bras and knickers on a chair.

'You hadn't told me you were married.'

'Well, not strictly married. Although she calls herself Mrs Upton we're just registered partners. Anyway whatever we call our relationship she reckons that she's the boss. Probably correct, I suppose, as she earns more than I do.'

'So ESA pays you but where does their income come from?' asked Mike as Simon turned to a cupboard and began to prepare their second snack of the day.

'ESA's a charity. We depend on donations. That's our strength really. The donors support us to provide services and keep the military out of civil matters. You know about the Ravenscourts at Westhead House but there are several large and hundreds of small donors across the east of the county. The school here holds a fundraising event each summer with fifty percent of the proceeds going to provide educational extras and the balance keeps the school bus on the road. People around here are very supportive.'

A message came through on Simon's notepad. He tapped in what appeared to be a brief reply then continued making coffee as the conversation turned to other topics – football, weather, journalism, as Simon steered the talk away from ESA. Four more times during the next few minutes messages came through, each one succinctly acknowledged until after the sixth and last brightening of the screen Simon put the notepad back into his pocket and looked across to Mike.

'That's the last one. All six mailboxes have reported. We've got five pick-ups to make; only Eastbridge has nothing for us today.'

Crockery rinsed and stacked for later washing – probably Marissa's influence Mike thought – they left the house, retrieved the ESA bus and took the short journey to Westleton's community shop. A green sack labelled ESA Mail and a large package were placed on the front seat to join the parcel picked up on the morning school run. Heading south the next stop was Middleton. Here the mail sack was again collected from the village shop which, together with a pub and café was housed in the now redundant school building, a casualty of rationalisation as the population of the area had fallen. After Middleton the green mail sacks were collected from Theberton (the garden of a Church Road house) and with no need to visit Eastbridge they turned westwards to East Green (a farm entrance) and Kelsale (another shop) before travelling direct to Saxmundham Mail Office in the High Street, not far from the ESA headquarters.

'Do this every day?' asked Mike.

'Yes, but not always this route. Alternate days we go east of the A12.'

'So what now?'

'Lunch.'

'Do you look in at HQ?'

'Not unless I have to! Show your face there and you'll end up with an extra task or two. Let's face it – you came for one day originally but now they've got you back again.'

Simon laughed at his own comment and then added, 'We'll go to the café if that's OK.'

With lunch over they took the short trip to pick up seven year old Annie and her mother from Benhall Green to make a clinic appointment in Saxmundham and then take her back home before returning to Westleton for the return homeward school run. After that Simon checked in with Michael Warren at the Leiston Unit base then signed off for the day.

'That's it then. Come on. I'll introduce you to Marissa.'

'What about tomorrow?'

'We've a treat for you tomorrow, Mike. That can wait. Now, though, its home and then the excitement of a fine Westleton late summer evening's entertainment. Don't forget your bag.'

The best that Westleton could offer, leaving aside a leisurely walk on the common or picking ripened vegetables or fruit from an allotment was a relaxing meal and a drink at the pub. Not a pub in a village hall, not a pub that shared its premises with a shop or a clinic but a genuine seriously old-fashioned country public house. And the food was good, the drinks great and the company excellent. Simon had an inexhaustible fund of amusing stories to entertain Mike and even Marissa smiled occasionally although she must have heard most of them before. Mike liked Marissa. She was an attractive lady, the attraction for Mike being in her capable, self confident character rather than in any visual beauty. As he sat listening to Simon a thought of Cassie came into his mind. He wanted to ask Simon if he would see her in the morning but decided it was best to wait and see and further thoughts along that line were abandoned when Simon's empty glass prompted him to get in the next round of drinks.

The next morning saw an early rise, the dull light entering the window as they had a quick breakfast suggesting that the forecaster's promised weather front had arrived and yesterday's bright weather had gone, giving way to gloom now and probably rain later. They took the ESA school bus to Westhead House by the now familiar route. Gianni Prince was waiting for them at Westhead ready to take over responsibility for the next part of Mike's day, leaving Simon to continue with the day's school run. Gianni was tall and slim, verging on skinny with short, carefully styled jet-black hair very much in contrast to Simon's shorter more rotund figure capped by his cropped brown locks. He also appeared to be a man of few words as he gave just a nod to Simon and the one word 'Hi' to Mike before Simon resumed his seat in the bus and moved off in the direction of Walberswick. The only thing the two men appeared to have in common was the wearing of identically coloured and logoed ESA T-shirts.

Gianni, followed by Mike, walked down to the edge of the broad. Cassie wasn't there; the ferry was in the charge of Reuben Court who appeared to be about the same age as Mike and on the way across made polite conversation by asking about his journalistic career. It was Cassie, however, who met them in the galley area of the cabin and prepared drinks as the three men walked through and sat in the day room. It was, Reuben confirmed, Cindy's day off.

At 0900 Heron, dressed just as Mike had seen her before in combats, joined the group. Her arrival was met by an expectant silence; she was clearly in charge this morning. When Cassie joined the group Heron outlined the day's operation.

'It's quite common,' Heron said, apparently for Mike's

benefit, 'for smugglers from the continent to come ashore at Minsmere Broad to leave or collect goods in or near abandoned houses or farm buildings and then make a quick retreat. Today we are going to follow up local reports of just such activity last night. We are, of course, just filling in where the police are unable to operate through lack of personnel.'

She continued to give an outline of the planned patrol that would take them south to Dunwich and Minsmere. Then leaving Reuben behind in the cabin to handle the communications part of the unit's work the four person patrol – three ESA operatives plus hitchhiker Mike – piled into an old, battered but still sturdy ex-army ATV parked at the rear of the cabin and headed south on forest trails. Cassie was driving whilst Heron gave directions and the still uncommunicative Gianni sat in the back with Mike. At a junction of tracks Heron instructed, 'Turn right' and Cassie took them down the new trail passing by an open area in the forest where a house and a set of cabins were surrounded by a high fence that was punctuated occasionally by large double gates that gave access from the track. All the gates were closed and the place had an air of disuse.

'That's an Army Camp called Forest Lodge. Not permanently occupied,' stated Gianni in a rare helpful comment.

It was Mike's first sight of a military location in the area and Gianni's comment led him to believe that ESA kept an eye on any such location that had the potential for future expansion of army activities. Soon they reached a surfaced but poorly maintained tarmac road and turned left on it for several hundred metres before slowing on the approach to a left hand bend. A roadside notice carried the message: *New Bridge Farm. Strictly private traffic only*. Cassie had slowed, not to negotiate the bend but to carefully follow Heron's instruction to turn right onto the centre track of three that met the road at that point. When he had first seen their ATV Mike had wondered at the use of such an ancient vehicle but the steep descent down this uneven track demonstrated its value. On reaching the broad at the end of their descent his belief in the suitability of the vehicle was complete. A low uneven causeway of stones topped by logs and in places part-submerged was negotiated easily if not comfortably by the ATV before it took to the gentler southern slope of the valley turning left across grassy fields and tracts of heathland to meet a coastbound surfaced road of good quality. A couple of kilometres along this road they entered the village of Dunwich. The first building on their left was the Dunwich Coast Heritage Centre. The building was not unattractive but had been criticized by some local people as being too modern and out of place in an ancient village. Mike had reported on the opening two years earlier and noticed how the subsequent tree planting and landscaping had softened the building's impact. At Heron's suggestion Cassie took advantage of the large almost empty parking area beside the museum to pull off the road and come to a halt. Heron half-turned in her seat and spoke.

'Right, then. I'll go and talk with the local borderguard officer. Cassie you go and see this eyewitness – here's the address – and Gianni, whilst we're away fill Mike in about what we're doing.'

Instructions complete Heron and Cassie climbed down, spoke briefly and walked off up the street. Then Gianni, without speaking, got out and followed by Mike sauntered across the car park and sat on a bench seat positioned near to the Heritage Centre entrance. Fortunately the grey overcast had so far failed to produce any rain and September had so far proved to be a little warmer than could have been expected. They sat without speaking, pleasantly relaxed with Mike waiting for Gianni to tell him about the day's operation. He had decided that, in contrast to his previous visit to the Leiston unit a month earlier, he would on this visit observe and listen to, not question the ESA workers. The previous day he had been unable to keep strictly to this plan as Simon's outgoing personality had drawn him into discussing the Association's work, prompting him to be inquisitive but today Gianni's reticence aided him in his resolve. He was tempted to goad his companion into conversation but elected instead to focus his mind on some tasks of his own that required attention in the coming days. But within seconds Gianni had turned to face Mike, his habitually dour look replaced with a broad grin.

'That Heron. Eh, Mike? She's more army than the army itself! She reckons if we outdo the army in what we're doing there's no need for them to take over from the authorities or us.'

They subsided into silence for a while before Gianni spoke again.

'We're a team. Heron, Cassie and me or Reuben when I'm not around. We look for smugglers or more often smuggled goods. Heron plans the operations and talks to the police, borderguard, etc. Cassie's the driver and good at talking to little old ladies who report unusual activities. I do the heavy stuff. Better than ferrying kids to school like Simon, eh?'

'What's the heavy stuff, then?'

'Better you wait and see. There may well be some of that later.'

With that they sat back in silence and it was not long before first Cassie and then Heron returned.

OK. Get in,' instructed Heron. 'I'll fill you in as we travel.'

Cassie took the wheel again and drove the ATV out onto the road travelling inland away from the village but soon took a left turn to head south across Dunwich Heath, parallel to the coast.

'The borderguard radar picked up an interesting echo about 2213 last evening. Close to the coast the vessel slowed near the entrance to Minsmere Broad and then speeded up again, travelling north for a little before turning out to sea. On its own this wouldn't necessarily be regarded as significant but there were other reports. Cassie spoke to a local resident whose son was out sea fishing last night. He thought he heard an unlit vessel heading for the broad's entrance at about that time, roughly a quarter past ten.'

'Piggyback or hit and run?' asked Gianni.

'Piggyback, we think. There were no reports of a high-speed vessel returning to the open sea. A piggyback,' Heron continued for Mike's benefit, 'is where a vessel drops a small boat and shades it from the radar until it reaches cover inland. In this case there may well have been an inflatable vessel that entered Minsmere Broad and was probably run aground on the inside of the spit to the north of the entrance. The boat could well have been abandoned but it's usual for the outboard motor to be removed and then hidden or taken away.'

'Couldn't the borderguard intercept the boat?' asked Mike, now that he had been brought into the conversation.

'The Dunwich Borderguard could alert one of the fast patrol boats. There's one based at Kessingland and one at Aldeburgh. But by the time they could reach Minsmere there would be little to see since smuggling is very profitable and the operators can afford vessels that are at least as fast as those of the authorities. They've been talking for some time about running airborne patrols but cost seems to be holding up that plan's implementation. Smuggling's on the increase so they'll have to do something soon. Last night the nearest borderguard vessel at Aldeburgh had already been deployed further south,' concluded Heron.

Scenario completed Mike turned to the window to notice that they had travelled the length of the road and were approaching the Old Coastguard Cottages that stood perched above Minsmere Cliffs overlooking the spit and the Broad mentioned earlier. The cottages were now the administrative centre for the Dunwich and Minsmere Coastal Ecology Centre and were as old as their sister building, the Dunwich Coast Heritage Centre, was new. Cassie parked next to a newer ancilliary building, the Centre's laboratory and waited whilst Heron informed the Centre's director of their presence on the reserve. That done they abandoned the ATV to walk to the top of a cliff overlooking a marshy area trapped behind the shingle spit with the wide waters of Minsmere Broad beyond. It took

Gianni, with the aid of binoculars, a few minutes to locate it but a small, inflatable open boat was just visible amongst the dune plants and bushes that had colonised the edge of the shingle barrier.

'There it is,' stated Gianni pointing in the direction of his discovery. 'Looks like a *Gemcraft* of some type; typical smuggler's boat. Can't pick out if it's still got its outboard power pack.'

They moved along the cliff to the right until Gianni could pick out the stern lodged against a large bush.

'There you are,' he said, handing the glasses to Mike. 'You can see the brackets where the power pack would have been fitted. It's gone now.'

Mike adjusted the glasses to his sight and could clearly see where the motor had been removed from its housing.

'So what do we do now?' he asked, handing the binoculars on to Heron. 'Do we go down there?'

'No,' Heron stated. 'That's a job for the borderguards. We need to see if the motor or any contraband goods or both are hidden anywhere around. The weakest part of any smuggling operation is the offloading and distribution of the cargo. If they make a rendezvous with a receiver and transfer goods to a truck or another vessel there's a high risk that they'll be seen by an army or borderguard patrol. Usually a trusted local person collects the goods, hides them nearby and notifies the receiver who'll collect when any activity by the authorities has died down. The smugglers – rarely more than two – lie low and are picked up later unless, of course it's a hit and run operation.'

The team returned to their vehicle. Again directed by Heron, Cassie took them across country via a series of barns and woodland areas that Heron said were typical of the places where goods had been stashed in the past. Despite Heron's prompting it was clear to Mike that Cassie knew the area well and had probably followed this route before. At each stop Gianni was sent out to investigate. This usually meant clambering over or under fences, looking for footprints or disturbed soil and vegetation and investigating piles of rubbish or stacks of containers piled against barn walls. After examining the fourth location, a barn at the end of a stony track backed by an area of woodland, Gianni turned towards the ATV and gave a thumbs-up sign.

'Go on Mike. See what he's found,' instructed Heron.

He walked over to the side of the barn adjacent to the wood where Gianni indicated a bundle wrapped in plastic sheeting that was almost covered from view by several bags marked with the logo of a well-known agro-chemical company. Just enough of the cover had been moved by Gianni to reveal part of a motor unit of the type often used to propel small, light vessels. Gianni carefully replaced the covers and as he did so Mike noticed that he was wearing protective gloves.

'Now let's look around. Goods are often stashed outside.'

A large water butt took Gianni's attention but it was empty apart from water. Moving around to the next wall they discovered twenty or so containers labelled as containing a proprietary wood preservative paint. They appeared to be unopened. Gianni carefully tried the lid of the first one on the top row. He grunted. It clearly had not been opened since leaving the factory. Then he ran his eye along the top row of ten. All unopened. He carefully lifted the last container in the row and examined the one below; just the same. Mike went to help lift off the remaining containers but Gianni warned him to stay back, holding up his arm and pointing at his gloved hand. Mike nodded his understanding and stepped back as Gianni crouched down and ran his eye along the lower rank of containers. Then he moved his gaze back, more slowly this time, and stopped just over half way. He stepped forward, took a container from the top row and gently tested the lid of the one below. Satisfied, he removed the lid using a small screwdriver from his pocket and looked inside before replacing it together with the covering vessel previously removed from the top row. Gianni turned, a broad grin on his face, and walked away whilst indicating to Mike that he should follow him back to where Heron and Cassie were standing beside the ATV. Gianni said just one word, 'Drugs'. When they reached the vehicle Gianni and Heron moved a few yards further away, deep in conversation.

'What happens now?' asked Mike, joining Cassie in supporting his back against the Land Rover.

'I expect Heron will let the borderguard have the details.'

'Do we do anything?'

'No. We'll probably wait around until the authorities get here as long as they're able to get here promptly. We don't touch contraband and we don't handle smuggler's equipment,' Cassie replied.

'Do you think anyone from the smuggling band was watching us?'

'It's possible. The borderguard could arrive here in two

or three hours time and find everything gone. That's why we wait as long as possible to hand over to one of their officers.'

Gianni sauntered back to join them leaving Heron speaking into her phone.

'OK. Borderguard will be here soon,' called out Heron as she walked back towards them. 'We'll wait till they arrive,' she added as she joined them. 'They shouldn't be long so we can then go back to see that their vessel from Aldeburgh picks up the smuggler's boat.'

Following the handover of operations to the two borderguard officers who arrived in a Land Rover similar to theirs (but unsurprisingly a rather more recent model) Cassie drove them back towards the Minsmere spit where the smugglers had beached their boat. For the first time that day she drove the route without prompting from Heron. It was about ten minutes after their return that the sound of a boat was heard moving up from the south, close to the coast and a few more minutes before the borderguard support vessel slipped in through the entrance to the broad. It stopped at the seaward end of the spit, unable to navigate the shallow waters nearer in. Two uniformed men got out onto the shingle whilst a third pegged a stay into the beach and after turning the vessel around tethered it to the stay and fixed a towing hawser to the stern railing. Meanwhile the smugglers' Gemcraft had been pushed into the water, pulled towards the waiting tug and then attached to it. Moving gently at first to navigate the narrow entrance the Borderguard vessel reached clear water, turned south and accelerated away.

'Good work,' said Heron, awarding the now departed

officers a compliment. 'They do a good, professional job. If they weren't so short on staff we wouldn't have to do these operations ourselves.' She paused and then continued, 'OK then. Lunch. Pub or back to base?'

'Pub,' chimed Cassie and Gianni in unison. Heron gave a rare smile suggesting that she had anticipated their reply.

'Mike?'

'Pub.'

'Pub it is then. Which one?'

'Dunwich is nearest,' claimed Cassie.

'Westleton Old Crown is better,' advised Mike feeling that for this part of the operation at least he was equal to the others.

'Crown's fine,' confirmed Gianni, with conviction.

'Mike, have you left any gear at Westhead or at Simon's?' Heron inquired.

'It's all at Simon's. Marissa will be there all day.'

'Right. Crown it is then,' decided Heron. 'I'll text Michael on our way and see if he wants to join us.'

Cassie took a track across the Reserve until they reached a lane named Mill Road that led to Westleton. Following a minor detour to pick up Mike's things from Simon's house they made the pub just as the promised rain arrived.

ESA matters were not discussed during lunch, not even when Michael – surprisingly accompanied by Kassim – joined them about ten minutes later. Mike stood and shook hands with both men and in reply to Kassim's question assured him that he had found the two days most useful.

Conversation returned to trivial matters, sometimes with two ongoing topics as Kassim and Michael talked between themselves. Then, with meal over, Heron, again taking up the mantle of team leader, herded Cassie and Gianni back to the ATV with Michael joining them for the journey back to base. Heron left without comment but to Mike's surprise Gianni slapped him on the shoulder and said, 'See you, partner.' Cassie just said. 'Bye,' but as she turned away she smiled and raised her hand in a parting salute.

Kassim explained to Mike that he was on his way back to Saxmundham so he would give him a lift back. During the journey they discussed Mike's visit, his forthcoming ESA article, scheduled for publication the Sunday after next and Mike's opinion of the work of the association. When they reached the ESA headquarters Kassim pulled into the yard at the rear of the building and parked beside Mike's car. Before he could thank Kassim and retrieve his bag from the rear seat Kassim made a statement that was quite unexpected.

'We would really like you to work with us again, Mike. Part-time. As much or as little as you liked. Nothing scheduled. Just as and when.'

Briefly there was silence, no eye contact, as both men looked ahead at nothing in particular.

'That's an attractive offer,' replied Mike, 'but first I'll finish this article and then I'll give it some consideration. Thanks for the invitation.'

Another slight pause.

'You're a Reydon boy, aren't you Mike,' said Kassim, turning his head to look at the younger man. Their eyes met. Mike smiled. It was definitely not a question and appeared to be rather more than a statement. It went to the heart of the matter and at that moment Mike knew he would be back. East Suffolk was, after all, his home territory.

As he stowed his bag and climbed into his own car Mike realised he was still wearing the ESA sweatshirt. He smiled to himself. He'd better get Mum to wash it when he got back; he'd probably take it back at some time.

As he travelled home to Framlingham Mike reviewed the situation. Yes he'd like to spend more days with ESA, now and then. But why? Why would he want to do that when his career, which he enjoyed, took up much of his time? Certainly he sympathised with ESA's aims and he would be quite happy to work with Simon again. Then there was Heron. He knew little about her and he had already wondered about the anti-smuggling campaign earlier that day. It had gone like clockwork which could have been the result of Heron's undoubted ability and experience but equally it could have been a set-up job. Was it a stunt to impress him and gain sympathetic publicity through his soon to be published article? Simon's programme the previous day was absolutely genuine. He was certain about that. But he had concerns about how far he could say the same about the supposed smuggler's boat and the contraband. Did Gianni find the stash just a little too easily? But again, surely they wouldn't involve the Borderguard in the operation unless it was one hundred percent genuine. Mike remained undecided.

And then there was Cassie. He had spoken with her only briefly but he kept reliving her parting smile and hand raised in salute as she left the pub. In his mind her actions carried the message, 'See you again.' And Mike knew he would be more than pleased for that to happen.

Saturday 17th January 2201. The Corner House, Denham, Buckinghamshire.

Stacy had spent much of the week working on plans to open up a new Café-Shop like the one he had run in Bourne End many years ago, before his move into politics. At present the main difficulty was in finding suitable premises near home. He had looked at possible sites in Beaconsfield and the Chalfonts but upon examination each one had proved to be a disappointment. Now, however, he was reading a memo outlining the need for the Restricted Areas legislation to be applied to urban areas as well as the existing coastal ones. Not all urban areas, of course, just those where the police needed a little more manpower to help keep law and order. Although he had been retired from Parliament for some weeks now it seemed that in matters such as this one his opinion was still well regarded – the memo and request for his advice had come from his successor in the Environment department.

The government's use of the armed forces to tackle dissident groups in certain coastal areas had been a success but the growth of copycat *brigades* in some major cities now needed attention. Unlike the coastal dissidents who at least had some sort of grievance against the authorities these urban brigades were simply out to control illegal operations such as protection rackets and the supply of drugs, alcohol and any other merchandise that could provide a reasonable profit. Already such gangs had set up small no-go areas in parts of London, Nottingham, Brighton, Wolverhampton and Gateshead and fledgling operations were known to exist elsewhere. The police, local authorities and sometimes even the emergency services were not welcome in these gangland enclaves. It was essential that normal control be established and if assistance from the military was needed to achieve this aim, so be it.

Satisfied, at last, that he had commented meaningfully on the draft proposals and that it would have broad appeal to a wide range of MPs he made a copy of his suggested changes and then sent an encrypted version to the FM's office at Westminster.

Stacy stood, stretched his arms, clenched and unclenched his fists a few times to relieve stiffness and walked across to stare out of the window. The weather was fair – the frost that had formed under the cloudless skies the previous night had gone apart from a few patches in shaded sections of the garden – leaving a cool but clear day. To relieve his tiredness and forget the chores of the past few days he decided that he would have lunch and then ride out in the early afternoon. He'd give Matthew a call but if his friend were unavailable he'd go all the same. He had ridden out solo on several occasions during the end of year holiday and now that he had retired he no longer felt that he needed to check with the ATU over such activity.

Arrangements having been made with Matthew he left the study and walked across the hallway to find Tallin replacing a rather pitiful display of flowers and unpleasantly smelly water that occupied a vase usually resident in the main lounge. Whatever else was left untended Tallin insisted on having a good array of flowers in the room where visitors were entertained. In Stacy's former line of business the more important the visitor the less notice they seem to have given him before turning up on the Corner House doorstep so she always needed to be prepared with some show of attractive decoration.

'Lunch, Stacy?'

'Something light. I'm meeting Matthew in a while. Let's get our own now and then we can go out to eat this evening.'

'I assume that means that you've finished hiding in your office for a while. How's it going?'

'My plans for a café or the government's imposing on my kindly nature?'

'Your plans, of course. I'm becoming rapidly disinterested with the goings on at Westminster.'

'It's going well but rather slowly. There's not a lot more I can do until I find decent premises available at a reasonable price.'

'Good. So a day out next week then? Monday? Tuesday? Before you're back on the property trail,' suggested Tallin presenting the facial expression and body stance that she knew Stacy found hard to resist.

'Monday should be OK. That's a date then.' He gave her a quick kiss that confirmed the agreement and then added, 'We'll talk about it over our meal this evening.'

Flower arranging complete, Tallin washed her hands, made her lunch and sat at the kitchen table with her e-reader displaying the novel she was part way through. Stacy joined her a little later. She looked up and smiled. They seldom ate lunch together and she was pleased to think that there could well be more times like this before her husband got bogged down with his latest business venture and all the irregularity of mealtimes that it would generate.

Lunch over, coffee cup drained, Stacy went off to change and then walked to the back door where he kept his riding boots in the small rear cloakroom that was reserved for the purpose.

'Bye, Tal,' he called out. 'Ring you on my way back.'

He walked out across the garden, through the gate in the garden wall and out into the stable yard. Tallin watched from an upstairs window. After a while he appeared with his horse which he hitched to a post, returned to the stable and soon after re-appeared with Matthew's mount. He led the two horses through the gate leading into the grounds of Oakend Grange, mounted his own horse and gently led Matthew's up the grassy lane that separated the Grange's formal gardens on the right from an area of the estate's woodland to his left. The path veered slightly to the left and at this point Tallin lost sight of her husband as he disappeared from view behind the trees. Tallin smiled, blew him a kiss although she knew he wouldn't see it and set off to tidy the kitchen and after that find something to wear for their evening out.

About twenty minutes later there was a chime from her PERC mobile. The caller was registered as Matthew.

'Tallin,' Matthew began – although it was unusual for him to use her full name – 'Has Stacy left? He wasn't at our meeting place so I came down to the stables and there's no Stacy and no horses.'

Tallin's heart missed a beat.

'Stay there, Michael,' she yelled down the phone. She charged down to the small back cloakroom, frantically grabbed an old coat to ward off the cold of the crystal clear air outside, kicked off her house shoes and stabbed her feet into a pair of old garden boots. Not even stopping to shut the door she ran out into the garden and followed her husband's route to the stables towards where Matthew was standing, waiting. He approached her as she came through the gate.

'I saw him go Matt! He had both horses. He's there somewhere. Perhaps he's been taken ill although he appeared fine when he left.'

'Should we call the police?' Matthew asked. He knew of a threat to a government minister although he didn't know any details.

'No,' replied Tallin. 'He's there somewhere,' she repeated, 'but if we can't find him in twenty minutes we'll get help.'

Tallin dived into the stable block, grabbed an elderly bicycle (one of a pair that she and Stacy used when they visited Matthew at the Grange) and set off up the lane with Matthew jogging in pursuit. They came to a halt where the lane joined the track from the Grange; the place where Stacy should have been waiting for Matthew just a short while earlier. They scanned the surrounding fields, hedges and woodlands. There was nothing to tell them where Stacy had been or had gone. The ground here was sheltered from the sun and although not frost covered was bone hard so preventing the formation of new footprints from either man or horse. Whilst he had followed Tallin cycling furiously along the lane Matthew had worked out a strategy for their search.

'Our best bet is to work around the farm boundary path. We'll split. You go left and I'll go over the far side.' He pointed across the field to where a gate opened onto a path and the road and again beyond that to an area of community parkland. 'We'll probably meet up near that gate.'

Tallin was gone. Negotiating her cycle along the rough path with some care – she didn't want to fall off and waste time – she headed around the edge of the wood on her left and then ahead picking up the field boundary that extended beyond the trees. She then aimed for a copse some 500 metres away looking left and right as she did so. On reaching the copse she left her bike, stood for a few seconds, listened and then quickly walked through the copse and back. Nothing she heard or saw gave her any clue to Stacy's whereabouts. Carrying on she cycled round to the right on her clockwise tour through open fields shorn of their summer crops but still yielding no clues. Almost halfway round, when she came to a junction of farm paths, she was brought to a halt when her phone rang. She grabbed it from where it had been handily placed in her coat pocket and breathlessly answered.

'Tal, I've found the horses.'

'And Stacy?'

'He's here but he's hurt. Where are you?'

'By the waymarker, opposite the gate in the hedge.'

'OK. Turn right and you'll see me down the track. About 400 metres or so.'

Potholes and ridges formed by the weather and farm machinery no longer deterred Tallin as she pedalled determinedly round the corner, redoubling here effort when she saw a figure straight ahead standing in the middle of the track, next to a patch of woodland. Braking hard she skidded, dropped the bike, jumped over it and ran forward.

'Where? Where for God's sake?'

Matthew pointed to his left, towards the track into the woodland but grabbed Tallin's arm when she started forward.

'No, Tal, the horses appear to be drugged and Stacy's badly injured. I've called for help – ambulance and vet. We mustn't touch anything.'

'Police. You must call the police. Now Matt! Now!'

She sat down, suddenly exhausted and held her head in her hands, dry-eyed and trembling. Matthew crouched beside her placing an arm gently around her shoulders in a comforting gesture and spoke calmly and quietly.

'The police are coming as well. They know it's an emergency. They'll be here soon.'

It took three silent minutes during which even the birds seemed to stop singing. It seemed longer but first the paramedics and then the local police officer carefully bumped their way down the track, directed by Matthew's wife Gaynor, who as the result of a phone call had been placed on gate duty to speed the vehicles down from the main road. Directed by Matthew the paramedics and policeman took the narrow track into the copse. Another wait. Then, just as Tallin raised her head at the sound of another approaching vehicle one of the paramedics emerged and beckoned Matthew over to join him. They talked briefly before he walked back.

'Can I see him?'

'Sorry Tal. No. I'm sorry but Stacy is dead. The medic can't say more than that but he's been advised by the police not to disturb the body before the police surgeon and a crime scene team arrive.'

'What happened, Matt. What's happened?'

'I don't know. We've got to be patient,' he told her as she stood looking down, sobbing quietly, one hand covering her face.

More vehicles arrived. First the vet – known to both Tallin and Matthew – then the police team who directly took charge. They were prepared. One of the Thames Valley Police vehicles was a mobile incident room. The vet soon returned. The two horses seemed to be just lightly sedated but further tests would be needed, she reported. She suggested that Matthew and Tallin, if she were up to it, took the horses back to the farm where she would give them instructions for their care.

The vet turned, spoke to a policeman and then ducked under the incident tape now placed around the copse. She soon returned carefully leading the horses, negotiated the tape and passed the reins of one to Matthew. Gently taking Tallin's hand she led the other horse away from the scene, back up the track. Tallin felt in no position to disagree. In contrast to normality she no longer felt in control of events; other people had just taken over and she had no power to resist them. As they reached the gate into the farm yard beside the Grange a large, official looking dark green limousine swung off the road and stopped for

Gaynor's instructions before moving on, more sedately, down the track. As it passed her Tallin turned her head and caught a glimpse of the back seat passenger. She was certain it was Mr Oakwood and at that moment she was sure she understood what had happened. Her blood suddenly ran colder. Her heart was frozen and felt heavier than she could ever remember and she knew that there was nothing more that she could do. All she could do now was to grieve and preserve him in her memory where he would never die and perhaps in good time she would carry on with one of the many interests that had filled her lover's days.

CHAPTER EIGHT
MORE NEWS

Friday 23rd January 2201

The Redditch and Bromsgrove Messenger
Find us at: info@randbmessenger.newsnet.gb
Friday 23rd January 2201

The Wedding of Alana Jane Buckhurst and Christian Carter Blake

Saturday 17th January 2201

Ms Alana Buckhurst, formerly of Redditch and Mr Christian Blake, formerly of Bridgenorth, Shropshire, were married in All Saints Church. Both bride and groom serve with the Mercian Regiment and are at present stationed at Bentwaters in Suffolk. The bride was accompanied by her sister, Ms Simona Harrow and Mr Blake was supported by his fellow officer Mr Quinlan Quays. A guard of honour was formed by soldiers of the Mercian Regiment stationed at their headquarters in Nuneaton. The service was conducted by the Rev. Claire Sudbury who is the minister in charge at All Saints and also civil registrar for Redditch.

The bride's parents, both well-known teachers in the

town, were present together with the groom's mother who lives near Montreal in Canada. A reception for the guests was held at the Studley Manor Hotel. Ms Buckhurst and Mr Blake will honeymoon in Canada, where Mr Blake has a number of relatives, before returning to their duties in Suffolk.

* * * * *

The Daily Register
London, Monday 19th January 2201
MINISTER KILLED!
Architect of Martial Law assassinated

Last Saturday afternoon Mr Stacy Kenton, formerly Minister for the Environment, was found dead on a farm estate adjacent to his home in Buckinghamshire. Much has already been reported by the media but the Register feels bound to set out for its readers the circumstances surrounding his death. A full obituary detailing his life and achievements appears on pages 3, 4 and 5.

The main facts that have so far been made known are that Mr Kenton was riding his horse over the farmland, a common pursuit he used for relaxation, usually in the company of a neighbour and long-time friend, Mr Matthew Park. It appears that the former minister was abducted and killed before he could meet up with Mr Park. Mr Kenton's horse was sedated but otherwise unharmed by his killers. The police have not revealed the method used to assassinate Mr Kenton but sources at Wycombe Hospital suggest he also was sedated but then given a lethal injection. No group or individual has so far claimed responsibility and the police are not revealing the progress or lack of progress they have made.

Mr Kenton's widow, Tallin Green, and the family have made no comment. Mr Park, friend and neighbour, described Mr Kenton as a true, loyal friend and a public servant who set out to help those in society who found themselves disadvantaged. Mr Park was amazed that Stacy Kenton had made enemies who were prepared to go as far as murder. The leader of the Opposition, Lewis Holborn, said that Mr Kenton had been a rare man in politics – a minister who gained respect from MPs of all persuasions. Spokesman for the South Chiltern Nationalist Party, John Goldhawk, said that it had been difficult selecting a candidate to replace Stacy Kenton when he resigned but that their newly elected representative at Westminster would do well to study the legacy left by her predecessor.

The Register has often supported Mr Kenton's policies through difficult times when harsh measures had to be taken. In general people living in coastal areas have welcomed the laws brought in by the Nationalists. Mr Kenton's death is a tragedy. Under different circumstances he could and maybe should have become this nation's First Minister.

Tallin looked up from reading the paper, one of several national and local editions scattered across the kitchen table.

'Support from *The Register*?' she said to no one in particular. 'Too late to tell the truth now! It may help to prop up your circulation but it's no longer any help to Stacy. Wherever he is I hope he puts in a complaint, Mr Editor.'

With a sudden feeling of anger she tore *The Register* in half and threw the pieces across the room. Then as her anger subsided as quickly as it had appeared she put her elbows on the table, her head in her hands and cried. Not the brief, quiet shedding of tears that she had experienced at the time of his death but a sudden upwelling of grief that shook her body from head to foot until she could cry no more.

* * * * *

West Wales Advertiser
Machynlleth, Friday 23rd January 2201
news@wwads.net.gb
ASSASINATION CLAIM

The Advertiser has been provided with a statement from a little known dissident group – The Penycraig Brigade. They have asked for this statement to be printed word for word. It is given below.

"We, the Penycraig Brigade, assassinated the former English government minister, Stacy Kenton at 1427 on Saturday, 17th January. Mr Kenton had done nothing to reverse the decimation of Welsh coastal communities over a number of years by consistently refusing to protect our coastline. We said in August 2199 that we would remove a government minister from circulation. Mr Kenton had been given every opportunity to reverse his government's policies but he did not, right up to the time of his resignation from the English parliament. The Penycraig Brigade always keeps its word."

A group described as the Penycraig Community Council did in fact send a statement to the Advertiser threatening a government minister in August 2199 but on police advice it was never published.

A spokesman for the Joint Coastal Protection Unit of the Royal Welsh Regiment and Dyfed-Powys Police confirmed that they were aware of this dissident group. They were, the spokesman said, a very small group incapable of carrying out such an operation. Their statement, published here, was probably just a publicity stunt. None-the-less the Joint Unit was closing in on those people thought to be members or sympathisers.

CHAPTER NINE
BATTLE STATIONS

Monday 2nd February 2201, Bentwaters

Alana sat at the workstation in her office, looking intently at the text on the monitor screen. It was time to make the monthly check on her Mission Statement and if necessary update it, particularly that part of it that outlined the action to be taken to meet the aims of her current deployment. Those aims had not altered since she had arrived at Bentwaters in July the previous year but the actions needed to meet them had. For about six months now her unit had been tasked with the investigation and control of those elements in the local community whose purpose was to defy the laws of the land. Smuggling was still the main problem and itinerant lawbreakers a nuisance but it was local dissidents that potentially posed the greatest threat. In particular she was out to frustrate the work of those who felt that the armed services should have no part to play in local policing.

She scrolled down to and then read through the section listing actions to be taken.

- Work in support of local people
- Observe and if necessary infiltrate questionable local organisations

·   Patrol the areas where dissenters are active to limit illegal activity and reassure the local population.

Alana checked through each strand of her programme. Firstly, working to support the local population. Her unit had set up social programmes – local people were encouraged to use base facilities and matches with local teams in several sports, an annual 5k and 10k fun run event at the Saxmundham carnival, adventure camps for youngsters in Rendlesham Forest and support for schools and youth groups had been organised. And of course the army had used local shops, pubs and restaurants.

Secondly there was keeping tabs on local organisations. At first the net had been widely cast but most of the groups they had studied had turned out to be quite harmless. Now they were down to keeping an eye on just five set-ups. Two of these were openly belligerent – a small handful of avowed dissidents who took part in small acts of disruption and violence. There had been for example one incident where a petrol bomb was hurled at an army ATV but there had been little damage and the perpetrators had been detained; there had been nothing of a violent nature recently. Still vigilance was the keyword to success here. By far the largest organisation – and the one that worried her most was the East Suffolk Association. On the face of it ESA was a local charity but there were certain elements among their organisation and personnel that concerned Alana. She regularly visited their HQ in Saxmundham where she was politely entertained with refreshments by the ESA leader, the urbane Kassim Wood-West. This group even supplied the army, police and borderguard with information about smuggling that proved to be both accurate and useful. Yet there was still something about this lot that caused her to mistrust them. They clearly undertook social work locally but why did they need an almost military organisation with unit leaders and area bases to do that sort of work? Alana had therefore placed a trusted civilian as an administrative assistant in the ESA headquarters office. Jasmine White worked there part-time on secretarial duties and provided her with a wealth of information regarding the charity's organisation. Alana now had a file listing all the personnel, their contact details, the unit to which they were attached and their normal duties. In addition to Mr Wood-West there were three names on the list that seemed to have an important place in the hierarchy – Michael Warren, Carlos Theydon and Jane Heron. They were full-time workers who did not actively take part in the operations such as school runs and ferrying people to surgeries or hospital. Jasmine had so far been unable to find out exactly how they spent their time whilst on duty. There was also a Frankie Parsons who ran ESA's northern unit and was openly aggressive when visited by her officers.

Area patrols were the core of the army's programme of control. High profile, overt operations had the purpose of letting everyone know that they were around, that they were active and that they were serious. The patrols gave reassurance to the law-abiding and a warning to others. The army's Ubiquitous Force computer programme, known as UB to the troops, had been developed for battlefield use but had been adapted to provide a format for these local patrols. Despite an apparently random pattern the computer generated patrol routes that covered every square kilometre of the Bentwaters territory frequently but without providing the opposition with a predictable pattern for either route or frequency. Covert patrols concentrated on what Alana termed *hot spots*, particularly ESA's base areas.

All this was fine and had proved effective but the situation had now changed with the assassination of Stacy Kenton. The claim that a Welsh dissident group had been responsible for the killing of a former government minister had given greater urgency to the army's work. From the First Minister to the Chief of the Armed Forces and down on to the head of the Army, Regiment chiefs and base commanders the message had been clear – No more slip-ups. All dissidents had to be identified and rendered inactive. Alana wouldn't have wished for anyone to be killed in that manner but Stacy Kenton's death gave her just the excuse she needed to set out a more ruthless programme. Scorning voice recognition she switched to manual operation and made a copy of her original file, changed the date to February 2201 and then added a forth point to her action list.

On proof of illegality take action to eliminate such activity, *with or without* police assistance.

Alana read the statement again and then scrolled down to make space for a more detailed account of the action she proposed to take.

Alana's PERC phone rang. It was Christian.

'Hi, Christian.'

'Just back home, Ally. See you this evening. When do you expect to be back?'

'Should leave off about 16.30. See you soon after that.'

Alana signed off with a kiss down the phone. Christian had been out on a night time operation with the anti-smuggling unit he operated. Alana didn't know the detail; they had a policy of leaving work at work. Christian wouldn't learn much about his wife's planned operations either although he could probably glean a little information from others drinking at the bar or in the canteen or on some other social occasion.

The computer responded to her typing by filling the monitor screen with the details of Alana's plan to deal with the small dissident groups in the area. When she came to her proposals for the East Suffolk Association she sat back and thought for a while. Her informant had given her details of ESA's organisation. Alana could probably have walked into ESA's Saxmundham HQ and obtained this information from Mr Wood-West but this would have made the ESA leader suspicious of her intentions. ESA was organised into three area units. The northern area was called the Wrentham unit and operated north of the River Blyth. They were based in an industrial unit in the grounds of Benacre Hall, just north of Wrentham village. The unit leader was Frankie Parsons who organised it as a quasi-military outfit that he preferred to call a brigade rather than a unit. Of the three ESA unit leaders he was the only one outspokenly anti-army. It was rumoured that if Frankie had his way he would damage army vehicles and equipment and bomb Bentwaters out of existence. Despite this belligerence the Wrentham lot were an obvious first target – they were a small group whose members could be picked off easily.

Further south the Leiston unit, based near Westwood Broad, differed from the Wrentham lot on several counts. There were at present ten or eleven operatives, double the number presented further north by Frankie Parsons and his four sidekicks. The leader was Michael Warren, a well meaning graduate of the original Aldringham Seven but his deputy, Jane Heron was another matter. Alana hadn't learnt much about this lady and that worried her, fuelling her suspicion that there was more to this unit than just their charity work. In addition to Ms Heron there was the presence of a journalist named Mike Cannon. It was true he had written articles describing the work of the army in countering dissident groups around Britain's coasts and then balanced it with an article about ESA but he now appeared to be working actively with the Leiston lot. Perhaps he wasn't as impartial as his writing suggested. The army could disrupt ESA by taking out key personnel from the Westhead based unit and splitting up the whole operation. However at present that would be a premature move. Until she knew what Jane Heron and that journalist were up to she would let them carry on as usual but keep a close eye on them.

To the south ESA's third operating group was the Rendlesham unit. The leader of this unit was the overall ESA boss, Kassim Wood-West. Kassim did not appear to be an enigma like Ms Heron. Alana had respect for him. He was welcoming, open, answered all her questions and provided the Mercians with information about smuggling. Kassim had a genuine concern for local people and the ESA charity certainly fulfilled a need but there could, of course, always be another deeply hidden side to Mr Wood-

West or a faction of his association could be involved in illegal activities. ESA could be a sort of Trojan Horse. This Rendlesham lot numbered about ten or eleven – the same as the Leiston unit.

OK, then. Mr Parsons had better look out. He was the first on her hit list. Alana drew up a strategy for operations. With any luck it would be approved without significant changes and then it would be all systems go.

Thursday 5th February, 2201. Westhead.

Since starting work as a volunteer with ESA, Mike had made himself available most Wednesdays, even to the extent of now being regularly rostered on the Leiston unit's post run. He was also now a relief driver for the school bus run providing cover for Simon when he was needed for other duties or was otherwise unavailable. He hadn't actually made the school run by himself yet but he had been on the minibus driving course – mandatory for school bus drivers – and had, just the previous day, received his certificate of authorisation. At first he had refused Kassim's offer for ESA to pay the course and test fees.

'Look Mike,' Kassim had said. 'We have the funds. Proceeds from Westleton School's Summer Fair pays for our petrol and servicing. Last year they raised more than we needed. They'll be pleased to help out.' With that Mike felt he could no longer object. It would be churlish to do so.

So Mike was now spending two, sometimes three days a week at Westhead, a Wednesday and one or two other days often, but not always, at the weekend. He fitted his ESA work around the demands of his freelance journalism. Sometimes he would stay overnight. Not in the cabin as he had expected but in the more comfortable accommodation at Westhead House where in addition to the kitchen the Ravenscourt family had made two rooms available to the ESA volunteers. Beyond the kitchen lay a small lounge and beyond that a bedroom with one single bed and two bunk beds together with an en-suite shower and toilet. Together the three rooms formed a self-contained unit with its own access at the rear of the house. Apart from a welcome from Mrs Ravenscourt during the first evening that he had stayed there he hadn't had any further contact with his hosts.

The previous day, Wednesday, he had helped on the school run greeting the pupils and assisting at each pick up or drop-off point as required. His regular mail run had been sandwiched between the two bus journeys. Now, today, after staying overnight he was up, washed and dressed, including regulation T-shirt and finishing his breakfast when there was a knock at the kitchen door. Without waiting for a response the door was pushed open and Carly came in carrying a cardboard box that she placed on the island bar countertop near Mike.

'Morning Michael.'

'Carly! I haven't seen you for ages. What brings you out into the country? I thought you were a town girl.'

'I'm from Bredfield, Mike. Rural Suffolk born and bred,' Carly countered. 'Now, Mike, you'll be needing these today. I hope they fit.'

Carly opened the box and took out a set of combats – jacket, trousers and cap together with a belt and a belt-pouch.

'Go and change,' she instructed. 'I'll make a cup of coffee while I'm waiting. I need to check that this lot are OK. I'm usually pretty good at guessing sizes.'

When Mike returned, cap in hand, Carly stood up, smiled, walked across and pulled the shoulders of the jacket so that they sat more comfortably.

'Fine. Now the cap,' she prompted.

Mike hesitated, looked sheepish and then put it on. They both burst out laughing.

'OK,' she said, eventually. 'Stay there. I'll be back.'

It appeared that Carly had a stock of clothing in her little van for she brought in three caps of different sizes on her return. After a couple of attempts they found one that fitted.

Don't worry, Mike. Simon sometimes does operations in combats and I've never seen him carry, let alone wear his cap. Now. I've a message from Heron. Keep your combats on and meet Cassie at the waterside at 0930. You're operating from the cabin today.'

A cheery smile and wave as she turned to the door and Carly, her box and a few spare caps were gone. Mike pulled off his cap – he hated headwear – and put the kettle on. He felt in need of another brew before he set out to meet Cassie and take part in the as yet unknown operation that needed him to wear the newly acquired gear.

1000 hours precisely. Heron led her group out to the familiar, battered old ATV. On this occasion there was no briefing in the cabin. Cassie drove with Heron in the front, beside her, and Mike in the back with Simon who was free from the school run as it was Gianni's day to drive the bus.

Cassie drove a zigzag course through the forest along the main woodland tracks that formed a rectangular pattern to the south and east of their base. Mike thought they were travelling generally coastward. After about ten minutes of a far from comfortable ride they stopped just short of a small clearing.

'Simon and Mike come with me, Cassie stays here.'

Heron took what looked like a tool box from the back of the ATV and led the two boys into the clearing. A rectangular plot, cleared of undergrowth, lay ahead. It was almost completely surrounded by forest apart from a gap in the left hand corner where the track exited ahead. At the end of the clearing a number of cans and small boxes were set up on a chest high wooden bench. Mike thought it looked like a fairground shooting gallery. He turned to give Simon a brief glance but his friend's expression gave nothing away.

'Welcome to *The Warren*,' said Heron who then put down the case, decoded the lock and opened it to reveal a pair of handguns.

'Christ!' whispered Mike, a comment that raised a broad smile across Simon's face.

'Ever shot before?' asked Heron.

'No. I haven't got a licence.'

Even Heron laughed out loud at that one.

'Neither have we so we're all in this together. Some smugglers visit our shores armed. Many of their companions around here involved in the distribution of contraband also have firearms; some legal many of them not. We need to be in a position to disable boats and vehicles if our patrols are in danger. Hopefully we would never end up in a gun fight. If we were licensed we would have the authorities snooping around checking up on us. They could even ask us to account for every shot fired.'

Introduction over Heron took up one of the guns and handed it to Simon.

'Is that a *Piata?*' asked Mike.

'I'm impressed with your knowledge. Yes, it is,' replied Heron. 'It's a *Piata GS.*'

The Piata was to Mike's generation what a Kalashnikov, a Luger, a Colt 45 or a Winchester had been to earlier generations and long finished wars and skirmishes from previous centuries. The Piata had become the first choice with professionals for both legal and illegal use around the world. It had been used by both sides in the Mexican and Russian Far East conflicts during the second half of the previous century. As had so often been the case in the history of such weapons the design that gave birth to the Piata had not been the product of a major military hardware manufacturer but the patented brainchild of a lone gunsmith, this time in Italy. His design was licensed to a Slovakian manufacturer who instituted small scale production until, five years later the Piata was adopted by the European Union. Since then its ubiquity reflected its ability to provide deadly pinpoint accuracy that could disable man or machine but whilst inflicting the least possible amount of damage.

Simon stepped forward as Heron motioned for Mike to move back a safe distance. Simon raised the Piata, focused his mind and fired. Direct hit on the left hand target. One by one he repeated the action, from left to right until all seven had been hit. He handed the gun to Heron, walked over to the bench, replaced five of the targets and selected two more from a box beneath the bench. Now positions were reversed with Simon retiring and Heron and Mike forward. Heron took the second gun from the case and retained the one that Simon had used for herself.

'It's not armed, Mike, and the safety catch is on. First we need to talk safety then we need to teach you firing skills. Are you up for that?'

'Yes,' answered Mike in what he hoped was a confident voice.

'OK, then.'

Heron talked earnestly and enthusiastically, drawing Mike into the ethos of target shooting. She was describing an attractive sport with all its skills rather than training Mike for a military combat situation and for a while any concerns Mike had about the ultimate purpose of the training were forgotten. After a while Simon was brought in to demonstrate the procedures for priming and then firing the Piata. Mike mimicked each action. Then he shadowed Simon and then again and again. After that he repeatedly produced the routine on his own, at first slowly and then with greater confidence until Heron stated, 'It's time now, Mike.'

Heron took the unarmed gun and Simon passed the other one to Mike. Knowing that it was armed made the gun feel a completely different weapon in his hands but Mike was determined to demonstrate that he had learnt his lesson well. He checked that Simon had applied the safety catch, checked that Heron and Simon were at a safe distance and then set about the routine that had been impressed upon him. When he was ready he raised the

Piata, aimed, concentrated and fired. There was a slight hissing sound, a dull thud and a small, dark, circular hole appeared on the trunk of a tree directly behind the left hand target but some way above it.

'Good! Well done,' commented Heron. 'Pretty good first attempt. Just a little high. Try again and remember that the shot hits the target where the sight is pointing when the shot is released. You aim correctly, the Piata does the rest.'

Mike thought for a few seconds, raised the gun again and with Heron's comment firmly set in his mind he aimed and fired at the second target. There was a 'clink' sound and the can spun around but was not propelled off the bench.'

'Great second shot. You're almost there. Elevation fine but don't shoot to wound. Fire to kill! Try again.'

Mike was a little un-nerved by the tone of this latest comment although he realised that Heron had simply used a metaphor for hitting or winging the target but unsettled, his third shot missed completely. With no further evaluation from behind he took a few seconds to relax, repeated the procedure and was rewarded with a satisfying 'phizz' accompanied by the site of the target can flying backwards off the bench and an almost simultaneous thud as it hit the ground. He heard the sounds of congratulation from behind him but didn't connect with them sufficiently to hear the actual words. He was absorbed in completing the process of disarming the Piata to show that his excitement at this success had not put the routine right out of his head. He turned, walked back, handed the gun to Heron and was congratulated by

Simon, who shook his hand warmly and Cassie, who had now joined them, who gave him a light kiss on the cheek. Then he sat down on a tree stump, a little shocked, rather surprised and somewhat relieved at the success of his last shot.

For three months, through the spring of 2201, Mike performed his ESA duties of collecting mail and delivering pupils whilst providing media articles to the national and local press and regularly attending target shooting practice, usually with Simon and Heron. He learnt to shoot from any position – standing, lying prone or squatting in a variety of attitudes – until he was proficient. He had target competitions with Simon and on rare occasions even managed to beat him. And he learnt to shoot on command and fire in one smooth, efficient action no matter in whatever stance he held the gun. Away from The Warren he gave some thought to the purpose of this training. It was quite true that smugglers were armed. It seemed sensible to carry arms when on anti-smuggling patrol yet so far Mike had no evidence that firearms were ever taken on these operations. He hadn't been part of the patrols recently and it was quite possible that the guns were stashed somewhere out of reach of the prying eyes of the authorities and they were picked up en-route.

The temptation was to ask Cassie, often the driver on such ops, but he didn't want to appear too inquisitive and so lose the trust of ESA friends and colleagues. He had spoken casually with Simon but honest or not he seemed to know no more about any other end purpose of their training than Mike himself. And Heron gave nothing away. Apart from being a superb organiser Mike still knew very little about this secretive lady.

Tuesday 12ᵗʰ May 2201. Bentwaters.

It was Tuesday. And everything was about to change. ESA the charity, the questionably benign tumour on the face of East Suffolk was about to be tested and eventually Alana Buckhurst decided, removed. Since Stacy Kenton's murder the rules had altered in favour of the work carried out by the military. Enhanced operations in other parts of the country such as West Wales had already produced good results. They were, of course, still operating under civilian laws but the local army units could obtain warrants to act against suspected or known dissidents more easily than before and of course in the Military Restricted Areas such as East Suffolk they could by-pass the police. In Alana's thinking they *were* the police. Government appointed law officers, the Magisters as they were termed, were the link between the army and the government and had the task of ensuring that armed service operations were kept within the law. A Magister had been attached to each local authority or, in mainly rural areas a group of local councils. In Suffolk there was one magister in Ipswich, one in Lowestoft for the Waveney district and another in Bury St Edmunds for the west of the county. The Mercians based at Bentwaters usually obtained warrants from Ipswich although Alana found the lady in Lowestoft more approachable and just the previous day had used her office to gain a warrant for today's operation against ESA.

Since ESA had formed a separate unit to operate north

of the river Blyth it had been Alana's aim to open a base of her own in that area. Operating from Bentwaters, some twenty-odd kilometres to the south it was difficult to respond quickly to incidents in that northerly area. And then there was Frankie Parsons, ESA's local unit leader or commander as he usually referred to his position. Outwardly the organiser of school transport, mail runs and ad hoc missions of mercy, Mr Parsons had taken it upon himself to be openly belligerent. He had been uncooperative and actively hindered the work of her patrols. Just the previous week a road had been blocked by an overturned truck that she was certain was a set-up, not an accidental happening. It delayed her soldiers and she was convinced it had the work of Frankie Parsons stamped all over it. Mr Parsons would have to go. The thinly populated area east of the A12 road was not completely under army control and that was a situation Alana was no longer willing to countenance.

'Good morning.' With these words Alana prefaced her talk to the detachment seated in front of her in the Bentwaters assembly hall. It was 0700 hours exactly.

'Today our regular patrol units are combining to secure one site in particular. The location is Benacre Hall.' On the map display behind her Alana highlighted a point adjoining the A12 just north of Wrentham village. 'The Sizewell based patrols will join us there. Their task will be to secure the entry points and boundary of the estate. We will take over the house and grounds – part parkland, part farmed. There are two aims for this operation. First, we need a more northerly base, permanently manned and the home for detachments patrolling in that area. Secondly the Hall is home to ESA's northern unit. The leader has provocatively called his rag-bag band of workers a brigade and has done what he can to disrupt our work. Although such things as parking on a narrow bridge and sending false reports of smugglers to the borderguard are only flea-bites such actions are deeply offensive. We'll disrupt his plans by requiring him to move out. I have a warrant signed by a magister to allow compulsory tenantship of the property. You will receive instructions as necessary when we move in. Any questions?'

'Is it just ESA we are evicting or are there staff at the Hall, Ma'am?'

'The owners of Benacre Hall are absent; they live permanently abroad at present. An agent has responsibility for the farm and the upkeep of the buildings and grounds of the estate. The Hall has three live-in caretaking staff who will remain and work for us. The ground staff and farm workers are mostly tenants living in free accommodation on the estate and they will also stay on under their contracts with the estate company. The army will employ extra civilian staff to work at the Hall and that should endear us to the local population.'

'Are we arresting Mr Parsons, Ma'am?'

'No. He and his staff are simply being evicted. ESA occupy a former industrial building on the site and we need that building as a workshop. We shall give them 24 hours to vacate their base. At 0900 hours, the time we are legally entitled to enter the site, a notification and copy of the warrant will be delivered to ESA headquarters in Saxmundham. They have a right to oppose the eviction but I don't believe they will. The process would be long and costly and in any case I can't see Mr Frankie Parsons wishing to remain as one of our neighbours.'

At 0758 Marcus Brent, as usual on a weekday, was travelling south down the A12 road towards his workplace in Saxmundham. As he passed through Frostenden he noticed an army convoy travelling north towards Wrentham – two ATVs and a minibus. He took little notice; army convoys had been commonplace on the A12 for several years now.

A little later at two minutes past eight, nine year old Lucie Kensal was standing outside Crossways Cottage waiting for the ESA school bus. The bus was due at 0805. Lucie's mother stood behind the front room curtains, watching so as to be certain that her daughter was picked up on time. Lucie could have waited inside until Sami Stockwell from ESA announced her arrival with a toot on the horn but Mrs Green had always impressed on Lucie that she should not keep Sami waiting. Just before the bus was due two army vehicles passed by, heading north towards Benacre village. Lucie waved to the soldiers and they waved back. Mrs Kensal had taught Lucie to be friendly yet restrained towards those in authority – teachers, the police, service men and women. The soldiers had been instructed to make friends with local people as their support would be half the battle won.

Luke Lancaster fixed the last section of irrigation pipe into the system ready for the expected dry summer months to come. He looked at his watch. 0810. He had been at work since soon after dawn and it was time for a break. As he walked back up the field towards the place where he had left his bag he saw the tops of several army vehicles above the line of the hedge. The vehicles were moving north towards Benacre Street. Army patrols were as common as starlings these days and Luke, more interested in a flask of tea and a sandwich didn't give the patrol a further thought.

On Mondays, Wednesdays and Fridays Lizzie Old worked at Benacre Hall, cleaning and cooking for the ESA people. She thought they did a good job. If she had been rich she would have supported their cause with donations but as it was she worked two days paid and one day free for Frankie Parsons. But today, Tuesday, she was heading towards the A12 and her other job in Kessingland. Still cooking and cleaning but this time in a retirement home. With the young people moving out of the area and the old people staying put she reckoned the whole place would soon be populated by geriatrics so she'd never be out of a job. Come to think of it though, by that time she would be one herself.

As her car approached Benacre Church, a little late at 0821, Lizzie had to brake and then overtake a couple of stationary army ATVs. She clicked her tongue in annoyance but was even more put out when less than a kilometre further on a soldier held up the traffic allowing another army convoy, newly turned off the A12 to cross her path and take the road on her left heading for North Lodge and the northern entrance to Benacre Hall. Alarm bells rang in Lizzie's head. One patrol was commonplace but two, including a minibus was less so. She couldn't stop there as the traffic backing up behind forced her to turn right at the main road but as soon as conditions allowed she pulled in at the entrance to the back road turn to Henstead, stopped, pulled out her PERC and called up her ESA boss.

'Frankie? OK it's me, Lizzie. Listen. There are a couple of army patrols in the area. One, including a fully laden minibus is heading your way down the northern approach to the Hall and the other was stationary in The Street, near the church. That was about five minutes ago. Reckon it must be rather more than routine patrolling. Let me know if anything happens. O.K?' Frankie replied briefly then Lizzie ended with, 'Thanks. Pleased to help.'

Her PERC stowed away Lizzie turned her car and pulled out onto the northbound carriageway to continue her journey. Frankie seemed pleased with her. She liked Frankie. Some people thought him rather forthright, even aggressive but she liked his blunt, no-fuss character. And anyway he was tall and dark and handsome.

At 0900 hours precisely, the time given on the warrant for the start of the army's tenancy, Alana's ATV led the other ATV and the minibus past the lodge, through the gates and into Benacre Park. By using the northern entrance and approaching the Hall, screened from the south and east by an area of woodland, the army hoped to be out of sight and sound to the ESA group housed in the small industrial area near the eastern boundary road. Turning left behind the Hall, Alana's group headed east and soon the three vehicles were able to take up their pre-arranged positions around the building labelled Unit 3. The twelve soldiers from the minibus secured the area as Alana walked briskly up to the door supported by the two officers from the second ATV. Without waiting she pushed the door open to reveal, beyond a small entrance lobby, a barely furnished space set out as an office containing a workdesk topped by a printer, three chairs, an empty waste bin and spaced around the walls some cupboards, shelves and cabinets that proved to be as empty as the bin. Turning towards a further lobby Alana saw three open doors revealing three further rooms. One was equipped as a cloakroom from which no-one had bothered to remove toiletries, the second was a kitchen and the last a bunkroom bare of bedclothes; a two-tier bunk, a mattress and an empty cupboard being all that occupied this final space.

She turned and gave orders to her two companions. Firstly a sergeant along with four soldiers was sent to organise a search for anyone who had witnessed the ESA operatives' departure. Alana sat at the desk and took out a handwritten list and turned to the lieutenant standing by the door.

'Here's a list of the ESA members operating from here. It includes personal phone numbers, home addresses and other contact details. Take Tufnell and Bond. Find each of these people and explain to them that the unit's operations are now under our control.' The lieutenant turned and left immediately.

Alone for a while Captain Buckhurst sat and thought. On the plus side ESA had abandoned their local base without causing any trouble. On the minus side it appeared that Mr Frankie Parsons must have been tipped off about the Mercian's arrival. They must have been better organised than she had previously believed. Not only had they learnt about the army plan but they had been capable of leaving promptly having cleared the building in what could have been not much more than half an hour. That degree of organisation impressed Alana. The army was, she decided, dealing with a group who were extremely well set up but what, she pondered was the purpose of this degree of organisation? It confirmed her belief that ESA was something more than just a local band of do-gooders.

At a little after 1030 Lizzie Old's mid-morning break was interrupted when matron called her into her office. An army officer sat in matron's chair behind her desk. Matron withdrew and Lizzie was not asked to sit down. The message the lieutenant brought was simple. If Lizzie turned up for work at Benacre Hall on Wednesday she would be employed by the army. If she failed to be there by 0930 her employment would be ended.

Luke Lancaster had also been contacted by the army just as he was setting off to make final checks on the newly re-laid irrigation system. A text message from the estate manager passed on some instructions from the military. Now, following those instructions, he had come to the Hall at lunchtime and, along with most of the estate staff he was seated under a large tent-like awning that had been set up in front of the big house. An army lady who introduced herself as Captain Buckhurst was explaining that the Mercian Regiment had taken over Benacre Park but that this change would not effect their employment or their domestic situation. Same job, different employer. When the lady had finished Luke got up, nodded to one of the gardeners and set off for the back of the tent where a buffet had been set out. It wasn't the first time he had heard that speech or something very like it. Mind you, he thought, hearing it from a fit, smart lady army officer was a sight better than listening to a load of old waffle from some fat old fart of a bailiff.

At 1520 as usual, regular as clockwork, the school bus pulled up outside Wrentham School. As usual the pupils were herded into Sami Stockwell's care by the duty teacher. But eagle-eyed, 9 year old Lucie Kensal noticed two changes. For one thing Sami was not wearing her "ESA cares" T-shirt. The green top with the logo had been replaced by a plain white shirt. And on the side of the bus the title "ESA Schoolbus" just read "Schoolbus". The first three letters had been obscured; a plain white label had been pasted over them.

Returning home from work at about 1545 as usual, Marcus Brent again saw the army. This time though he gave a little more attention to what he saw. Between the staggered turns, Benacre Street to the right and then Henstead to the left, stood an army ATV, pulled back off the road. Beside it stood an alert soldier holding a rifle, studying the traffic as it passed. Marcus, believing it to be in response to some small, unimportant local trouble put the scene to the back of his mind and continued homewards listening to some of his favourite music on the car audio.

Tuesday 12th May 2201, 1730 hours. Westhead.
    'Sorry I'm late.'
    Kassim Wood-West put his briefcase on the table and

sat in the only remaining free chair. Opposite him across the table in the Leiston unit's Star-cab base sat Michael Warren. To his right was Heron and to his left seated on the bench seat with his back to the window was Frankie Parsons.

'OK, Frankie. What happened this morning.'

'Sod the army. Sod the bloody army.'

Frankie took a few seconds to compose himself then speaking more steadily he began to describe how the events had unfolded. He spoke in a broad West Country accent. No-one knew much about where he came from before ending up in Suffolk but he had been in the area for at least ten years.

'Lizzie phoned me about 0930. The larger convoy she described sounded like trouble. Patrols don't usually go around mob-handed. Jacob and I set about *Operation Retreat* – it took about twenty minutes. We left them nothing. The computer is in the van. Jacob removed two of the drives – both have been destroyed just leaving the record of names, personal data, duty rosters and the like. I reckon the army know that stuff already anyway. As we were finishing loading of the van the people at North Lodge phoned to tell us that the army were camped outside there on the approach to the Hall. A few minutes later we left via the farm entrance. We were able to get out close on the heels of a cattle truck and just in time too! As we turned south we saw some army vehicles in our rear view. Fortunately we've regularly changed our vehicles and their registration plates so we weren't going to be picked up quickly. I took a roundabout route via South Cove and Jacob rang the others to tell them to carry on with their duties but avoid Benacre if possible. That's about it really.'

'So, Heron,' said Kassim turning to his right, 'what do we know about Lizzie and the rest?'

'I've spoken to them all in the last couple of hours. Jacob Latimer's over at Westhead House, feeding himself no doubt.' The three men smiled. 'Lizzie's decided not to work for the army – I won't repeat how she described their offer – but she won't move away from Benacre because of her family and her other job. She'll stay a supporter so I suggest we find her something she can do for us, but based at home. Sami will keep on with the school bus and could be useful in reporting on the Mercian's activity from their new base. Anitra Woodside will move down here as will Jacob. And Warwick Baker, the communications man could be a help to the Rendlesham lot. He's young, got no ties.'

'Frankie. What about you?' asked Kassim.

'If you want a fighter on your hands I'll stay. You know my agenda. If not, I'll be off. There's plenty will welcome me.'

'Stay, Frankie. See how it goes,' counselled Michael with his first comment.

'Frankie and I don't get on,' said Heron. 'You know that Kassim. His being here won't work.'

'Frankie can stay here for the moment,' decided Kassim. 'He can billet at Westhead with Jacob and Mike when he's around. Frankie will nominally be part of my HQ staff. We'll see how things get along before we make a final decision as to how to use the displaced staff.'

There was a short silence.

'OK then. I must go now,' continued Kassim. 'Michael,

I'll be in touch later this evening. Keep operations here going normally as far as possible, Heron. I think the army will want to settle in up at Benacre before trying anything else.' Kassim paused and looked to his right. 'Coming Frankie?'

Kassim and Frankie got up and left the cabin.

'I don't like this, Heron,' commented Michael. 'It's bad enough having to accommodate Frankie but he's a problem better dealt with if we can keep an eye on him. The army have really started something; I don't believe they'll stop here. They're hell-bent on proving that they have the upper hand. It's the local people – our friends and supporters – I'm worried about.'

'There are things we can do, Michael. The work must go on even if we have to reorganise things. You and Kassim have done so much for so many years. We won't let you down.'

Heron gave him a quick supportive kiss and moved off to the galley, it being Cindy's day off, to prepare food for herself, Michael and Cassie who was expected in at any moment. After a short break she would end her stint at the cabin by dealing with the duty rotas for the next day.

Wednesday 13ᵗʰ May 2201, Westhead

When Mike arrived at Westhead to start his Wednesday schedule he found things mostly as he had left them the previous week except that everyone carried an air of disappointment or concern. Even Cassie, sitting in the kitchen at Westhead House, said little and Mike found it difficult to coax from her the beguiling smile that had been such a defining mark of their relationship. The reason for this unusual gravity was immediately clear when, at Michael's request he crossed the Broad and walked into the cabin to find Heron deep in conversation with a man whom he confidently assumed was Mr Parsons himself. Michael got up from where he was seated and motioned for Mike to return to the galley and take a seat. When coffee had been provided by Cindy, who diplomatically left soon after, they sat together and Michael explained about the goings on of the previous day. The one good thing, he told Mike, was that Heron and Frankie were actually speaking with each other. They were deciding how far Frankie's operations could be undertaken from Westhead especially as the army had contacted Kassin to say that the school bus service to Wrentham would be returned to ESA operation the next day.

'You'll have two companions when you stay over at Westhead. Frankie and Jacob are now billeted at the House but you could always sleep and eat here at the cabin if you preferred. I don't think Frankie will stay long; he likes to be in charge wherever he it and that won't happen here,' explained Michael.

'What will the army do next?'

'Possibly nothing. Frankie was a fool. Good leader, good organiser but he shouldn't have goaded the authorities. From what I hear the Captain in charge of that army unit doesn't like being crossed.'

'So we carry on as usual?'

'Yes. There's still plenty of work to do. Mail run today isn't it Mike?'

'Yes. But first Heron wants to talk to me.'

Mike finished his drink. As he got up to take his mug to the sink Frankie walked purposefully past him without any sign of greeting or acknowledgement and Heron followed him to take the seat vacated by Michael Warren.

'After your round, Mike, get some rest and be back here by 2130. There'll be no moon to speak of so I hope we can do a spot of night shooting.'

For the next couple of weeks the Leiston Unit continued to work as usual. One of the refugees from Benacre Hall, Jacob, operated ad hock operations from Westhead to areas north of the river Blyth and when needed relieved Sami on the school bus run into Wrentham. The army did not appear to have any further interest in these operations.

One Thursday towards the end of May a note on the kitchen table at Westhead House proclaimed that Frankie had gone. It didn't give any further information. No-one knew where he had gone but somehow everyone thought it wouldn't be the last they heard of Mr Frankie Parsons.

After a couple of night sessions Heron seized the opportunity given by a break in the dry early summer weather to hold target practice in the wet on a rainy, blustery Thursday afternoon. Mike now felt that he would be capable of using a firearm effectively under almost any condition but he'd not been asked to help with any smuggling patrols and continued to have doubts concerning the true purpose of this training.

CHAPTER TEN
DINGLE POINT

Tuesday 2nd June 2201, 1134 hours. Framlingham

On the first Tuesday in June Mike was at home in Framlingham, checking the article he had just completed for his next week's regular New Times column but was interrupted when Heron called him up. It was a rare occurrence; Heron preferred to contact her team by electronic text.

'Mike. Smuggling operation tonight. We need an extra body. Could you come in this evening rather than tomorrow morning?'

Mike hesitated.

'We really do need you,' cajoled Heron.

'OK but I couldn't be with you until about 1900, 1930ish.'

'Fine. Wear combats. See you later then.'

Tuesday 2nd June 2201, 2230 hours. Westwood Broad

Heron and Mike set off from the cabin at 2230. So much for being an extra body, thought Mike; smuggling patrols usually numbered at least three, usually four. Instead of using the ATV they hiked through the forest in the direction of the shooting range, Heron walking ahead with confidence. They walked silently. Heron occasionally stopped and listened and now and then pointed out a hazard in their path as illumination from the moonlight was limited by a largely cloud covered sky. Heron, walking just a little ahead of Mike, navigated through experience and without the need for a spotlight. On reaching the clearing Simon and Reuben materialised from the woodland each carrying a back pack, Simon with a Piata holstered to the right of his waist.

Heron squatted down under cover of the trees and motioned for the others to do the same.

'For Mike's sake I'll outline what's happening. This is a smuggling operation but we're doing the smuggling. We could quite legally buy these items but the army would soon learn of our purchases and come asking questions. Now, here's the plan. A small boat carrying arms and ammunition will rendezvous with us at about twenty past midnight. It should be out there now. Unloading on the coast would be, as we know, impossible. There are now borderguard lookout posts at Southwold Gun Hill to the north and Aldeburgh Church to the south but they're no real problem unless they are able to pass info to the helicopter patrols that were recently put into place between Yarmouth and Felixstowe.

Mike wanted to ask questions but he knew to keep quiet. The throb of an approaching helicopter interrupted Heron's briefing so she waited as the low-flying aircraft passed along the coast about a kilometre to the east, its searchlight cutting the deep grey of the night with a swath of brightness. It continued up the coast, northwards, leaving Heron to continue.

'The boat will slip into the narrow break in the coast at the entrance to the broad whilst the helicopter is on its northern leg. When the borderguard return our craft will be hidden in the shadow of the cliff to the northern side of the cut. Even with their searchlight approaching from that direction they shouldn't be able to recognise the boat. As the helicopter moves south the boat will be able to rendezvous with us at the end of Dingle Point, unload and be out to sea safely before they return. The southern leg takes between eighteen and twenty minutes from the time the helicopter passes over the cut until its return. But after every eight passes the interval increases to about thirty minutes. We use that time for this operation.'

Much preparation had obviously gone into organising this event. Heron had been well briefed about the airborne patrols and Mike guessed that Cassie's absence the previous week had probably been so that she could check the timings and regularity of the patrols and gain information about the manning of the two borderguard posts. The only unknown factor was the possibility of an ad-hoc army foot patrol straying into the area.

On Heron's command the four of them moved forward around the edge of the clearing, through the wood and down towards Dingle Point, the promontory that separated Westwood Broad from Dingle Broad. Mike and Reuben stayed in the cover of a small clump of trees whilst Simon and Heron checked the timing of the patrols to establish that they conformed to the routine pattern previously used.

After a little over an hour, just as Mike was beginning to feel both cramped and bored Heron spoke quietly to Simon who returned to the woodland and sent Mike out in his place. He followed Heron forward a few metres and they went to ground in a small dip positioned behind a low ridge that would give them enough cover when the helicopter passed nearby on its next northerly leg. She passed him a gun, probably, Mike thought, the one that Simon had been carrying. He automatically checked it and waited for instructions. As they lay there Mike considered that somewhere out there, beyond the helicopter's gaze was a small vessel waiting, gently rising and falling with the swell, her crew making the same observations as they were.

Then Mike felt Heron's breath on his neck and turned slightly to face her.

'Have the Piata ready, armed and safety off. I don't expect we'll need to use it but if we do respond only to my command of *"Shoot!"*'

In an operation such as this Heron did not want Mike to be left to use his own initiative. Left to his own Mike's decision time would be far too long to make any shot effective. Her order would be clear and unambiguous. Anyway there was only one leader, one decision maker in this operation, and if necessary she would require Mike to make an instinctive reflex action following her command. They flattened themselves and lay still whilst the helicopter returned, passing near them on its southbound patrol.

Within five minutes Heron had moved forward, silently disappearing into the darkness and at the same time Mike heard a gentle crunch on the pebble ahead, almost drowned by the sound of the waves breaking on the coast. The boat, previously unseen in the darkness, had arrived at the point. Simon and Reuben moved past Mike and merged with the darkness before reappearing carrying their previously empty back-packs puffed out by the items collected from the boat. They wordlessly retreated to the cover of the trees followed by Heron who again settled down beside Mike. She lay, head raised, looking through a pair of night-vision glasses. A scraping sound again and the boat was on its way back to the open sea. Mike assumed they were waiting to check that the boat had cleared the shore before the borderguard patrol returned.

At first feint and then gradually louder the whirring sound of the rotor blades approached from the south, the near-black inky darkness of the sea increasingly illuminated into a light yellowish-grey fluorescence as the bright sweeping arc of the aircraft's spotlight scoured the surface below. The plan was for the boat to again hide in the shadow of the cliffed side of the cut until the helicopter moved northwards leaving it free to make its escape. Twenty-two minutes exactly. The bonus of two added minutes meant that the little boat would have had plenty of time to move into the shadows of the southern edge of the channel. Mike sensed Heron's body relax as the bright beam passed to their left but she suddenly tensed at a change in the note of the aero-engine as the helicopter banked, turned and circled inland behind them before regaining its coastal position and taking up a station, hovering some way to the north of the cut. The manoeuvre broke the expected pattern of the patrol and suggested that the observer had noticed something worth investigating. After a few seconds during which time Mike and Heron

did not move the engine note changed again as the
helicopter turned once more, tightly this time, and began
to move southwards but inland of its usual course, almost
directly towards them. The boat would be safe but the
sweep of the searchlight could well pick them out. Second
by second the darkness-banishing light approached. Mike
lay unthinking, frozen, mesmerised until he was suddenly
aware of perfume and perspiration and breathing close to
his right ear as Heron moved her body to touch his.

'Light, shoot!' she yelled over the increasingly loud
throbbing of the rotor blades.

It was an order that required a reaction, not to be
questioned but obeyed. A hiss, a whine, an explosion
and the light was extinguished just seconds before their
position would have been clearly lit up.

'Move! Cover!'

Mike reacted equally speedily to this second command
setting out in a crouching run with Heron just behind him,
covering his back. His eyes took a little time to adjust to the
darkness after the brightness of his target and he stumbled
a little, almost falling, but managed to reach the forest
before the circling aircraft, auxiliary light now switched on
turned back to seek the source of its temporary blindness.
Fortunately the helicopter crew concentrated on the now
abandoned promontory giving Heron and her team time
to retreat with the courier boat having had plenty of time
to reach open water unobserved.

Simon and Reuben were ready, packs on their backs
and when Heron moved to the front of the little group
they followed her wordlessly keeping to the woodland
cover and avoiding the clearing to their right. After about

three minutes Heron stopped and they squatted on the ground. It seemed to Mike that their retreat also followed a well rehearsed plan.

'Good. That went well. That lumbering old borderguard plane won't find us here. Bentwaters, though, have a smaller but much more modern Transmanche Kestrel. That little bird has heat seeking and laser probing capabilities. There are only two ways to defeat that amount of sophistication; merge with a group of other people or disappear a long way below ground.'

Heron took out her PERC and pressed two keys.

'That'll be a programmed code,' whispered Simon to Mike. 'The recipient back at base, that's Cassie, will receive a totally innocuous text but they'll know what it means. There are several escape plans for our operations and that text will tell her which one Heron's using.'

'OK. We have at least ten minutes if they send out the Kestrel. For the moment we wait here.'

They waited still and silent until, a couple of minutes later they heard the unmistakable sound of their battered old ATV bouncing along the forest trail rather more quickly than was usual despite the lack of illumination. Cassie pulled up about 100 metres from their position. Mike, following the other three ran and jumped in the back with Simon and Reuben as Cassie took off, turned and without further instruction gave them a rather uncomfortable ride as she navigated the forest tracks heading towards base. At first as they travelled without headlights Mike found the journey rather nerve-wracking but relaxed a little when he realised that Cassie now had the shadows to mark the route ahead as the sky had partly cleared to reveal a half circle moon. Not a drive to be taken for the first time at night but Mike guessed that Cassie had certainly tried it out in these conditions before.

Of the available ten minutes three had elapsed before the arrival of the transport and probably another three during their return to the point where Cassie slowed and stopped near a waymarker post at the side of the tack – a feature of the landscape that could have gone un-noticed were it not for the number '6' painted on the post that appeared almost luminescent in the moonlight. Heron turned to face the three in the back.

'Simon. Help me with the cargo. Reuben and Mike stay here.'

Simon lifted one of the backpacks from the ATV, handed it to Heron and then retrieved the second before setting off left between the trees. Muffled sounds a little later gave no indication as to what was happening.

'One of our arms stashes,' commented Cassie, speaking for the first time.

By the time the two returned empty-handed eight minutes had elapsed. Cassie drove on to a point about 300 metres shy of the base hut. Heron issued the next instructions.

'Cassie take Mike back to base and explain to him what happens now. I'll follow you in. Simon and Reuben take the ATV. Head for the road and stay overnight at your place in Westleton, Simon. OK? Remember the story is that you're heading home from Blythburgh. No need to hurry when you hit the road.'

Heron jumped down and moved to the back of the vehicle where she took the gun from Mike. Cassie left the driver's seat free for Simon and shepherded Mike towards the hut whilst Heron watched until the ATV moved off in the direction of the Westleton Road. At that moment the feint sound of a helicopter could be heard. She had guessed correctly. The Bentwaters' Kestrel had been deployed and was now travelling up the coast towards the site of the reported incident. By the time it tracked back inland Simon and Reuben would be safely in Westleton and the others back in the cabin.

'Right,' said Cassie when they were in the cabin and the door closed behind them. 'Shower thoroughly. There's a change of clothes in the bunkroom and your old clothes should be bagged up before you shower. They'll need to be destroyed to eliminate any chance that the army forensic people could link you to the shooting. I expect the army will pay us a visit sometime tomorrow so we'll take your combats over to Westhead when we take the rubbish early in the morning after we've slept. The army don't know the area well enough to come knocking before it's fully light.'

Mike showered and changed. By the time he returned to the main room Cassie and Heron were seated at the table with hot drinks in front of them, playing cards as though they were filling in time, passing an evening during which nothing exciting had happened.

'Get a drink if you want one then come and join us,' called Cassie.

In the kitchen Mike caught sight of the time – 0037. It was Wednesday and in only a few hours he would be heading out on the school run. He was tired but the thought of food and drink overcame his need for sleep. With hot chocolate and a sandwich prepared Mike returned to the main room and pulled a chair up to the table.

'You'll sleep here tonight,' said Cassie, rather unnecessarily. 'Simon will deliver the school bus to Westhead in the morning. We girls will take the bunk beds so you can settle down here on the bench. I'll bring you some bedding. Before that Heron needs to explain things a little.' Mike turned his gaze away from Cassie and towards Heron.

'I'll start with Simon and Reuben. Their alibi is simple. They were fishing up at Blythburgh and returned home just after midnight. The ATV was kitted out with fishing gear and lanterns and there are people in the village who will say that they had seen them. We couldn't leave the ATV here with a warm engine indicating recent use. You, of course stayed over after a meeting because it was too late to get home and return for the school run in the morning. You could, of course, invent a story involving Cassie if you preferred,' said Heron making a rare attempt at humour. 'I don't think we will be worried by the army but they may use the incident as an excuse to question us and look around here. As far as the Bentwaters lot is concerned they'll probably think that the shooting was just done by smugglers who were defending themselves. However, we need to be prepared if they come visiting.'

'So everything went OK even if there was a hiccup in the plan but what are these armaments for?' asked Mike, feeling that following his involvement he was now owed an explanation.

'Being prepared, Mike. Being ready for whatever

happens. So far we've had just two guns for training and defence and never found ourselves in a position where we've had to use them. But we know things are changing. There have always been smugglers but as you know in some coastal areas dissident gangs have armed themselves; similar gangs could set themselves up here. The army have always been active against these anti-government brigades but since Stacy Kenton was killed they seem to be seeing trouble everywhere, even putting the squeeze on harmless charities such as ourselves. So far they've got rid of Frankie's unit but there could be more to come. For the moment it's the smugglers who are likely to cause us trouble and if we have to mount more patrols we shall need more arms for our protection. The arms and ammo have come in from Belgium. At present we don't see the need for any further deliveries.'

Wednesday 3rd June 2201, Westhead.

It was 1651 and with the school run complete Mike parked the minibus at Westhead House and phoned Michael at the cabin to report the day's work complete.

'Good. Thanks Mike. Can you spare the time to come over here now? There are things to discuss.'

'That's OK. I'm ready to come over now.'

'I'll get Reuben to come straight over for you. See you soon.'

Mike sat on the low wall outside Westhead House and looked out across the bright sunlit water watching Reuben launch their little ferry. First there was the powered crossing then with the motor cut the craft was punted in through the reeds. Mike stood then walked down the bank to exchange a few words of banter and take his place in the boat. They were silent as Reuben concentrated on reaching open water but with the motor gently pushing them across the broad conversation resumed.

'Know what this meeting all about?'

'Routine,' replied Reuben. 'Rotas and duties. That sort of thing. You know what Michael's like. Takes his position as unit leader very seriously. Has to do something to support his rank particularly as Heron actually runs the show!'

In addition to Michael those assembled for the unit meeting were Reuben, Mike, Cassie, Simon and James Court, Reuben's brother who was the unit's IT officer but only on a part-time basis. Only Heron was missing which was unusual but her absence wasn't mentioned and housekeeper Cindy, duties complete, had left a couple of hours before. The main item on the agenda was Michael's request that Mike and James work for the unit full-time. Payment would be no problem although he realised that there was no way that they could match Mike's income if he were to give up journalism. There was, Michael continued no reason why Mike shouldn't write his columns at Westhead whilst not on duty He was sure the Ravenscourts could find him a place for him to create a small office. James agreed that he could put in another day or even a day and a half but Mike explained that without his days away from his ESA duties he would lose contact with the people and the events that were the basis of his writing. Some progress then Michael had decided and the meeting ended just after 1800 hours after dealing with a handful of routine matters. Michael, Reuben and James were ferried back by Cassie before she returned to sit with Simon and Mike. For a while they discussed the possible reasons for Michael and by inference Kassim wanting Mike to offer more time to ESA. Then with no conclusion reached they had a bite to eat and watched television until with the end of the news broadcast at 2030 they tidied up, locked up and left. Once across the broad Cassie set about tying up the boat and Mike walked up the bank with Simon who gave a farewell wave before driving off towards his home in Westleton hoping that he would be back before Marissa returned from her aerobics class in the village hall.

'I'll stay over tonight. Coming in for a drink before you head off home?' Mike called out to Cassie as she walked up the bank towards him.

'Yes,' she replied, smiled and added a further affirmation, 'OK,' before lightly taking his hand as they walked around the side of Westhead House to reach the ESA quarters at the back, entering through the small entrance lobby to reach the kitchen. Cassie put her jacket on the back of a chair then turned to fill and switch on the kettle whilst Mike disappeared only to return a few minutes later dressed in shorts and a non-ESA T-shirt and carrying a bottle of wine. Cassie turned to look at him as he entered the room.

'Anybody would have thought you planned this rendezvous Mike,' she said. Ignoring the comment Mike asked, 'Tea or the red stuff?'

'It had better be tea.'

'Why's that?'

'I'm still officially on duty until 2100. I'm not supposed

to drink; you know what Michael's rules are like!'

Mike put the bottle on the table, walked over and gave her a kiss. A brief kiss. He drew back, noted her reaction and kissed her again. This time he held her head and pulled it closer and they kissed longer and more passionately than before.

'Wow, Mike!' Cassie exclaimed when she had regained something like normal breathing. 'What's brought that on?'

'Well I was just filling in time. If I now pour two glasses really slowly we'll be ready to have a drink just as you officially come off duty.'

Cassie grinned and kissed him for the third time in as many minutes.

'OK. I'll turn off the kettle. Wine it is.'

They drained the bottle whilst eating a light meal from what was available in the refrigerator. Leaving plates, cutlery, glasses and food packaging on the table Mike stood, took Cassie's hand and led her willingly to the bedroom. It was clear to each of them that the other had a strong desire to make love. Mike had for some weeks wanted to find the right time to fuck Cassie and she had guessed his intention when she noticed the increasing tightness of the material at the front of his shorts.

'Are you OK about this?' he asked.

'Yes,' she replied. 'Absolutely. But first I need to visit the bathroom.'

When she returned she was dressed only in her panties. Mike thought he might not be able to make it through to penetration without coming first but in the end their love-making turned out well. Satisfied he lay back with a deep sense of pleasure; a mixture of excitement and relief whilst

Cassie idly traced circles on his chest with her forefinger. After a while they each in turn made use of the bathroom, Cassie first, then Mike who returned to sit on the bed and lean forward to kiss her lightly on her breasts and mouth.

'What do Michael's rules say about sex between ESA volunteers?' Mike asked.

Cassie laughed.

'Not encouraged, I think but not banned either. In any case if there is such a rule I'm glad I've broken it and, who knows, I may break it again sometime soon.'

'With me?' teased Mike.

Cassie reached out, tousled his hair playfully, turned over and went to sleep. Mike used the lower bunk.

Thursday 4th June 2201.

Mike slept deeply for a while but in the early hours of Thursday morning he was wide awake again. At first he lay still listening to Cassie's gentle breathing then for a while he relived the events of the previous evening until the excitement that filled his brain transferred to his limbs and he found it difficult to find a comfortable sleeping position. Cassie gave a little sigh and stirred.

'Are you awake?' he asked, gently.

'Yes.'

She turned on her side to face him. The moonlight invading the room was sufficient for Mike to see her lips form a smile and the attractive way her dishevelled hair fell across her face.

'What do you know about Heron?' he asked.

The question came out of the blue. Cassie thought to

tease him with a display of mock indignation that some other female had invaded his thoughts so soon after their love-making but she instinctively knew that it was a serious question; a matter that was of concern to Mike.

'Who's asking? Mike the famous reporter, Mike the ESA volunteer or Mike the lover?'

'I'd just like to understand who I'm working with. That's all.'

'Well,' Cassie prefaced her answer after a few moments thought, 'I don't know how much you know but here goes with the info I've picked up. Her name is Jane Heron. She may have middle names but I don't know of any. She's from East Suffolk but I don't know where she was born and she never talks about her childhood. She married Franc Heron and moved away, somewhere abroad I think. Her husband was Australian so it could have been there. Anyway her husband died or walked out or something and she came back this way. She was already with ESA when I joined. Always been a leader; always full of ideas with the energy and enthusiasm to see things through. If you ask about her past she manages to say as little as possible and steer the conversation onto something else. That's all I know really.'

'OK. So why the firearms? What's the real plan?'

'Heron thinks ahead. Her main aim is to preserve ESA. At present she sees weapons as a necessary evil, an insurance for the continuation of ESA's work. But if anyone interferes – smugglers, the army, police or anyone else the tactics may have to change. Heron believes in ESA as it is but she wouldn't give up on supporting local people if the government tried to clamp down on our operations.'

'Could she lead us into trouble?'

'I don't think so; she's not a hothead like Frankie,' replied Cassie. 'She wouldn't do anything to hinder our work and there's always Kassim to keep the lid on things just as he did with Frankie.'

'There are rumours that Frankie has joined up with a fairly militant group in Yorkshire.'

'Frankie would join any group that would allow him to organise things. That group in Holderness are welcome to him. At least Heron thinks about things before she acts or asks others to follow her instructions. She's not gung-ho like Frankie.'

At that moment the moonlight that had been hidden behind the clouds for some minutes made a re-appearance and flooded the room, lighting up Cassie's face. Mike got up and moved over towards her for a kiss but Cassie, sensing that he could easily be aroused again responded with a quick peck and a brief, 'Goodnight' before pulling the cover around her and snuggling into the pillow in search of sleep. Mike smiled to himself and briefly stroked her hair, gently, before following his lover's lead and settling down to sleep for the few hours before Cassie needed to return to work operating under the edicts of Michael's rules.

Friday 5th June 2201. Westhead House.

No more excitement with guns, no further attention from the army. It had been back to routine for the Leiston unit. When Mike returned to Westhead after the last school run of the week he parked up the bus and as usual reported back to base before returning home. He had only just reached his car when his text to Heron was answered by a voice-call.

'Change of plan Mike,' she explained. 'Kassim's called a meeting at the house. It's rather important so just come in round the back as usual.'

Mike re-locked his car. Despite the forthright character of her leadership it was unusual for Heron to summons Mike to extra duty in this way; she was appreciative of his non-ESA commitments and usually asked if he was available for extra sessions. This meeting, Mike decided, must be important. He made his way up beside the house but as he turned towards the entrance he met Kassim, Heron and an unknown man standing outside the back door. Kassim turned and spoke.

'Hello, Mike. I'm glad you're available. We're meeting in the kitchen. Go straight in.'

There were more ESA staff in the room than he had previously seen all together in one place. In addition to Michael Warren, Simon, Cassie, Reuben and James Court and Gianni from his own unit there was Carlos whom he hadn't seen for some weeks and Beth Stamford from Saxmundham HQ. A little apart, to one side, stood a group of three girls and two men. Of these five people there was only one person he recognised. The presence of Vandra Mornington suggested that this group was a contingent from the Rendlesham unit. Towards the back of the room Karen Ravenscourt stood with her husband James. They were the owners of Westhead House and major supporters of ESA. It was clearly an important occasion for all these people to be called together.

Mike moved towards the back and squeezed in next to Carlos. They chatted quietly for a few minutes during which time two more people arrived – Jacob Latimer and an unknown girl to be followed by the three who had been standing outside. The room was warm. Someone opened a window and the outside door was wedged ajar to allow a welcome movement of air into the room. Heron perched herself on the work surface near the sink and when Kassim, standing, looked across at the assembled company the room fell silent. Mike noticed that Kassim, usually formally dressed for business was, on this occasion, sporting no tie, no jacket and the habitual darker colours of his clothes were replaced by a plain light-blue shirt and light sports trousers. It appeared that rather than presenting himself as the leader of ESA he just wished to be seen as one of the group.

'Thank you for coming. Some ESA staff are unable to be here but what I have to say couldn't wait until we could arrange for everyone to attend. Firstly may I introduce Callum Royal.'

Kassim turned and motioned to the man standing behind him, just inside the door. Mr Royal gave a slight nod of acknowledgement to the assembly.

'Callum,' Kassim continued, 'is a solicitor we use to make sure our operations do not inadvertently break any rules. He also helps us by explaining the ever changing laws that the government applies to the work of local authorities, the police and the armed forces. One such situation arose today and I need to tell you what has occurred.'

Kassim paused briefly as though gathering his thoughts on a complex matter of some importance.

'Earlier today the army made a two pronged attack

on our operations. Not directly that is; we don't have to stop any of our work. I'll let you calculate what you think their motive is for yourselves but here are the facts. When I arrived at our HQ just before 0830 there were two army vehicles parked outside in the High Street. The detachment's senior officer got out and followed me in when I opened up. Some of you know the confident and forthright lady Captain who runs operations out of Bentwaters.'

Heron made a barely audible comment as though she were talking to the kitchen tap beside her but one that seemed to reflect her well known dislike for Captain Buckhurst.

'Her visit,' added Kassim, 'was to inform me that the County Council in Ipswich has passed responsibility for licensing school bus and other community transport schemes over to the army. The army will act as the council's agent. Clearly it makes sense for Suffolk to save money by using an agent that has access to some central government purse. I asked her if it was the army who suggested the change or the County who approached them but she claimed not to know as such negotiations were carried out through the base commander; she was just the messenger. ESA have been given temporary licences until the end of June after which we need to re-apply but she saw no reason to expect refusal at that time. Until 1st July our vehicles can be inspected at any time by the army and after that date any infringement of the licence such as late running or poorly maintained vehicles could see fines or even an end to our operations.'

Kassim paused and looked around.

'So with care we should be able to carry on as usual,' suggested a man who was not known to Mike.

'Yes. Nothing she said indicated otherwise. But other action taken by the army today may suggest something different. You all know that the Forest Lodge compound 2k south of here has now been upgraded from a part-time training camp to a permanently staffed base. A similar base was this morning set up in Chillesford, in the grounds of Kiln Wood House, about a kilometre from our long standing base in the village. Unlike Forest Lodge or their long-established Sizewell outpost or the detachment now stationed at Benacre Hall there seems to be no practical reason for establishing this newest base. It's only 3 or 4k from Bentwaters. Their first action was to harass our operations in the Rendlesham area. The school bus into Tunstall was stopped twice. Once with pupils on board when the route and timing were checked against our license and later, outside the school when a cursory mechanical examination took place. The army patrol involved allowed Saskia Hill, today's driver, to contact me before the inspection. As I had just had Captain Buckhurst's visit I told her to cooperate fully.'

'What do you reckon the purpose of all this is?' asked Simon.

Kassim's prompt reply indicated that he had already given considerable thought to the matter.

'It could be seen as a jittery response to the increasing activity by paramilitary brigades in some other areas. However, I think otherwise. The Mercian's are beginning to put a squeeze on our activities. It appears to be carefully planned. The army are suspicious of us and are not just going to sit around and tolerate us. They'll harass us until they have obtained a high degree of control over our activities. First they close down our northern unit, now they have turned their attention to our workers in Rendlesham. Since they now hold the licences for our school bus operations they have every opportunity to keep us under surveillance. The army clearly suspect that we are a front for more sinister activities.'

Kassim paused. There was silence, apart from a little foot shuffling whilst people thought about Kassims's words.

'Is there anything we can do?' asked a voice from behind Mike.

'I vote we stay squeaky clean. Carry on, give no offence and gain the army's trust,' the reply came not from Kassim but from Simon. 'We shouldn't jeopardise our work by upsetting them.'

'If we do that they'll gradually stifle our activities. They need to be kept at arm's length. Let them know that we look after our own people. Let them know quite clearly that we don't welcome interference,' came another reply.

'Yes, Simon and Yes, Gianni. We need to walk the tightrope between those two paths,' stated Kassim. 'I've spent the day talking to our own people, both staff and supporters including Callum here and our hosts Karen and James and we have formulated an outline plan. Under the regime popularly known as *Martial Law* we are now living in a Military Restricted Area and there's little point in arguing with the army. In the past we have kept up a dialogue with the military on the basis that if we cooperated with them they would leave us alone. Up to now that's worked well but as of today my normal avenues of contact directly with Bentwaters have been withdrawn. We can still leave messages with their general office but I'm unable to speak directly to the officer who had previously been detailed to liaise with us. We've always been a widely spread organisation and the army seem intent in picking us off and gaining control of one unit at a time. As a result we need to consolidate as a single unit with more people working full-time out of here, Westhead, and in the cabin over the Broad. Outlying ops – school runs, mail pick-ups and medical transport will continue but run from operatives homes rather than a unit base. I shall give the army a list of our operations, vehicles, drivers and their assistants as soon as things are sorted out. There's lots to think about. We'll break for about forty-five minutes now so that you can talk about this plan Tell me it's crazy if you like but we need to decide our strategy soon before the army takes further steps. Meet in here again at 1900 unless of course you need to go. There are just three essential points to remind you about.'

Kassim looked around before continuing.

'Firstly the army have access to realtime satellite and drone surveillance. They could pick up an image of Simon in Westleton and follow our minibus on its school run. They could check who had attended this meeting and have a list of when each of you arrived and left. The only thing stopping them is the cost of employing operatives to monitor the videos. They haven't got the manpower for 24 hour coverage but that doesn't mean they don't sometimes make use of the technology.

Secondly they have a legal responsibility to help

keep law and order but we are able to challenge any of their actions in civilian courts. Callum will look into the possibility of challenging their right to be in control of school bus licences.

And finally our operations are also controlled by the law and we have very clear duties to fulfil as a charity. Our duty is to serve the people of East Suffolk and there are no laws to say we cannot discharge our duties. OK. See you back here at 1900.'

A shuffling of feet, the scraping of chairs on the floor and the low hum of localised conversations was followed by further movement as the officers and operatives of ESA formed themselves into ad hoc groups. Some took chairs to form tightly knit groups whilst others sat around the table or stood in twos or threes. Yet others stepped outside into the warm evening air and sat on the lawn or strolled around the grounds of Westhead House. Only Heron remained aloof from the proceedings, collecting a bottled drink from the chiller cabinet and making a seat for herself on the low wall that separated the lawn from the paved apron behind the house. Heron appeared unconcerned by events; it was as though she would just carry on as usual no matter what decision was made.

A little after half an hour later people began to drift back inside. Groups split up, pairs or trios of friends settled into quiet conversation, trading views, until Kassim took up the same position as before and the low tones of conversation subsided allowing the gentle sounds of the evening to invade through the open door and window.

'Who'd like to start us off? Any volunteers?'

Momentarily quiet descended on the gathering whilst recent recruits gave time for more senior members to speak. After a few seconds of turning heads and shuffling feet Simon stood up.

'I think quite a few of us support the idea of forming a single group so that the army can't pick us off like they did at Benacre with Frankie's lot. If work in outlying areas can be organised from here we can react quickly to any army action. The army are not going to find a reason to close down a registered charity and any such action by them would have to be sanctioned by the courts. I vote we take on board Kassim's plan.'

There was brief applause from one area of the room and a low buzz of comments that seemed to indicate general agreement.

'Thanks, Simon. Anyone wish to qualify that?'

'I also reckon it's a sound plan.' The comment came from Beth Stamford who worked as an admin assistant at Saxmundham. Mike had seen her but never heard her speak before. 'But we have to keep up our contact with the army,' she added. 'The best way to stop their interference is to constantly re-assure them that everything we do is legal and open to their inspection.'

'Hold on a minute!' There was the sound of a chair being pushed back across the floor as Vandra Mornington stood up. All eyes turned towards her. Vandra was the sort of person who attracted attention as she was not only known for her forthright views that sometimes bordered on rudeness or even vulgarity but also for her strikingly handsome, some might say beautiful face and her short well cut jet-black hair that contrasted with the trademark deep red gloss applied to her lips. 'Trust a clerk from HQ to come up with some form of appeasement. No! We cut all ties with Buckhurst's military police and just get on with what we all joined ESA to do; serve the local people.'

'I second that.' There was no need for anyone to turn around to identify who had come out in support of Vandra's comment. Gianni had one of the most distinctive voices of those present, his words delivered with an accent that proclaimed his pride in his Italian ancestry despite belonging to the fourth British-born generation of his family. His opposition to authority was also well known. 'I'm not going to make friends with any army people. They haven't done us any favours. We should let them know that we don't take kindly to interference. If they start interfering we should play them at their own game. Perhaps Mr Callum Royal could earn his money by challenging their actions in court.'

There was a self-conscious ripple of applause that quickly subsided as Vandra and Gianni's supporters realised that they were in a small minority.

'Not an unreasonable view,' stated Kassim. 'We should bear it in mind. And I'm quite serious about that Gianni. No one's views will be swept under the carpet. Anyone else wish to comment?'

The room was again quiet for a while.

'With those comments in mind then a small group of us will thrash out the future organisation of ESA. I'm suggesting Michael, Heron, Carlos and myself. Vandra – your welcome to join us if you wish – and Callum will be present as an adviser. I hope as many of you as possible can be here again at 1900 hours next Tuesday when we hope to have a draft plan to put before you. After that we'll need to see each of you individually to find out if you're in or out and decide on your rôle in the revised set-up. All being well any changes should be up and running in about a week. Thank you everyone and particularly Karen and James for your hospitality and support. I'll wish you all 'Good evening'.

Mike sat opposite Cassie at the kitchen table, his right arm stretched out and his hand resting lightly on hers. The last low rays of the setting sun cast alternate oblique shafts of light and shadow across the walls.

It was the first time Mike had been to Cassie's gran's house in Walberswick. Normally, if staying over night he would bunk down at Westhead House or occasionally across the broad in the cabin but on this occasion, with so many others staying after the meeting, it had seemed convenient for them to leave others to the arrangements provided by Karen Ravenscourt and make their escape. On arrival Grandma Vale had fussed over Mike, made them a meal and then gone out to visit a friend, leaving them alone.

For some time they talked about the evening's events and broadly agreed that for ESA to survive Kassim had put forward a pretty good plan.

'I was surprised at Beth Stamford chirping up. I've never heard her speak before; whenever I've been to Saxmundham she's just given me a quick smile and carried on with her work.'

'She spoke sense, though. I think Kassim was pleased for her comments to counteract some of the others. But you couldn't have been surprised at Vandra,' added Cassie.

'I was surprised that she was relatively polite in putting her view across. She once called me an '*establishment spy*' and suggested that my real employers were '*that lot at Bentwaters*'. Of course I've left out the expletives she used in consideration for your sensitive nature.'

Cassie leaned across the table and gave Mike a quick kiss on the cheek.

'That's sweet of you,' she said with a smile and then gave him a gentle clip around the side of the head. 'There,' she concluded. 'Is that sensitive enough for you?'

'Point taken,' he replied, grinning. 'But I really do think that Vandra is a bit of a liability to ESA.'

'Very forthright our Vandra,' replied Cassie, now back in her seat. 'But have you ever seen her at work? She's one of the best operatives we have. Her services out of Leiston run like clockwork.'

'That's as may be but it doesn't mean I have to like her,' he concluded.

For a few moments they sat silently, listening to the chorus of birds bidding farewell to the last few minutes of daylight. Cassie sensed there was more Mike wanted to say. She placed her hand over his and slid it up to gently squeeze his forearm and looked directly at him.

'And?' she said.

Mike smiled.

'Heron.'

'I reckon you spend more time thinking about her than you do me,' she said with mock indignation. 'You're not still fussing about guns are you?'

'Not fussing exactly. I just can't make sense of all the

training and the need for all those guns and ammo.'

'I've told you before, Mike. Anti-smuggling patrols,' stated Cassie as though she were repeating a well rehearsed mantra, 'and contingencies.'

'What contingencies?'

'Like the one you were involved in with the helicopter.'

'Yes, but as far as I know we've never used arms against smugglers and that could be because we don't want to let the army know we have weapons. So on that basis we don't need guns and therefore we didn't need to smuggle any in and I needn't have been put in that position to shoot at the helicopter anyway.'

Cassie didn't reply for a few seconds then stood up and reached for her PERC mobile.

'Stay here a minute, Mike,' she instructed. She tapped in a number and with the phone to her ear she walked out into the hallway half closing the door behind her. After a further few seconds Mike could make out the low tones of one side of a conversation but without knowing what was being said. Half a minute later Cassie returned, placed her mobile on the table, resumed her seat and sat with her arms folded, looking across at Mike.

'I've just spoken with Heron. She says I can tell you this mister clever journalist. You're right that it's not just smugglers who may eventually be at the receiving end of our weapons. One contingency is that armed dissident groups may well set themselves up in this area as they have done elsewhere – rather like the lot that killed that government minister. Another is the feasible but as yet unfounded chance that the army may decide we are too much anti-government and then act against us. Heron thinks that one of those is quite likely to happen as has already occurred in places like west Wales and Lincolnshire. Kassim doesn't see these threats as an imminent problem but he *is* worried about smugglers. Personally I think using guns if the army came for us would be a disaster but I can see the wisdom in being ready for smugglers and dissidents. So far we're preparing for defensive action; most definitely defensive and certainly not offensive.'

They sat with their own thoughts for a while until Mike broke the silence.

'We must make sure the army don't have any reason to stop our operations. As long as our operations don't suffer we should do as they ask. And we should show them we have the support of local people. We need to put out propaganda and keep our supporters informed and on our side.'

'I agree Mike. I know that will help ESA survive but it may not be enough; in the end it may not be up to us.'

CHAPTER ELEVEN
A SIGNIFICANT DEATH

Friday 12th June 2201, Westhead

A week later Mike sat at his desk in one of the two cabins newly erected in the grounds of Westhead House. Busy tidying away after a day's work he was interrupted when Carlos opened the door and ushered in a girl dressed in usual ESA attire – a logoed T-shirt and drab green trousers. Mike recognised the girl from the ESA meeting the previous Friday.

'Mike. This is Anna Chalk. She joined us recently and has been working with the Rendlesham lot for about three months. She's been sent here to make up our complement in Hut 2. Now I must shoot off so show Anna around and make her welcome and I'll be back in about an hour to settle her in.'

With that Carlos left leaving Anna standing a little awkwardly in the doorway.

'Take a seat Anna,' Mike said adding a welcoming smile. 'Anywhere you like. I'll be finished with this in a couple of minutes and then I can fill you in about what goes on around here.'

Anna walked across the room a little self-consciously

and sat in one of two easy chairs in the corner of the hut beside the work surface that supported a small sink, a water heater, a few storage containers and a small cupboard. It was a rudimentary kitchen but sufficient for their needs as it acted only as an annex to the main kitchen over at the house. She looked around at the desks and office equipment as Mike finished pushing papers into folders and dropping them into a desk drawer. When finished he sat back, stretched his arms, put his hands behind his head and turned to look at the newcomer. Some months ago he would have been drawn to Anna's attractive face and neat figure, her nearly blonde hair tied back in a businesslike knot and her seemingly quiet, possibly shy personality tempered by a slight smile. But now in Cassie he had found an attractive maturity that the younger girl lacked. He smiled.

'What brought you into ESA then?' he asked.

'Aunt Claire, really. You know – Claire Bois – she does school runs and things around Chillesford. I used to help her out in school holidays then worked part-time when I left school. Jobs are hard to come by around here and I could only find part-time work doing clerical stuff in a small Woodbridge factory. Anyway, the bits and pieces I did with ESA were more interesting than my main job. Aunt Claire got me interested in ESA and so did you.'

'Me?' asked Mike, surprised.

Anna coloured a little but recovered quickly to explain.

'Yes. Your articles. Aunt is always giving them to me to read. You're so enthusiastic about the work ESA does. So that's how I got interested and when this job came along I was pleased to take it.'

'Well,' responded Mike, 'I'm glad my ramblings seem to have done some good.'

Anna smiled again.

'So now let's show you around.'

He ushered her out into the garden, walked up the newly laid path towards the house then stopped and turned around.

'Our hut is Hut 2. Communications. We keep in contact with all the operations in outlying areas like your Aunt Claire in the Rendlesham area and Vandra Mornington in Leiston. Vandra used to be part-time like me but since the shake up she's taken the minibus test and now does the school run into Leiston full-time. We also keep our supporters informed and the third aspect of our work is to keep in touch with the police and the army as far as we can. Let them know what we are doing. My job is to supply media information. If the army don't want us to speak to them at least they can read my press releases. We use newspapers, radio, television, e-post, texts, blogs, networking sites and any other method we can find. We can't expect our sponsors to give us money and then hear nothing about how it's used.'

He turned a few degrees to his left and gestured towards a second identical prefabricated hut set a little further back in the garden away from the house.

'That's Hut 1. It's the admin headquarters. Kassim works from there with a couple of assistants. He liaises with all the section heads and also with Michael Warren who now heads up our fundraising team at our old HQ in Saxmundham. Simon, who is in charge of local operations uses this as his base although most of the time he's out working. Gianni – I'm sure you know him – and Saskia Hill who used to work with your aunt Claire are also part of Simon's team but when they're here they usually use the house,' he said as he turned and headed for the back door to the ESA accommodation. 'There's a kitchen, a lounge, a shower room and sleeping quarters. It's our rest and recreation area. I'll take you in and show you around then leave you there to wait for Carlos. He's our boss so it's really his task to show you what we do in Hut 2.'

'You haven't mentioned Heron. Where does she work?'

'Good question!'

Mike stopped, turned to face Anna and gathered his thoughts for a few seconds.

'Come around here,' he said guiding Anna around the side and out to the front of the house where he stopped and pointed out over the broad. 'Heron has her own section and works from the cabin you can see across the water. So we have four sections – Administration and Communications in the huts, Operations in outlying units such as your Aunt Claire in Chillesford and Heron's Intelligence unit in the cabin over there plus, of course, Michael's fundraising.'

'What's Intelligence for?'

'That's another good question. I'm not totally sure of the answer. It's a new aspect of our work. We've only been putting Kassim's reorganisation into operation for the last three days so I've been busy in Hut 2 and haven't been over there yet. I imagine one of their major tasks is to keep an eye on what the army is doing. As I said earlier I have to let everyone – the army, the police, the local authority, our supporters, everyone – know that we are doing a good job so that there's no need for further action by the military. But if that fails Heron's unit may hold the key to our taking a different course of action to maintain our independence.'

'Why should the army dislike us? We're only helping provide services. I can't see any harm in that?'

'The army are unable to take us at face value because of what's happening elsewhere in the country. They see any well organised and active charity as possible cover for illegal activity whether it's just a little bit of smuggling or serious disruption by active dissidents. We may not have armed paramilitary brigades in Suffolk but the activities of those in places like Cumbria and Lincolnshire have cast a shadow down here and the situation hasn't been made any easier since copycat gangs have set up no-go areas in city housing areas. Since Stacy Kenton's assassination the army seem to imagine that dissidents are everywhere.'

They stood quietly for a while before turning back to the house.

'We'll go in and have a drink if you wish and you can ask me anything else you'd like to know. Most of us are also active in operations sometime during the week. I do a mail run and also back up on the Westleton school runs when needed. Carlos should be back in about half an hour to show you your tasks.'

Wednesday 12th August 2201. Westhead.

Following on from a brilliant June and July the month of August had so far been disappointingly cool, colder than Mike could remember but returning to Westhead one Wednesday after taking a two day break his spirits were raised by the bright sunshine, the promise of a clear, warm day and the chance to end his separation from Cassie – she'd been on duty with Heron's team whilst he had been back in Framlingham completing his monthly column for *UK Today*. As Mike parked up and walked around Westhead House, heading for Hut 2, his mind turned for some unknown reason to the day about a couple of months earlier when he had shown Anna around ESA's new HQ site. He had told her he knew little of the work that was organised in the cabin across the broad but now, several weeks later that was no longer the case. Cassie, as had been expected, had been allocated to work with Heron's group and he now had almost daily updates on the activities of the Intelligence Unit. As far as he could tell Cassie told him everything about her work and it appeared that she did so with Heron's blessing. Sometimes it felt as though Heron was actively keeping him informed for some reason.

'Hi Mike. Back to peddle more colourful propaganda for the ESA cause?'

Mike was brought back to reality by James Court's cheery welcome. They stood and talked outside Hut 2 for a short while before James went on his way and Mike climbed the two steps and walked through the open door. Anna was at her work station. She turned briefly and gave him a smile before continuing with whatever she was doing. Carlos as usual was nowhere to be seen. Mike wasn't quite sure what Carlos did half the time as the three of them, Anna, James and himself seemed to run the section perfectly well whether their boss was there or not. Mike opened a window vent then collected a drink from the small chiller cabinet. The chiller had been provided by James to augment the previously rather limited facilities available without having to take a walk across to the house. Then he settled at his desk. There were three messages marked up on the monitor screen. He ignored the note from the Anglian Times and was about to open the mail from Councillor Southgate of Ipswich when he noticed that the third message was from Heron.

'Well that's a rarity,' he said to himself. 'It can't be very important; she usually phones when she needs an instant reply.'

It was a brief message.

"Today's Anglian, Page 5. Speak later."

Mike was a little surprised. Heron knew that one of the first things he did each morning was to scan national and local media on-line to find out if anything published was relevant to ESA. So he stuck to his usual routine except that he started with the Anglian Times rather than the nationals and scrolled right past the front page headlines and went straight to page 5. Half way down he found the item that Heron must have already noticed.

'Ambush Death of local Soldier'

Bentwaters. Tuesday 11th August 2201

"At a news briefing arranged for 1600 hours today the commanding officer of the Bentwaters Army Base, Colonel Westbourne, announced with regret the first death in action suffered by the Mercian Regiment during their current campaign. Although he declined to give details the CO stated

that Captain Christian Carter Blake had headed a small detachment attempting to intercept a smuggling operation on the coast north of Southwold early that morning. No other soldier had been injured. Captain Carter Blake leaves a wife, Captain Alana Buckhurst, also of the Mercian Regiment and based at Bentwaters. It is expected that the funeral service will take place in Captain Carter Blake's home town of Bridgenorth in Shropshire. A memorial service will be held at Bentwaters on the day prior to his funeral."

Mike sat quietly staring at the screen, uncertain how to react to the news. At first he thought the worst. The Mercians now had an excuse to further disrupt ESA. But on the other hand it was just one less soldier, until he was replaced, and the circumstances of his death were nothing to do with them. Then again this news probably supported Heron's belief that they themselves needed to carry arms for defence when out on patrol monitoring the activities of smugglers and other illegals.

His PERC beeped.

'What do you think, Mike?'

He told Heron what had just gone through his mind.

'I think you're right,' she said, 'on two counts but we can't just dismiss this as the inconsequential death of a soldier. I'd like to discuss this further so you had better come over. I'll send Cassie to fetch you in about twenty minutes but don't spend too much time hidden in the reeds kissing or whatever it is you do.'

Heron rang off leaving Mike with a slightly warm feeling in his cheeks, a flush of embarrassment despite the fact that his relationship with Cassie was perfectly well known to anyone in ESA who cared to be interested. A kiss whilst hidden from view, or so they thought, on their leisurely passage through the reed bed on the north side of the broad was, they had believed, their own little secret. On this occasion though their crossing was relatively rapid and on arrival at the cabin Heron made no further comment. They found her sitting with the rest of her team – Reuben Court and Frazer Oak – around the main table. Frazer, who had been a part-time ESA helper in Leiston for some years but had joined the full-time staff at the reorganisation moved along to allow Mike to bring up a chair whilst Cassie joined Heron on the bench next to the window.

'You all now know what has happened. Now we need to work out what may happen as a result of this soldier's death and decide what our reaction needs to be. It may make no difference. The checking of our vehicles and operations may just continue as usual but whilst I have some sympathy for her loss I reckon that once the grieving is over that bitch Buckhurst will pull out all the stops to crackdown on those who she feels were responsible.'

'That's not us though. Why should we be worried?' asked Reuben.

'That's exactly the problem we face. She almost certainly doesn't know who killed her husband so she could well imagine we were involved.'

'Who do you reckon was responsible then?' continued Reuben, probing his boss's thoughts.

'Almost certainly he was killed by smugglers. I don't think the army invented that part of their story as a cover for some other secret operation, unless of course Frankie Parsons has moved back south again to wreak havoc.'

The members of her team smiled politely at Heron's rare joke.

'I'll explain how the smugglers now operate,' she continued. 'Landing goods or people from boats has recently fallen out of fashion. The army, police and borderguard, with a little help from us have become too good at catching them. Now the goods are dropped or off-loaded from light aircraft. It's quite simple. For example there's a company that flies out of Norwich Airport and regularly files flight plans for trips to Southend or Rotterdam. Sometimes they fly several times per day carrying passengers, light goods or mail. The smugglers know this. The borderguard don't have the resources to check every flight. The smugglers file a similar flight plan, all above board, but en-route deviate a little to fly into or drop goods at some remote site in Suffolk. Unlike the boats that tended to use a small number of havens the planes can drop into many dozens of places not far off the air corridor. We know of sites that have been used at Covehithe, South Cove, Walberswick, Eastbridge, Sudbourne and so on down the coast.'

Heron stopped to take a drink from her mug.

'The weak point,' she continued, 'is always with the ground party that make the pick-up and pass it on to the next link in the chain. Being the most exposed part of the operation they are the most likely to have to defend themselves and make sure they aren't caught or recognised. We know that they are frequently armed which is one reason why we have abandoned our anti-smuggling patrols for the time being.'

Heron took another drink to allow this point to sink in.

'So what happened early yesterday at Coney Hill, Benacre was that Captain Carter Blake managed to get very close to the heart of an operation but met his match when he attempted to prevent the pick-up from taking place.'

Heron sat back and waited for reactions. Mike wondered how Heron knew so much detail; had she been there and if so how did she know about the drop site? Did she have inside intelligence from an army informer? He was intrigued and a little disturbed to hear the amount of detail Heron gave. She certainly hadn't gained it from the news report although probably the army had put a limit on the amount the media could broadcast leaving the reporters knowing rather more than they were allowed to tell. It was more likely, he decided, that Heron's source was a news reporter than an army informer.

'If Carter Blake got that close the army must have a good idea who the smugglers were and that surely leaves us in the clear,' decided Frazer.

'Not necessarily,' answered Cassie, speaking for the first time, 'If he came across the operation by chance the army may not know very much about those responsible for his death. We are one of the local organisations who are large enough to have the manpower, the vehicles, the local knowledge and the network of supporters to carry out illegal activity on this scale. The army may suspect us of either being actively engaged in smuggling or either supporting or condoning such activities.'

Heron leant forward and looked at each member of her team in turn.

'So,' she stated, 'we have to be prepared. A couple of

weeks, perhaps, and then I'm certain that Buckhurst and Co. will step up their ops and keep a very close eye on what we're doing. There are just four of us allocated to this unit to cover a huge area and learn as much as we can about army operations. At present that's OK but if things escalate we'll need more hands on deck. Kassim is determined to keep ESA operations outside the control of the military and as far as possible in local hands; our hands. Our system of ad hoc patrols works well for now but we may have to step up our work and that will mean more bodies working with this unit.' She turned to look at Mike. 'How busy are you in Hut 2, Mike?'

'We're well staffed. My own routine work can be done in about ninety minutes on many days.'

'Could you delegate that?'

'I reckon I could train Anna to do most of it. She could be competent in about a week, certainly in ten days I guess,' calculated Mike.

'Good. Hopefully we can train you and James from Hut 2 to work with us so that we could call on one or other of you if needed. Similarly I could use either Simon or Saskia Hill from our local operations with Gianni as a back-up. Ideally I'd like a pool of ten trained people available to our unit. This list gives us nine. Any suggestions?'

'How about Anna?' questioned Cassie, 'Mike reckons she's a quick learner.'

'I think Anna would be ideal,' confirmed Mike, 'but what about Carlos? Would he be happy knowing that he could be sitting in Hut 2 all on his own?'

'Leave Carlos to me,' said Heron. 'It would do him good to have to settle down to some hard graft every now and again.' Her comment was met with knowing smiles all round. 'So, Mike, would you like to help us out in this unit?'

He looked across at Cassie who smiled and gave the slightest of nods.

'Yes. In theory that sounds fine. But with what kind of operation would I be involved?'

'I reckon you know more or less what we do here Mike but you should ask Cassie. She'll fill you in on the detail. Come back tomorrow and let me know what you think.'

Wednesday 12th August 2201, 1937 hours. Walberswick.

Cassie came out of the kitchen in Grandma Vale's cottage, put down a coffee mug on the table and placed a second in front of Mike.

'You haven't said much about the meeting earlier.'

'No but I've been doing a lot of thinking.'

'Heron respects you, you know that don't you,' stated Cassie.

'Yes. I know. But at the moment I'm more concerned about us. What you told me over dinner, about your operations, could have been said some days ago. Before Carter Blake's death. I thought we talked about everything.'

'I'm sorry Mike but Heron told us to be quiet about the possible need to expand operations until people needed to know. At the time it was just a long term contingency but the soldier's death brought the plans forward. It's true she spoke to me on my own and it's true she mentioned that you could be involved but at the time it was just an outline plan in her mind. There was no point in shouting about half-baked plans.'

'That's fine. I take all that on board and I'm not really annoyed with you but I'm also not sure we should cross the path of the army. Prevention is better than cure and I'm working on preventing any conflict arising. The pen, as someone once said eons ago, is mightier than the sword.'

'That's all very good but what if the army take it into their head to act further against us. We have to be prepared. Surely you can see that.' Cassie leant across and gave him a kiss. 'We're not on opposite sides Mike, just working from different angles. Heron's just asking for a little help from you. Anyway, what do you think you'll tell her?'

'I'll go along with this plan for now. But I'll reserve judgement. Mind you – if the situation does change and if she puts you in any danger I'll be out of there, taking you with me.'

'I think that's your obtuse way of saying sorry for your earlier grumpiness. I accept your apology. Anyway thanks for your concern but I can look after myself. I don't need protection.'

Mike reached across, pushed back some hair that had fallen across her face and squeezed her hand.

'Fighting talk is it now? Should I go back to Framlingham and leave you to it?'

'If you like but Grandma's out for the evening and I'd rather like you to stay.'

They kissed.

* * * * *

Thursday 27th August 2201
Alana rarely took a back seat when travelling by

car. There were few drivers she trusted and even when travelling with those that she did trust she preferred to sit in the front. Most drivers, though, found her regular commentary from the passenger seat pointing out real or imaginary hazards or her frequent bulletins regarding navigation quite irritating. Those people who had to travel with her preferred to sit quietly in the passenger seat happy in their knowledge that she was in fact a very good driver. Returning from Christian's funeral she was however pleased to sit in the back and leave her driver, Corporal Richmond, to do her job. It was Colonel Westbourne who had insisted that Alana took a staff car and a pool driver although she was going on a purely civilian journey. Alana was dressed in civvies but her driver was sporting her No.2 uniform in plain airforce blue – a colour adopted by all the armed forces to be worn by a service man or woman whilst on military duty but attending a civilian function; a uniform sporting only a discreet shoulder flash indicating rank – no ribbons, no medals, no sashes, no regimental insignia - in sombre contrast to the No.1 full dress uniform that had been worn the previous day at Bentwaters when a memorial service had been held for their dead comrade.

Alana also felt that she had taken a back seat during the funeral, cremation and reception. At the funeral of course all eyes had initially been on her as she took her place at the front of the church but she could not compete with Christian's niece Scarlett Blake aged 7, her hand held throughout by her older sister, 12 years old Sapphire, as she told the assembled mourners how much Uncle Christian had meant to her. It was the first time that Alana had heard a spontaneous, gentle ripple of applause at a funeral and for the first time since Christian's death, for just a few minutes, her heart had been filled with gladness. At the crematorium a feeling of equality pervaded as each mourner focussed on the committal of their son or brother, husband, uncle or cousin, friend or colleague. But it was at the reception, hosted by Christian's parents at their palatial home, that Alana felt most alone. Everything had been arranged by the Carter Blakes; she hadn't been part of the planning, she hadn't been asked to choose a hymn or a prayer or to suggest flowers to decorate the church. At first the guests at the reception each sought her out to express condolences or sympathy but soon, plate or glass in hand, the mourners separated into small groups either seated in the conservatory or standing outside on the terrace or the lawn. The Carter Blake clan formed by far the greater part of the assembly. They had come together from widely dispersed homelands in at least a dozen countries and, formalities complete they set about catching up on family news, renewing acquaintance with remote family members and meeting for the first time with new wives, husbands, partners and offspring. Alana spent time with her own parents and a few others of her relatives before tiring of the event and phoning Richmond to bring the car up to the house. Her original plan had been to return to the hotel near Market Drayton and travel back to Suffolk the next day but, with formalities over and several hours of summer daylight left she decided to return direct to Bentwaters that evening.

The car sped smoothly eastwards unhindered by heavy commercial traffic. At first, sitting alone in the back, she had thought sadly about Christian; her Blakey. After about forty minutes or so she had dozed, lulled by the gentle, even sound of the tyres on the tarmac but at about the hour mark she had awoken and asked Richmond to pull in at the next service station. They parked up and walked to the concourse to find a *'CoffeeHouse'* where Alana ordered coffees, black for herself plus a sandwich and with cream for Richmond together with a cake. They sat in chairs at a table rather than on stools up at the bar and as with the hotel the previous evening Alana insisted they referred to each other by forename. She asked Cerys why she had joined the army and enjoyed listening to her driver's succinct but informative account delivered in a pleasing, gentle Welsh accent. She found Cerys, who was probably a few years younger than herself a pleasant companion and for the first time in her life Alana could understand that some girls could be attracted to a lesbian relationship. But it was only a passing thought, not a desire on her part and after a few further minutes of small talk they returned, refreshed, to their car.

'Front passenger seat, please Richmond,' instructed Alana with a return to formality.

'Yes, Ma'am.'

Alana was now back in the driving seat of her life if not of the car in which they were travelling; her natural tendency to give instructions had returned but her instinct to take total control continued to be masked by further thoughts of Christian. As they headed on towards Suffolk with the sun beginning to set behind them she knew that providing a fitting memorial to Blakey lay in her hands. It hadn't been in the formality of the regimental memorial service the previous day nor had it been in the meticulously organised funeral in Bridgenorth; it would have to be seen in her ability to finish the work they had started and deal decisively, once and for all, with the outlaw activities blighting East Suffolk. And there was another thing that gave her the strength to look to the future rather than dwell in the past. Christian Carter Blake had died knowing that in a few months time a son or daughter would be born; a living memorial to his existence on this Earth. But with baby on the way she would need to act quickly to deal with the local dissenters in the area around her base at Bentwaters.

A few kilometres further on Alana spoke for the first time since embarking on this leg of their journey.

'Pull over at the next convenient place, please Richmond. I'd like to drive home from here.'

CHAPTER TWELVE
THE NOOSE TIGHTENS

Wednesday 2nd September 2201. Westhead. 0930

It was Anna's turn to be duty officer in Hut 2. The four communications officers, Carlos, Mike, James and Anna took it in turn to sit in the office to record and if necessary deal with any incidents notified by ESA members or supporters or the authorities. On Monday Anna had been duty officer from 0700 to 1620. Having already done her stint for the week she was not a little annoyed to find Carlos waiting for her when she arrived at eight-thirty this morning asking her to cover the rest of his duty that day as he had to be at an unspecified place elsewhere. Carlos, who always seemed to be needed urgently elsewhere when there was work to be done did not wait for her reply but headed directly for Hut 1.

So far it had been a quiet week. The display above her workstation gave a three day rolling record. On Monday when she was last on duty there had been just two incidents to record – a routine army check on the school bus at Westleton after the morning school run and a note that Francesca Hyde (who operated out of Chillesford) was on holiday next week and her duties would be covered by Anna's aunt, Claire Bois. Tuesday's sole report was from Heron's intelligence unit to say that the Mercian Regiment had increased the vehicles housed at their Forest Lodge outpost with the two usual ATVs being augmented by two 12-seat troop carriers, a flat-bed truck and a further three ATVs, all arriving between 1030 and 1100 hours. Wednesday's space was so far empty.

Duty Officer was, by its nature important but could in no way be regarded as an exciting or an engaging occupation. So Anna completed her routine tasks listing down start and finish times as the ESA operatives reported starting or finishing a duty and by ten-thirty she had made herself a drink, eaten the chocolate bar that she had brought as part of her lunch and resorted to touching up her makeup and looking up the previous day's sports results on the interweb. But just before eleven these peripheral activities were interrupted by the alert tone from her message box. She opened up the note. It was from her Aunt Claire.

'Chillesford. 1034. School bus check by army patrol. Damaged seat belt in unused, cordoned off seat. Bus impounded by army. Please send replacement vehicle for p.m. run.'

Anna posted the incident on the display board and copied it to the Operations unit in Hut 1. The second message came at 1122. Michael Warren had been visited at the Saxmundham ESA fundraising office by another army detachment. Armed with a warrant from the Magister in Ipswich they had examined the premises and briefly skimmed through electronic and paper records. Computers had been locked and files containing written records sealed pending the promise of an actuarial inspection the next day. In the interim, he was informed, any updating of records needed to be completed manually using individually numbered sheets that the army provided. Each sheet would have to be accounted for during Thursday's visit. Anna copied the message to Kassim in Hut 1. Making an assumption, based on experience that messages were hardly ever received between twelve and thirteen hundred hours she decided to wait another quarter of an hour and then take her break in the rest area over at Westhead House; it would be nice to chat to someone as she had been alone for the three hours since Carlos left. But within a few minutes footfall on the steps outside heralded a rare visit from Heron.

'Army being a nuisance this morning I hear,' she stated as she crossed the room and pulled a chair over to sit near Anna.

'Two reports on one morning are not that rare but they do seem to be more belligerent than usual,' agreed Anna.

'I could do with a coffee, please Anna. I'll wait here a little while in case anything else occurs.'

It crossed Anna's mind to wonder why Heron should think another incident likely but the thought was soon forgotten as she made two coffees, offered Heron a biscuit from the container that housed James' supply and became engaged in answering questions about the scope of the work undertaken here in Hut 2. With refreshments consumed and Heron showing no signs of moving Anna collected the mugs and plates and took them across to the small galley area. As she was unloading the crockery the message alert sounded again. She quickly put down her load and hurried back to her workstation but not before Heron had turned to it first and opened up the message.

'1153. Leiston. Saskia Hill. Army patrol at Eastbridge. Followed school bus on our roundabout run to Leiston. Blatant shadowing – no attempt to conceal their purpose. After drop-off followed me home. Asked to see licence and other papers. Asked why I was driving, not Vandra. Told them they had been informed of the change at the end of last week. Vandra's gone to her sister's wedding. Army very polite. Apologised for taking up my time.'

'What do you think their game is, Anna?'

'Seems to me they're telling us to watch our step. They've got their eye on us.'

'Certainly it's that but they've been doing that for months now. In fact ever since Stacy Kenton was assassinated. There must be more to it than that. I'm certain this escalation is more than a one-off blitz. If it continues it will prove that they're out to disrupt or destroy us for some reason. These army people seem to see dissidents and illegal operations everywhere they look. Kassim will need to consider these reports very carefully. I'm off to Hut 1 now.' And without a word of farewell or thanks for her welcome Heron was off again.

Wednesday 2nd September 2201. Westhead. 1507

Returning to Westhead after ferrying the replacement bus to Claire Bois in Chillesford, Mike and Gianni parted by the garage – Gianni reversing his car and heading back home to Wenhaston whilst Mike made his way to Hut 2. Expecting just Anna and possibly James to be there he was surprised when the open door revealed Carlos and Heron and all of her team except Cassie perched on stools and chairs and any other available surface. With a questioning look on his face Mike moved clear of the door and stood, leaning against the wall to the right of the doorframe. Carlos looked up and nodded to him.

'Bit of an emergency meeting. It's Heron's shout so I'll leave her to do the talking.'

Heron stood up. Heron could never be a chairperson, keeping order; Heron was always the main item on the agenda at any gathering except when Kassim was there, usually the only item when she was in charge. Typical Heron, considered Mike but, and he smiled at the thought, it was a rare occasion to witness Carlos being upstaged.

'There have been four incidents involving ourselves and the army today,' Heron pronounced. 'Most of you have been informed about the first three through Anna's messages. Checking a school bus is routine; taking it out of service is a first. That journey has a passenger list of 18 pupils. The bus seats 22 and the defective seat was clearly marked and cordoned off and Claire had even shown the army the booking note for the replacement seat belt fitting in Woodbridge on Friday. Another first is the army using a Magister's warrant. OK, I accept that they must have had one when they took over from Frankie at Benacre Hall but they didn't need to use it then. Now shadowing a whole school bus run is also new but perhaps the most worrying development of all happened just an hour ago. Cassie was returning home after a short break away, cutting off the A12 at Yoxford and heading over towards Westleton. Approaching the Middleton turn-off she joined the back of a queue of traffic – most unusual on that road unless there has been a traffic accident. It turned out to be an army roadblock. The check was brief – just visual, saloon and boot. Cassie wasn't in uniform or fatigues and there was nothing to suggest she was part of ESA. Less than a minute's stop and she was waved on her way. Now this is definitely a first as the army have never taken random action before; they've always hit specific targets. When Cassie asked why they were being stopped she was told they were looking for three armed men suspected of a robbery in Saxmundham but the local media have no information about such a raid.'

Heron paused to emphasise the importance of the information she had just given them. Continuing, she said, 'Today's activities may be a one off but I believe it's the start of a new campaign by the Mercians. Static roadblocks rather than mobile patrols are a worrying new tactic. Up to now our unit's patrols have been able to keep tabs on the army's activities but now we need to put into operation the plans I explained to you a little while back. Kassim, Carlos and I have decided on a scheme for patrols that require me to co-opt you Communications people – James, Mike and Anna – to help out. I'm sure Carlos can draw up a rota to make sure that work here is covered whilst one of you is available at any time to help me out. The rota should also arrange for a second person to be available in case of an emergency.'

Carlos smiled an acceptance of the task but his eyes and body seemed to say *I've already done that; I don't need you to tell me how to do my job!*

'What are you asking us to do on these patrols?' asked James.

'You'll find out by working with Cassie, Reuben or me at first. We'll show you how we operate. Any other questions?'

'Won't the army be suspicious if we're seen out and about more than usual? And won't that make them even more paranoid and more likely to crack down on our operations?' asked Mike.

'We have a plan to cover that,' explained Heron. 'In addition to our planned ops such as the school runs we do a lot of ad hoc work such as the hospital journeys or home and garden maintenance for older people. Our patrols will all have a cover story; they will appear to be undertaking a task that is a plausible and legitimate activity. The location and personnel will be varied so that the army can't pick up a pattern in our operations.'

Heron looked around for signs of a response or further questions. There were none.

'OK Mike. If it's OK with Carlos come over to the cabin tomorrow morning and we'll get you started. Anna and James can start later on, James on Friday and hopefully if it fits in with Carlos I'll see you, Anna, on Monday or Tuesday.'

Heron slipped down from the table where she had been perched and made her way directly to the door as Reuben and Anna moved chairs aside to let her pass. When she had gone Carlos asked for their attention and from his monitor projected the current week's Hut 2 staff rota onto the large wall-mounted screen occupying the wall behind him. The revised schedule showed that Mike was now free the following morning and James the next day, to work over in the cabin. After pointing out the changes he ended with a quip. 'We're always one step ahead here at the nerve centre of ESA operations. I reckon after an hour with Heron's lot you'll be asking to come back over. And Mike – if you do come back bring Cassie with you; we could do with someone really bright to help us out here.'

Thursday 3ʳᵈ September 2201. The Cabin.

'Where and when we patrol will be decided each morning. That often means an early start so those on patrol duty will need to be ready to start their planning by 0730. I expect we'll need to mount some sort of operation most days. How we patrol will be up to the team leader; each sortie may be different,' explained Heron, by way of introduction to her team, on this occasion augmented with the addition of Mike. 'Reuben,' she continued for Mike's benefit, 'has been patrolling, usually with Cassie but sometimes Frazer, for three weeks now and they have developed some good techniques. So, Reuben,' she said, turning her head towards him, 'explain to Mike what we do.'

'There are two types of patrol work. General foot or vehicle patrols that hope to come across the army and then report back to base. This method's a bit hit and miss. So whenever possible we go out following information supplied by ESA members and supporters. We had a report from one of our friends yesterday about an army roadblock but in fact Cassie had already reported in about it. As Heron said yesterday, our patrols are disguised as normal ops so we try to plan ahead. Sometimes we need to respond quickly to information about the army's movements so we have a plan ready and adapt it as we go along. You'll see what I mean when you come out with us next week.'

'OK, Reuben. Any questions, Mike?'

There was a short silence. Mike shifted his position on the bench, looked up and asked the question that he knew Cassie was expecting and he guessed Heron was half expecting as well.

'Do we patrol with arms?'

As usual Heron was unfazed by the query, understood where Mike was coming from and readily provided an answer.

'Patrols out gathering information will almost always avoid contact with the military. I can see no purpose in going out armed. If you were caught in possession of firearms, particularly unregistered guns, ESA would be in a whole load of trouble. We would be in the proverbial shit and that's what these patrols are trying to avoid. However if army action intensifies, as I feel it may, we'll possibly have to think about the matter again. We have five highly trained and competent firearms operatives – yourself Mike, Reuben, Cassie, Simon and myself. We need to be ready but we're not planning to start a war. We just need to be to have the capability available to us.'

Reuben spoke again. 'Will Simon be part of our patrols?'

'Not at present. He's far too valuable an operations officer but he could be made available if necessary. Heron looked at each team member in turn. Mike had sat back and folded his arms to indicate he was happy with what he had heard. 'OK,' she concluded. 'Mike, you join us next

Tuesday, the eighth, to go out with Reuben. Be here by 0800.'

Friday 18th September 2201

Having been out with Reuben then Heron and then Reuben again during the previous two weeks Mike had developed a good idea of how Heron needed her patrols to operate. His duty rota had now settled down to working two days and one morning in Hut 2, one of the full days acting as duty officer, plus another half day on patrol with the Intelligence Unit. The duty rotas set out by Carlos generally worked in well with Heron's requirements although Mike had a sneaking suspicion that the odd occasions when manning problems did occur were manufactured on purpose by Carlos in response to the put-down Heron had handed out at the meeting a couple of weeks earlier. Cassie was, of course, also involved in these patrols and she had taken James or Anna along with her on some occasions. Frazer Oak usually acted as anchor man, based in the cabin, maintaining a link between the patrols and Heron and those in Hut 1 and Hut 2.

So this week had seen Mike on duty in Hut 2 on Monday but continuing, under protest, for an extra hour when Carlos claimed to be in conference with Kassim. On Tuesday he had been on patrol with Reuben but taken Wednesday off to attend to his journalistic responsibilities before returning to Westhead on Thursday for further work in Hut 2. He had not been home to Framlingham for some time and when not working for ESA he often stayed at Grandma Vale's cottage in Walberswick. When Cassie was on duty the cottage was quiet and her grandmother left him alone to get on with his work.

Tuesday's patrol had been classified as *'low risk'*. That meant that ESA uniforms were worn and marked ESA vehicles were used (van, truck or minibus depending on the task) with a crew of two – one of the original team and one of the new recruits. The journey was, or at least looked like a normal ESA operation. Today Rueben took an ESA van and once they had reached the road they had turned south through Westleton and on along Leiston Road to reach the village of Theberton. Their task had been generated by Hut 2 and the text on Reuben's PERC directed them to a farm where they had collected livestock samples to be taken to the veterinary centre in Sternfield, just outside Saxmundham. Task complete they travelled on to the fund-raising office in Saxmundham High Street and took advantage of Michael Warren's hospitality and his supply of coffee and biscuits. After a general chat between the three men, together with Beth Stamford the administrative officer, they returned to their van and Reuben asked Mike a question.

'Now Mike. Today's patrol. Do you reckon it was a normal operation or a cover for collecting information about the army?'

Mike thought for a few seconds. It seemed genuine enough. The farmer had been expecting them, had the sample case ready for collection and the vet's centre had thanked them for bringing the expected delivery promptly. He tossed a coin in his mind and gave his answer.

'Genuine.'

'Wrong! It was a set up. The farmer is an ESA supporter

and so is the head of the veterinary centre. The whole thing was put together a couple of days ago by Heron and Frazer. But that's good. If *you* didn't see it as a set-up I'm sure your average soldier would be equally fooled. Most army people wouldn't want to risk messing about with biological materials in sealed containers sporting a bold HAZARD label!'

'Very good but what was the purpose of this jaunt then?' asked a puzzled Mike.

'On the way here we passed a building site near the rail level crossing west of Leiston. Like normal construction sites it was bounded by two metre high panels but unlike most commercial sites there were no boards advertising the builders, the owners or the purpose of the work. It's a ninety-five percent certainty that it's an army development. That rail line is important. It supplies the Power Station at Sizewell with goods and equipment and also provides a link to the army guard post that was built nearby. On the way back we'll take a look at this new construction from the other side; it could well be a new outstation for Bentwaters.'

Having left Michael to his work they had returned by a more northerly route towards the level crossing, been stopped briefly by an army road block near the construction site and returned to base after making a short diversion to the village of Middleton to make a mail collection – totally genuine, Reuben had assured him. The task had ended with the sending of a report to Heron. New army guard post, almost certainly, was the gist of Reuben's message. The army were increasingly making their presence felt across East Suffolk.

Today, Friday, Mike had been called in for an extra patrol duty with Reuben. He had been instructed to turn up in what Heron termed 'neat casual' attire – no ESA t-shirts, no combat gear. In Heron's absence Reuben led the briefing meeting for Mike and Frazer in a rather less formal manner than that employed by his immediate boss and not in the cabin but in the more relaxed surroundings of Westhead House.

'Medium risk today, Mike. You've been promoted. We're going up around the A12 road. Now as you know ESA don't usually work beyond the main road so we have to make this trip look really genuine as in fact we seldom have tasks to carry out in the area. Come outside and see our transport.'

They walked around the house and out to the garage area. The seven vehicles in residence were an ESA marked van and a truck, the reserve minibus, three private cars including Mike's belonging to ESA staff and, new to Mike, a black GM Avenger pick-up truck.

'So which is ours?'

'The Avenger!' replied Reuben with enthusiasm.

'Is it yours?'

'No. I wish it were but I couldn't afford even a ten year-old model. No,' he repeated. 'It's ESA property but if the police were to check the plates today they would find it registered to Mr Justin Caton Garden of Coles Hill Close, Wenhaston. He's a friend of Gianni.'

'So what are we doing with his truck?'

'We're not. Come on Mike – you're a little slow this morning! It's *our* vehicle but for today it's taking on a different identity. It's the same make and model as Mr

Garden's pick-up, same colour and just one year older. We've borrowed its identity. With Mr Garden's permission of course.'

'Which of us is going to play Mr Garden then?'

Reuben laughed. 'Neither of us, really but if asked, though, I'm Mr Garden. I know quite a lot about him. I know he travels around Suffolk mending IT and other electronic equipment and that he has clients in Southwold, Halesworth and Saxmundham. Perfect cover for us to cruise around and see what the army are up to. Anyway, jump in; we've got a couple of appointments to get to.'

They said goodbye to Frazer who left to take up his anchor-man role back at the cabin and took their seats in the Avenger, Reuben driving, and headed towards the Westleton Road where they turned north, heading for Blythburgh. Mike sat quietly, thinking. He was rather excited by the prospect of an operation using the subterfuge of impersonating a willing accomplice but at the same time a little concerned at the element of danger this type of operation introduced. Once they were on their way Reuben explained the task ahead.

'So here's the plan. The A12 road from Blythburgh southwards to Saxmundham and Wickham Market forms the landward boundary of our operating area. We sometimes work across the A12 but none of our regular school runs or mail collections operate that far inland. The East Suffolk Restricted Area, now *Military* Restricted Area, also ends at the road so there's less call for our work over there. What we don't know is how far the military recognise the boundary in practice although we do know they patrol the road regularly. That could be just for show.

We have a number of appointments connected by a route that zigzags across the area giving us a good chance of coming across any army patrols in the area.'

On the approach to Blythburgh they crossed the old A12 to join the recently diverted main road to the west of the village. Here they turned left again and set off travelling along the northern boundary of the Restricted Area towards Saxmundham.

'Do you know anything about repairing computers and so on?' queried Mike.

'If no one asks I don't need to know anything.'

'And if someone does ask?'

'I know a little and I reckon I'm able to pull the wool over the eyes of any soldier lowly enough to be sent out on routine patrol. Anyway leave the talking to me – for today you're just the lad learning the trade'

Traffic was light, mainly private cars but after a few minutes they were passed by an army ATV heading north on the opposite carriageway.

'One of the Forest Lodge vehicles. I spotted it there when we passed by the other day. Two man crew,' stated Mike.

'Could be patrolling. In which case it will probably continue up to Benacre and turn back. Let's find out.'

Reuben drove on for a short while then, near the mid point of a straight section of road he pulled into a layby on the left.

'Shouldn't we pull off the road so that we're not noticed? We could drive up behind that copse and observe the whole stretch of road from there,' suggested Mike.

'Mike. This isn't your routine low risk patrol. This is

the real thing! True we are observing the goons but we're also testing new ways of dealing with them. We're going to stay here until they find us.'

Having no answer to that Mike sat quietly and waited to see whatever Reuben had planned for his meeting with the military. Reuben sat back, zapped the window down and sat quietly for a while as though thinking then turned, reached back and pulled forward a bag that had been resting on the rear seat. He pulled out a drinks flask and a food container.

'Tea?'

Mike smiled and nodded.

Five minutes passed pleasantly with warm late-summer air filling the vehicle, a passable container of tea and a couple of biscuits providing refreshment and relaxed, casual conversation passing the time until an army ATV, recognised by Mike as the one he had seen earlier, came into view and pulled in behind them. The rear view mirror showed the driver, an army sergeant, looking alternately up and down and presumably recording details of the ESA vehicle before getting out and walking up to Reuben's open side window.

'Good morning sir. We're checking vehicles because there have been a number of smuggling operations in this area recently.'

Not that same tired old excuse, thought Mike.

'Could you confirm your vehicle registration, please sir?'

'Isn't that a police matter?' asked Reuben.

'This is a Restricted Area, sir. Here we are responsible for such investigations.'

Reuben obliged with an answer, continued to deal with other questions and provided documents to confirm his identity and ownership of the vehicle. At each stage the sergeant tapped information into his Infopad.

'And where are you headed, sir?'

'We're between jobs,' explained Reuben, pulling a list from the dashboard locker that showed that they had earlier been to install new equipment for a lady in Blythburgh. The task was booked for 0900 to 1000 but they had finished early so had made a brief stop for a drink before moving on to their next appointment, a media centre malfunction in Darsham where they were due at 1030, he explained. Satisfied with the answers and a check having been made to the Central Vehicle Registration Centre, the sergeant thanked Reuben for his cooperation, accepted the offer of a business card headed *J C Garden, IT specialist*, returned to his vehicle, had a brief discussion with his colleague, pulled out and moved on towards the south.

'Thank God it wasn't the police,' commented a relieved Reuben as he similarly checked for traffic then pulled out and followed the military vehicle towards Saxmundham.

'Why's that? Why would the police have been any worse?'

Reuben chuckled.

'Because, mate, the one thing I haven't got is Justin's Driver's Licence and you know what the police always ask for first!'

Turning off after about two and a half kilometres they headed into Darsham to keep their 1030 appointment; not to actually fix a media centre but to spend forty minutes or so in the house of an ESA supporter with a workbox, an array of tools and partly dismantled equipment providing a scene of suitable activity for the eyes of anyone who cared to visit.

'Knowing the army,' explained Reuben, 'our friends would probably be instructed to keep to their pre-arranged patrol route but equally well they could call up another pair of squaddies to check up on us. Paul here has this media centre and whose to say it wasn't a straight forward job that now just needs reassembling?'

'So what next, Boss?' asked Mike.

Reuben picked up and studied his job list. 'Bramfield, then Wenhaston and then home and if we see the sergeant on out travels we give him a toot on the horn and a cheery wave.'

Mike was impressed. Vehicle, documents, job list, equipment, cooperative ESA supporters. Everything had been arranged almost to perfection. But there remained one concern. Back in the truck he expressed his concern.

'They know your face now, Reuben, and probably mine as well. They may even have a picture of us. And what if they check up with the real Mr Garden?'

'True. Next time we'll need to do something different. The army have better things to do than double check on a seemingly everyday occurrence such as a citizen going about doing his lawful occupation. In answer to your other question have you ever thought about cosmetic surgery?'

Reuben laughed and Mike smiled as the truck moved out onto the road heading towards their next scheduled appointment.

Baiting the military was certainly not part of ESA policy. Kassim did not condone it as he was aware that the practice could become popular among the younger workers and detract from the association's core activities. Heron was even more opposed to such pranks. Despite being the most vehemently anti-military member of ESA she was also quite clear in her mind that they should not do anything that would give the army a further reason to hinder or control their work.

The first incident had not been planned but resulted, not surprisingly, from an idea thought up by Gianni. Almost everybody associated with ESA knew Gianni. Tall, strikingly black-haired, independent and fiercely loyal to those he thought deserving of his loyalty, Gianni was for the most part quiet, even morose but when the time came he could speak passionately in support of those things closest to his heart. His loyalty was first and foremost to his family and secondly to the wider Anglo-Italian community in England. Generations had passed since there was a Prince family member with more than fifty percent Italian blood in their veins and in Gianni's case after five generations it had probably been diluted considerably further than that. Although originally settling in Norfolk his ancestors soon spread out and a sizable number of his relatives were to be found in and around the town of Halesworth so that from a geographical point of view Gianni's homeland lay in Suffolk rather than the area around the town of Trapani in Sicily. Given that he was an ardent supporter of his family's adopted county it was not surprising that, with the political situation as it was, Gianni should naturally have taken a dislike to the army muscling in on law enforcement in the area. The fact that Simon was friendly with Gianni was, at first sight, rather unexpected. Simon was quite unlike Gianni in that he was outgoing, easygoing and friendly with everyone. Whereas Simon was always smiling, Gianni was more likely to scowl or on a good day carry a brooding look on his face. But they both enjoyed a joke.

Since the recent reorganisation of ESA the overnight accommodation at Westhead House had been more in demand than before and even the cabin on the other side of the broad had to be pressed into use on occasions. As a result Simon and Marissa Upton now and then had house guests at their home in nearby Westleton. On one particular evening Gianni had been staying with the Uptons so that he would be available to take the school bus down to Woodbridge for its annual service the next morning thus avoiding a fifteen kilometre round trip to and from his home village of Wenhaston. After a meal Simon and Gianni spent the evening in Westleton's pub, the Crown. Simon seemed to know everyone in the pub and after what seemed to Gianni like an interminable time spent in handshakes, slaps on the back, exchanged greetings and the occasional joke they eventually settled down with their drinks. After a couple of minutes two men, one probably in his early 20s and the other a little older had walked into the bar and greeted the barman, Gerry, by name. The older one of the pair, speaking with a Midland's accent, had then ordered their drinks.

'Know them as well?' Gianni had asked, mischievously.

'Never seen them before. I reckon they're army; you can always tell army people,' replied Simon, adding, 'probably part of the new detachment at Forest Lodge. Not much for them to do of an evening there and this is the nearest part of the civilised world to their base.' Simon had laughed at his own comment.

About an hour's drinking and chatting had passed before the two ESA men called it a day recognising that Gianni needed a fairly early start the next morning. They had thought nothing more about the two army men until on leaving and walking out through the car park Gianni had noticed an army ATV backed in under the shadow of a wall at the rear of the hardstanding area.

'What do you think, Si?' he had asked, pointing towards the vehicle, a grin on his face and a sparkle in his eye, caught by the light of the illuminated pub sign.

'That ATV will be locked. You can't just drive it around the corner for a joke.'

'I'm not planning to drive it anywhere. And when they get in they'll be able to drive it away like normal. No. What I'm thinking is that from where they're parked they won't be able to see the gate until they pull forward and turn.'

'So we shut the gate.'

'Yes. But we also lock it!'

Simon had then walked back into the pub, a smile forming on his face. At the bar he had a quiet word with Gerry, an old friend from his schooldays, resulting in the receipt of a piece of paper with a five digit number written on it. This code when tapped into the keypad would lock the gate, a process introduced a couple of years earlier when a group of itinerant travellers had invaded the car park with motorhomes and stayed there for several days until the authorities were able to evict them. Now the gate was locked half an hour after closing every evening. By the time Simon had returned Gianni had shut the barrier so with the code applied the two had then walked back to Simon's leaving the ATV in enclosed isolation.

Next day although Simon had not found out the result of their prank news of it had spread around the younger ESA staff. With retelling the story first invented and then exaggerated the discomfort of the two soldiers and then spawned plans for further similar action. Opportunities for some simple practical jokes would surely arise although some of the more militant members dreamed up schemes that were only a little short of being classified as guerrilla warfare. Perhaps it was a result of the mundane nature of much of ESA work that caused the excitement but unlike many overinflated ideas that soon burst, leaving nothing of value, Gianni's prank gave rise to a series of incidents where the Mercians were caught at the end of some well crafted practical jokes. Rules soon developed and a form of competition evolved. There was to be no injury to soldiers, no damage to vehicles and definitely no cost to ESA itself. This left just the ability to inconvenience the army by causing them to deal with an unexpected event rather than continue with their own planned duties. And that was where the competition came in – any incident posted on the kitchen notice-board at Westhead was measured for success by the length of the delay imposed on the opposition.

Two weeks after Gianni organised the pub prank the leading act was down to Saskia Hill, Simon's number two for operations out of Westhead House. Saskia lived in Darsham. She had left the school bus at Westhead late one afternoon for Simon to take home in preparation for the next day's run and after showering and changing had collected her own car and started on the journey home. As she pulled out onto the track leading to the Westleton Road her PERC sounded a text alert. At first she felt tempted to leave it. If it had been urgent the caller would have made the effort to speak with her. It could wait for a while – after all it wouldn't disappear. She had travelled a little further before giving a slight click of annoyance with her tongue and pulling over onto an unofficial rough lay-bay created by the cars of walkers and bird watchers and the like. She had decided to stop just in case the message was important. The text was from Anna in Hut 2 giving the latest update on the army's activities and among the information was a note about a roadblock on Bowman's Lane – part of her route home. Normally Saskia didn't reply to texts – in her mind it only started a never-ending cycle of comments of ever decreasing value but on this occasion the timely warning allowed her to plan a diversion around her usual route so she texted Anna a reply using just the single word '*Thanks*'. By the time she had reached and crossed the Westleton Road however she had abandoned any plans to make a diversion that gave a less direct journey and decided to sit out any minor delay caused by the roadblock. A little further on, though, she had developed a plan to turn any delay that she suffered to her own advantage.

Anna's information had placed the army checkpoint just south of the bridge over the stream, about half way down the lane. The army had a clear view down to the south but to the north of the bridge the lane turned sharp right before a left hand bend restored its original direction. Any incident that occurred further up the road would be hidden from the soldiers and it was an incident that Saskia was planning as she turned into the top of the lane. There were two practical ways to block a lane. One was to arrange for a herd of cattle to leave their field and take to the highway but as a farmer's daughter she had no wish to alienate a family friend or neighbour and Kassim had emphasized that no action was to be taken that could harm the reputation of ESA or it's supporters. She was, therefore, just left with organising a car breakdown. Having only a rudimentary knowledge of the workings of a vehicle engine – she knew only enough to have passed her minibus test – she doubted that she could make any tinkering with the motor look like a real breakdown. So that just left that old standby – the flat tyre. Pulling into a wide field gate entrance she let the trailing car pass then climbed out and let air out of the rear left tyre. Not a complete deflation as she had to move the car partially onto the road and she didn't want to damage anything. She had chosen a good spot. The lane was narrow at this point but her car could be seen easily by approaching vehicles from either direction. She had taken out the spare wheel and started to jack up the car when, despite it being a lightly used lane the first car arrived, travelling up from the bridge. It was surprising how quickly chaos built up. Someone from a few vehicles back came to size up the problem and helpfully suggested that rather than change the tyre in the middle of the road she inflate it temporarily so that they could move the car into the gateway. By the time this Good Samaritan had returned with his compressor a soldier had arrived to find out why the last car he had despatched had got no further than the first bend. With the soldier's help the wheel had soon been fixed and Saskia's little runabout had been moved safely to the side of the road. The soldier, having abandoned his duties became a temporary traffic cop and for a few minutes was engaged in releasing vehicles from the hold-up, one at a time, alternately until the traffic was flowing freely again. After assuring well-wishers that her car was now OK to at least make the short distance home Saskia had pulled out onto the southbound side of the lane aided by the soldier who had temporarily held up traffic to allow her manoeuvre. She had waved her thanks to him and as she returned her hand to the steering wheel noticed the dashboard clock click over to 1737. It had been 1701 when she initially pulled off the road so she reckoned it would be OK to claim 36 minutes for the hold up and post it on the Westhead kitchen noticeboard in the morning. It was the first time anyone had been able to claim a disruption of over half an hour. Saskia smiled and as she travelled past the roadblock the smile turned into a broad, toothy grin. It wasn't so much the record that gave her satisfaction but the fact that the two other members of her team, Simon and Gianni, couldn't even meet that figure between them.

Saskia's record didn't last long. She naturally felt disinclined to show her face to the military again for some time afterwards and took care to listen to the bulletins issuing from Hut 2 that allowed her to be aware of any new roadblocks or patrols. So Saskia withdrew from the competition and so did all the others when an unbeatable five hour delay for the army resulted in Kassim issuing an order that the mischief had to stop. The fact that a supply truck accessing the Mercian's Forest Lodge outstation turned down a totally unsuitable forest track about 400 metres short of the correct turning and then became stuck in deep mud could well have been down to poor army navigation or it could have resulted from the fact that the army's direction sign seemed to have been relocated shortly before the incident. No-one at ESA actually claimed responsibility for the incident. So the practical jokes were relegated to the annals of ESA's past although some people thought that Gianni may have had the last word on the episode that he had started. And in any case, by then the nature of the confrontation between ESA and the army had changed.

Thursday 24th September 2201, Hut 2, Westhead.

Carlos, who on this rare occasion had actually made himself available for his shift as duty officer in Hut 2, looked at the map on the wall and uttered a single word expletive. James had just updated the computer generated map showing the location of army roadblocks and suggested that Carlos take a look at the revised display projected onto the large wall screen. As a rule Carlos did not swear so it wasn't surprising that the rest of his team, Mike and Anna, left their workstations to see what had prompted this comment.

The map, covering ESA's operating area, was overlain by circular and triangular symbols. The key at the foot of the map explained that the circles lined the routes of the army's mobile patrols and the triangles marked the position of their static roadblocks. When such army activity was reported to Hut 2 its location was plotted on the map using a yellow circle or a triangle, each outlined in black. If a patrol area or roadblock was retained for a second day the number 2 was added to the centre of the symbol and the computer automatically updated day three, day four and so on as long as the symbol remained on the map. When the Mercian's abandoned a roadblock site or a patrol route the symbol was downgraded to an uncoloured outline but when an army activity persisted past day seven the colour of the symbol changed to blue and the numbering was discontinued.

Until recently most of the blue symbols represented regular patrols on the periphery of ESA's area – along the A12 main road, for example – and also on the road and rail route leading from Saxmundham to the power station and army outpost at Sizewell. Today the previously few permanent roadblocks between the A12 and the coast had suddenly multiplied to provide what was in effect a second line of control further into ESA territory. For James it was a steady encroachment that he had been monitoring as he added new symbols to the map each day; for Carlos, who had been away for a couple of days, the change must have looked far more dramatic.

'Looks like they're gradually surrounding us, creating a stranglehold,' suggested Anna.

'Right,' agreed Mike, 'but I don't understand why. OK. I can understand that they need to keep an eye on us because some so-called *brigades* in other areas have armed themselves in defiance of the government and its policies but we're just a charity so why pick on us in this heavy-handed way? Apart from the smugglers there aren't any other illegals around at present so it must be us they're after.'

'Whatever their motive is, we just carry on. We have a duty to our clients and our supporters. I'll need to bring Kassim up to speed. Could you cover my duty please Mike? Thanks!'

Carlos left, James returned to his computer and Anna headed for the door with a cheery, 'Bye', on her way to cover a mail run for Saskia who had a clinic appointment. Mike, aggrieved, mumbled under his breath but as requested sat down at his workstation to await any incoming messages. But at that moment it was the message sent out by the map that concerned him more. His mind tried to reconcile the existence of an established, respected charity with the facts that a senior ESA member trained selected staff to use firearms and a local army officer seemed to believe that the charity was not quite what it seemed on the surface. At present he couldn't make sense of these conflicting aspects of his ESA life but he determined to unravel the conundrum one day soon.

Friday 25th September 2201. The Cabin.

For about six weeks now the weather hadn't been at all like the popular view of late summer. There had been one or two days with blue skies and high temperatures but the weak ridge of high pressure never developed enough to prevent the alternate cold and warm fronts from bringing cool, windy days and grey, wet muggy ones until everyone had decided that a fine spring had morphed into an early autumn without the benefit of an uplifting few weeks of glorious weather in between. And then it had all changed. The previous Monday had dawned clear and warm after a reasonably fine weekend. When Tuesday came the population of East Anglia had been pleased to welcome a second bright day and by the end of the week people were planning an outdoor weekend and some were referring to the settled spell as an Indian Summer.

It had recently become the habit among younger ESA members, particularly those without husbands, wives, partners or the ties of parental duty to meet at the waterside cabin and relax for a little after work at the end of the week. On this particular Friday Reuben, Cassie and Frazer, released from their duties by Heron were seated outside the Starcab on its shady northern side overlooking the broad. They were joined from across the water by Mike, Gianni, Anna and Saskia. After collecting cool drinks from the cabin they sat, mostly quietly, putting thoughts of the working week behind them. By and large ESA matters weren't discussed on Friday evenings but Saskia, who hadn't been around Westhead during the week, raised the matter of the recent army activity.

'What's all this about an army noose around ESA?' she asked.

Nobody else appeared keen to develop this topic but eventually Reuben replied.

'Well that's a neat way of describing the situation but it's not actually as dramatic as that. We're not heading for a siege situation. We can still move about.'

'Perhaps the military are reinforcing their boundary and will now leave us in peace in our own area,' suggested Cassie, ever the diplomat.

'Well, that's it then!' exclaimed Gianni, wishing to lighten the tone. 'We'll declare independence for East Suffolk. To hell with the army and the government too.' Everyone laughed. 'And,' he continued, 'we'll be known as IESA. "I" for Independent.'

They idly chatted about what sort of government they'd form.

'Kassim for President, obviously, and Heron for First Minister,' suggested Frazer.

'No. Certainly not,' countered Cassie. 'President is a figurehead position without real executive powers so we'll give that to Michael Warren, he's our elder statesman. Kassim must be First Minister aided by Mike, here, for Foreign Affairs, Vandra for Home Affairs and Heron should be i/c the military.'

'What about Carlos?' asked Reuben mischievously.

'Communications and Transport,' replied Mike referring obliquely to Carlos' tendency to be out and about for much of the time. They laughed and the little group continued to bandy names about linking them to ever less likely responsibilities until Anna suggested that their new nation would require a flag.

'Every country has a flag. What should ours be like?' she asked.

'Heron's knickers,' said Gianni who since his initial suggestion had been quite quiet. His comment raised the biggest laugh so far.

Monday 28th September 2201. The Cabin

Next Monday morning, about four metres up a tree

trunk a pair of knickers were indeed displayed open to
the view of anyone crossing Westwood Broad to reach the
cabin. When the intermittent gentle, warm breeze fanned
the fabric it was possible to pick out the letters I.E.S.A. in
uneven letters written across the garment. Heron ignored
it. No-one knew if the pair belonged to her or at least if they
did they weren't saying. But Heron was pleased about one
thing – a new solidarity and sense of cheerfulness seemed
to have been born among the ESA staff. The improvised
flag did not last long but two days later a genuine emblem
did appear. The early morning breeze that Wednesday
morning regularly pushed the material out to near its
true rectangular shape to exhibit three horizontal stripes
– light blue above then green in the centre with dark blue
below. A gold semi-circle took centre place on the upper
blue. The design was admired but no-one appeared to
know who had created it or what the flag might represent.
It was late on in the day as the staff gathered in the garden
behind Westhead House before Gianni admitted that he
had been responsible.

'So what's it all about?' demanded Heron.

'Simple,' explained Gianni using an exaggerated Italian
accent and arm movements. 'Top blue is sky, green for
woodland and lower blue for the sea and the broads. It's
a picture of East Suffolk! And then there's the sun rising
over our newly independent state.'

For a few seconds there was silence before the
explanation was greeted with a spontaneous round of
applause and a few admiring comments. Gianni for once
in his life appeared a little embarrassed until Mike broke
the spell of universal approval.

'Good God, Gianni, we'll have to make you First Minister now!' Everyone, including Gianni laughed and someone slapped him on the back in congratulation.

Friday 23rd October 2201

It was the second time in a week that Mike had been asked by Heron to carry a firearm when he reported for patrol duty at the cabin on Friday morning. The first time was on Tuesday evening when Heron had led an anti-smuggling patrol. With the larger smuggling organisations continuing to favour air rather than coastal handovers this side of ESA's work now took up considerably less time than before. It was fairly easy to patrol the half dozen probable landing sites for seaborne contraband unlike the possible aircraft landing sites that ran into three or four times that number and if locations for dropping goods from over-flying aircraft were considered the number of locations to keep an eye on ran into dozens. Even so to patrol the ESA area on the off-chance of spotting illegal trading would have been like trying to locate the proverbial small needle in a very large haystack and as such it would have constituted a clear misuse of ESA's manpower. With the withdrawal of the major organisations from the coast the field was left open to small local gangs. Fisherman and other boatmen engaged in smuggling could easily disguise their operations as part of their everyday work. Small amounts of drugs, currency, arms, ammunition, jewellery and so on or even people could be passed from one boat to another or from boat to vehicle disguised as part of a legitimate cargo. Once landed on some remote stretch of one of the broads or estuaries the contraband could be ferried onward with, for example the day's fish catch, down the A12 road to somewhere such as Ipswich and the next point in the distribution chain.

On that particular evening the ESA patrol had been lucky. Heron now only ventured out with the support of trustworthy intelligence and that Tuesday the tip-off had been good and they had been able to video the gang, their boat and their vehicle at a remote mooring on Blythe Broad west of Walberswick. Mike, Cassie and Gianni had been in good spirits as they had begun the twenty minutes walk back to their vehicle whilst leaving Heron to report to the Borderguard and catch them up later. And their firearm had remained holstered and unused. But before Gianni could head off in the ATV to drop Mike and Cassie at Grandma Vale's their mood had been rather dampened when Heron caught up with them.

'Good work,' she had said, 'but we have a problem. When I phoned the Borderguard hotline I learnt that the service had been ended. Cut off. Just a message stating that, *"This service has been discontinued."* No change of number. Nothing more.'

'We can tell the police, though,' Cassie had suggested.

'Yes but the police haven't the manpower to deal with it and by the time the info has been passed on to the military the initiative will have been lost. The best I can do is to give the information to Beth in our Saxmundham office since the army call there quite regularly to check up on us. It's about the only line of communication left open to us.'

'That's OK then,' Gianni had pointed out, adding, 'Isn't it?'

'Yes and no. The real point is that this is another step in the military crackdown. They don't want us doing anything that appears to impinge on their operations. They're not definitely accusing us of being engaged in illegal activities but telling us all the same that if we are so engaged we'd better look out; they've got the measure of us. That Buckhurst woman has become a right nasty bitch since those smugglers got her husband. I suppose I can't blame her really.'

But today it was Mike, Simon, Anna and Frazer who were rostered for the patrol and were sitting around the table in the cabin waiting for Heron to give them their orders. Reuben sat in an easy chair within listening distance of the meeting. He was not part of the patrol but would be taking over Frazer's usual role by staying in the cabin in case an emergency arose. Cassie was not on duty. Mike had left her up, but not dressed, taking a leisurely breakfast. Heron finished sorting through a pile of papers and looked up.

'Mike's in charge today. Normally I'd give him the lowdown and leave him to organise things but this patrol's a little different. We're trying out some new techniques so you all need to hear the details.'

Heron paused to let the point sink in.

'Most of our daytime patrols use two or occasionally three of you,' she continued. 'The larger the patrol the greater the chance of drawing the Mercian's attention. Today we are having a dummy run to try out new ideas but also as a practice for collecting a delivery from an air drop next week.'

Frazer half turned his head towards Anna and raised

his eyebrows. It was a surprise to him. He didn't know they collected anything dropped from aircraft. Simon who was never surprised at anything Heron planned just withdrew his hands from the table and placed them on the bench beside him whilst Mike hardly moved although it was news to him as well.

'We need four people so that one of you – I'm suggesting Simon, mans a safe-house location. That means,' she said turning to Anna and Frazer, 'that if anything goes wrong we have a point near the patrol area that acts as a rendezvous or point of contact. The person at the safe house has a use-only-once handset to make contact back here. As far as we know any extremely brief coded message sent by these handsets cannot reveal either the source or the destination of the message. I also routinely give Beth in Saxmundham a brief outline of what we're doing so that someone away from Westhead knows what's going on.

'So that leaves three of us to patrol.'

It wasn't clear whether Mike was asking a question or making a statement.

'No. There'll be two on patrol – you Mike and Anna – with Frazer acting as a forward guard or lookout. Take a look at these and you'll see why.'

Heron passed around four copies of an aerial photograph that clearly from the logo included bottom left had been taken from a well-known interweb site.

'Why not show us these using the net page directly, Heron, so that you can change the view or zoom in and show detail?' Anna queried.

'The army keeps tabs on the websites we visit. They could, for example, be monitoring Kassim or Carlos as we speak. If we kept using our terminals to get aerial or ground views of this area they could guess what we were up to and intercept us. We did it on a purely legitimate operation once and they turned up just as we arrived. It was in fact a completely innocent trip to the coast taking some elderly residents from Leiston to enjoy the seaside near Dunwich.'

They all smiled.

'So now,' Heron explained, 'we get some of our supporters to provide them. One copy was printed off by a landowner in Thorington just over the A12 and outside the Military Restricted Area. He then copied it a further three times. You'll understand why as I tell you the task for today.'

Heron stopped and took a sip of water whilst the others studied the "overheads" as the satellite images were popularly known.

'Here we go then,' she resumed. 'Take the ATV, cross the Westleton Road and turn off for Hinton. The safe house is here where I've marked a red circle. Your cover is that you are helping to build an extension to a barn, a project that is bone-fide and actually going on at this moment. If any one cared to check with the County planning department they would see that the whole project is above board. Simon and the ATV stay there. OK?'

They nodded.

'From here a green lane, bordered by hedges and trees provides cover up to this woodland,' she pointed to the overhead, 'that then gives cover right up to the road, the A12. Now, as you know the main road is patrolled by the army and all the side turnings to the south have at some time or other been roadblocked. Frazer will stay here as lookout to warn of any activity that could jeopardise the operation. Of course this is just a dry run; we don't expect any trouble. Mike will decide exactly where Frazer will be positioned depending on the cover and the view of the road available at the site. Now. Look carefully at where this tongue of woodland extends almost up to the road. At its northern end there is a stream that parallels the road westwards for about three hundred metres then passes under the A12 in a culvert to reach the northern side. We think it should be possible, Mike and Anna, to pass from the wood and under the road without gaining attention from the army's mobile or foot patrols. This is your first task – to assess the feasibility of this route.'

'When this op is carried out for real,' interposed Mike, 'are we sure that the delivery as well as ourselves will be able to get through the culvert on the return leg?'

'Yes,' confirmed Heron, 'The delivery will be small packets of ammunition.' She looked directly at Mike as was her habit when answering his questions and he hoped that his face did not tell of his concern at hearing this information. As far as he knew they had plenty of ammunition. In all the time he had been aware of the use of firearms he knew of only two occasions when a gun had been fired. The first was at Dingle Point when he had extinguished the helicopter spotlight and the other, reported to him by Cassie, happened on a recent patrol when Simon had shot at the tyres of a smuggler's ATV. And the expenditure of ammo at firearm's practice had been greatly curtailed now that Heron had her fully trained team in operation. Mike determined that when he returned from this patrol he would definitely have a word with Heron and push her to find out once and for all if there was an as yet undisclosed covert reason for arming ESA.

'Now, Mike and Anna,' said Heron, bringing Mike's attention back to the matter in hand. 'You'll take up the guise of hikers; two friends, man and wife, boy and girlfriend – whatever you like.'

Anna blushed, lowered her eyes and gave a slight smile.

'We have maps, food, walking boots and clothes for you. The delivery point for our air drop is here – a small farm airstrip. Our contact keeps two planes here but it is also used now and then by other local fliers and visitors. Traffic into this airstrip is unlikely to be monitored by the army but in case it is we have a cover story for the flight planned for next week. You don't need to go all the way to the farm today, just cover the first two kilometres or so north of the A12 and then turn off west to take this alternative route back.' She indicated the route marked on the overheads. 'And look for possible places for hiding the delivery if that were to become necessary. Mike will be armed – not that it will be needed today of course but this is a mock run, a simulation of the real thing so we'll treat it as such. All clear?'

Her audience nodded.

'You should be able to leave in about twenty minutes. The ATV is loaded with building equipment and tools and walking gear for Mike and Anna. Usual ESA dress can be worn up to the safe house. For the real operation we'll give you identity papers but you won't need them today. Good luck and I'll see you on your return.' With instructions completed Heron got up and left the cabin. She didn't say where she was going; Heron never did.

Having left Simon and the ATV at the construction site and changed into appropriate gear Mike, Anna and Frazer had followed the green lane, passed through the wood and reached its edge about 400 metres from the A12. They located a ditch that gave Frazer a good view over the land towards the road, both to the north-east and down towards Saxmundham and, with the trees and the sun behind him he was well hidden from view. There was little chance of his being spotted by an army patrol or of the sun reflecting off his field-glasses to give away his position. The journey to the barn at Hilton had been uneventful and the walk to their present position had also been undertaken without any problems.

They rested, ate lunch and observed the mobile army patrols along the main road. Nothing unusual to note; the soldiers were keeping to the regular pattern they habitually employed. Mike, satisfied with what they had seen, waited for the next Mercian patrol to pass by on the north-eastern leg of their route then after another few minutes set off down through the tongue of woodland. Anna followed and as planned on leaving the cover of the trees they crouched down and kept to the course of the stream until reaching the culvert entrance. The opening was a little overgrown but the concrete passageway under the road was large enough for them to navigate simply by bending down. Mercifully free of rubbish the only obstacle was the stream itself which, swollen by recent rain meant that there was no possibility on this occasion of keeping dry feet. But even so, Mike estimated, it would be quite possible to carry small packages through the tunnel on a real operation even if there had previously been sustained heavy rainfall.

So far, so good. Exiting on the northern side of the road a degree of cover was provided by a belt of trees along the highway which they followed until reaching open country and locating the path needed to take them towards the airfield. They knew Frazer would be following their progress but at each stage of their journey they took care to hide themselves from his view. If Frazer, who knew where they were headed couldn't spot them then the military had no chance. On leaving the cover of the trees Mike and Anna moved onto a permissive path that ran beside a private track headed downhill until it crossed a stream and then made its way gently uphill towards Hall Farm.

In their guise as hikers they were able to relax as the journey proved uneventful and rather pleasant. Mike liked Anna; not in the way he was drawn to Cassie of course but as a companion she made their task less a chore, more a relaxing day out. Naturally they had work to do imagining the reverse journey with a load of contraband, estimating their ability to cover any eventuality thrown at them during the forthcoming operation. But as the clouds above thinned and broke Mike felt lucky compared with Simon who at that moment would be getting down to some serious construction work to validate their cover story and Frazer who had to remain alert for a couple of hours in his lookout position. Mike and Anna had definitely drawn the long straw and Frazer, holed up in a ditch, the short one.

Finding the point previously indicated by Heron at their briefing they turned off left and surveyed the alternative route for their return. This new path ran up to the A12 parallel but to the west of the one by which they had descended. There was little cover at first but once they had crossed the road they would benefit from almost uninterrupted woodland cover until they reached the safe-house. Their incarnation as hikers seemed to have worked well. A lady walking a dog, a farmer on a cultivator and another pair of walkers, somewhat older than themselves, all appeared to accept Mike and Anna at face value. They walked on up towards the A12 and with the road only a few metres away they were almost at the point where Mike figured they would be at their most vulnerable. They waited for the next passing of an army patrol, a southbound vehicle, waited a few minutes more and were just about to cross to the southern side of the road when the throb of rotor blades heralded an approaching helicopter. Coming into view the aircraft could be identified as an army Kestrel following a steady course parallel to the road but fortunately some way to the south ensuring that Mike and Anna, crouching in a roadside ditch, would not be noticed. Its steady south-easterly course suggested that the crew of the helicopter were not interested in looking for a pair of hikers and it was soon out of sight. The incident, however, cautioned Mike to take great care when crossing to the next convenient area of cover.

'It looks as though we're OK now but just in case I'll stay here and cover you until you reach the safety of the wood opposite,' he instructed.

Anna checked for traffic then crossed onto the opposite verge and picked up a track that ran between two fields but was soon bordered by the wood on its eastern side. As she approached the trees Anna turned and raised her hand, the signal that the area was clear of army or police or any other problem. To an onlooker it would have been interpreted as a signal to her partner that the road was clear of traffic and safe to cross. Mike made a final check on the road but slipped back into cover when he heard the helicopter returning. Breaking cover again as the sound of the rotor receded Mike looked up and was horrified to see that Anna, half way up the track, had been surrounded by a group of five soldiers. Two were examining her backpack and a third was clearly asking questions. After a couple of minutes the group moved up along the path leading Anna to a point hidden from Mike's view by the woodland that bordered the track. She had not been pushed or manhandled and when asked to move she would have had little option but to do as requested. Fortunately the army did not seem to realise that Anna had travelled to this point with a companion.

Mike, quickly checking for traffic crossed the road and ran in a crouching position across the field to the left of the track and entered the wood without attracting attention. He was tempted to run on, crashing through the leaves, twigs and small boughs that littered the woodland floor but his training stifled the desire to reach Anna as soon as possible so he moved steadily, almost silently, towards the point where he thought she could be held. Sounds – talking and the noise of footwear crunching on the unconsolidated gravel surface of the track caused him to slightly alter his course until the light beyond the woodland edge became brighter so that sight as well as sound filled out the picture of the activity beyond. Taking cover a few metres from the scene Mike was able to make out an army troop carrier parked at the far side of the track, facing down towards the road with a group of about seven or eight uniformed soldiers standing at the rear. To his right, about a hundred metres down the track another vehicle – some form of ATV – stood on the track with a smaller group of people beside it. Moving cautiously through the wood, parallel to the track, Mike was soon able to make out Anna in the second group, her bright blue jacket and fair hair standing out from the drab uniform of the soldiers. She stood facing down the track engaged in conversation, probably an interrogation, with a tall sergeant facing her. Between them and looking on with her back to the wood stood a lady captain. In Mike's mind there was no doubt. This had to be the officer that Heron habitually referred to as, '*that bitch Buckhurst*'.

First, observation. He needed to know what the army were up to. Best scenario was that after the questioning Anna would be free to go and would make her way back to the safe house. And he would follow. But doubt crept into Mike's mind. He doubted that a routine patrol that simply stopped, interrogated and then left their victim free would employ so many soldiers and be commanded by such a high ranking officer. It appeared more likely that Anna would be requested to attend a local police station or even be arrested and taken there in the troop carrier. Depending on how this action was organised Mike could possibly create a distraction and rescue Anna and with this in mind he took out the Piata and readied it. At that stage he didn't know how he would make use of the gun but at least it provided him with one option if needed.

The captain moved nearer to her sergeant and spoke briefly. The soldier then guided Anna so that she stood with her back to the vehicle. Sensibly she did not offer any opposition. Mike watched. So it had to be Plan B. But Plan B soon morphed into Plan C when the sergeant tied some material around Anna's head in the form of a blindfold. Mike's whole body tensed but soon his concern deepened further. The sergeant was despatched to stand with the other soldiers whilst Buckhurst or whoever it was took several steps back and reached for her handgun. And at that moment Mike knew in reality what was meant when a person said that their blood had run cold.

An execution or a mock execution or a bullet zinging past her ear as a warning? Which? Mike had no time to calculate the odds. As Buckhurst raised her gun hand Mike did the same and got his shot in first. The captain's gun left her hand, looped away to the right and went crashing onto the gravel track as the captain's body crumpled and fell to her left. Almost before her body collapsed onto the grass beside the track Mike had holstered his gun and was up and running towards the edge of the wood.

'Anna, run!' he yelled grabbing his bewildered colleague as she stumbled forward, pulling her into the cover of the woodland. They ran as best they could with Mike guiding Anna with one hand and using the other to pull off her blindfold. It was difficult to assess their position and form a strategy as they picked their passage through the trees but as their headlong push for safety slowed to a regular trot Mike came to realise that they had gained a lead over any pursuers. He assumed that the stunned soldiers had initially run to the aid of their injured captain before the sergeant, taking charge, would come to the conclusion that any attempt to follow them would be futile. It was unlikely that the army would feel confident about following them into a wooded area unknown to them and the detachment had too few soldiers to stake out the perimeter of the wood in the hope that they could contain their quarry. Road patrols and the overflying helicopter could be called on for assistance but by the time the reinforcements were available the army would probably work out that the best way to apprehend these outlaws, whoever they were, was to mount roadblocks and use helicopter patrols before darkness set in. This gave Mike and Anna a realistic chance of reaching the safe-house and the whole patrol of making it back to base.

First task was to contact Frazer. Mike sent him a single letter message and followed it up 10 seconds later with a second. The two letters and their separation time formed one of that day's agreed codes. In plain language it meant *'Get the hell out of there and back to the safe-house'.* Twenty minutes later Mike and Anna reached the edge of the wood at the head of the green lane. Hopefully Frazer had already passed this way sometime earlier. They waited at the top of the lane with the barn in clear view whilst Mike forwarded a second message containing just one letter, this time to Simon. After two minutes a figure walked out of the barn. It was Frazer. He walked across to a hedge and threw the contents of the bucket he was carrying into the ditch at its base. Exactly thirty seconds later the sign was repeated. Two people – Simon and Frazer – were at the safe-house. As Frazer turned away from the hedge for the second time he placed the empty bucket upside down at the barn entrance indicating that it was clear for them to return.

'Off you go,' instructed Mike, almost in a whisper. 'Good luck, Anna.'

She turned, gave Mike a quick kiss, turned back and was gone. He did not follow her passage along the lane nor did he wait for any sign of her arrival at the safe-house. She would be fine; Heron had trained her well.

Instead Mike turned and made his way back into the wood. His mind was a mixture of emotions but after a few seconds whilst his thoughts seemed to have become frozen a natural instinct to ensure his own survival became dominant. He needed a strategy for survival. He had read somewhere or perhaps seen it on video that assassins had two priorities after completing their task. First they must get rid of their weapon, as soon as practicable and then put as great a distance as possible between themselves and the crime scene. True or not, wise or not, with these tenets in mind Mike retraced his steps towards the main A12 road.

PART TWO

THE FUGITIVE

CHAPTER THIRTEEN
OUTSIDE THE LAW

Saturday 24th October 2201

He awoke. Early morning light seeped into the room from beneath the partly lowered blind at the east-facing bedroom window. Waking in a strange bedroom for the first time was often presented in novels as a time of confusion and disorientation but Mike was quite clear where he was: A house in the village of Bramfield owned by Dale and Colette Church. He had reached their house the previous evening. He wasn't sure about the time of his arrival but it was probably somewhere around 1930. He had eaten, watched the evening news and then had a broken sleep of about nine hours with the wakeful interludes spent replaying the previous day's drama.

Getting rid of the gun had been quite simple. There had been no empty buildings where it could have been secreted, no streams or lakes to throw it into and although burying it would have been possible even a half decent attempt to camouflage the site would have been discovered by an observant soldier or an army sniffer dog. Traversing the wood, covering the same route used earlier in the day, he had noticed a hole in a tree about five metres above the ground just above a point where a branch left the trunk. He left the Piata up there, embedded in dry leaves, twigs and debris. At least he wouldn't be found carrying the weapon. Then he had struck out towards the road and headed for those parts of Suffolk that were outside the Military Restricted Area. He couldn't hope to be safe there – he had committed a crime – but he would feel better away from an area where the army seemed hell-bent on harassing the local population. The previous day's reconnaissance had stood him in good stead as he eased through the culvert beneath the main road and made his way north-westwards towards the village of Bramfield on the Halesworth Road. Although the distance had been no more that four kilometres the journey had taken him more than two hours, diving for cover every time he heard a helicopter or light plane and for each stage of his journey he had spent time looking, listening and waiting until he was sure that the way was safe. There had been several possible overnight billets in the village. Although outside their main operating area there were ESA sympathisers and supporters throughout this part of East Suffolk and a number of them had been actively recruited to give accommodation when needed although they probably expected notice of some days or weeks before their guest's arrival. The Tower family had children and it would have been too much of an imposition had he stayed there. Chay Limehouse would have welcomed him but asked far too many questions. So he had ended up at the Church's cottage; a welcome and no questions about what he had been up to, no desire to know what had caused him to request their hospitality.

There was a knock on the bedroom door. His host looked in and smiled.

'Hope you slept OK. The bathroom's free and there'll be some breakfast for you in about half an hour.'

Mindful of the need to be moving on as soon as possible Mike carried his thoughts about his immediate future on into the shower. The TV news the previous evening had given a brief account of the hunt for the person who had shot a soldier near the A12 road north of Saxmundham. No detail was given of the exact location of the shooting, the rank of the soldier or the gender of the fugitive. The report reminded him of a similar news item he had heard back home in Reydon, almost six years earlier. Mr and Mrs Church had made no attempt to relate the news item to their unexpected visitor, at least not before he had retired to bed. He doubted that the army were really that ignorant of his identity. The lack of detail was, he concluded, an attempt to play down the seriousness of the event.

Breakfast. Food and drink consumed Mike made signs that he would need to be on his way.

'Back to Framlingham I expect,' stated Mrs Church, indicating that she had no real need to know his immediate plans.

'Yes,' agreed Mike.

'Do you need anything for your journey? Food perhaps?'

'Thanks. A couple of apples and a bottle of water if you have them, please.'

'I thought so. Here's a little bag I've packed up for you.'

Mike opened up the present and found the apples and water, a block of cheese, some biscuits and two bananas.

'Thanks. Thank you very much and thanks for the nights sleep.'

'You're welcome.' Mr Church extended his arm. They shook hands. 'Good luck, Mike,' he concluded.

Mike picked up the pack that Heron had provided for his hiking disguise, added Mrs Church's parcel, turned, walked out of the front door and set off down the road. On any other occasion he would have turned and waved a goodbye but this time he just strode on his way. It seemed appropriate. He was cutting the ties that linked him to his previous life.

'Distance. Distance from the A12,' Mike said to himself. 'At least fifteen kilometres today. Avoid Framlingham. Travel west.' He spoke the words quietly to himself as though trying to programme his future. 'Not too fast, though,' he continued. 'But must take care.'

At this stage his destination was as unknown as was his future in general. He simply had no idea where he would finally end up or what he would do when he arrived there. At this stage he could do little more than plan his journey to the next bend in the road or the next corner on a path; he couldn't contemplate what lay beyond. For the first few kilometres Mike obsessively avoided habitation and people. Even crossing a minor country lane was a major event as he looked, listened and looked again before stepping out and checking again when reaching the other side before carrying on. Fortunately navigation was not difficult since he had learnt a lot about the area since moving to Framlingham. In the early days of his residence in his new home town he would take every opportunity to explore this part of Suffolk that lay away from his natural haunts near the coast. On travelling to Halesworth, for example he had discovered four different ways of making the return journey so that the villages and hamlets of mid-Suffolk where now quite well known to him. On this journey, however, whilst using the surfaced roads as a navigation aid he preferred to take advantage of the cover provided by roadside hedges and areas of woodland and stick to little used paths and tracks where there were fewer chances of being seen by motorists, pedestrians and farm workers. Fortunately, despite heavy rainfall a couple of days earlier, the autumn dry spell had given a firmness to the ground that helped to speed his progress. But realising that it would not be long before he reached alien territory he set about studying the sun's position and the disposition of shadows in an attempt to form a navigation technique for use in the coming days. From time to time he referred to his trusty watch. To many this timepiece was an anachronism, replaced by the ubiquitous Personal Communicator but for Mike, in his present situation, his faithful PERC would have been a distinct liability. It was the first item he had ditched – even before the gun – as it would have given his location away by constantly logging into the nearest base station. Fortunately his watch had recently been fitted with a new longlife battery so if, heaven forbid, he was on the run for a couple of years, he would still have the services of a reliable timepiece. He reached a point on his journey where the position of the sun, together with his stomach suggested it was lunchtime but his watch told him otherwise. One more hour before stopping. It was imperative that he eke out what little food he had until he could find a way of obtaining provisions on a regular basis.

1300 hours eventually came. Time for a break and food.

He noted a thin line of trees set a little way back from the road on the south side. It would give him a reasonable amount of cover, sufficient to render him invisible and prevent the now bright sunlight from exposing his position to passing traffic. He was also concerned to be out of sight of aircraft although he had seen none throughout the whole morning. A few more days, a week perhaps and leaf cover would, he thought, be decidedly thinner but for the moment it was just about sufficient to provide cover. He checked for traffic and people on foot and seeing none crouched down and ran the few paces needed to gain cover.

A slight hollow positioned behind a tangled bush just inside the wood offered Mike a convenient place in which to take his break. The temporary respite from the need to be constantly vigilant brought a measure of relaxation, a change in mood and a switch in his thinking. For the first time that day he thought about those he had left behind just one day before.

There was Anna. He had been responsible for the operation and he had failed. He hoped that Anna was safe. If he really thought otherwise he would have been tempted to walk into the next police station along his route and hand himself in but for the present he felt confident in the safe-house procedure operated by Simon.

And Cassie. Mike sat quietly, thinking about the relationship that he would in all probability never be able to resume. For a few minutes his spirits plummeted and a black unthinking void took over his mind until gradually, from somewhere deep in his thoughts came the realisation that for the sake of Cassie and Anna and Simon and ESA the best thing he could do was to stay away, as far away as possible and hope that his actions hadn't jeopardised their cause.

Then there was Heron.

For some reason Mike hadn't included her in his initial list of those he had now left behind. He liked her, he admired her but she neither commanded the complete respect he had for Kassim nor the friendship he had for the likes of Simon or Reuben or even Gianni. For some reason Heron had erected a barrier around herself, a filter that only allowed through certain emotions, in either direction, denying the possibility of her taking the ultimate step to comradeship.

Hunger. Mike's mind was dragged back into the present. He halved his food supplies, ate lunch and turned his thoughts to how he should move on. What, he considered, did the army know? What was the worst scenario?

Question : Did the army know Anna's true identity?

Answer : Yes.

Question : Did the army know who had attacked their officer?

Answer : Again, yes.

Did the army know where he was? Probably not. Their immediate move would have been to scour the East Suffolk area and visit ESA bases. Next they would have assumed that he would have wished to make a speedy getaway or possibly take refuge at home. So the A12, north and south would have been watched and Framlingham visited. After that, with no result, they would probably be at a loss as to where they should look next. They would hope that a region-wide if not a nation-wide circulation of his details would lead to every policeman and borderguard official being on the lookout.

So what did this mean for him? It meant so far so good and carry on. He hadn't seen or heard any search helicopters but he didn't doubt that they would be around soon. And if his photo wasn't in the newspapers and aired or screened during every news programme it soon would. So it was time to be on his way again. He was one step ahead and he needed to stay that way. And somehow he had to get hold of a newspaper whilst avoiding showing his face.

The afternoon proved uneventful. Using the same tactics as before Mike travelled on until he realised that the light was beginning to fail and he had about forty to fifty minutes in which to find a safe place for the night. The late October weather was still quite mild and mercifully dry and he reckoned that the cloud cover that had increased since lunchtime would prevent the night-time temperatures from falling far below double figures. Not yet confident that he could be safely housed for the night he began to scour the landscape for a woodland sanctuary. Approaching a village – Badingham the sign told him – the road kept to the contour on a valley side with a wood covering the land down to a stream on his right. Mike stopped, looked, listened, moved on and repeated his surveillance until he was satisfied that he could enter the woodland unseen.

The gloominess of the wood took him by surprise and he was forced to slow until, with his eyes fully adjusted, he was able to find a reasonable resting place. In a clearing in the undergrowth he positioned a couple of fallen tree boughs to make a boundary to his sleeping area and laid the waterproof sheet, conveniently included in Heron's pack, on the ground between them. Picking up his jacket, previously taken from the pack, he put it on and during the last of the daylight ate the rather meagre remains of his food supply leaving nothing except a little water for breakfast. Meal over Mike hung his bag on a branch above head height up a tree, made a pillow by arranging a pile of dry leaves under his groundsheet, pulled his jacket tightly around him and settled down for the night. At first sleep eluded him but without the attraction of a TV, his PERC or Cassie's conversation tiredness eventually lulled him into a deep, dreamless sleep but not before the word 'torch' had been added to the list he was making in his head of items needed for his journey; a list that in addition included map, newspaper, water and food.

Sunday 25ᵗʰ October 2201.

After a morning's trek, dodging habitation and having had only a frugal breakfast of a couple of apples from an overhanging bough and the rest of the water Mike had no option but to look for a reasonably sized village with the amenities that could meet his needs. He decided that Earl Soham, a place that he had travelled through on journeys into and out of Framlingham but had never visited, would fit the bill. In common with his recently adopted home town this village and several others in the area had benefited from recent economic and population growth.

The washroom of one of the Earl Soham's public houses allowed Mike to clean his face and hands, dampen his hair and finger-comb it into reasonable tidiness and use a mirror's image to help improve the appearance of his crumpled clothes. He hoped his rather extravagant use of the scented handwash would help overcome the stale smell of clothes that had been unchanged for a couple of days. Half the remaining cash in his pocket bought him a light lunch and a much needed drink at the bar which was sufficiently well populated to give Mike the hope that he did not particularly stand out from the locals and other visitors. Refreshed he left the pub, glanced left and right and chose to continue on along the street westwards in search of his other requirements, a comb having been added to his overnight shopping list. The main village shop, a general store, seemed to be an appropriate starting place. The notice outside stated that opening times for Sundays were between 1130 and 1600 hours but one glance inside as he passed showed an unfortunate absence of customers. Too risky, he thought. The shopkeeper or an assistant would hear the door open, look up in anticipation, follow with interest his progress as he browsed around the stock and face him with a smile and a friendly word of greeting as he approached the paystation. Nor would he be able to hang around outside waiting for the shop to fill with customers since a passer-by may well recognise his face and match it with a photograph they may have seen on TV, their PERC, computer screen or in the morning paper. The sun had broken through after the dull but dry morning so he stopped to take off his jacket and stow it in his backpack before continuing down the road whilst considering his next move.

About 100 metres beyond the shop he turned left into an alley that gave pedestrian access to a car park. Mike spotted a pole-mounted camera to one side that was probably used to identify parking infringements but in his experience could equally well have been a dummy. Unable to take a chance he threaded his way, head down through the lines of cars and empty spaces, heading for the exit road opposite. His bowed head may not have totally avoided the camera but by chance it did allow him to look into the cars as he passed. He was surprised to see that in an age when only very old vehicles or very basic new models did not have a factory installed navigation system there should be, on back seats, dashboards or parcel shelves, various generations of road atlases. Just what he needed. But not here, under the eye of the camera. The exit road led to a residential street with older style houses along one side and roadside resident's parking bays beside the pavement. Mid-Sunday afternoon presented a scene of quietness and inactivity broken only by two swooping birds and the distant sounds of a children's playground and a football match. Mike walked casually yet steadily along the line of cars parked parallel to the kerb, targeting the older vehicles in the line. Gently and with as little arm movement as possible he tried the rear door handles of the chosen cars. Locked and again locked and again but at the fourth attempt there was a click and the door opened. Mike looked down. No road atlas. He swore briefly and almost silently and moved on. The next time, though, just three cars further along he was in luck. Mike grabbed the atlas and a newspaper from the back seat. He wanted to run but leant nonchalantly against the door until it clicked and then without looking around walked on in what he hoped was a quietly purposeful manner. Just past the last car a side road led back in the direction of the main street.

He turned left, stopped briefly to fold the atlas and push it and the newspaper into his backpack then completed his circuit back to the shop. Three shoppers, Mike becoming the fourth was hardly a crowd but with limited time before closing and a belief that it was not a good idea to hang around he walked in and scoured the shelves for his needs. Fortunately the single sales person was busy serving at the paystation. Two bottles of water, biscuits, tomatoes, cheese and a tin of sardines would see him through to the next day. He formed a queue by standing behind the previous customer and diverted the shopkeeper's attention away from his face and onto his purchases by placing them promptly on the counter and immediately concentrating on finding his money in the pocket of his backpack. He could have avoided any contact with the staff by using autopay but he couldn't run the risk that his paycard would be traced to this location and in under an hour just a few kilometres down the road he would be met by helicopters, ATVs, soldiers and well trained dogs and his freedom would be over. He paid, mumbled his thanks, turned and headed for the exit.

As the shop door closed behind him he felt a degree of relief and, realising he had been holding his breath for a few seconds, exhaled and began to walk steadily westwards but soon turned southwest at the next road junction towards the village of Otley beyond which his geographical knowledge would become decidedly sketchy. After Otley it was out into the unknown. He was tempted to stop and look at the newspaper but decided there was time enough for that and at present he wanted to put distance between himself and the last person who had seen him and could possibly describe him to the army or the police. He planned to walk for a couple of hours and then look for somewhere to sleep but after just half that time a brief sunny interlude gave way to increasingly low cloud and a few spots of rain. Mike pulled his jacket out of his pack, shrugged it on and pulled it around himself against the damp. As he did so the splatting sound of the rain on paper drew his attention to the newspaper that had been pulled out with his jacket and had fallen to the ground. Whilst bending down to retrieve it a gust of wind unfolded the paper and he was momentarily held in a stooping position as he noted the headline on the front page.

Sunday Record
25th October 2201
TRAGIC ARMY DEATH
Search for outlaw gunman

Ignoring the intermittent but by now large drops of rain Mike grabbed the paper and squatted down at the edge of a field, his back to a roadside bush. For the first time on his journey he lost interest in passing traffic and looked at the print in front of him. However rather than the printed word it was the picture illustrating the article that grabbed his attention. There was no caption but Mike had no doubt about the reason for the photograph. Captain Alana Buckhurst had been pregnant and the tragedy was not hers alone but that of a mother and her unborn child.

Mike was physically sick. A feeling like panic gripped him and for a while he was unable to focus his mind, his thoughts consisting of a jumble of images and emotions.

However as the feeling subsided he felt an urge to find out all he could about the event in which he was a major player but about which he knew so little. He opened his eyes, lifted the paper and began to read.

'Captain Alana Buckhurst of the Mercian Regiment, based at Bentwaters in Suffolk, was shot on Friday afternoon whilst manning a roadblock near the A12 road north of Saxmundham. Badly injured, Captain Buckhurst was airlifted to hospital in Ipswich where it was discovered that her unborn child had died, probably from the trauma of the incident. Alana Buckhurst herself died from her injury about midday yesterday.

The Record can reveal that this incident is even more tragic than it first appears. Just over two months ago Captain Buckhurst's husband, Christian Carter Blake, also a Mercian soldier, was killed whilst taking part in an anti-smuggling patrol not far from the site of this new incident.

No statement has been made by the army except to express profound sadness at the loss of such a talented officer. Captain Buckhurst had spearheaded the army's campaign to deal with dissidents in the East Suffolk area.

Suffolk Police explained that at the time of the incident the army were questioning a member of the East Suffolk Association (ESA) – a local charity. It is thought that the assassin may have been associated with ESA. A search for the weapon has so far proved unsuccessful.

The Record believes that the army has reason to suspect that this charitable group has a more sinister agenda than the services it undoubtedly provides to local people. A member of this Association told the Record that in the face of *army pressure ESA had recently cut down its operations and some workers were made redundant by a reorganisation. It is possible that one or more of these former staff members blamed the army for their loss of work and felt it necessary to take some type of action.'*

Mike finished the article and realised that the rain had become more insistent as large drops had left a random pattern of damp marks on the paper. He squashed the paper into his bag, zipped up his jacket and looked around. Aided by the heavy overcast the daylight was beginning to fade and he had no heart to carry on. Pushing around the bush he scaled a low wall, reached the road and trudged along in full view of the traffic, disregarding his previously observed rules about self preservation. At the first opportunity he would rest up for the night and in the morning consider his position in the light of the information supplied by the Sunday Record.

Monday 26ᵗʰ October 2201.

Mike stirred. He became aware of daylight seeping down in rays through gaps in the wall of the building where he had spent the night. A quick look around confirmed that it was a large barn that he had stumbled into, wet and hungry, the previous evening. He stretched his limbs and pulled himself up stiffly from the corner where he had slept fitfully in a half-sitting position. Dry and warm enough his billet had been an improvement on his previous night's forest residency yet the woodland floor, adapted to his needs, had made a more comfortable bed than the wooden board he had found in the semi-darkness the previous evening.

It was 0807. His trusty watch told him it was later, much later than he wanted it to be. It was not that he needed to be anywhere in particular but he had to be away from this barn and any nearby habitation as soon as possible. He packed up and left. Just ten minutes after leaving his overnight stop he found a field corner, hidden from the lane and with enough cover to allow him to settle down and eat breakfast. He had food enough. He would be OK for lunch and an evening meal as well and at a push could eke out his rations to cover tomorrow's breakfast. After a few mouthfuls his mind again turned to planning ahead and he even flirted with thoughts about his final destination and his long-term future. A desire for self-preservation that he hadn't previously known he possessed had brought about a degree of optimism that had replaced the feelings of depression induced by the news in the Sunday Record. With the rain gone and despite there being a cool breeze, the early morning brightness also helped to lift his spirits. Mike took out the road atlas, looked through it and slimmed down the reference material by discarding the pages representing Scotland, Wales and northern England. He concentrated on the two page spread showing the land from London to the North Sea deciding to skirt Ipswich to the west, hopefully reaching Bramford or at least Claydon by nightfall. He desperately required a wash and if possible a shave and his clothes were well past being ready for replacement but he had no real idea of how to achieve these needs. He packed up, removed any signs of his having been there and set off.

On this, his third day as a fugitive Mike found travelling easier. The modus operandi he had developed to avoid detection became second nature and the route map now firmly fixed in his mind aided navigation. With a destination planned for today he set about considering two other aims – obtaining his immediate needs and his long-term future. He travelled largely on autopilot and by lunchtime, taken at the edge of a wood north of Ipswich, he had begun to put a plan into place. His shopping list had grown and near the top was the wish to find a newspaper, preferably The National Guardian, on as many days as possible as he needed to keep up to date on the authorities' effort to locate him. After his snack he set off again heading for his overnight stop with the hope that before reaching it he would be armed with food and news and possibly also a torch. Somewhere, he thought, there must be a pub where a rather scruffy itinerant like himself wouldn't appear too much out of place.

And there was. Rather run down, with faded décor and worn upholstery neither the staff nor the clientele of the Swan Inn seemed to pay much attention to Mike after he had made use of the washroom. He didn't seem to be out of place at all. He had just enough money left to buy a light meal and a few items to bolster the next day's rations. And surprisingly someone had left a copy of the rather upmarket National Guardian in this rather ordinary little hostelry. As he sank his teeth into the somewhat indeterminate filling of his reasonably warmed pasty Mike opened up the paper and found the section he needed – the Brigadewatch update – in its habitual location occupying the lower half of page Two.

The National Guardian
Monday 26th October 2201
BRIGADEWATCH : The Suffolk Army Death

'The ongoing search for the assassin who killed the Mercian Regiment's Captain Alana Buckhurst last Friday has concentrated on investigating the East Suffolk Association – a local charity set up to provide services in the severely depopulated areas of coastal East Suffolk. For some time the army has suspected that ESA had become a cover for armed resistance or more likely that a secret wing or unit of the group was planning such action.

The civilian being questioned at the roadblock just before the incident has been identified as ESA member Anna Chalk who operated from their base at Westwood Broad. Army intelligence has established that two regular members of ESA have recently been absent from their usual duties, present whereabouts unknown. One of them is the nationally respected journalist Mike Cannon, aged 30 (photo right). Whilst not at present connecting Mr Cannon directly with the shooting the police are keen to talk to him about his time working with ESA. Both the police and the army declined to give the identity of the second missing ESA member.

Any person with information about the shooting should contact either

Saxmundham Police (police.suffolk.gov.gb)

or The Mercian Regiment at Bentwaters (mercians/ bentwaters@mod)

or alternatively the confidential Brigadewatch Infoline (bwatch@natguard.media.gb).'

CHAPTER FOURTEEN
THE JOURNEY

Wednesday 2nd December 2201. Denham, Buckinghamshire

He had been on the road for just a little over five weeks – a little more than a full month. Not actually on the road for all that time since he had been at his present 'lodgings' for almost a week and earlier in the month he had stayed near Harlow, Essex for around a fortnight. For most of his journey he was happy to pack up promptly and leave his overnight accommodation to move on again quickly but there were also times when he had felt confident enough to hang around and stock up on basic necessities, particularly clean clothes. Now, here in Denham, he was again in a similar situation but in addition to obtaining supplies Mike also needed to decide on a final destination and plan the next part of his journey.

For the present though he had his most comfortable accommodation to date. Light, heating, a water supply, a table, a stool and a camping stove together with some reasonably comfortable bedding added up to luxury compared with the deprivations he had suffered throughout much of the autumn and early winter. When he had arrived here the previous Monday evening the weather had been so unpleasant he had considered squatting in the large apparently unoccupied house that was the main building on the site. He had spent the first night uncomfortably in his small tent more or less hidden from view against a narrow strip of woodland that lined the northern boundary wall to the estate. Experience had taught him to treat apparently abandoned buildings with caution. Ten days earlier during his travels on reaching Broxbourne he had observed a boarded up house for over an hour before deciding it was safe to use as overnight accommodation. But just as he was about to leave his observation position a couple of people, probably a man and a woman and probably in their early twenties, he guessed, had walked up the neighbouring alleyway, reached over and unlatched a side gate and made entry by moving a board from a ground-floor window and climbing in. At the late hour of 1947 he had little time to search around and little chance of finding somewhere convenient. He had spent the most uncomfortable night of his journey in a goods wagon at the back of the railway sidings. The experience had led him to take a seemingly abandoned tent from a camping and caravan site the next day.

Following his first night in Denham he had soon dismissed the large boarded-up house in favour of one of several outbuildings. A wooded framed and clad building with a tiled roof had been his choice. From the outside it appeared to be a stable, an impression confirmed by the interior layout and the equipment stored there. Soon after midday he made his entry by forcing open the top part of one of the stables' eponymous two-part doors and set about making a passable bed area and sorting through a store cupboard to provide himself with a lamp and a heater, rather ancient items but useful ones considering the good supply of fuel cartridges also available. For the remaining daylight hours he had inspected the fabric of the building, covering gaps in the woodwork so that no light from his meagre lamp would attract the attention of evening and nigh-time travellers along the bounding roads.

Periodically he had kept observation on the adjacent house. Peering cautiously through the gateway in the wall that surrounded the garden at the rear of the house he had taken stock of the situation. Clearly a little derelict the owners or their agent had boarded and barred the ground floor windows but apart from a couple of cases of boarding the upper floor windows were unprotected. By the next morning Mike had decided that the house had no residents either legal or illegal and although he no longer thought of this house as a billet he considered it worth entering to see if there was anything of value for him either to improve the stable or to help with his future travels. Above a small porch at the back a boarded but unbarred window occupied a medial position between the ground and first floors – probably, he assumed to give light to a landing on a staircase. After a few minutes observation he climbed a drainpipe beside the porch, gained the sloping roof and, balancing rather precariously worked away at the corner of the boarding. Fortunately it was simply screwed into the window frame and its removal proved no problem for the hefty screwdriver Mike had found amongst other tools stored in the stable block. He used the screwdriver as a lever to prise out the screws rather than fuss about removing them in the usual manner. Opening the window vent however proved more difficult, in fact impossible. He had then attempted to break the glass, a noisy task that in Mike's mind could have attracted the attention of anyone within a half kilometre radius. Even two minutes later, though, no-one had appeared to investigate his breaking and entering and this method had also failed. Finally he was forced into prising away the surrounding beading and carefully easing out the glass unit which gave him just enough room to clamber in and drop onto what was indeed a landing. There was enough light from an un-boarded upstairs windows for him to see his way down to the gloomy ground floor interior.

As he anticipated the flicking of light switches brought no illumination but as his eyes grew accustomed to the gloom he was able to pick out a few useful items. The kitchen provided a wooden stool, crockery and cutlery and he rescued a small table from a lounge. He was tempted to take everything he might possibly need but on reflection he decided that a single plate, knife, fork and spoon would have to suffice as he wasn't expecting to stay long; he planned to move on as soon as he had formalised his plans and the weather improved. More in hope than expectation he had examined the possibility of leaving by the back door in the porch. Surprisingly the turning of an old-fashioned key and the sliding of three bolts left only the need to give a hefty pull for the door to open and the daylight to flood in. For a few seconds he was worried that he hadn't taken the precaution of checking for a door alarm system but fortunately no such protection seemed to be installed or working. Mike was pleased. He didn't fancy pulling the table and other items up the stairs, out through the window to then be carried over the porch roof and down to the ground. He was further heartened when the light let in through the door highlighted the contents of a door-less cupboard under the back stairs, just inside the porch. A spade, two pairs of riding boots, an old coat hanging on a hook and various pieces of cleaning equipment were of no interest but by moving a couple of brooms and the spade he uncovered a small camping stove – one that could be powered by the fuel cartridges already to hand in the stables. Luxury! For the first time in weeks he would be able to save a little money by avoiding cafés and restaurants and indulge in his own simple cooked meals.

Cautiously Mike had ferried his finds across to the gate-less arch in the garden wall and then out to the stables, checking on each trip that he was unobserved. Fortunately the stable block screened the back of the house from the road and even though it was winter the closely planted trees and hedges along the road gave a good degree of protection so that he was unlikely to be seen as he shuttled to and fro. Thankfully the house itself protected him from the worst of the persistent wind that carried with it brief but frequent sleety showers. Task completed Mike had re-locked and bolted the porch door, climbed the stairs to the landing and exited through the window on to the porch roof. Retrieving the beading from where he had left it on the roof he threw the pieces inside onto the landing, pushed the glazing unit back into place and after moving the boarding back into position he used the handle of his screwdriver to hammer home the screws. It was enough, he considered, to protect the window unless it was attacked by a particularly ferocious gale and hopefully if one did occur he would be long gone. Mike didn't expect to go back into the house again.

During that evening, after eating a cold meal – using the stove would have to wait until he had obtained suitable food the next day – Mike had used the luxury of an hour's lamplight to do some writing. Once a journalist, always a journalist! For paper he used the margin strips from newspapers and he still had one of the two pens he had put in his backpack before leaving Westwood Broad that fateful day back in late October. For reference he used the newspapers he had collected en route and the rather tatty and much folded remains of the road atlas he had taken from a car in Earl's Soham. The journalist was about to start his first journal.

That evening he had written out the stages of his journey. Day and date were checked with the aid of the Brigadewatch newspaper articles he had collected and the location of overnight stops retrieved from his memory with the aid of the maps. On subsequent evenings he had compiled a list of his overnight billets, recorded notable events in his quest for survival, made a list of cars he had 'borrowed' and recalled his efforts to obtain food and clean, dry clothing. Tonight, however, he was ready to turn his scrappy lists into a more detailed account of his travels. He didn't want to record everything; there were many forgettable days when nothing notable happened apart from the footslog of making his way safely westwards. Earlier in the day he had ventured out to the edge of the nearby village and purchased a notepad and a pack of pens from a small general store and now he was ready. He headed the first page and then added some detail.

Accommodation

Old cottage near Bramford. *My first night in a bed, first*

really comfortable stopover so stayed a second night.

Allotment shed in Earl's Colne. *Now in possession of a screwdriver I was able to remove or lever off simple locks. Fortunately this one could be unscrewed so was able to replace it reasonably well in the morning.*

Construction Sites, Takeley and Potters Bar. *Not ideal but at least dry. Relocatable cabins used by workers stood enticingly out of reach behind fences with multiple electronic locks and alarm systems but large wooden store cupboards were easily entered and gave protection from the rain and wind that marked the weather in early November.*

Railway wagon, Broxbourne. *Worst billet so far! Open to the rain although some protection from the wind. Cold. Hardly slept. Better than nothing but several nights spent sheltering in woodland were better than this.*

Caravan site, Harlow. *Best accommodation before these stables. Tucked away at rear of the site I had choice of seven touring caravans stored there. Main site had about forty caravans with an air of permanence about them. Few occupied this time of year and staff confined themselves to their office, never ventured beyond inhabited area. Entered site at dusk through gap in perimeter fence and left soon after dawn. Way in concealed from view of nearby road by bushes and brambles. Stayed six nights.*

Casting his eyes back over his draft list on the newspaper margins Mike decided that a couple of barns and various woodland hideouts didn't add anything to his narrative so he left the account there. He arranged the paper, pen and reference material neatly on the table, extinguished the lamp and when his eyes had become accustomed to the dark he made the few paces to his sleeping space and turned in for the night.

Thursday 3rd December 2201

The weather that had kept Mike largely confined to the stables over the two previous days relented overnight. Cold, snow flurries and brisk winds had given way to a calmer, brighter and drier atmosphere but it was still cold. Having had plenty of time to think Mike knew exactly what his next steps would be. Food supplies were paramount but he had increasingly given thought to his onward travel plans. So far he had only been able to explore his immediate surroundings. The lane to the north of the estate stood in front of an area of woodland and parkland stretching to the north and east and beyond that, his road map told him, there was a large lake with watersports facilities. The road that ran past the front of the house was called Durden Road, its northward extension being the route by which he had arrived in the area whilst to the south according to a signpost he would be able to reach Oakend Village and the rail station. So far he had only ventured to the edge of the housing area where he had noted a pub, a school and three shops including the store that had provided his notepad. The road names here seemed to be aviation related. Vickers, Hawker and De Havilland he recognised as very early aircraft manufacturers. Cessna he thought may have been American but Auster and Miles were unknown to him. Mike thought that at one time this area may have included an airfield and under more normal conditions he would have been happy to spend a little time researching Oakend's history.

Today he walked down Durden Road towards the village. This was not the type of country where he needed to keep out of sight behind hedges. In an urban area he had to appear confident, seemingly part of the community and in Oakend that meant wearing casual but reasonably smart clothing. At the start of his journey his apparel had become stained, creased and torn by wire fencing, brambles and the need to sleep rough but gradually he had discarded garments as they became soiled and dishevelled and found ways to replace them. He had already documented the origin of his replacement clothes in the rough notes prepared for his journal.

Clothing

T-shirt, Saxted. *My first new clothes came courtesy of a farmhouse washing line in Saxted near Earls Soham. A smart, newly washed T-shirt that suggested the wearer had possibly attended an American university was taken after observation of about thirty minutes. There were socks and other items that could also have been stolen and I almost did but at that moment formed an important rule. Only take one item or two small ones at most from each location. Hopefully the owner would not actually miss anything or just believe that it had been mislaid.*

Shoes, Leisure Centre, Harlow. *I expected that someone would ask me for a sight of my ID card, a card I didn't possess. But after being allowed through the reception area to make use of the toilet facilities I was free to move around the leisure complex and found that the place was a treasure trove. Walking into a men's changing room I reluctantly passed over a fine waterproof jacket in favour of a pair of* shoes. The jacket would have to wait for another day. I could imagine that the owner of the shoes would think that they had been kicked along the floor somewhere and after an ineffectual search he may have thought that they had been picked up by mistake and were by now resting in someone else's sports bag. For the first and only time I had broken my golden rule and returned to the leisure centre for a second time. It was three days later. Found a nice leather jacket in good condition, walked out wearing it and immediately departed Harlow, heading for Broxbourne.

Supermarket, Harlow. Heavily populated and extensively stocked, supermarkets were a great attraction. In addition to clothes there was food on the shelves and vehicles in the car park. If fifty or so cars in Earl's Soham had provided at least four that were unlocked imagine the chances presented by the six-hundred or so cars parked there on a busy Friday evening. I spent a good hour examining the possibilities. Firstly I found that most clothes were electronically tagged. Since then I've worked out a way to remove these tags but at the time it presented an insurmountable drawback. Then there were surveillance cameras, both inside and out and if they didn't catch me then the security staff could. As it was I didn't come away empty handed. My reward for sixty minutes work was a woolly hat (and a packet of biscuits) taken from an as yet unloaded trolley parked behind the open boot of a car whilst a mother was securing her young child inside. I later felt that I had behaved badly but at the time it had been a reflex action.

So dressed in the Harlow jacket and shoes and new trousers that he expected would have at some time been missed from a market stall in Cheshunt and with these acting as a cover for his rather less smart underclothes, Mike stepped out into Oakend heading for the rail station. As this urban village was still under construction he guessed that the sight of an unrecognised newcomer was not at all unusual so he smiled at or briefly greeted people he met on his way. As he moved towards his goal the side streets with aviation names gave way to roads named after writers (Austen Avenue, for example, on the left) or cathedral cities (York Way on the right). Whilst travelling from Suffolk he had passed several similarly named housing areas. He could imagine members of a county highways committee, tired after a long meeting, rubber stamping the first collection of names suggested then grabbing their coats and briefcases and gratefully heading home. If not cities and writers it would probably have been flowers or garden birds or trees.

Within twenty minutes he had passed through the village centre, purchased a newspaper (unfortunately only the Daily Record was available) and was within sight of the railway line straddling the road on its bridge; the station being signposted to the right along an approach road parallel to the railway embankment. The station was an unstaffed local halt. Mike removed a timetable leaflet from a box at the entrance and took his place on the platform with half a dozen other people waiting for the next train. His timetable listed this as being due at 1117, originating at High Wycombe and travelling on to London – a fact confirmed by the electronic platform display that also stated that the train was on time. It was one of the regular trains providing a half hourly stopping services on this route. As the 1117 arrived Mike stood, waited and then mingled with the disembarking passengers and left the station with the crowd. There were no staff, no ticket checking systems and to his relief no police presence of the type he knew now regularly guarded many rail stations in and around London.

The rail passengers split into two groups, one peeling away from the exit around to the car park but Mike followed the remainder up to the village then turned into the door of a café he had noted on the way down. He ordered a coffee and sat at a vacant table for two from where he could see the door, the window and anyone passing outside. He wasn't expecting to notice anyone in particular; it was a precaution born out of habit. An earlier customer had left a newspaper on a nearby chair. Reaching across to collect it he saw that it was today's and that it was the National Guardian. There was nothing in the paper about the search for the killer of Captain Buckhurst and nothing about ESA which he hoped was good news. In his current position, however, he couldn't be sure that no news was in actual fact also good news. After five minutes reading, with his mug empty, Mike ordered a meal that resembled an all-day breakfast; he wouldn't need to cook that evening, he'd just do with a sandwich somewhere around 1800 hours. Meal finished he left the café, abandoning his unread Daily Record and taking with him the Guardian.

So far his day had been unusually law-abiding. He had purchased, not purloined a newspaper and he had paid for his lunch although it could be argued that the money itself had been stolen as his newfound wealth had been left in a wallet found inside the last car that he had 'borrowed'. But all that could well change with his new plan for onward travel. If he was to get to his next destination, now decided as being Oxford, he would need transport either by road or rail. Train travel was feasible. The timetable indicated that a local train to Beaconsfield or High Wycombe would make connection with the fast service to Bicester where he could change to an Oxford service. But the motorway lay a little over a couple of kilometres to the south and that would allow him to travel directly to his destination by car.

Mike had borrowed several cars during the course of his journey. Without them he would still be some way off his present location. He had quickly learnt that as with 'shopping' there were a few rules he needed to follow. Firstly he had to be patient. In Earl's Soham he had found the car that provided his road atlas after only a few minutes searching. After that it hadn't proved to be so easy. In Harlow he had spent eight hours of one day without success and had to move to another part of town the next day. And choice was limited as only the oldest vehicles had been built without modern security systems such as fingerprint or voice recognition. However second and third-hand owners often failed to reset the security and just depended on a keycard or keyfob for locking. It was these cars that were most vulnerable to the thief and were paradoxically more likely to be left unlocked. Once inside Mike found that starting the car was quite easy using a small electronic gadget that Simon had given him to use on ESA vehicles in an emergency. It may not have been legal but it was certainly effective.

When patience was rewarded it was necessary to limit expectations. Long journeys were out of the question as the vehicle had to be abandoned before its absence was noted. So Mike usually limited himself to a thirty minute drive, certainly a maximum of three-quarters of an hour.

The most important rule, however, was to chose a different location for his theft each time. Any repetition could lead to a pattern and attract attention from the traffic cops. An industrial estate to the northern side of Potters Bar, home to several small businesses had seen his first successful attempt to obtain transport. Most of the buildings had parking bays to the front for staff and visitors but on one side of the estate units F12 to F18 had this facility at the side with access around a windowless back wall. The first three units housed modern cars, medium to high end models, none above about three years old. It was a similar story with E15 except for one older model of a once extremely popular type, its styling noticeable in comparison with its sleek modern neighbours. Despite its age – the registration plate suggested twelve years – the type was still seen in quite large numbers and would not stand out as an oddity on the road. It had been 0944 and if the owner worked an eight hour shift it might not be missed until 1600 or 1700 hours or at least until 1200 if revisited at lunchtime. The car had opened without trouble. It was not the quickest but possibly the easiest time he had in finding a car.

He had driven the car, blessed with a well-charged battery, along the M25 motorway, a journey that had been mainly trouble free until, with bad weather closing in he had abandoned it in the village of Herongate just off the slip road at junction 17. There had however been one rather scary moment near the start. Within a couple of kilometres of his theft he had taken a road signed 'M25 Junction 24' to meet the back of a slow moving traffic queue. After about four minutes of stop/start he saw the clear signs of a police roadblock up ahead, near the junction. He didn't think that they were looking for him or even the car he had borrowed but without proper ID and other paperwork he couldn't risk a police interrogation. Signalling in good time he smoothly turned left into a side road as though he was a resident of the area. Despite the urge to head away as quickly as possible he had sedately doubled back through Potters Bar to run parallel to the M25 and join the motorway two junctions further west. He hadn't previously seen a roadblock since leaving Suffolk: He had clearly strayed too near to London with its increasing problem of urban brigades who copied the attitudes of the more belligerent of the coastal gangs. Mike made a note to move away from the metropolis as soon as possible.

With these experiences behind him Mike planned to borrow another car and make a recce of the route onto the M40 road and his escape route to the west. Today he wouldn't need to join the motorway itself but he needed to gain all the information he could so that the journey, when he decided to move on, would proceed smoothly. Forewarned, as the saying goes, he said to himself, is forearmed.

Whilst waiting for the 1117 London train earlier in the day he had time to study the station car park. The station entrance, forecourt and car park were covered by surveillance cameras. All, that was, apart from an apparently recently laid extension characterised by its jet-black surface and clean white lining to the rear of the parking area. On his return after lunch Mike slipped into a wooded area beside the approach road where he was able to observe cars arriving and leaving. The area near the station was full with cars left by the morning commuters so that any newcomers were forced to use the newer spaces to the rear. Two possible cars and a truck were parked there together with a number of unsuitable newer ones. On the point of moving out from his cover to try an elderly blue saloon Mike was forced back again when another, newer blue car pulled into a free space nearby. The driver – a young woman, possibly not long in possession of a driving licence – quickly left her car, seemingly without locking it and hurried back towards the station. Lost from view for a moment Mike scanned the platform and caught a glimpse of her distinctive blonde hair just as the 1347 train pulled in. When the train pulled out the platform was empty.

Within a minute he was inside the car and moving towards the entrance. Fortunately the barrier raised automatically on his approach. Blondie must have set up a pre-paid account and the barrier read her details from a 'toll box' in the engine compartment. On gaining the road he turned right, passed under the railway bridge and followed the direction signs to the motorway but avoided the direct connection at Junction 1, preferring to take the old road through Gerrards Cross, towards Beaconsfield and Junction 2. Here he turned southwards, crossed the motorway slowly, taking in the scene and then motored back through the villages on its southern side. At the station he returned the car to the space where its owner had left it but then mischievously backed it into a vacant spot one row behind.

The trip had proved that he could get a car, travel to

Beaconsfield and head up the motorway to Oxford. He could but he wasn't going to, at least not immediately. He had noted armed army personnel observing the slip roads with some of their number stopping and checking vehicles. They must have had their reason. Armed soldiers on an unknown local operation alarmed him. It was time to move on and at that moment rail seemed to be his best option. But first he needed money, various items of clothing and, if at all possible, an ID card. But getting that third item wouldn't be easy.

Walking back through the village Mike firmed up the shopping list in his mind. It was a little like preparing to go on holiday except that the cash in his pocket gave him a dilemma. If he spent the money (and there was quite enough for his intended purchases) he would have very little left to continue his journey. He didn't wish to leave a trail of petty thefts between Oakend and wherever he ended up. And there was little time left now for him to obtain enough money to enable him to complete both his planned purchases and his journey should he decide to leave in the morning. If only he could get hold of an ID card he could obtain and use the credit available with a store card but having failed in this quest so far during his journey from Suffolk it was extremely unlikely that he would succeed during the following fifteen hours or so. So it had to be splash the cash now and take a chance on replacing the money later as he travelled on towards his planned destination.

Oakend's shopping area started with a parade of units along the main road. Walking up from the station Mike passed, on his left, the café he had visited that morning, a general store including a Post Office, provider of his Daily Record, a hair salon, a land agents and a bank. Immediately after this last unit a broad entrance gave access to the pedestrian area accurately, but unimaginatively named The Square. Mike turned left past the bank and into the entrance of the ubiquitous ECOS store. Convenient. All his requirements available under one roof at a reasonable price and only one payment would be needed, a payment that could be made conveniently at a self-service checkout. In increasing numbers in recent years large stores no longer agreed to handle cash but ECOS wasn't fussy. It would take payment however it was offered although possibly no longer allowing a farmer to exchange his purchases for two hens and a clutch of duck's eggs. Unfortunately without an ECOScard or some other trading account he had no access to credit or cashback facilities.

Mike stood momentarily inside the door to get his bearings. Signs hanging from the ceiling indicated food sales to the left, clothing and stationary to the right, pharmacy straight ahead and electrical goods upstairs on the first floor. Starting on his left Mike took a circular journey around the ground floor. Two bottles of water, a bar of chocolate and two bananas were added to his shopping basket before he headed to the pharmacy for a comb, deodorant and first-aid plasters. Then it was up the travelator to look for a razor. So far Mike had kept as far away as possible from what passed for civilisation in Britain and had not taken too much care with his personal appearance. But his latest plans suggested that such lack of care would have to change. There was a wide choice of shaving appliances available but he chose a small lightweight travel version with a variety of adaptors that the blurb on the outside of the box claimed would suit all sockets and electrical systems around the globe. Then it was downstairs and on to the clothing section.

Temptation. Mike longed to provide himself with a completely new smart set of clothes. And he had the money to so do if he kept to budget brands but he had to remember that as he was moving on he should only purchase clothes that he could wear on his person or stow in the limited space offered by his well worn backpack. There was no point in leaving anything behind when he eventually set off. So being painfully practical he picked up two shirts, a pack of underpants, three pairs of socks and a woollen hat that could be worn by any twenty to thirty year-old male (and some ladies as well) to keep out the cold and damp conditions expected at this end of the year. After successfully negotiating the checkout he left ECOS, ignored the adjacent stores, exited The Square and turned left onto Durden Road and the route back to his billet. By shopping carefully he had saved enough to provide himself with food for another couple of days.

Nearing a road junction where his homeward route met DeHavilland Drive, Mike, looking ahead noticed passengers leaving a bus. As he arrived at the stop the bus pulled away heading for Rickmansworth and Watford leaving a young woman, newly alighted from the bus, pushing her baby carrier towards him through the space between the bus shelter and the wall of the adjacent house. He stepped to his right to avoid her but in passing around the shelter and making his way along the pavement's edge he kicked something that skidded a short distance away in front of him. He looked down and saw a tan-coloured wallet. 'ID card', was his first thought as he picked it up but he was to be disappointed. There was a National ID Card but its owner was dark haired, rather older than himself and getting on for two metres tall. However the initial let-down was eased by the sight of crisp new banknotes. He took just enough to cover his initial travel plans and noted the owner's address as 21 Miles Close, one of the 'aircraft' roads. He turned left into DeHavilland Drive and found the close a little way up on the right. The door bell at no.21 brought no reply but he was able to leave the wallet with a neighbour, newly arrived on the driveway of no.23 and brushing aside the suggestion that he left his contact details turned back to DeHavilland Drive (in fact a crescent) to continue on the return route to his present home.

That evening Mike continued with his journal. Before settling down to write he had kept to his habit of checking the contents of his backpack. Spare clothes, a little food, the torch he had found in the stables, his new razor, comb and first aid plasters and his now tatty but still useable maps. He decided not to take the tent as he would hopefully not need it again and with check complete he stashed his backpack, jacket and woollen hat by the door in readiness for any emergency evacuation. It was a reflex precaution; he didn't have any reason to think it would be needed that night in particular.

His next set of notes were to be a summary of information from the National Guardian's daily *Brigadewatch* articles. He worked through the cuttings he had saved, sorted them into date order, circled the references he needed and transferred the details to a single sheet of lined notepaper. He headed up the page and added the required items, each listed under the reporting date rather than that of the incident itself.

BRIGADEWATCH

Tuesday 27th October.
Death of Alana Buckhurst confirmed. East Suffolk Association investigated. Mike Cannon named as suspect.
Friday 30th October. *Anna Chalk arrested.*
Tuesday 3rd November. *ESA headquarters and local offices raided. Computers, backups and files removed. ESA work suspended. Army take over civilian operations using existing personnel. ATVs and other vehicles impounded.*
Thursday 5th November. *Frankie Parsons, Holderness Brigade, Yorkshire sentenced to 21 years for carrying and using a gun.*

Mike hadn't seen news of Frankie's arrest and hadn't particularly followed the fate of other groups and brigades. The news, though, drew his attention to The Tariff applied when sentencing brigade members. It was listed in a box at the foot of the page.

Brigade sentencing tariff
from 20th July 2201
National Council Notification 01070353

Active members, 5 years
Carrying an illegal weapon, 15 years

Damage to Army/Police equipment, structures or vehicles, 15 years

Using a weapon, 21 years

Killing an Army, Police or Borderguard officer, 28 years

Leading or organising a Brigade, 28 years

All sentences carry nil remission.

15 year sentences include the last 5 years in a Rehabilitation centre.

5 year sentences include the last 2 years in a Rehabilitation Centre.

Mike continued his list.

Tuesday 10th November *Cassandra Vale, Reuben Court, James Court arrested.*

Tuesday 17th November *Kassim Wood-West, Michael Warren, Simon Upton, Vandra Mornington, Beth Stamford, Saskia Hill arrested.*

Saturday 21st November. ESA brigade trial and sentencing.

Kassim Wood-West *Brigade leader 28 years*

Cassandra Vale *Carrying a weapon 15 years*

Reuben Court *Carrying a weapon 15 years*

James Court *Active member 5 years*

Saskia Hill *(absent) Active member 5 years*

Simon Upton *Active member 5 years*

Claire Bois, Anna Chalk, Vandra Mornington & Beth Stamford *Members rehabilitation*

Michael Warren *Member released*

When Mike had first read this list he had been both saddened and angry. Kassim did not deserve to be imprisoned for what could well be the rest of his life for apparently just knowing what was going on. Kassim himself would of course have felt it his duty to take full responsibility. Michael Warren, Vandra and Saskia had nothing to do with guns or illegal operations and should never have been arrested in the first place. And Cassie. Sweetheart Cassie. He would gladly take her place if he could but if he did turn himself in they'd both be inside. Despite a recurring desire to go to the nearest police station and surrender he felt it his duty to remain free and thwart the army for as long as he could.

There were some notable names missing from the *Brigadewatch* reports. Over the last month he had seen no mention of Carlos or Heron or Frazer Oak. The only other information of interest was a map showing areas of current brigade activity but it was the areas displaying least activity that interested Mike more. And one of those areas was north Oxfordshire.

CHAPTER FIFTEEN
JOURNEY'S END

Thursday 3rd December 2201. Denham, Buckinghamshire

Mike glanced at his watch. 2237. He had been writing for rather longer than he had planned. He stood, stretched and tidied his papers.

'Shit!' he exclaimed, loudly and with feeling.

He was reacting to a loud, thumping crash that had broken the previous almost complete silence. The noise was close enough to make Mike jump and drop the papers from his hand.

Silence, darkness.

The silence was profound and the darkness a result of Mike's instinctive reaction to extinguish the light from his lamp.

He stood still and listened.

Nothing.

He stepped cautiously towards the door, opened it part way and stood in the gap he had created. The half moon behind the stable and the part-clouded sky allowed him to remain hidden in the shadow. With his shoulder to the wooden structure he moved slowly to his right, edging around towards the moonlit space between the stables and the house. He looked across the gap to see what may have caused the noise but could see nothing. He was about to move back when a missile of some description crashed into the façade of the house to his left with a sound of breaking glass followed by a thud as the projectile crashed to the ground. For some reason the house was under attack. Mike crouched down and waited. Moments later the purpose of this activity became a little clearer. The third missile followed on a similar trajectory to the second. As before he heard the crash but no thud followed this time as the missile lodged itself in the space previously occupied by the now broken window. Within seconds there was a flash followed by a plume of smoke and the sky was lit up by unseen flames.

Mike didn't need to stay around for any further action to prove that his occupation of the stables had become untenable. He turned, skirted the building in a low crouching run, grabbed his bag, jacket and headgear and looked to escape through the shadowed area before making a brief dash across the moonlit paddock and into the cover offered by the trees that bordered the lane. He had just left the safety of the shadow and vaulted the paddock fence when he heard a familiar sound.

An army helicopter.

For the second time that evening Mike swore aloud to himself. He was half way across the paddock when the searchlight swept across him as the chopper circled and banked around to his left. With the throbbing sound subsiding he made the relative safety of the woodland strip and scrabbled northwards through it for a few metres before crouching down against the low boundary wall to wait and see how things developed and think about what he should do next. If he knew anything of army practice there would be ground troops on the scene before long. Although he hadn't consciously thought about it he knew that the missile attack hadn't been aimed at him. The action had probably been taken by some person or persons aiming at providing a decoy; a group hoping to escape from the area by diverting the attention of the authorities towards the burning house. Mike had learnt from newspaper articles that some copycat urban gangs were in possession of shoulder mounted missile launchers and guessed that this was how they had targeted the house. Perhaps they were the same people being sought by the army who had set up the roadblock he had seen earlier in the day. It seemed that although the armed forces hadn't been looking for him specifically they had most certainly now found him. Whilst waiting to see how events would unfold Mike had time to muse briefly on the fact that a helicopter with a searchlight had been a recurring feature in his life so far but such thoughts were cut short when he heard the sound of vehicles on the road.

Two army personnel carriers passed behind him and a little further up the road turned into the estate on the track that serviced the stable area. Although out of view to him it was evident from the sounds that a number of soldiers were being disembarked and soon the addition of light from the returning helicopter provided assistance in their deployment. More noise, further away, gave the impression that fire fighting forces were also on the scene. Then, in addition to all this activity a third army vehicle passed behind Mike and slowed to a halt just by the entrance. Raising his head slightly he saw two soldiers jump down. They moved round to the rear of the truck, let down the tailgate and removed items of equipment. It was difficult for him to understand this activity until a spotlight came on and by moving slightly to one side, into a shadowed area, he could see that the two men were constructing a roadblock. He had just decided to try a breakout over the wall and back down the lane when his plan was put on hold by the sound of another vehicle – a civilian car he guessed – entering the lane and coming towards him just as the army vehicles had done earlier. After passing his hideout this vehicle was brought to a halt by one of the soldiers now acting as a guard whilst his colleague continued the construction. On request the driver got out and was being questioned by the soldier when the fire, previously just a dull glow in the windows of the house, burst through the roof with a great roar that sent both driver and soldier ducking for cover. Mike momentarily thought that the English language did not contain a word that adequately described the ferocious sound but seizing his chance he scrambled over the low stone wall, rounded the car with its door still open and its engine still running and jumped in. Selecting *drive* the vehicle lurched forward with a surge of acceleration, narrowly missed its owner then, with a crashing sound, pushed aside the partially completed roadblock. Mike was certain the second soldier must have fired at least one shot at the departing car but beyond the spotlight's pool of illumination the lane was dark and he had been able to extinguish the car's headlights leaving only the sound of the engine as a guide to the vehicle's location. He was well on his way down the lane and safe for the immediate future.

The lane was narrow, dark and unknown to him. It was scary driving down a road he hadn't travelled before, in the dark and with the lights off. More frightening was the appearance of the helicopter tracking him from above. He recognised the aircraft as a Ra77 – a Russian design but licence-built in Britain and the deadliest search and destroy helicopter around. It came from the same stable as the lumbering old search and rescue Ra50 hand-me-downs used by the Borderguard in East Suffolk but this most recent addition to Britain's airpower was an entirely different craft. It was even more capable than the Transmanche Kestrels used by Bentwaters. A guided shot at one of his wheels would end his journey not long after its start and also his prospects for escape but, fortunately, the route he had been forced to take followed a zigzag course of lanes bordered by well-wooded country. It was difficult for the helicopter pilot to keep his craft close to the car and its height above the trees further limited the opportunities to take accurate aim at his quarry. It was like a game of hide and seek apart from the fact that the seeker hadn't counted to 100 before he started and Mike had no idea where he was going to hide. Complete annihilation would have been possible of course but a crater where the road had once been, bordered by an extensive ring of charred vegetation would have created ammunition that would have provided a field day for those in the media and in parliament who were opposed to the army's activities.

His cover, though, lasted for less than a couple of

kilometres. Ahead he saw the country open out on either side of the road. As the searchlight swept the area in front of him Mike picked out not only the railway embankment ahead and his lane passing through it under a bridge but also, fleetingly, a fenced field and gateway on the left. Escape by road was no longer an option, he realised, as he would easily be picked up on reaching the motorway if not before. His only option for getting out of the area was to travel by train. By breaking hard and swinging the car through ninety degrees with a thud and a splintering sound the car came to a halt part way through the wooden gate near the left-hand pillar of the bridge. With the helicopter now ahead of him and banking hard in an effort to reconnect with its quarry Mike jumped from the car, dived under the bridge and once through turned to his left and ran along beside the wooded embankment following a field edge and heading for the lights of a housing area some 500 metres ahead. The helicopter returned, located the car and circled around its position, its steadily increasing radius causing Mike to occasionally dive for cover. By running, crouching and weaving around obstacles he came ever nearer the buildings until the sudden barking of a dog caused him to pull up sharp. Which was fortunate. He unexpectedly made contact with a previously un-noticed high metal chain-link fence but luckily without any great force. With access to the roads beyond now denied he had little choice but to turn left around the fence and enter the wooded area that reached down from the fence towards the railway tracks at a point where the embankment gave way to a cutting.

Once under cover Mike paused briefly to catch his

breath and review his situation. Heron's words of wisdom came into his mind. If he wished to become inconspicuous he had two options. He could hide well away from his pursuers but this instinctive first option was a non-starter. Helicopters with searchlights and body-seeking equipment would soon locate him if the army personnel and dog handlers failed to follow his trail. So option two it was. One body among many. The army didn't know who they were looking for although it wouldn't be long before they found his journal notes at the stables and were able to put a name to their quarry. So the rail station it had to be, hoping it was well populated even this late at night.

A hum on the rails presaged the approach of a train on the track closest to him. A country bound local service accelerated away from the station with the lineside trees creating flickering dark shadows alternating with brightness as the carriage windows passed. Half an hour until the next stopping service if his memory of the timetable was correct. He needed about fifteen minutes to scramble along the wooded slope, five minutes for surveillance near the station and, if the coast was clear, another five in the toilets cleaning up followed by another very nervous few minutes waiting for the train.

Mike started towards the station. He glanced back and noticed a red traffic signal controlling the track nearest the trees and a green light for the adjacent fast line. He scrabbled further along his route with the noise of the returning helicopter and the sound of heavy road vehicles somewhere behind creating a sense that his pursuers were closing in around him. A train passed London-bound on the furthest of the four tracks and then after a short period of relative quiet there was a new, different sound; a heavy monotonous throb. Not the high pitched whirr of a chopper but the deep, ponderous sound of a powerful locomotive. Two searching headlights marked the advent of a pair of huge engines. As the train came into view Mike noted that it was not speeding through on the green light but creeping towards him on the local line, presumably shunted there to allow an express train to pass. The squeal of breaks confirmed this thought as the locos passed and the tanker wagons that formed the train were drawn to a halt.

His next move was a reaction rather than a logical move. As a Midlands bound passenger train passed speedily by on the adjacent track Mike scuttled quickly down the side of the cutting and taking advantage of brief moments of illumination from the passing train, jogged along the gravel beside the stationary train until he could jump onto the metal steps built into the end frame of one of the wagons. He hauled himself up and managed to sit down wedged between the body of the tanker and the handrail that extended above the wagon's floor and, facing backwards, braced himself for the acceleration he hoped would not be long in coming.

It came in less than a minute. The convoy of tanker wagons edged slowly forward, delicately hauled by the powerful but controlling locomotives up front. A helicopter came within earshot above the railway but some hundred metres behind the train and probably, Mike thought, above the station. As he was taken away Mike felt increasingly safe in the shadow of the huge tanker truck coupled behind the one that now gave him refuge. The moon, uncovered by a passing cloud, temporarily gave sufficient light to illuminate a large rectangular label on the end of the tanker in front of him. The word TOXIC in large black letters stood out above three square boxes containing information. The first box was filled by the standard orange flame symbol indicating flammable contents. The second sported chemical symbols and names that Mike neither recognised nor understood and the third box gave a company name, a London address and an emergency telephone number.

Mike summarised his situation. Taken at face value it wasn't very encouraging. Firstly he was on a train without knowing its destination. Secondly he was sandwiched between two containers whose contents could potentially burst into flame or chemically attack him. Thirdly in case of an emergency he had a contact telephone number but he didn't have a phone.

Perhaps not a good situation but then he had never heard of a tanker train exploding and anyway it was definitely better than being hunted down by aggressively trained dogs or the piercing searchlight of the Ra77 as he stumbled across the Buckinghamshire countryside. And he didn't expect a ticket inspector to come clambering along the wagons to ask if he had a valid pass for travelling.

To his relief his transport's snail-like progress became converted into a steady acceleration as the previously idling engines of the locomotives increased their power to produce a steady purposeful beat and take the train past the signal, now green, then first with a swing to the right and then another to the left pick up speed along the fast track heading to the west.

He let out a great sigh of relief. There was nothing he could do now but let the train travel on and wait. He desperately wanted to sleep. He tried to relax but a tingling sensation gripped his head and then, like a wave, washed through his body and down into his extremities. Despite the drive along the winding country lanes having lasted for only a few minutes the concentration of mind and vision could not easily be relaxed and the subsequent crouching, twisting run along the embankment had left every muscle in his body taught.

Gradually, however, the environment exerted its influence on him and his horizons broadened. The cold night air freshened him and the darkness calmed his mind and the friendly hum of the engines way up ahead helped him to relax. The train slowed, switched tracks again and trundled past a stationary train standing in darkness at a brightly lit station platform. They were passing through High Wycombe. Mike guessed that the train must be the local service he had seen earlier from his cover beside the railway. It now stood at the 'up' platform ready to become the first train back to London in the morning. Past the platform end, under the glare of car park lighting he observed the last few passengers now warmly enclosed in their vehicles clearing condensation from their windscreens and thankfully making their way homewards.

Back onto the main line and accelerating to operating speed the train forged westwards into the night. The motive power seemed not to notice the steady climb up to the summit of the Chiltern Hills, heading onwards with hardly a change of engine note and in the same manner descending the gradient the other side towards Princes Risborough. There was nothing to slow progress as Mike's wagon passed through the darkened station. Were it not for a single illuminated sign, standing out like a nightlight in a child's bedroom, giving its location away, Mike would not have known how far he had travelled at that point. He checked his watch and found that it was eighteen minutes past midnight. He welcomed the new day in the hope that it would be a new day, new beginning.

The night air cooled further. Mike shivered and pulled his jacket around him although it was little more than a symbolic act; it did little to help keep him warm. With hindsight he knew he should have bought a woollen jumper during his shopping spree at Oakend's ECOS store. For a few kilometres he dozed on and off, lulled by the steady motion and the monotonous sound of the wheels on the track. During conscious moments weak moonlight occasionally lit up trackside buildings and caused isolated trees to stand out as inky black silhouettes, passing between the lunar brightness and the moving train but his vision was limited by the bulk of the tanker wagon coupled behind his own and such scenes were insufficient to raise awareness and keep him from sliding back into sleep.

Then the train braked, slowed, changed track and stopped. Mike was woken by the stillness and relative quiet. The train sat immobile. He could see very little and heard only the gently idling throb of the two engines up ahead. Five minutes passed. It didn't seem like journey's end. Then another couple of minutes. Still nothing stirred. Finally Mike stood up and stretched moving first to his left and then to his right before peering around the edge of the wagon. Ahead he saw only a dull light from the cab of the rear locomotive; no buildings, no station, not even a distant colourlight signal. There was no road visible and nothing to tell him where he was. For a moment Mike considered abandoning his transport but on reflection he hadn't travelled far enough. It was only a little over half an hour into the new day and he had calculated that he would need to travel on until at least one o'clock before reaching a suitable destination, one far enough from his last billet.

Why had they stopped? Had the crew been sent a message to halt so that the police or army could check the train for a stowaway? So far there were no signs that they had. No uniformed welcoming party, no transports, no helicopters, no dogs.

Perhaps it was journey's end. But there was nothing to suggest that it was a location set up to receive a cargo. And the train was still intact with the two idling giants at its head.

So either it was waiting for a faster train to overtake or it was just a mundane occurrence such as a rest break. Mike knew nothing of railway worker's terms and conditions but he supposed there were some rules akin to those applied to lorry and coach drivers on the road. It was probably best just to sit out the delay.

Mike could have slept again but he needed to be alert in case anything untoward did happen. As it was, at about one o'clock – just thirty minutes after they had stopped, the engine's tone changed, the locomotives crept forward, the couplings took up the strain and the cargo wagons moved steadily along the siding before switching to the main line and resuming their journey heading north-westwards through Oxfordshire. It was now time to consider journey's end. At the next opportunity he would, he decided, leave the train and look for somewhere to hole up, hopefully at or near Bicester. After that Mike had only vague assumptions about his future. Heron's training again provided the key. He would need to lie low for a while, hide away, then if all was quiet he would find some well-populated area where he could integrate himself into everyday life.

But not at Bicester! The train was pulled relentlessly through that town's railway station.

0115 came and went as did 0130.

And not at Banbury either. Slowing a little as it passed through the station the train soon resumed its accustomed canter towards the Midlands. Mike became a little concerned that Oxfordshire would pass into Warwickshire and Warwickshire would morph into the West Midlands but much to his relief getting on for ten minutes out of Banbury he felt a deceleration and heard the hiss of brakes being applied. To his left he could pick out nothing in the darkness but to his right he saw the silvery path of a waterway intermittently reflecting the pale half-moon as passing clouds trundled across the sky or lineside vegetation gave way to a broader view. The train finally pulled to a halt. This time there was no need to stop and think. Grabbing his pack he checked the adjacent track for traffic. Nothing. He climbed down, turned, jumped onto the gravel, checked again for any oncoming train then crossed the parallel track, climbed a low embankment and dropped down to the edge of the water.

Mike paused for a few moments, his mind temporarily frozen. He really didn't know what he was going to do next. From being carried along with few decisions to make he was suddenly presented with a choice – the path beside the water could be followed to the left or the right – and there was no overwhelming reason why he should choose either. He was like the donkey stuck between two equally attractive bales of hay. He stood for a few more seconds hoping that something would appear to make up his mind but there was nothing. Then he turned. For some reason that he didn't understand he had selected left and headed off in the same direction as the now departing train.

As he walked carefully along the waterside path he looked around for anything that could provide shelter; a place that would give some cover and enough comfort to allow him to sleep. If he didn't find anything soon he imagined he would simply reach a point where nothing could stop him from lying down beside the path, curling up and subsiding into oblivion. He was not far off that point when the small clumps of vegetation that marked the water's edge on his right-hand side were matched by similar patches to his left. The railway line had now veered away and been replaced by a smooth moonlit silver-grey surface similar to that found to his right. The path he was following now curved gently to the right and took the form of a causeway between two bodies of water.

And then he saw it.

In dark contrast to the brighter moonlit water a bulky, seemingly featureless object sat at the side of the path to the left about 200 metres ahead. It appeared to be about the size of a large family saloon car but as he approached it the shape took on the features of a small boat, covered by a tarpaulin. Mike assumed that the craft was either laid-up for the winter or had been left there, abandoned, but whatever the case as far as he was concerned this was journey's end. The vessel's cover was tied by bands that went under the hull to securing points on the far side. These ties held the tarpaulin securely but there was a fold near the front where the cover passed around what Mike assumed to be a cabin or cockpit. He eased the flap out from where it had been tucked away and managed to crawl in through the gap beneath it. Once inside he was able to use the torch from his backpack to see that the vessel's superstructure comprised a windscreen and a tiny open-fronted cabin. There was, though, enough space to provide a small but not too cramped hideaway. It was dark and appeared dry although there was a slightly damp, musty smell but given the complete lack of an alternative it would suit his present needs very well. Momentarily Mike thought of searching for anything he could use as bedding but fatigue took over. He put his backpack down as a pillow, took out a bottle of water and had a quick drink, checked the time – 0227 – switched off his torch and settled down, still in his jacket and travelling clothes. He was cold and hungry but above all, tired. Gradually his body provided a degree of heat to the cocoon that was his jacket and his leg muscles that had at first tightened up somewhat painfully, began to relax. Within fifteen minutes the muzziness in his head had spread to the rest of his body. He slept. Fitfully at times but he slept.

CHAPTER SIXTEEN
ENDGAME

Friday 4th December 2201, Oxfordshire

1538 clicked over to 1539. Mike had been asleep for well over twelve hours. He had slept fitfully at first – he remembered checking his watch at 0250 and again at 0322 but after that could remember nothing until he became conscious of the cold and the stiffness in his legs and the darkness of his environment; a darkness broken only by a few pinpricks of light creeping in through holes in the material that formed the cover to the boat. He lay there thinking for a while before checking the time again. It was 1546. Hunger overcame the feeling of cold. He felt around for the water bottle, found it, drank the remaining content then threw the empty bottle onto the floor, picked up his backpack – unopened since his arrival apart from removing the water – and clambered out through the flap before jumping down onto the waterside path.

It was, thankfully, a little warmer than the previous time he had stood there. The night-time chill had given way to a milder daytime with a cloud cover that gave a light drizzle and a temperature that was a few degrees higher than those of the previous few days. Mike looked around. Opposite his refuge, across the path, he saw the waterway. Almost certainly, he decided, a canal. He turned around. The boat that had provided him with shelter lay at the edge of what appeared to be a small lake, its edge largely masked by reeds and small bushes. Perhaps it had been constructed to act as a pound to hold the water that served to keep the canal level constant. Or it could have been a sort of lay-by for vessels using the cut. Mike could see another though half sunken craft over the other side and two others further along. He moved back to his boat, pushed the tarpaulin flap back in place then, standing with his back to the boat again considered the possibilities offered each way along the path. After a few seconds he nodded to himself, turned up the collar of his jacket against the damp, picked up his bag and set off to his left as the early December light began to fade. At first he stretched his arms and legs to relieve the stiffness induced by his cramped sleeping conditions but soon settled into an easy walk along the path in his chosen direction.

Ahead through the gloom he had seen a group of buildings spaced either side of the canal and a bridge beyond. A couple of vehicles had crossed the bridge whilst he had been considering his options. It would take about ten minutes he had calculated for him to reach this outpost of civilisation. After that he had no clear idea of what he would do. His aim was to find food and return to the boat for the night, have a good sleep and get up in the morning to start his new life. But for now all he could think about was his search for food.

As he walked towards the buildings the light from vehicle headlights made the layout of the land a little clearer. The canal veered away to his right to pass under the road bridge. To his left, beyond the water, lay the rail line that had brought him from the south and ahead there was another road that emerged from beneath the rail line to carry vehicles across his view and up to a junction near the bridge over the canal. Reaching the end of the lake on his left a signpost directed his footpath away from the water's edge and up steps to this road. Here he turned right onto the roadside footway and finding the way more even he was able to settle into an easy stride. To his right now, occupying the space between the road and the canal were several large single-storey buildings occupied by businesses; some in darkness, others with yards bathed in light. More buildings lay a few hundred yards ahead and although as yet he couldn't identify their purpose his spirits were brightened by the hope that one of them could offer the traveller some kind of hospitality.

The industrial area gave way to a collection of about half a dozen houses that, judging by their style were of quite recent construction. Most were in darkness or suggested occupancy only by a low level of lighting, all doors and windows closed tightly against the cold and gloom. Yet one was contrastingly bright, a result of some early Christmas illuminations. But it was a larger, well-lit building just beyond this development that now attracted Mike's attention. As he approached the road junction the almost leafless branches of a tall tree, shaking slightly in the breeze, moved to reveal a traditional pub sign proclaiming this building to be 'The Wharf Inn'.

Mike thanked his luck.

He turned in through the car park and headed

for the porch-style entrance. The outer doors opened automatically, closing behind him to reveal an inner door that also opened as he approached giving access to a lobby serving a bar and a restaurant together with restrooms to left and right. Mike turned right, pushed open the door sporting a male logo and went straight into a toilet cubicle. On exit he washed his hands and studied himself in the mirror over the basin.

'No! This just won't do,' he said out loud to himself.

Unkempt hair, stubble covered face, dirt-smeared forehead and dishevelled jacket would almost certainly result in his ejection from the Wharf Inn before he had eaten; more than likely before he had even ordered. Mike said a brief silent prayer of thanks reflecting the feeling of relief that he hadn't needed to pass through the bar to reach the washroom, opened his backpack and took out two items. Apart from his jacket and his watch they were his most prized belongings – his razor and comb. Mike washed his face and dampened down his hair. The sound of someone pushing open the door caused him to temporarily scamper back into a cubicle but he was soon out again looking for a razor point. There was none but he was grateful that the model he had purchased in Oakend provided a variety of adaptors to ensure universal use. In the case of the Wharf Inn he had to resort to the light socket adaptor and it now being late on a winter's afternoon, with customers thin on the ground, he was able to complete his shaving in the resulting barely lit washroom without interruption. Bulb restored and light back on he took out his new shirt, also courtesy of ECOS, stowed his jacket in his backpack and put the new shirt on over the old, creased and stained one he had worn for the last thirty-four hours. A quick attempt at hair styling and the mirror now reflected a young man not exactly smartly dressed but presentable enough to buy a bar snack if not really dressed for a three course meal in the restaurant.

Mike emerged, walked through to the bar, nodded to the bar staff and studied the menu.

'A pint of Atherstone's, please, a ham sandwich and a packet of crisps – cheese and pickle if you have any, please.'

Mike was constantly bemused by the fact that draft beers were still dispensed in non-metric units whilst their bottled equivalents had always been measured in litres. The food and drink he had ordered would give a quick fix. He would relax, consider the menu and order more food later.

With food and drink served he moved to a table in a corner facing the bar. For once he didn't adopt his news reporter rôle and stop to study the clientele; he was far more interested in his food. But despite his hunger he resisted the temptation to dive straight in. He took the meal steadily – a sip of beer, a mouthful of sandwich eaten slowly, a couple of crisps. Then repeat. And again. Towards the end of this snack he looked up to take in his surroundings. The bar was set out in a traditional rather than modern manner and at this time of the day there were few punters. Two ladies who could well have been mother and daughter presided over the bar with the younger doing all the serving but turning to talk with the other, seated on a stall, before returning to deal with another order. A young couple were seated with drinks by the fire, studying large menu folders and probably would place their orders electronically before taking their places in the restaurant later. Two men were seated at the bar with glasses of beer talking alternately to form an animated conversation with occasional asides to the ladies behind the bar and the only other customer was an elderly, rather untidily dressed lady seated beside the fire. She was the only person who appeared to need an outer coat in the almost overpowering warmth. In contrast to her Mike felt quite smartly dressed.

Nobody appeared to be interested in Mike.

He ordered another beer and a hot pasta dish.

As he sipped at his second pint the warmth of the inn and the effect of the alcohol brought a feeling of comfort to his body unlike anything he had felt for many days. It was now 1707. He hadn't heard anything from his pursuers for about eighteen hours and as far as he knew they were no nearer finding him now than when he had last seen them in Buckinghamshire. They could still be about 100 kilometres behind him. It was now, he decided, that he should stop running. Mike determined there and then to stay in this area and steadily, a little at a time, build a new life for himself and if that involved further visits to the Wharf Inn he wouldn't be at all disappointed.

When his meal was finished Mike sat for a while, exchanged a brief greeting and a few words about the weather with a middle aged man who had brought his drink over to an adjacent table then packed the remains of the previously purchased snack food in his bag. Nodding farewell to the neighbouring drinker he strolled across to the bar, thanked the two hosts, visited the washroom and made his way out. As he made his way back along the waterside path Mike felt more relaxed and cheerful than he had done for some time. The hospitality, warmth and sustenance of the Wharf Inn was in part responsible but he also had a feeling that fate was on his side. And one particular piece of good luck was that so far he had not been asked for a sight of his ID card. Obtaining one now went to the top of his 'to-do' list. Although adept at living reasonably well without one he knew that for the next steps in creating his new life he would have to give the impression of being a regular, law-abiding member of the community. And he would have to manage without his recently acquired habit of stealing money and clothing and cars.

It was still cloudy, still drizzling and away from the streetlights and buildings almost pitch black. He had to take care navigating his route home but he had not drunk too much and the cool evening air had sharpened his senses sufficiently for him to be able to take the short walk in his stride. On reaching his temporary sleeping quarters he climbed in, re-set the tarpaulin flap and in the dark almost fell as he tripped over the empty water bottle he had abandoned earlier. Mike smiled. It was almost like being at home.

Saturday 5th December 2201. Oxfordshire

He woke. His faithful watch told him it was early. 0718. Although not yet fully light he could see the muted pinpricks of light forming imaginary constellations in the firmament that was the cover above him. Although cold and stiff of limb Mike felt much better than the last time he had woken up in the boat and with good fortune he would not need to return for a further night. Rousing himself he half-stood and after taking a couple of paces opened up and pushed back the flap to let in the weak daylight and peer out. He was welcomed by the promise of another cool, but this time fine, December morning.

He had vague plans for the day but first he needed breakfast. He started with a Wharf Inn cheese sandwich, now rather dry but still quite pleasant and a packet of crisps that fortunately hadn't suffered the same deterioration. He followed this up with a chocolate bar that had originated in Oakend and a bottle of water. As was his habit he started his day by packing his bag which together with his jacket he left on the path when he clambered out of the boat. There was no hurry. He tidied his clothes, combed his hair with his fingers rather than bothering to find his comb and then walked forward to sit on the bank that formed the canal's edge to ponder his next move. But thoughts of the future became relegated to the back of his mind as he studied the view in front of him.

The sun, an orange-red orb was hanging, suspended in the lightening eastern sky and appeared larger than he had ever seen it before. The lowest part of its rim touched the gentle contours of a low hill, not anchored to it but gently rising as though it were freeing itself from the earth's attempt to hold on. In the foreground stood a tree and an attendant herd of hardy cattle shunning the warmth of a heated byre. Both tree and cattle formed coal-black silhouettes, stock still but seemingly hovering above the ground, tree trunk and cattle legs hidden by a low swath of white mist.

All was still.

Then a car's silvery-blue headlights silently crossed the scene in the background and a little later a small flock of birds traversed the sun's bright disc, left to right, rising as they passed by.

All was still again until the silence was broken by the gentle sound of a small duck making its zigzag course across the cut. It was a beautiful scene. Mike struggled in his mind to remember when he had last been so mesmerised by such a scene. This was a vision that spoke to his soul.

'*Welcome,*' it said. '*Come and stay.*'

But it was not Suffolk. It had all the elements that marked the Suffolk landscape – earth, sky, water and the fire of the sun and the shadows and the brightness.

But that did not make it Suffolk.

Missing were the forests and the ocean. The still, steel-grey water of the cut reflected the sun, trees and cattle, disturbed only by the wake of the little duck but despite its serene beauty at that moment Mike's eyes saw instead the grandeur of the winter waves pounding the steep cliffs at Easton a little north of his home village of Reydon and the majestic ranks of trees that formed the Dunwich Forest ranged behind the Starcab building at Westwood Broad.

At that moment Mike's mind was made up, his future decided. He had settled on the only reasonable option open to him. He turned, walked over to the boat, tucked the tarpaulin flap back into position and leaving only a discarded plastic bottle to mark his tenancy he picked up his pack, slung it across one shoulder and turned to trudge south along the footpath.

It took Mike about ten minutes to reach a point where a road bridge crossed the canal. The volume of traffic early that Saturday morning suggested that it carried an important route. He clambered up the steps that mounted the embankment and stood on the bridge that spanned the canal to his left and the rail line to his right. He paused, thought and then turned to his right to head south along the road that he expected would take him to the town of Banbury. A few hundred metres further on his belief was confirmed by a signboard placed on the opposite side of the road facing a side turning joining from his left. Banbury was signed in the direction in which he was headed. The arrow pointing the opposite way indicated Coventry and Leamington Spa.

With his direction confirmed Mike increased his stride to a comfortable length – he had no need to hurry – and he continued his way south. There was a temptation to hitch a ride but before deciding about that he needed time to work out the details of the plan he had just formulated for his immediate future. He had more than enough money to take the bus that he assumed linked the towns mentioned on the signpost but before heading directly for Banbury he needed the more limited facilities of a village. Not any old collection of houses but a reasonably sized settlement with at least one public house and a handful of shops.

A bus appeared from around a bend. The single-deck articulated vehicle purred purposefully towards him until he was able to read the destination displayed above the windscreen. Coventry. Presumably the service had started in Banbury or possibly even further south in Oxford. If so he expected such a trunk route would offer at least an hourly service. Twenty minutes further down the road he saw the next road junction, this time the minor road led off to his right. A signpost indicated the name of a settlement reached by this road but before he could get close enough to read the sign his attention was taken by the sound of another bus, this time approaching from behind him. He turned. It bore the same red and blue livery as the Coventry bus but this one carried the destination Banbury. It was indicating a right turn. As it passed the bus slowed, stopped at the junction, waited for oncoming traffic to turn into the side road then turned to the right itself.

The place named on the signpost was previously unknown to Mike but, he reasoned, if it was large enough to attract the bus service away from the main road it should certainly contain all the services required for his immediate needs. He crossed the main road and started along the side road heading towards a church tower just visible above the trees and rooftops some half kilometre ahead. Soon he reached the first few houses on his left and these in turn gave way to a gaggle of buildings marking the start of the village proper. To the south, on his left, lay a modern estate of houses but the main street was like a time warp – an old fashioned village, no building less than 200 years old. As he walked on he became more confident that diverting along this way had been the right decision. This place, he thought, would do very well.

The pub was closed. No matter. Opening time was 0900 and despite his hunger he had things to do before he ate. He was tempted by the snack foods available at the village shop opposite but the sight of the adjacent bus shelter concentrated his mind on one of his other requirements – finding details of the bus service to Banbury. He counted seven would-be passengers as he crossed the road one of which, a lady, was studying the timetable. He was relieved to see this display. Back in rural Suffolk travellers were expected to obtain travel information via their personal phones. Mike, of course, hadn't had the use of a phone since leaving there in rather a hurry all those weeks ago. He waited behind the lady, smiled when their eyes met as she turned, and stepped forward. Conveniently there was a real-time display showing the next service due.

Time due: 0855

Route: 24A

Destination: Leamington Spa

Time expected: 0858

Things were no different here, he thought. Buses in Oxfordshire ran as late as anywhere else but he had to admit to himself that apart from operating the ESA school minibus it had been a few years since he had actually used a public bus service. In his professional life the car had been preferred and, where longer distances were necessary it had been train or plane. He touched the icon for southbound services and was rewarded with information for the next bus in that direction.

Time due: 0912

Route: 24

Destination: Banbury via Hardwick Park

Time expected: 0912

Mike took back his thoughts about the punctuality of the number 24 bus service. The 0912, though was too soon for his needs. He scrolled down. 0942 and 1012. He could certainly manage the 0942 but depending on what other facilities the village provided he would happily leave departure for the further half hour. Turning back across the road he continued on his previous direction towards the church, its building now largely hidden around a left-hand bend, just the top of the spire visible over the rooftops. Mike didn't believe that the church in particular held any interest for him but you never knew what could lie around a bend and anyway he had a little time to spare before returning to the pub. As he rounded the bend the 0855 bus for Leamington came towards him. He checked his watch. 0857. The bus had managed to pull back a whole minute; perhaps it would be able to reach its final destination on time.

A narrow side road was signed as the route to the church. Mike turned and walked along it.

"Christmas Fair. Saturday 5th December. from 0900"

A banner announcing the event was stretched out above the open double doors to a surprisingly modern building adjacent to the contrastingly ancient church. Cars were parked around the hall and goods were being unloaded and carried inside. The Fair could just be worth a visit later on, Mike thought. He turned, smiled to himself and retraced his steps to the pub. A clean-up and a meal would put him in a good mood, set him up for the day and leave him ready for the bus to Banbury.

0935. A shave, a wash and an attempt at tidying his clothes was followed by a good breakfast. Mike downed a traditional plateful of bacon, egg, sausage, mushrooms and fried bread. It may not have been a gourmet meal but he had just had his best breakfast for a long time. Mike walked up through the village again. This time he approached the church hall with purpose in his step. When he arrived the people forming a small queue were passing steadily through the doors. The queue was formed, as Mike found out when he joined the back, by a lady asking each visitor to take part in a raffle.

Shuffling slowly forward there was plenty of time to observe the proceedings. Children, parents, groups of teenage girls and elderly couples: There was a good representation of the population of the village. The situation was perfect – noise, bustle, crowds but that would be of little account if the person he was hoping to see wasn't there. Then as he stopped, smiled and turned to register his five chosen numbers for the raffle, out of the corner of his eye he saw a possible chance. To his right there was an open doorway to an adjacent hall and by the door a board carried a notice:

ART EXHIBITION

Entry to the Fair had been free, providing the rather persuasive lady with the raffle was discounted, but for the Art Exhibition a small fee was requested. The money was being collected by a youngish looking man seated at a table just inside this side hall.

Not quite perfect, thought Mike. Height OK, weight perhaps a little on the low side, hair shorter but not a problem, wrong eye colour but you can't expect everything. All things considered though, pretty good.

Ignoring all the stalls and booths in the main hall he

made his way across with the few strides needed to reach the exhibition's guardian.

'Sorry. Can you change this?'

Mike presented the ticket seller with a high denomination note obtained from the wallet in Oakend.

The man paused, counted the cash in the cash box and shook his head. This early in the day it didn't amount to much. He lifted the cash tray out and counted the notes in the well below. Still not enough. Reaching for his jacket, stowed on the back of his chair, he took out a wallet but its contents still failed to reach the total needed for the necessary change. He put the wallet back and gave Mike a quick smile.

'Wait a moment, please. One of the stallholders will have change. I'll try the Prize Draw – they usually win the competition for the most money raised.'

The custodian of the art exhibition pushed back his chair, moved around the table and pushed through the throng in the main hall. Mike looked around, gave it five seconds and then dived into the abandoned jacket, took out the wallet, found what he was looking for and returned the wallet to the interior jacket pocket.

When the man returned he was concerned to find that the potential patron for the village Arts Society display had disappeared. The stranger wasn't in the exhibition hall. He checked the cash box and found both coin and notes just as he had left them. He waited for thirty minutes, issued tickets to a handful of interested parishioners all of whom he knew by name then decided what he would do with the large amount of change he had previously placed in an envelope now sitting next to the cash box.

'Far too much to issue tickets for. It'll have to be a donation,' he said to himself.

He placed part of the cash in the box, dispensed the relevant number of tickets then screwed them up and put them in his jacket pocket. The remaining cash he exchanged for notes, of which he now had enough, put the notes in the envelope and wrote DONATION on the outside. Satisfied, he placed the envelope below the cash tray and looked up to welcome the next patron, greeted him by name and accepted from him the correct fee for entry. Soon after that when his relief appeared, he stood, collected his jacket and following a brief conversation he made his way to the café area at the end of the main hall.

At about the same time that the Arts Society treasurer was taking his wallet out from his jacket to pay for a mug of coffee and a bun Mike was seated towards the back of the rear section of the Midland Travel service 24 articulated bus. He had purchased a low denomination travel card from the shop near the bus stop, crossed the road to the southbound stop outside the pub and boarded the on-time 1012 bus to Banbury. In his jacket pocket was a National Identity Card for a gentleman fairly similar in appearance to himself. The card had been issued in the name of Mr Mark Steven Hills. Mike reckoned that he would need to make use of it at least once in the next couple of hours.

Passengers were picked up from outside isolated houses and lane-end bus stops but, shunning side turnings the bus remained resolutely headed southwards along the main road. After about fifteen minutes the route passed over a motorway and the previously rural landscape changed dramatically. To his left Mike noted an area of factories and warehouses but on the right a housing estate was packed in almost up to the motorway, the edge of its cutting seemingly acting as a barrier that contained the outward spread of the town's growth. Then, on reaching a roundabout his bus turned into a small bus station adjacent to a large, modern retail centre with an extensive car park. The indicator panel towards the front of this section of the bus showed the name of this stop just as it had for every other stop on the route. On this occasion, however, in addition to the label that read:

Hardwick Park Retail Centre, there was a spoken message:

'Next stop Banbury Interchange. This bus travels non-stop to Banbury Interchange. Passengers for intermediate stops please use Service 207 from Stand 3. Passengers for Oxford please use Service 49 from Stand 1.

About half the passengers left the bus for the retail centre or one of the connecting bus services. Mike had time to quickly assess that Hardwick Park did not have anything useful to offer him. He was not looking for large national chain stores or any of the restaurants or fast-food outlets that advertised their presence by large, colourful signage universally accompanied by a well-known logo. Mike would be better served in the town centre.

Shoppers with bags bearing the same well known names soon filled many of the seats so recently vacated and two minutes after its arrival the bus pulled away and manoeuvring carefully picked up a dedicated bus lane that continued south, swung to its left to cross the river then turned right to run parallel to the rail line before easing into the correct bay at the Interchange. Many of the passengers leaving the bus headed straight for the exit labelled 'Town Centre'. A few followed the arrow and logo embellished sign labelled 'Rail Station' but Mike's agenda led him towards the back streets to the south and the smaller businesses, unable to afford the cost of setting up in the town centre, that resided there. A trawl along streets dotted with small cafes, general stores, a wedding dress shop, a stationers and the like brought him after about six minutes walking to an old-fashioned, one-man owned and operated barbers shop. He went in.

The barber – named Bob if the sign outside were to be believed – gave him a friendly nod and continued to work on his only other customer. Mike took one of the surprisingly comfortable chairs that lined one wall and looked to see if Bob provided any newspapers or magazines. He did. But above the magazine rack was an item that immediately attracted his attention. It was a telephone but more to the point it included a directory. Mike stood, looked over to Bob, indicated the telephone with a nod of the head and an enquiring look and received an affirmative nod in reply. His interest was in the directory rather than the phone. The list of instructions for the directory told him to press the 'ON' symbol. He did. Next step was to select an initial letter for a Family Name. Mike pressed 'H' on the keypad and was presented with a list headed by Haagan. Step three was to use an arrow to scroll down to reach the name he required. He did. And there it was; the entry for which he was searching.

Hills, M.S. 7 Glebe Court, Mollington.

In the absence of any other similar entries he assumed that this was the Mr Mark Steven Hills whose identity he now hoped to assume. The entry was completed with a telephone number.

Mike highlighted the entry (Step 4) and pressed 'PRINT' (Step 5) to obtain a small printed ticket that he put in his pocket before picking up the Daily Register and returning to his seat. About ten minutes later, by which time the waiting clientele had increased to three, Mike was welcomed over by Bob and his hair, rather longer and more unkempt that he usually liked to keep it, was tamed and trimmed. Bob worked to Mike's frequent and rather exacting instructions and had little time to ask what Sir was doing this weekend or was Sir new to the area. But Bob was rewarded with an unusually large tip that led him to wish Sir a very good day with the hope that he would see Sir again soon. Mike knew that he would not.

Standing outside the barber's Mike worked out his position in relation to the town centre then moved off left, turned right and soon reached his new goal. As he walked he was looking out for two particular stores and it wasn't long before he found one of them. He turned and crossed the pedestrianised area towards it whilst dodging around busy Christmas shoppers focused on their own next objective and groups of people standing and talking animatedly before breaking up and, with season's greetings filling the air, going their various ways. As he walked he repeated to himself the information he had gained about Mr Mark Steven Hills. At that moment Mr Hills was back at his desk selling entry to the Art Exhibition to an elderly lady whom he had never seen before but who passed over the exact money and had no intention of borrowing his ID Card.

Everyone knew *McAndrew's* the health and beauty store. Mike had often used the Framlingham branch. He knew of two in Ipswich, had used their airport shops and, if he had the time to think could probably have come up with a dozen or more High Streets up and down the land where he had seen their well-known green and purple sign. Reaching the entrance he walked in, hesitated, looked around and then walked past the perfumes and the opticians and headed for the tattoo parlour at the rear. Taking a seat, he joined a queue of three others waiting their turn. After a few seconds a receptionist handed him a catalogue and a disc numbered 37 indicating his position among those waiting. At that moment the indicators over two doors to his left proclaimed that numbers 32 and 33 were being attended to. He opened the catalogue. There were two pockets inside the front cover. The first held order forms so Mike extracted one for his own use. The second held sheets of paper, blank except for a fine blue-grey grid. They were provided for clients who wished to draw out a design of their own but Mike ignored them as he already knew exactly what he required – no explanatory sketches were needed. The first few pages illustrated mermaids, dragons, super-heroes and the like followed by birds and flowers and then a great variety of Celtic, African and Polynesian influenced designs. At the foot of each page there was one of three straplines, repeated in sequence throughout the catalogue:

· All clients need to show an ID Card.
· Clients aged 16 and 17 need their order to be endorsed by a parent or guardian.
· Clients aged 8 to 15 are limited to Transfer Tattoos only and must be accompanied by a parent or guardian.

Continuing through the pages Mike passed over lovehearts and cherubs, football club logos, name banners for popular music groups or artists, lightly clothed ladies, naked ladies, hunky men and much more before finding, near the back, a list of male and female forenames and another list of type styles. He noted a number code from the first list and a letter code from the second and using the pen provided filled in his order form.

'Next, please. Number 37.'

Mike walked over to the receptionist's desk.

'ID Card please.'

Mike handed over his 'borrowed' card.

'Thank you, Mr Hills.' She said, smiling professionally. 'Your address, please.'

Mike quoted this detail gained during his visit to the barbers. The village of Mollington included in the address had been one he had noted during his bus journey earlier. Another smile, a brief discussion as to the size, position and colour of the tattoo and with the details added to Mike's order form they came to the question of payment.

'Cash, card or transfer?'

'Cash, please.' Mike handed over the correct fee.

'Would you prefer a man or a woman practitioner?'

'Either. Whoever is free first, thank you.'

'Fine,' she said with another matching smile. 'The monitor will indicate the relevant practice studio. Please take a seat and enter when your number is displayed.'

A little over an hour after entering McAndrew's Mike was back mingling with the lunchtime Saturday shopper on the street outside.

Now for his last task. Some decent clothing. Mike

decided he had been rather ragged, often dirty and sometimes cold for far too long. He sat on a seat tucked into the angle between two buildings and counted the remaining money from his pocket then sat back to enjoy the crowds and the Christmas evergreen decorations and, above the street, the pageant of as yet unlit festive lights strung between the buildings. He felt remarkably calm. It wasn't quite happiness but more an acceptance of his situation and a belief in the plan he was working to complete.

Last task then. Carrying in his mind the amount he had to spend Mike walked up one side of the shopping street, wandered through a shopping mall and then returned to the main street where he selected a clothing outfitters not previously known to him. It was not part of a national chain nor a high quality, highly priced men's outfitters but rather a middle of the road outlet where the prices, rather higher than those of a national supplier were offset by superior service. 'Greendales' was just what he was looking for.

In height and weight and stature Mike was mister average. Unlike brother Frank, who appeared to be a throwback to some giant generation of ancestors, Mike had always been able to walk into a store and find something that would fit. As with clothes it was the same with shoes. Mr Mark Hills would seem to have the same advantage. The two assistants on duty – trade had slackened a little with the onset of lunchtime – greeted him discreetly but, whilst standing ready to help, did not force their attention on him as he browsed and eventually selected his new wardrobe. A medium weight dark-grey suit, a smart pair of leisure shoes – again grey but of a rather lighter shade, a plain white T-shirt, some underpants and a lilac shirt were rounded off with a pair of maroon socks.

'Fitting room, Sir?'

The question was complemented by a manual indication. Mike replied with a smile and a nod of the head. He tried everything on, changed the shirt size when he discovered that the suspected loss of weight sustained during his journey was in fact a figment of his imagination, and added a black belt to the pile of goods he presented for payment. If the assistant was surprised that cash was offered for an amount universally settled by card, he did not show it.

'Would you like to add your name to our mailing list, Sir?'

There had been no request for a view of his ID Card but this was a subtle probing for information non-the-less. Mike declined, explaining that he was a visitor to the town and didn't expect to remain long in the area. To the assistant's slightly expressed bemusement Mike returned to the fitting room and a few minutes later emerged dressed in his new outfit, the old clothes stashed in the store bags provided with the purchased items. Only his trusty jacket remained from his previous attire.

'Can you dispose of these, please?' Mike placed the bags containing his old clothes on the counter.

By the time the assistant had thought to suggest that he use the recycling bin in a nearby car park Mike had turned, exited and disappeared into the crowds outside.

Mike felt ready for a new life now. ID Card, smart haircut á la Mark Steven Hills, nice clothes and, hidden away, a tattoo. But just one thing more. Most importantly he wanted to start his new life feeling comfortable and satisfied after a good meal. Despite the sun the early afternoon December temperature was quite cool – something like 7 or 8 degrees he guessed; hardly sitting out weather! Even so there were a couple of people seated at a table in a sunny spot outside a coffee shop and, after ordering food he took a large mug of coffee outside to an adjacent table to await the rest of his order. Two freshly made prawn salad sandwiches and a large chocolate gâteau arrived some five minutes later. The sheltered position, the direct sunlight from the cloudless, windless sky and the hot coffee kept him just about comfortable. Mike relaxed, cherishing a few minutes sitting quietly now that his plan was almost complete. He gave the waitress a handsome tip when she came to clear his table. Pleased but bemused she smiled and wished him a pleasant weekend.

He was refreshed and ready.

It was time to go.

Mike walked over to an advertising cube – a large square box raised to eyeline height on a pedestal base. Three sides were given over to the advertisements, the fourth presenting an interactive town centre plan. He scanned the location list beside the map and tapped the legend indicating Police Station. An illuminated spot shone on the map, brightened, enlarged and retreated to its original size. Another touch point, this time labelled 'Route from here', gave him the information he needed. He had no need to touch the 'Refresh' button but immediately turned, walked past *McAndrew's*, turned into a side road and saw his destination ahead.

Oxfordshire had provided its police force in Banbury

with a rather grand older style building, the entrance gained by walking up a shallow flight of wide steps. The outer door gave way to a lobby occupied by an armed constable who appraised the visitor but saw no reason to question his entry. The inner door opened automatically so Mike walked in, passed through a body scanner and continued directly past a seated waiting couple to the desk opposite where a sergeant, previously intent on studying a CCTV monitor, turned his chair and looked towards him.

'Yes, sir?'

'I've got an ID Card that I found.'

He passed Mr Hills card through a slot below the desk screen. The sergeant studied it carefully.

'Thank you, sir. I'll just log the details if you care to wait.'

The policeman brought up a form on his desk monitor and swiped the card so that its image appeared in a rectangular box on the screen.

'Where was it found, sir?'

'On the paved area outside *McAndrew's*,' he lied.

'And your name and address, please sir.'

'Joshua Michael Cannon of Framlingham in Suffolk. I'm a member of the East Suffolk Association and I'm wanted for questioning about the death of Captain Alana Buckhurst, an army officer with the Mercian Regiment.'

Before Mike had finished his announcement the sergeant had touched his keypad and made the slightest of nods towards the armed officer in the lobby. A security gate moved across to cover the entrance and a grill descended in front of the desk. The couple who had been seated behind Mike were ushered out through a side door and for a few seconds there was silence.

Then, suddenly, action.

Doors opened to left and right of the lobby with two policemen entering through each. There were no firearms visible but Mike guessed that they were all armed. One officer from each side walked over ready to restrain him if necessary but the handcuffing and body search and the obligatory statement of their right to arrest him and his to remain silent were carried out without fuss. His captors must have made a further signal when those formalities were complete as a door behind the desk opened and the sergeant was joined by a tall grey-haired man in naval uniform.

It was well known that to conform with the "Martial Law" legislation the police were overseen by military personnel able to sanction emergency action. In 'quiet' areas such as rural Oxfordshire, these supervisors were often newly retired officers, some of high rank, who spent more time on the golf course or writing their memoirs than taking serious action. The naval officer (retired) at Banbury was probably overjoyed to have an emergency with which to deal. This incident's retelling, possibly with a little embellishment, would certainly be worth a few beers or possibly the odd dinner over the coming festive season. It wouldn't take much to raise a simple arrest to the level of a major incident.

After a brief conversation and the naval gentleman's signature on a form two of the officers escorted Mike away, photographed him and placed him in a cell. Provisionally he was charged with the theft of a National Identity Card. Mike declined the services of the duty solicitor, declined an offer of food but gratefully accepted a mug of tea.

When recording the arrest the sergeant noted that among other distinguishing features Mr Cannon had a tattoo. It was located on his left upper arm, was 6 centimetres long and consisted of a one word upper case legend in royal blue. It read 'CASSIE'.

CHAPTER SEVENTEEN
SENTENCE

The day after Mike's arrest was Sunday so it was not until the Monday, the seventh of December that he was taken to the court in Oxford. At this hearing he was remanded in custody on two charges:

- Theft of a National Identity Card at Farnborough in Oxfordshire on the 5th December 2201.
- Theft of a motor car at Oakend in Buckinghamshire on the 3rd December 2201.

As was usual in such cases he was remand so that other charges could be considered. At a further hearing two days later he was again brought to the court and charged with the murder of Captain Alana Buckhurst at Darsham in the East Suffolk Military Restricted Area on the 23rd of October, 2201. The two earlier charges were dropped and Mike was again remanded, this time to appear before a Martial Law Tribunal at the end of February.

Tuesday 23rd February 2202, Crown Court, Winchester

Mike stood in the dock with two policemen stationed behind him.

The tribunal members filed in from a side door and sat

behind a bench with e-pads, notepaper, pens and bottled water available to each. Opposite Mike, seated and facing him were, on the left, two uniformed gentlemen, one from the army and one from the air force. To the right were a lady and a gentleman in civilian clothes. The centre position was occupied by the chairwoman. She was a judge and was dressed accordingly. Her name displayed on a plaque in front of her pronounced her to be Lady Justice Farringdon. The court was completed by three officials seated in front of the bench, facing it, with their backs to Mike, plus two soldier, standing, one either side of the bench.

'The prisoner will remain standing throughout the proceedings,' announced the chairwoman. 'As Mr Cannon has proclaimed his guilt,' she continued, 'it only remains for me to outline the circumstances surrounding the crime and to determine the appropriate period of custody prescribed by the government's tariff. This court, Mr Cannon,' she explained, looking directly at Mike, 'has no jury and I alone decide the sentence after receiving advice from my four colleagues.'

There followed a brief account of the circumstances surrounding the death of Captain Buckhurst, read by a court official and a second statement, a deposition provided by Mike himself, read by a second official. Then there followed a discussion between the chairwoman and the other members of the tribunal. This took the form of Lady Farringdon asking each member in turn for their verdict on what sentence should be handed down. During this discussion it occurred to Mike that perhaps he was unlucky to have appeared before Justice Farringdon. She had reportedly rebuked an advocate in a case of unlawful killing along the lines of, *'Manslaughter, Mr Swiss? A dead man is a dead man; a killing is a killing. The cause of the killing is immaterial here, don't you think, sir?'*

The members of the bench sat back in their seats and the chairwoman gave a nod of her head towards the third court official who stood, turned and pronounced, 'All rise.' In fact only the other two officials and the two policemen behind Mike needed to follow this instruction.

'The tariff for murder is 28 years in prison. And this was undoubtedly murder,' stated chairwoman Farringdon. 'However this killing was inflicted in very unusual circumstances. Although Mr Cannon was carrying a weapon it was not a premeditated crime. I believe Mr Cannon was provoked, not directly by the deceased army captain but by the situation. I therefore sentence Mr Cannon to the lower tariff of 21 years. Case complete.'

Mike had been in court for just 14 minutes.

Wednesday 24th February, 2201

The media were not present at the tribunal sittings. Not at Winchester, nor in Swansea and not in York. True they would be given official transcripts but these were often not released until a day or two later or three if a weekend intervened. Providing no whispers were available from court officials or police officers the press had to rely on meagre information and a bit of constructive embellishment. The New Times account was therefore rather limited but used material from Mike's earlier appearances in Oxford. The Daily Register had no such problems. It was their stock in trade. Where there was limited information (and sometimes where there was none) they just invented their own copy under an eye-catching headline.

The Daily Register
Wednesday 24th February 2202
Britain's toughest judge goes SOFT

The front page headline set the tone for the article. It was based on a whisper from a court official. The register proclaimed that as the people's champion it was upholding the desire of every right-thinking citizen to expect criminals to be given the longest deterrent sentence available to the judge. Mike's name was not mentioned, neither were the salient points that resulted in his prosecution.

The New Times
Wednesday 24th February 2202
Former New Times Journalist Guilty

A more thoughtful approach marked the article headlined on page seven. Details of the sentence, their reporter explained, would be given when they had received the official tribunal transcript. The editor obviously considered the proposal to upgrade the A14 road to motorway standards between Ipswich and Cambridge and on to the A1(M) road to be a far more important front-page story.

PART THREE

FRIENDS & TRAITORS

CHAPTER EIGHTEEN
KASSIM

Saturday 27th March 2224, Fordham, Cambridgeshire

Mike awoke with two headaches. The first was clearly physical, characterised by a regular, pulsating pain in his forehead with related symptoms that included a dry, unpleasant taste in his mouth. This headache was no doubt the result of careless over-drinking the previous evening, Friday, at the party given by his publisher to celebrate the re-launch of his book. In marked contrast the second headache had no physical manifestations. Completely out of the blue just one thought was filling his mind and vying for dominance with his hangover. It hadn't occurred to him before but it had suddenly become quite clear. He had been betrayed. Why hadn't he seriously considered it before? Anna, Simon, Heron and the rest involved with that last ESA operation had all been betrayed. Back in Suffolk, over twenty-two years previously, when he had shot Captain Buckhurst, there must have been a leak of information to the army. How else could Buckhurst and her troops have ended up at the right place to intercept himself and Anna? And in any case he wouldn't have expected an army captain to be taking part if they had been intercepted by a routine patrol. The information he had mulled over for years, at first in prison and more recently as he wrote his book, had subconsciously reached a conclusion that was now firmly stuck in his mind.

Both headaches were rendered a little less potent by his need to visit the toilet, freshen his face and find a black coffee and a little food. Mike reached the kitchen via the bathroom, zapped the TV and with coffee made he stood warming his hands around the mug, looking out through the kitchen window southwards, across his small garden towards the flat farmland beyond. The television flickered soundlessly behind him, unwatched. Easter sunshine brightened the early sign of crops in the fields that were backed by a line of trees, remnant of an ancient linear windbreak. The sky extending above the flat Cambridgeshire landscape was almost cloudless and already bright. It was getting on for 1100 hours. Having moved into the house in Fordham village only the previous November Mike still found his new home area threw up previously unseen vistas with the changes brought about by variations in the weather and the season.

The Hunningham apartment had served him well but with money earned from on-line sales and the first print run of his book he had been able to afford this modest 200 year-old cottage in Fordham a few kilometres north of Newmarket. Hunningham had been fine whilst he was concentrating on writing the book but now he wished to be in contact with a greater range of people and places. And after eight months of freedom he no longer needed to report to the police each week. His search for a new home had been focused on the junction of the old M11 and A14 roads. Now, of course with the A14 upgraded and with motorways renamed Expressways whilst he had been in prison he must learn to call them E11 and E14. But whatever labels were applied it was that location he had homed in on. A trawl of villages around Cambridge brought nothing in his rather lowly price range but moving further out he had found just what he needed. The E14 road, just 5 kilometres from his new home was the artery that led conveniently westwards to his sister Gayle in Kettering and east to his homeland of Suffolk. He could easily visit old ESA friends, his father who still lived in Framlingham and brother Frank who, with partner Shelley, had remained in the old family home in Reydon.

Turning away from the window he became aware of the soundless TV picture and was surprised to catch a brief shot of himself in the preview to the upcoming news bulletin.

Mike zapped up the volume.

An economic report, weather related travel problems in northern France and the capture of an absconding criminal formed the main items that Saturday. Then there was a break to allow a review of the weekend's upcoming sport but the first of the minor news items that followed was a report on the re-launch of his book.

"This was the scene at the Wellington Hotel in London yesterday evening. Following the surge of interest in the Martial Law era promoted by recent television programmes marking the 20th anniversary of its end, a major work describing that period has been re-published. Midland

Publishing's Rupert Church brought together media representatives for the re-launch of Mike Cannon's book 'Outlaw'. Our arts correspondent Arvinda Lewisham spoke to Mr Church.

'How has a modestly successful book, published last November for the Christmas market suddenly become so much in demand?'

'I think the events recorded by this book have now been put in the historical context of our recent past. Many of us remember the events of twenty, twenty-four years ago and many of those born since the event are now old enough to take an interest. One critic said of the book: It reads like a novel but with the authority of someone for whom the events were totally real. *The book tells a good story and is a classic record of the times."*

Ms Lewisham signed off and a new topic took over the airwaves. Although he had been standing beside Rupert during the interview Mike had not been asked to comment. He turned down the sound and turned to make breakfast, one that was substantial enough for him not to have to bother with lunch.

It had been Rupert's idea to title the book "The Outlaw". During a meeting towards the end of September they had talked about marketing arrangements and discussed the title.

'Yes,' Rupert had said. 'Mike Cannon's Diary is OK as a working title. It is a diary of sorts I suppose. But people don't go for diaries of unknown people. You have to be a politician to make money out of a diary or possibly some high ranking army bod. But only First Ministers or disgraced ministers do really well out of their journals,

Mike. I'll publish it as "The Outlaw". Short, intriguing title, don't you think?'

So it was that on Thursday 6th November 2223 sales of *The Outlaw* by Mike Cannon first saw the public carrying copies away from bookstores or forwarding their details on line, expecting next day delivery or obtaining a downloaded e-copy with the advantage of a publication day discount. But however they were purchased each copy carried the same fly-leaf dedication:

"To my sister, Gayle Church (née Cannon) without whose help this book would not have been completed, let alone published".

Rupert Church had been a small town publisher when he had met and married Mike's sister Gayle. She had applied to Midland Publishing for employment as an administrative assistant. Fortunately Rupert was shrewd enough to follow up his wife's suggestion to take a look at her brother's manuscript. She had described it to Rupert as a money-spinner and when Rupert read the manuscript he had agreed. At first it was a rather modest though perhaps surprising success. This was in part due to Rupert's plan to catch the Christmas market and his clever pricing of the download version. For all his brother-in-law's know-it-all pomposity Mike had to agree that he had a good commercial head on his shoulders. From a small, one-room company located over a dry cleaners – a clichéd location as Rupert would later gladly point out – the sales of *The Outlaw* had allowed Midland Publishing's move to an industrial estate on the edge of town and the use of a light and airy four-roomed unit. A receptionist and a storeman were added to the staff and the approaches from aspiring authors had quadrupled. Things were ticking over nicely with *The Outlaw* still bringing in a useful but lower income when the unforeseen happened. National TV Channel Two aired its documentary on the 20th anniversary of the ending of 'Martial Law' and against some atmospheric shots of the Suffolk coast the programme had included a short interview with Mike and a couple of extracts from his book read by a well-known actor. Even Rupert couldn't have dreamed up such a fine piece of free advertising. Orders streamed in from home and abroad, a reprint had been put in hand and Gayle had taken on two further assistants. And now there was the film – probably.

'We're not quite there yet,' Rupert had confided in Mike, 'but a couple of the big boys are after the rights. Keep it under your hat for the moment, though.'

Rupert had always been high on drama. Under different circumstances Mike and Rupert would probably not have been friends but his brother-in-law had one major plus point in his favour; he made sister Gayle very happy.

A mole. It must have been a mole who betrayed their organisation. Mike couldn't imagine that anyone who truly believed in the work of ESA could do such a thing. It made sense that whoever had given information to the army must have been planted by them as a spy in the first place. Mike had banished his first headache by using a hot drink and some pills but this other problem was not going to be solved so readily. He pushed crockery and cutlery into a pile, cleared the kitchen table, turned off the TV and walked through the lounge and into his office. Computer on, *M C Diary* folder accessed, *ESA members* file opened and within a couple of minutes he had printed off a dozen copies of the ESA staff list correct for the time of the last reorganisation; the time when they had concentrated operations at Westhead House.

Mike could have copied the list into a new file and worked at it on the computer but that wouldn't have been the best way. A comfortable chair, a table to spread papers on and a beer or coffee close at hand were, in his experience, required to tackle a problem such as this one. On his way back to the kitchen he collected rough paper, pens and a road atlas which along with his lists he put on the table. Starting with a beer, he decided, was not a good idea; it would be better to use it as a reward once he had made some progress or at least decided how he was going to go about this investigation. He picked up the list of ESA members.

ESA Members/Reorganisation/June 2201

Somewhere in the list was the name of the person ultimately responsible for Buckhurst's death and his 21 year incarceration. Mike read slowly through the list. Kassim, Michael Warren, Heron, Simon, Cassie, the Court twins, Anna, etc, etc. Mike really hadn't a clue. His recently formed resolution went out of the window and he fetched a beer, took a couple of sips and read the list again. He still had no real idea how to go about recognising this mole or traitor. Perhaps he was wrong about the whole thing.

But the more he thought about it the more he remained convinced that ESA had been betrayed.

Mike got up and, hands in pockets, walked through the lounge, stopped, stared through the window and then returned to the kitchen, looked out at the opposite aspect then returned to the table. He needed to be methodical. He picked up one copy of the list and put it down again, picked up a pen and held it, poised over the top name.

Kassim Wood-West. Cross or tick?

No doubt! It couldn't have been Kassim. Mike put a cross beside his name. Kassim had been removed from the list of potential traitors. Apart from Mike's own name there were twenty-four more names after Kassim. He continued down. Michael Warren – cross, Simon Upton – cross, Heron – cross and so on. When he had finished only one name had been given a tick. He had never liked Vandra Mornington and as far as he could tell she had never liked him. She had once called him a *media spy* and she was one of the more outspoken critics of Kassim's last reorganisation. Perhaps she felt aggrieved that her views had not been taken into consideration and that she had been shunted out to do bus duties in Leiston rather than being at the centre of things at Westhead. But he was just guessing; just trying to justify his decision to implicate the one member of ESA whom he hadn't really got along with at all. As far as he could see all the others were totally patriotic to the cause. Tick and cross, he decided, wasn't analytical enough.

Mike took his walkabout again but this time after about five or six minutes he had a handle on a process that could at least take the investigation forward. He took another sip of beer.

'Thinking about motives at this stage doesn't help,' he said out load to himself, 'so what angle should I take?'

He paced further on and then stopped.

'Knowledge. Who knew about the operation?' And of those who knew who had the opportunity to inform the army? Yes! That's the way forward. Knowledge and opportunity.'

Back at the table he screwed up the first marked-up copy of the list and took a second one from the pile. He poised his pen again over the top name. Kassim. Then beside the names he drew two columns and headed them with the two factors he had identified. Repositioning his pen over Kassim's name he thought briefly and placed a tick in each column. Yes, Kassim would surely have known what Heron was planning and he almost certainly could have been able to contact the authorities. Before the crackdown he had been constantly in touch with the army, the police and the borderguard. Mike felt sick at the thought that he could implicate Kassim but consoled himself with the thought that there would be others with two ticks by the time he had finished and that didn't mean they would all have been traitors.

Once again it was one down, twenty-four to go. The list was arranged in groups, each section relating to one of the ESA operating units. He moved on to his own unit, the one based in Hut 2. So Carlos was next. Carlos would have known that Mike was possibly on an operation since his name would have been missing from the duty rota but he doubted that Heron would have given him details as to where he and Anna would be at any given time. Heron always worked strictly on a 'need to know' principle and Carlos didn't need to know. But he would have had opportunity. Carlos was always in and out, difficult to pin down but opportunity without knowledge didn't really add up to betrayal. Mike gave him a cross and a question mark and then decided to remove him from the list completely. Anna was next. She obviously had the knowledge but Mike had been with her for most of the day so there had been very little opportunity to pass on any information. Mike ticked her for knowledge, hesitated then remembered that there had been a space of about twenty minutes between the briefing and the operation, time enough to contact the army with details of their route. He placed another tick in the second column. Mike hesitated before continuing. He found the exercise quite distasteful but in the absence of any other method he decided he must carry on.

The task itself was quite straightforward. He was dealing with facts. But there was one major problem when it came to applying the criteria objectively to Cassie. She hadn't been on duty that day and hadn't been in the Starcab or even, as far as he knew, at Westhead. Of course Cassie knew that he was on an operation that day but he couldn't say for certain that she was completely unaware of the task that Heron had given him. She could have had all the opportunity in the world but if she didn't know what he and Anna were up to that would have been irrelevant. Mike just didn't want to include her but after some minutes thought and a break to make a coffee he put a question mark in the first column and a tick in the second. When the list was complete nine names had been marked with at least one positive tick. Two of those were not directly connected with Heron's operations and he had no reason to think that this couple had knowledge of that fateful patrol. He had included them for different reasons. Vandra was still in his reckoning just because she seemed to have a reason to dislike him. Beth Stamford, working from the Saxmundham office had always been on the fringe of ESA operations but she had been Kassim's link with the authorities until the reorganisation and had possibly kept up communications with the army after that. It was possible that she had been working undercover for the army. Mike wondered if his thoughts were flying off wildly on a tangent away from reality but for the moment he had to entertain any possibility however far fetched.

He added a third column, headed it 'Motive' and added ticks for Vandra and Beth.

Name	Knowledge	Opportunity	Motive
Kassim Wood-West	√	√	–
Anna Chalk	√	√	–
Heron	√	√	–
Cassandra Vale	?	√	–
Reuben Court	√	√	–
Frazer Oak	√	√	–
Beth Stamford	?	√	√
Vandra Mornington	?	√	√
Simon Upton	√	√	–

For the first time in his life Mike felt that he understood the meaning of the word *anguish*. Even including those names on the list made him feel disloyal. Friends such as Kassim, Heron and Simon had shown nothing but support for the ESA cause and nothing but friendship towards him. Mike picked up a pen and struck off those three names. His list now consisted of six names, two of them with some sort of motive. It had been a difficult task but perhaps sifting through just this abbreviated list would prove to be even harder; he wasn't even sure how or where to start. However he knew of one person who could quite possibly help him to step out along the course he had chosen to follow and eventually uncover the truth about the events that occurred all that time ago.

Tuesday 30th March 2224

Mike tugged the zip on his jacket up along its full run and pulled the collar up around his neck. Leaning against the rail, gazing into a grey overcast sky that was punctuated by spits of rain being hurried along in the wind, his mind was temporarily free of the questions that had been chasing around inside his head for the last couple of days. He had boarded the Isle of Wight ferry at Lymington and was headed for Yarmouth. It was a journey that had now becoming routine. He had first visited Kassim in prison on the island a little under a year ago. At the time he needed to gain the former ESA leader's approved for his book project. He needn't have worried: Kassim was all for him telling their story.

Since then he had made four further visits and this

was the fifth, the last three more as a supportive friend. One time he had tried the alternative ferry link from Portsmouth to Fishbourne on the other side of the island but had immediately reverted to the Yarmouth route for his next visit. Its main attraction was a direct bus service to the prison gate. He could, of course, have taken his car across on the ferry but he couldn't be bothered with the fuss of waiting to disembark behind lines of other vehicles and then having to find, and pay for, parking at his destination.

'Nice to see you again, sir!'

Had he become a commuter? A smile and a cheery comment from the ferry company lady as he left the vessel added to his relaxed feeling as did the sight of the waiting VectisBus service 8A – Cowes via Newport – in the little bus station just beyond the port gate. Mike made an effort to maintain the mood but try as he might the purpose of his visit eventually took over his thoughts until by the time his transport had taken its allotted two minutes stopover at Newport's bus interchange he was actively planning how to conduct his visit.

Kassim had been sent to Albany prison to serve his sentence. Albany was one half of the island's prison, the establishment now given over to long-serving prisoners from the martial law era. Parkhurst was the other unit and was reserved for those serving 28 years for killing a member of the security forces – a police officer or someone from the armed services or a borderguard. Compared with Parkhurst, Albany was one step down in security and at least one grade up in prisoner facilities. For his first visit

Mike had followed other, experienced visitors through security and into the waiting room. Unsurprisingly the arrangements were not dissimilar to those shown in film dramas and those he himself had witnessed whilst in Burton Green. At the given time the visitors filed into an adjacent room and Mike was directed to a group of four chairs placed around table 7 – the same number as marked in his visitor's pass. Within a minute the low hum of conversation had erupted into a clamour of greeting as the prisoners filed in and peeled off to the table assigned to them. Kassim had extended a hand in formal greeting before he had sat down and they had spent the next half hour in catching up on the previous twenty-two years.

Mike had been interested to know whether Kassim had other visitors from the ESA days. 'Not many,' had been his reply. Before the 'Amnesty' a couple of relatives – cousins from Yorkshire – had been along but it was a long journey and they now only came once a year, on or near his birthday. Simon Upton had been along several times and Heron had arrived out of the blue some ten years or so after he first arrived but he told her that whilst she was on the police wanted list she should stay away. Kassim didn't know how she had been able to obtain papers for this visit and had avoided being referred to the authorities. After the amnesty she had been about half a dozen times and even Carlos had turned up once. Mike had asked if Kassim had an address or any form of contact for Heron and Carlos but he had replied that he hadn't asked and he hadn't been told. But there were weeks and sometimes months when no-one came to see him.

The second visit had been along similar lines. The

same routine applied but there had been a completely different conversation. Mike had planned to ask for Kassim's approval for his book at the time of his first visit to Albany but somehow the time had been taken up with other matters. In retrospect he was pleased; the casual friendly atmosphere of that visit had set up a situation where Mike could confidently raise the matter of his book at the second. Kassim had enthusiastically and without hesitation endorsed his work. But on his third trip to the island's prison a new visiting pattern had been established that had since become the set routine. Same entrance, same security regime but after examining his pass the officer had directed him to a small side room. There were two other visitors there when he arrived and three further people arrived soon after.

'Mr Michael Cannon, please.'

On that occasion he had been the last of the small group to be called up to speak with the officer seated behind a simple desk. He had handed over his pass. The officer had looked at it, looked up at Mike, placed it on his desk, opened a drawer and taken out a small, clear plastic folder. From this folder he removed a new green coloured card apparently identical in all other respects to the old blue one lying in front of him. He compared the two cards, placed the old one in the folder and put it back in the drawer.

'Welcome to the green club, Mr Cannon. You're a privileged man,' he said, handing the new pass to Mike, his face failing to show any emotion that even slightly matched the words of his greeting. Procedure complete the warder stood and led the cohort out of the room, down a corridor, through a door, along a short path sheltered by a canopy and into a building that appeared to be of more recent construction than the main building they had just left.

'Mr Euston's visitor. Room 5.'

A lady officer called for, then escorted the visitor away, returning to repeat the process for each of the other visitors in turn.

'Mr Wood's visitor. Room 2.'

Mike noted the use of the abbreviated form of Kassim's name and assumed that the fuller version had never been officially registered or entered on a National Identity Card. He followed the officer along to Kassim's accommodation. As he stepped into the room the door clanged shut behind him and he involuntarily half-turned to glance at it.

'No need to be jumpy, Mike!' Kassim had said, smiling. 'You can leave any time you like – it's never locked. They've checked you out during previous visits and now you're a trusted man. I could walk out of here if I wished but there's no point really – I wouldn't get very far.'

For this visit to Room 2 he had waited in the side room as usual but today he was one of only three visitors sitting there. He spoke briefly to a man he hadn't seen before and nodded in greeting to the third visitor, Mrs Euston, the lady who had been there every time he had been to see Kassim.

'Regular as clockwork, she is,' Kassim had told him during a previous visit. 'Comes from somewhere in Scotland; every week for years. She's got two teenage sons who sometimes come with her. We were first given green card privileges about seventeen years ago so you can work out what privileges Karyn Euston had enjoyed on her visits!'

Formal handshakes long since dispensed with Kassim simply said, 'Hi!' and directed Mike to the guest chair with a movement of his hand.

'Tea or coffee?'

Kassim moved across to the little alcove where basic hot drink making equipment was provided and set about making two teas.

'So what makes you a privileged inmate?' asked Mike.

'They think I'm reliable, I suppose. For many years I've kept all their rules without arguing. But it's more the visitor's character that counts. You've been rehabilitated so they no longer think of you as an ex-con,' answered Kassim.

Mike thought that Kassim's room was not dissimilar to student accommodation he had seen in universities. Around from the door, against the next wall there was a bed with storage draws beneath. Then on moving his gaze further around he noticed a desk supported by a three draw pedestal, the desk itself topped with a basic media point and a monitor. The fourth wall, opposite the bed, contained two open-fronted alcoves – the one from which Kassim now brought out the refreshments and the second furnished in a rather cramped, utilitarian manner with a washbasin, a shower and a toilet. His visual tour ended at an open-fronted wardrobe occupying the space next to the door. Certainly it was rather better appointed than any prison cell he had occupied including the final quarters he had enjoyed along with the fairly relaxed regime at Burton Green.

Kassim placed one mug on the desk near Mike and the other beside it whilst he pulled out the desk chair and angled it to face his visitor before sitting down.

'So author and now TV star. I wouldn't be surprised to see you in films next.'

Mike smiled.

'Maybe,' he replied, 'but before that happens I may take up another profession. I reckon I need to become a detective.'

As expected there was no immediate reaction from Kassim. It was his habit to wait for further detail before committing himself to a comment or a reply or even a changed facial expression; he had always been very careful with words. Mike opened the folder he had placed on his knees and took out the prepared list of suspects. He handed it over. Kassim reached for and put on the reading glasses he now used, sat back and read the list. When he put the list down he looked directly at Mike for a few seconds then closed his eyes whilst thinking before posing a question.

'Why are you so sure you were betrayed?'

It wasn't that Kassim doubted Mike's conclusion. Kassim knew that being asked to endorse the names on the list required him to be certain that he understood the basis for their selection. He had spent barely a minute checking the names but he knew Mike must have lived with the problem day and night for some time now.

'The army operation was too neat. It was an ambush, not a random piece of good luck by a regular patrol. It was too high profile. Buckhurst wouldn't have led a routine operation like that. There was a troop carrier parked there.

For a routine roadblock it was seriously overmanned.'

Kassim nodded.

'OK. I see how you have constructed the list and I assume you would like me to check through it. First, though, I'd like to know how you are going to work with the list when it's finalized. Who are you going to check out first?'

'I haven't got past compiling the list yet.'

'Then I think we should give it our attention. You don't want to come to a sudden halt as soon as you've finished compiling your list of suspects; you'll want to get straight on with the job. How about working out who the most likely candidate could be?'

'If I knew that I wouldn't need the list in the first place. It would probably be easier to eliminate the least likely candidates first.'

'That does seem the best way to go about it.'

'Working through the list is all very good in theory but take the inclusion of Vandra for example. Its quite likely she didn't even know what Heron was up to – I've only put her there out of spite – but so far I don't even know where she is and no one I've spoken to has much of an idea of what happened to her when ESA broke up.'

'So, do you have an alternative?'

'If as you suggest I need to get going on the investigation so that it doesn't stall then I'll need to talk to people who knew most of those on my list fairly well back in ESA days. And hopefully also someone who knows of their whereabouts since then. I reckon Simon, still in Westleton and Claire Bois, who last time I heard was still in Chillesford are my best bets.'

'Good. I think we can see where this is going now. I'd better check the list again.'

He picked up the paper and checked through the candidates one more time. For a while Kassim lifted his eyes as though thinking before taking one more glance at the list and then handing it back to Mike. He removed his glasses.

'The list seems sound and with the possible exception of Vandra based on good reasoning. But you compiled it with your ESA hat on. It's nearly a quarter of a century since you first came to visit us at ESA. For the last year since leaving prison you have been engrossed in the ESA years but just for a minute forget your membership of our group and go back to that first visit. Put your journalist hat on. Now, would your list be the same?'

Mike knew that it would not. Should he deny his affection for his former colleagues and look at the problem objectively he knew he would have to reinstate Kassim, Heron, Simon and possibly others who met the criteria he had selected. But it would be difficult to talk to Simon as a suspect rather than a witness. There was no need for him to answer Kassim. He just nodded a couple of times and gave a wry smile.

'It's not an easy task but I can certainly talk for myself. Put me on the list,' directed Kassim, 'and leave me there until you have good reason to cross me off. I certainly had knowledge of the operation – Heron had given me details the previous evening. And although few others knew of it I still had some contact with the Bentwater's people right up until the end. I rarely used my contacts but after you had gone it certainly helped to keep ESA members relatively safe. Perhaps more than anyone else on your list I had every opportunity to direct the army towards your location.'

Returning to the mainland on the ferry that evening Mike found a sheltered, quiet spot away from other passengers and reinstated Kassim, Heron and Simon onto his list. He toyed with the idea of removing Vandra's entry but couldn't decide one way or the other so her name remained. And then there was Beth Stamford. Kassim hadn't mentioned her although she had been part of his HQ staff at Saxmundham for quite some time. This seemed a little odd. Whilst he sat there, considering her inclusion, Mike absent-mindedly emphasised the tick against her name in the motive column, repeatedly drawing over the symbol several times.

None down, nine to go. But at least he now knew where he was going.

CHAPTER NINETEEN
SIMON & MARISSA

Thursday 1st April 2224, Westleton.

It was April Fool's Day and apparently no-one had thought to tell the weather that summer was officially some way off yet. Simon had resisted the urge to uncover and clean up the garden furniture at the start of the week when March's cool windy weather had given way to blue skies and temperatures in the mid teens. But just four days later with a centre of high pressure firmly anchored over the near continent and the thermometer rising steadily he had been unable to put the chore off any longer. Now at 1100 hours and with the temperature into the low twenty degrees Simon, Marissa and their guest Mike were seated around the newly cleaned circular wooden table, basking in the welcome sunshine.

'More coffee?' asked Marissa.

'No, that's fine, thanks,' replied Mike.

'I assume you've signed the petition,' said Simon.

'What petition?' asked Mike, feigning ignorance.

'For Kassim's release, idiot.'

'No. Not yet. I will, of course, but as you can guess I've been rather busy recently.'

'No time like the present.' Simon got up and went into the house, returning a short while later with a notepad that he placed on the table in front of Mike.

'Just search for *jaffa.legal.gb/kassimwoodwest.*

Mike shuffled his easy chair forward so that he sat comfortably in front of the computer and entered the address. Page one gave him a brief story about Kassim – his life, his work with ESA and his prison history. There followed the statement with which signatories were being asked to agree. At the foot of the page there was a link to the petition. Mike brought that page up and scrolled down the list of names as a counter, top right, gave a running total but at such a speed that it just presented a blur until it stopped at the next empty space. The total stood at 17,215. Mike tapped the blank entry space and a palette appeared asking him for his name, address and National ID number. When completed the palette disappeared and his name filled the next space on the petition and the counter clicked over to 17,216. A new window flashed up thanking him for his interest but warning him that if any entered details were found to be incorrect the entry would be deleted. Mike was temporarily tempted to enter Father Christmas, Lapland or the name of some well-known children's cartoon character but a sense of seriousness brought his mind back from the brink of frivolity. As he focused back on the petition he noted the counter clicking over to 17,218. Two further names had been added to the list.

'OK. So we think that Kassim has served quite long enough and should be released immediately but what do these Jaffa people have to do with it?'

'J.A.F.F.A.,' said Marissa, spelling out the initials.

It stands for '*Justice and freedom for all.*' Our solicitor dealing with the appeal belongs to the organisation. They are a charity and they set up petitions for free. If the call for Kassim's release does go to appeal they will support us and provide legal aid.'

'It was JAFFA,' added Simon, 'that fought for and won your remission as part of the general amnesty for Martial Law offenders. Unfortunately the Justice Department baulked at reducing the twenty-eight year sentences. I suppose they had to make some sort of stand regarding the leaders and the killers and their compromise was, '*We're showing compassion but we're no pushover.*' Now there will be no general cut in the twenty-eight year sentences but the appeal system may still consider special cases,'

'So you reckon Kassim's a special case?'

'Absolutely! Our solicitor and another from JAFFA are convinced that their clients are less culpable than the others in Albany. In fact if their crimes were graded Kassim and one other prisoner, Carole Debden, would be at the foot of the list compared with, say, Cameron Euston. Mr Euston ran the Solway Brigade. He didn't kill anyone but three of his cohort are also serving twenty-eight years but over in Parkhurst – one killed a boarderguard, the other two ambushed an army patrol and the ensuing gunfight ended with three dead soldiers. His brigade was responsible for damaging army vehicles and stealing military equipment. When the tariff was drawn up for sentencing dissidents it was very prescriptive and didn't allow much room for varying the longer sentences. If you led an illegal brigade or similar organisation you got twenty-eight years and that was that.'

'I've met Euston's wife Karyn in Albany but I don't know anything about this Carole Debden.'

'Apparently she organised and led a charity group providing services in some part of Dorset. It was organised something like ours; it had similar aims. But they had to contend with a local armed gang who harboured rather more political aims so Carole Debden's group armed themselves in self defence. As far as we can tell they never fired a shot in anger.'

Marissa had collected the coffee cups and slipped back inside the house as they were talking. She returned to the door and called out, 'Lunch almost ready, Si. I think we'll need the shade for the table; it's already hot.'

Simon got up, an audible but unintelligible comment mumbled as he walked off towards the garden shed in search of the called for sun umbrella. Coming out carrying a fitted cover for the table Marissa asked Mike to help by fetching plates and cutlery from the kitchen. They were, she told him, piled on a tray on the work-surface by the oven. No sooner had he arrived there and picked up the tray than Marissa was back.

'A word please, Mike,' she said taking the tray from him and placing it back on the surface. 'When you phoned and asked if you could come over you suggested Friday but I asked you to bring the visit forward to today. Remember?'

'Yes.'

'Well, Friday wasn't good because Simon has a hospital clinic appointment.'

Mike took a step back and leant against the units. Questions about Simon's health immediately flooded into his head but he let her continue.

'It all started five or six weeks ago when Si came back from Saxmundham; he'd been to the gym as per usual on a Tuesday evening. He grumbled that he hadn't felt like reaching all the usual levels within his regular routine. He thought he must have picked up a cold or something and it would all be OK in a couple of days. Well there was no cold, no sore throat, no cough, nothing like that. He seemed his usual cheery self but as weeks went by he found he could do less and less at the gym, less walking out with the dog. So he went to see Doctor South.'

Mike remembered Doc South. He was surprised that he was still practicing, even that he was still alive.

'Anyway, Doc sent him to Ipswich for tests. The results were inconclusive but showed some abnormalities. Tomorrow he goes back for a scan and some more tests.'

'I hadn't noticed anything. I had no idea.'

'On the face of it he's fine. Most of the time he's his usual active, jolly self around the place but when he comes back from rooting around in the shed he'll be short of breath.'

'I reckon I'd be lacking energy and humour after trying to find anything in that shed of yours,' quipped Mike and immediately regretted making light of the situation but Marissa smiled and he knew he hadn't offended her.

'Let's get these things out,' she said and turned towards the door, picking up a tray of food on her way through.

Meal finished, meetings with or hearsay about old friends reported and discussed, coffee cups drained and refills offered, it was time for Mike to come to the point of his visit and raise the question of ESA's betrayal. He turned, extracted a folded piece of paper from the jacket he had draped over the chair, unfolded it and handed it to Simon. His friend read the heading and ran his eyes down the list before returning to the top and examining each entry more carefully, much in the way Kassim had done just two days previously. Marissa took the opportunity to clear the table. Simon looked up.

'You're not serious are you? About me, I mean,' he said in mock indignation.

'Deadly serious, I'm sorry to say, mate.'

Simon's face changed. His frown deepened and his eyes and mouth became set in an unusually serious fashion. He then looked away, raised one arm and flopped it back onto his lap and let out a sigh before turning his head and looking straight at Mike.

'It's not on, Mike, after all we've done together; all the hospitality Marissa and I have shown you. You must know I wouldn't betray ESA.'

Mike was tempted to explain himself straightaway but just in time he decided that he should say nothing; just sit it out. From experience he knew that Simon's next move would determine whether his comments were deadly serious or just a wind up. He sat, relaxed, looking straight at his old friend. The stand-off lasted just a few seconds but seemed much longer. Then Simon laughed. Mike grinned and they performed a high five. Sparing over they could get down to the serious business of the list but Mike needed to make just one more observation before they did.

'Good one, Si. But you're still only the number two wind-up merchant behind Gianni!'

Simon grinned and pushed the list into the centre of the table between them signalling that the discussion should begin.

'You were not on my original list. Neither was Kassim, nor Heron. I went to see Kassim earlier this week and he pointed out that since he fitted my criteria, knowledge about the op and opportunity to snitch to the army, he had to be on the list until I could prove otherwise. So I added his name and for the same reason I had to add you. And Heron.'

Simon turned the list around so that he could see the names.

'Kassim, no. He couldn't betray the cause he had founded. Anna, also no, unless she was a mole planted by Buckhurst and the whole thing about her supporting ESA was a charade. If so they would have had to give her the correct sentence to make it look good but then somehow reduce it. Do you know how long she served?'

'No. But thanks. That's a really good line of enquiry. Since the Tariff was harshly applied, with very rare exceptions, that could be a good pointer to the traitor if they were an army backed mole. Anyone not serving their full sentence should go right to the top of the list of suspects. I'll have to check everyone out. At least I know *you* spent the full 5 years put away.'

'To continue,' Simon said, returning to the list. 'Heron, again no. I just cannot imagine her betraying ESA. She was so passionate about our cause although it is true that she hated Buckhurst. Cassie, no. And Reuben and Frazer were both solid supporters.'

At this point Marissa returned from her chores but

recognising the seriousness of their discussion pulled a chair back from the table and sat, reading by the house wall, a little way off.

'OK. But Frazer interests me,' stated Mike after a brief pause. 'There are about three and a half hours of that day when we don't know exactly what he was up to at his observation point. He was on his own, knew what we were doing, exactly where we were and had the opportunity to contact the military. And for that matter I don't know what you were doing for that time, either, Si.'

'Building a barn extension, actually. I was taking my job of providing the cover alibi very seriously. Anyway there were always three or four workmen with me at any time.'

'What contact did you have with Fraser?'

'After you let me know that Frazer was in place at his observation spot I called him up with a coded message every half hour. He always replied promptly but I didn't actually speak with him until he phoned, after your message, to say that he was coming in.'

'So then the workmen are your alibi. But we still can't be absolutely certain about Frazer.'

'Do you really believe that Frazer could betray you then come back and behave as though he were one hundred percent behind our cause? His behaviour gave me no cause to think that he was anything except completely loyal. If he had been our traitor I reckon he would have defected immediately, not return to the barn. The army would have been ready to pick him up.'

'I tend to believe that you are right but I still need to be totally convinced. I reckon you're off the list, Simon, but until I've had a chance to speak with him, Frazer stays.'

'Now, what about these two girls?' Simon asked, dabbing his finger at the foot of the list. I think Vandra's there for personal reasons. Did you ever see her at work, Mike? If you had you probably wouldn't keep her on the list. She was probably our best operative but as you know she hated poseurs and imposters and she thought at first that you were one.'

'Poseur, Si, or imposter?'

'Imposter. Everyone else knew you were, and still are, a poseur.'

If Mike had been able to lay his hands on anything like a cushion he would have aimed it at Simon's head but in its absence he gave him a gentle kick on the shins. The banter took him back to ESA times and for a few moments he felt as though he were back in those days again.

'Beth Stamford. I didn't really have much contact with her. Shy and hard-working as far as I remember. I don't know enough about her to decide if she fits your criteria or not.'

'My main cause for concern about her is that for some time she was Kassim's official link with Buckhurst. Right up to the reorganisation when the units were concentrated at Westhead House she was the person who routinely told the army what we were up to. Kassim always said that he didn't want an army patrol interrupting our work so he always let Buckhurst know what we were doing. Even Heron's anti-smuggling ops were reported so that we wouldn't be ambushed in error. After the reorganisation, of course, you were mainly working out in the sticks,' added Mike, taking a dig at his friend, 'so you may not have known what was going on but those of us in Hut 2 knew all about these things.'

Simon did not rise to the bait. 'So did she continue reporting after that, right up to the end?'

'I don't know. I think we pretty much cut our contact with the authorities although I'm sure Kassim had some emergency connection to fall back on but I don't know if he used her. She was working for Michael's fundraising at the time. She could, of course, have maintained links with her old contacts.'

'Seems like Beth's still very much on the list then.'

'If it were me I'd leave it be, Mike,' said Marissa, joining in for the first time. 'You know, water under the bridge. And in any case, what would you do if you found this traitor?'

'I had thought that writing the book would have closed the ESA chapter for me. For a time it seemed to have done just that. But now it seems that I need to complete the story. It's like decorating a room and then, just when you think the job's done you come across a little piece you've missed. You have to finish it off. As to what I'll do when I find the person, well, I don't exactly know. In fact I don't know at all. At present I feel just knowing will be enough.'

There was little more to say.

They talked about Suffolk again, about how things had changed over the last few years, about new theories on controlling coastal erosion and about projects based on those theories being trialled near Lowestoft. And they discussed how the local council were organising local services and whether Marissa should stand to be elected to the council at the forthcoming elections. When Simon and his wife turned that discussion into a disagreement with Marissa denying vociferously that she had any talent for or interest in that rôle and Simon insisting that she would be a brilliant councillor, Mike knew it was time to leave. He gave Marissa a light kiss on the cheek, thanked her for the meal and then hugged Simon in their habitual embrace on parting. As he did so, looking over Simon's shoulder, he caught Marissa's eye, slightly inclined his head towards his friend and raised his eyebrows questioningly. Marissa replied with a slight nod. She knew Mike needed her to keep him informed about the results of Simon's forthcoming visit to hospital.

CHAPTER TWENTY
CASSIE

Thursday 29th April 2224, Middleton, Suffolk

Mike wasn't at all comfortable attending funerals. He hadn't been to many and this was, on reflection, only the third one where his presence was requested or in this case, required. His grandmother, mum's mum, had died when he was 16. Her death had been expected despite her relatively young age of sixty-one as she had been unwell for as long as he could remember and cared for in a hospital for much of her last two years. Mike had spent his time during that ceremony observing barely recognisable relatives, providing them with characters that matched their appearances and then weaving their imagined personalities into a fantastic story. The other funeral had been a couple of years later and sadly had been for a seven month old baby, the first child of a cousin whom he had never seen and new little about. They had to attend, his mother had told him, to support her sister, Aunt Grace, since the circumstances of the infant's death were so tragic. But today's funeral was very different.

He had reached the church early. Mike expected the church to be packed but that wasn't why he was among the first mourners to arrive; he had a reserved seat. He had been asked to give a eulogy and he needed to be relaxed; he didn't want to run the chance of having to rush in at the last minute.

Mike could still not believe that just four weeks earlier he had been sitting with Simon in his garden and that only three weeks ago he had been exchanging banter with a weak but cheerful Simon in Ipswich hospital. Just seven days after that his friend had lapsed into a coma and three days later he was dead. Mike had helped Marissa by contacting former ESA members using the database he had built up whilst checking details for his book. Many had been tracked down quite easily as the majority had stayed in or near the East Suffolk area although a few had dispersed across Britain or abroad and a handful like Heron had just disappeared. Carlos had not been located until quite recently in a reunion that had occurred quite by chance. On a visit back home to Framlingham Mike had taken his father for a drink at The Vine. And Carly had been sitting there, at the bar, just as she had been all those years ago when they first met. Carlos, she explained, had managed to avoid being arrested or charged in connection with his time at ESA. He had moved from place to place, job to job, unable to settle until he met a lady who owned a small market garden outside Cambridge. Carlos and his partner developed the business, expanded onto another site and had plans to do even better in the future. Mike had asked where they lived and Carly had dictated details for him to enter into his PERC. It turned out that Carlos now lived near Fulbourne, a village just twenty kilometres and two junctions down the E14 road to the west of Mike's Fordham home.

The funeral was taking place in Middleton, Simon's home village a couple of kilometres south of Westleton. Simon had not been a particularly religious person and had requested the so-called 'neutral' or not specifically religious service that about eighty percent of people in Britain stated in their wills as the preferred option for their send off. The vicar at Middleton, who by chance was also the local Registrar for Births, Marriages and Deaths, knew the Upton family well and had helpfully left little organisation for Marissa herself to complete before the day.

Mike stood at the edge of the churchyard backed close up to a strip of trees and watched the mourners arrive. As they walked through the gateway and up the path to the porch few turned to look in his direction for which he was thankful; greetings and small talk could wait until later. A good proportion of the people he had contacted had been able to attend and now became part of a casually formed procession approaching the church door. Local residents such as James Court and his wife Anna Chalk from Walberswick and James' brother Reuben, now resident in Leiston, walked down slowly with Anna's aunt Claire, having arrived in good time. Then Carly Theydon and her brother Carlos (not a cousin as she had originally informed him for some reason known only to themselves) arrived together with a lady he assumed must be Carlos' partner. He had spoken with but hadn't seen Carlos for many years and with an almost complete loss of hair, a lean fitness and a contented, relaxed set of facial features, so much in contrast to his ESA persona, Mike thought that he could have passed him in the street without recognising him. In contrast Gianni Prince seemed hardly to have changed at all. Gianni's presence was a little unexpected as like Carlos he had been unable to settle down after ESA's demise and when Mike had contacted his relatives still living in the area they had been unable to pass on his present location, only able to say that he was abroad, possibly in Italy. Somehow the sad news must have got through to him. As he walked up the path Gianni looked up towards Mike, raised a hand in greeting, changed it to a thumbs-up then continued on into the church. Unfortunately every attempt to persuade the prison authorities to allow Kassim to attend had foundered on the strictly enforced 'Relations Only' rule for such day release.

It was, however, for the unexpected that Mike was principally scanning the arriving mourners. He was looking for a sight of the three people who were named on his list but as yet had not been located. But there was no sign of any of them. Not Vandra, not Heron, not Beth, although the chance of Beth Stamford being there was extremely unlikely as he had no reason to believe that she would attend the funeral of someone that she probably knew only by name. 'Women,' he thought. 'Totally unreliable.' But then he had to change his mind.

There she was.

Slim, upright and incredibly attractive despite the intervening years and the sombre colours of her clothing. Mike realised that in reality it was Cassie he had been waiting to see all along. Cassie eclipsed all other current hopes or expectations even after all these years. Watching her progress towards the church he was easily able to swap his present view with that of the girl he had first seen standing on the little beach in front of the cabin, waiting for the approaching boat, about a quarter of a century before. And he knew he was still in love.

A bell tolled in the church tower. Five minutes until the service was due to start. A few people were still arriving – probably family friends and villagers who wanted to slip in at the back. Mike joined them but once in the church walked towards the front and took his reserved seat just behind the principle mourners – Marissa, Simon's parents, Marissa's parents and close relatives from both sides. The Reverend Jack Watford stood, walked to a position behind the coffin and waited for silence.

* * * * *

Twenty-five minutes later the coffin and the principle mourners were on their way to the crematorium in Ipswich and Mike and the remaining mourners filed past and shook the hand of the Rev. Watford whilst thanks for attendance and comments of appreciation for the service were exchanged. For a while small groups stood in the churchyard talking then gradually thinned out and dissolved as a new informal procession followed a course away from the church heading towards Mr and Mrs Upton's house or one of the cars parked by the small green in front of the cottages that backed onto the churchyard. Mike detached himself from a group comprising Carly, Carlos and his partner and two former college friends of Simon. He had briefly spoken with Gianni, who rushed off to visit relatives still living in the area but not before he had promised to contact him at the weekend. Mike looked around, hoping that he had managed to have a word with all his old friends and then noticed Cassie walking towards him, smiling.

'Coming to the Upton's?' she asked.

'Yes, but I'll just make sure I've spoken with everyone before I leave.'

'I'm going with Anna and her group so I'll see you there. I'd like to have a chat sometime but not at the house. I'm staying overnight with Anna and James at Walberswick and flying back north from Norwich tomorrow morning. Why don't you come to Anna's as well? Their Ellie is away staying with a friend.'

Mike hesitated before replying.

'Only if you want to, of course,' Cassie continued.

'Yes,' he decided. 'That would be good. But I wouldn't want to leave it too late before hitting the road.'

'Why not stay? Grandma left me her cottage. It's mine now. You'd be welcome to stay there. I rent it out for much of the year but it's empty at the moment.'

She smiled appealingly.

'OK, fine. I'd like that. After the Upton's I'll give you a lift up there.'

Another smile, a little nod of agreement and she was gone. His eyes followed her as she made her way towards and then through the church gateway.

'Mike.'

He froze for a second or two before turning. Not because it was unusual for anyone to call out his name but because he recognised the voice. It belonged to someone he had not seen in the church for the funeral, someone who may have squeezed into the porch at the back with the latecomers and then exited promptly before the coffin and principal mourners filed out.

Mike turned and saw Heron standing almost exactly in the place where he had stood to observe the congregation arriving before the service. She had put on a bit of weight and gained a few flecks of grey in her hair. He assumed that they were natural. And her face was a little lined and showed signs of an outdoor life. But what hadn't changed was her supremely confident stance and the look in her eyes that after all these years demanded his attention.

'Well done, Mike. Congratulations on becoming a celebrity. I'm sure you don't need my endorsement but I agree with every word of your story. They were good times with good people and you were one of the very best.'

The Heron he remembered hadn't been that free with compliments. She seemed to have mellowed a little.

'I had hoped to run the draft in front of you before it was published but no-one seemed to know how to get in touch with you.'

'I left East Suffolk for good when the Mercians came for us. I've been around, here and there, but now I'm settled and basically I've cut all ties with places and people down here. I don't want to live in the past. But Simon was special enough to come back just this once. I reckon I may come back for your funeral – if I'm able to outlive you that is. After all I probably owe you that much.' She gave a slight smile.

Mike assumed she was referring to the day when he had shot at the helicopter over Dingle Point.

'Have you been to see Kassim?' he asked although he already knew she had been across to Albany.

'Yes.'

It was just one small word but it was spoken with a finality that indicated she had no wish to develop the topic. She looked away from him for the first time during their conversation. When her usual confident gaze returned she said, 'It's difficult knowing that he's been shut away like that all this time.'

They stood silently for a few further seconds before Heron stepped forward, gave Mike a brief, light hug and a kiss on the cheek and was gone. Mike didn't turn round until he was certain that she would be out of sight.

The evening spent with Cassie, Anna and James turned out to be one of the most pleasant few hours of his life since leaving prison, in fact since the day when he had to flee East Suffolk twenty-three years earlier. In the days leading up to Simon's funeral he had worried about meeting Cassie again. It wasn't the first time he had seen her recently; he had been to visit her in her remote home in Moidart, Western Scotland when he was checking on the details for his book. Not once but twice he had been to the coastal cottage in Glenuig that Cassie shared with her partner Cameron. These visits had taken on the character of a meeting between two old friends, separated for years. Each visit had been brief and Cameron had been around for most of the time; they didn't have any intimate conversations. Mike had tried to stop regarding Cassie as a former lover; she was now just a friend although it was difficult to accept the fact that Cassie had taken Cameron's surname even though they hadn't been married or even registered a partnership. Perhaps it was a sensible step though, now that she was living in a staunchly traditional community. Even so it seemed totally unnatural to think of her as Cassandra Westferry. But he needn't have been concerned about seeing her on this occasion. As he and Cassie left Anna's quite early, on the pretext of Cassie's early morning flight, and walked next door he didn't entertain thoughts that entering Grandma Vale's cottage would turn the clock back. Two nearly middle-aged friends staying over before making their separate ways in the morning seemed quite reasonable. Without trying they seemed to have found a new relationship that was both comfortable and natural.

'Tea, coffee, beer, something else?'

'Tea will be fine. Thanks.'

Cassie turned away to make the tea. Mike sat at the table. It was the same table they had sat at as lovers, resting one hand on the other's, looking at each other and thanking Grandma Vale's wisdom for arranging to be absent for a few hours. That first evening at the cottage hadn't been the only time they had made love there but it was the one that had stayed in his mind. Now it seemed more natural to gain comfort from the feel of the warm mug of tea cradled in his hands or the warm smile of his host sitting opposite.

'So Cameron didn't come with you?'

'He would have done, had I asked, but he knows few of the old ESA people and had never met Simon. And in any case we couldn't really afford two return flights.'

'You never told me how you met him.'

'Your two visits to us were quite brief. Had you been able to stay longer we could have talked some more. It's no secret. As you know women with a fifteen year sentence were sent to Springfield in Essex, part of the City of Chelmsford really. The prison was old, derelict and due for demolition before extra places were needed for us 'fifteeners'. There were no men there. They were sent to Gressenhall in Norfolk. The last two years of our sentence was spent in a rehabilitation centre. The authorities appeared to take a delight in sending the rehab prisoners as far away from home as possible so Saskia Hill, also in Springfield but as a 'fiver' and I were despatched to Kinlocheil. Saskia had avoided capture and sentence for about ten years but that was long before the *Amnesty* so when they caught up with her she had to serve her full five years. When we arrived in Scotland it was cold and wet and the hills were covered in snow but Sassy and I learnt to love the place. Our rehab programme was aimed at teaching us to take up disciplined employment. I didn't work with Saskia – she was in forestry but I was allocated to the fish farm. So was Cameron.'

'You didn't have any say where you worked then?'

'We didn't have any say in anything but we weren't badly treated. Food was good and quite adequate. The jobs thing was alphabetical. It was like being at school. Vale and Westferry were usually together in any dividing up of the inmates into groups.'

'So you and Cameron worked together and stayed together after release.'

'Yes. We enjoyed the work and the area around. Spring and autumn are unbelievably beautiful when the weather is fine. There were seven of us at the fish farm but only Cameron and I stayed on when the others scuttled home. We took the offer of a year's paid employment to supervise newcomers and little by little we increasingly enjoyed each other's company. When the contract ended the centre was being run down so the government put the fish farm up for sale. The new owner took Cameron on as manager. So I had the choice of staying up there or returning to Suffolk. But I didn't know what Suffolk would hold for me and you were in prison and would be for several more years. I couldn't just waste all those years.'

She was silent for a while and Mike could find nothing further to say. Cassie looked away and then back to Mike. There was a gentle smile on her face but a tear in her eye.

'Do you think I was selfish?' she asked.

Mike hesitated and carefully composed his answer.

'Selfish? Possibly, yes. But you weren't wrong. You chose a life in Scotland and a life with Cameron for the right reasons and I know you're happy. So too am I. We both have good lives now. So, no regrets.'

She nodded and looked at him. Mike sensed something wistful about her look, her thoughts somewhere else but in less than a minute she was back in the here and now with a smile on her face.

'OK, Mike. When you phoned to ask if I were coming down today you said we needed to talk. What's this all about then? You're still not going on about Heron and guns are you, after all these years?'

'No. that's no longer important although I still harbour a small question mark over all that training. A couple of firearms to deal with a doggy situation with smugglers would have been OK but the amount of arms we amassed you would have thought we were going to take on the army.'

'Right. Time to put this one to bed. Heron always thought we needed protection. She confided in me once, just after you had shot at the helicopter at Dingle Point. Before that she was having doubts about her policy of arming ESA members but your shot confirmed her original thoughts about protection. But she kept the training to just a select few. You need to realise that Heron regarded ESA as her family. After Dingle she said that she thought of you and me as the younger siblings she never had. The arms policy was simply aimed at protecting her family. In addition to smugglers the army were a threat as you were later to find out and there was also the real possibility of armed groups based in the Thames Estuary and Norfolk heading into our own area. There never was a hidden agenda, just a need to keep everything as low key as possible. We shall never know if the policy was right as Buckhurst's death and the subsequent army action put pay to ESA anyway. You just need to see the whole thing through Heron's eyes.'

'That makes a sense of a kind and you were closer to her than anyone. Let's forget that topic. Now, what I wanted your opinion on was this.'

Mike took his list from his jacket pocket and passed it across. As he had done with Kassim and Simon he gave no introduction but let the document speak for itself.

Cassie read through the paper in front of her and then said, 'Let me get this right, Mike. You think that you were ambushed because someone had betrayed you and you're seriously considering Kassim and Simon and Heron as traitors.'

'Miss out the word *seriously* and you've got it about

right. Unless I've had a huge oversight I'm only serious about one name on that list. Unfortunately I don't yet know who that one person is. I was hoping you could help me whittle the list down a bit.'

Cassie looked through it again.

'No one stands out. Obviously I would remove Kassim and Heron immediately. What thoughts have you had on the others?'

'I agree about those two, principally because of their single-minded belief in the ESA cause and I would also add Simon to that group. Not just because he's no longer with us but because when we spoke about it I believed his version of events. Marissa told me she knows – sorry knew – when he was telling half-truths and listening to him whilst he was talking to me she was quite certain that his account was genuine.'

'So that leaves me, Anna, Frazer, Reuben, Beth and Vandra. I reckon you can cross Reuben off. He was perfectly happy, even pleased to see you today and he often visits Anna and James. He wouldn't be keen to do that if he had a guilty conscience.'

'Yes. Seeing Rueben today means he goes to the foot of the list with you and Anna.'

'So I'm still on the list!' Cassie exclaimed in mock indignation.'

'Of course. But only in the sense that Kassim is still on the list.'

'I've got an alibi and a witness. I was off duty and here, at home. I did some washing. In the afternoon I took Grandma to Saxmundham for shopping. Now for most days that I worked for ESA I couldn't give you details of what I was doing in particular but for that one day I can. On our return I was just making a cup of tea when Reuben rang to alert me of the situation. I went straight over to Westhead '

'You would have had plenty of time to contact the military and rushing over to Westhead could have been part of your cover.'

'Yes, but what could I have told them? Of course I knew there was an operation; I was in effect Heron's number two i/c but you know she never let on about patrol details to anyone unless they were taking part. I honestly had nothing of value to tell them; it was only later that I learnt where the incident had taken place.'

'And your witness?'

'Well witnesses actually. James next door was on late duty in Hut Two. He was leaving for work after lunch just as I was going out to Saxmundham. We spoke briefly. And whilst in Saxmundham with Grandma I met Michael.'

'OK. But how can you be certain that each of the events you have described actually happened on that day. After all this time memories could have been transposed from other days. It was a long time ago!'

'Because of the news about Buckhurst's death and your escape. I can still relive the whole day. It formed a capsule of memory in my mind that I've revisited time and time again and the details haven't changed one bit.'

Cassie gently laid her hand on Mike's. They were silent for a while and then he brought his thoughts back to the list.

'So in effect that's five people that have been moved to the *not at all likely* section at the foot of the list. I've spoken with Simon and you and you've both convinced me to remove your names completely. I shall go to see Frazer when it can be arranged – hopefully in the next couple of weeks so if I'm then able to remove him from the list that'll just leaves the two girls, Beth and Vandra and of course Heron.'

'Heron? I thought she had been relegated to the '*not likely*' group.'

'She really shouldn't be on the list at all. Everybody tells me to take her out of the reckoning. Nobody can give me a reason to leave her on the list. Everyone I've spoken to regards her as the definition of a true patriot and I've always agreed with those people. Until today that is. Now I don't know.'

Why today? What's happened?'

'I saw Heron at the funeral.'

'No! You couldn't have done. She wasn't there. I looked.'

'That's what I had thought but she spoke to me at the end, a little after you'd gone. She didn't say much. Just a sort of hello and to point out that she had broken completely with Suffolk and only returned out of respect for Si.'

'So you don't know where she's living or what she's doing?'

'No. Nothing. Enigmatic as ever.'

'Would she have sought you out if she had betrayed you?'

'For anyone else an appearance like that would have gone a long way to proving their innocence but with Heron things may not be quite what you expect.'

For a short while they both pondered the quandary that

was the person called Heron but with no further thoughts on the subject Cassie summed up their discussion. 'You just have to keep going with the investigation. It doesn't matter too much who's on the list as long as you find the traitor. Good luck with your search, Mike. Let me know how you get on and if you ever need to chat about it give me a call.' She picked up the mugs and put them on the side for washing later then turned back to the table, walked over to Mike and gave him a kiss on the cheek.

'Don't be a stranger,' she said. 'Come up and see us. As I said, autumn's a great time to visit. And if you'd like to then why not bring Marissa along with you? Anyway I'll be off to bed now. I've set the alarm early so that I can be ready for James when he comes round to ferry me to Norwich in the morning. There's no need for you to hurry up. Stay as long as you like and just take the key back to Anna. She'll set the intruder alarm after you've gone.'

Mike slept in Grandma's old room. As far as he could tell a new bed was the only change that had been made to the room. As he undressed he caught site of the tattoo on his left arm. Subconsciously he had kept it covered whilst Cassie was around. Now, he thought, was not the time to rock any boats. Perhaps one day he would have it removed, but not quite yet.

CHAPTER TWENTY ONE
FRAZER

Wednesday 12th May 2224

He hadn't driven into London since coming out of prison. He'd been to the capital on several occasions but had always arrived at his destination by rail even though he had driven to the railway station first. Newmarket was now his nearest rail station but he preferred Cambridge where he could access a much more frequent service to London's main eastern terminus at Stratford City but with parking at Cambridge limited and expensive he had also on some occasions driven further down the line to Bishop Stortford or even Epping. Using a slower, local train service didn't bother him. Mike's destination today was Fulham, to the west of central London. So today it was the car, all the way.

It had been difficult to make arrangements to meet up with Frazer. Every time they spoke or exchanged texts Frazer had been somewhere different, usually abroad. Single, no ties, a London home in up and coming Fulham and with the desire to move nearer to the city centre where costs were higher than anything Mike could ever consider; that was the high-flying Frazer today. How he came to be the trouble-shooter for Air London, a well-known major player in the air transportation world, nobody had been able to tell Mike but his main strength seemed to be in sorting out the volatile employment situations sometimes encountered abroad. One day Munich, the next somewhere on the Gulf and after that Sao Paulo or Lusaka seemed a fairly standard itinerary. This week though Frazer was off duty.

'E11, *junction 1, slip road right to A100 south,*' the Routesafe navigation lady instructed Mike, adding helpfully, '*On slip road stay in left-hand lane.*' The speed limiter in Mike's four year old Seat Cantabrian saloon picked up the signal beamed to it allowing the car to make a smooth turn around the tight left hand curve until, released by the unseen control it was able to accelerate to a suitable speed to join the carriageway of the Inner London Ring Road, the A100. On the map the A100 seemed less like a ring, more like a misshapen rectangle with curved corners and as a result had, soon after its opening, become known as The Box. An expressway in all but name the six lane highway had been built to provide a circuit around central London north of the Thames. It absorbed incoming traffic from the radial feeder expressways and sent those vehicles no longer needing the facilities of the capital spinning off homeward out along the same distributers.

Mike drove south. His Routesafe chimed in to warn him that he should avoid the new inside fourth lane that led to the A200 road that headed south across the river Thames via the newly constructed New Tower Bridge. The ring road itself arced right and headed westwards along what had once been Thames Street and the Victoria Embankment, hugging the riverside until diving into a tunnel whose course curved beneath and around the Houses of Parliament, home to the National Council. Daylight soon reappeared along Millbank from where the road ran along the Chelsea Embankment and Routesafe provided its next timely instruction as Mike approached the south-western corner of The Box to reach the Chelsea Interchange.

'500 metres, slip road right, onto roundabout and take fifth exit.'

Mike followed the instructions and reached the roundabout. 'Take fifth exit,' he was reminded, followed by, 'New King's Road, signed Fulham and Wandsworth,' with an addition noting that, 'Inside lane closed after 200 metres for road reconstruction. Keep left.' Again he was able to follow the instruction without difficulty and headed towards Fulham.

'800 metres slip road right signed Eelbrook. Lane 1 for Parking, Lane 2 for putting down and picking up, Lane 3 for through traffic.'

Ahead of him Mike saw the imposing façade of the Eelbrook Tower, his destination that morning. There was a short pause and then Routesafe issued its final instruction. 'Turn right now.'

Mike took lane 1 signed Tower Parking and then followed the sign indicating Parking Floor B (Floor A was full) and found an easily accessed place to leave his Cantabrian quite close to an exit door. Now the Routesafe lady's instructions were replaced by those of Frazer explaining where they would meet. These had been provided by audio-mail but Mike hated walking around with a voice talking in his ear so he had transferred the content to text on his PERC which he carried in his pocket should he need a reference.

'*OK, Mike. You're parked. Take any exit and you'll see a bank of lifts opposite.*'

There they were – six lifts – a bank of three with red indicators numbered 1, 2 and 3 over the doors and to their right a further three with blue indicators for lifts A, B and C.

'*Take the express lifts, that'll be A, B or C.*'

Mike stepped into the waiting pod C. A and B were somewhere above him moving up or down the tower.

'*There will be four floors indicated on the panel. Ignore 30 and 31, take 32. You'll get out into a foyer. I'll meet you there. OK?*' finished Frazer.

Yes. It was OK. The lift took off smoothly giving Mike the sensation of being suspended in the air. He looked down and moved his feet. They were, he found, firmly grounded on the floor and soon a more natural feeling returned. Being the only passenger he was taken directly to floor 32, the Restaurant Level. Leaving the pod to travel one further floor to the Viewing Gallery, if required, he stepped out into the foyer.

The Restaurant label for the floor was a bit of a misnomer. There were in fact six eating places although only three could truthfully be called restaurants, the other three eating places being more suitably labelled, one as a bar, the other two as cafés. 1150. He was a little early and no-one he saw in the foyer was Frazer. From a starting place with his back to the lifts Mike turned left to make a clockwise tour of the eateries. The first entrance gave access to a medium-priced restaurant that was followed, further along the same wall by an open-fronted café offering customers stool seats at long bars once they had paid for and collected their food and drink. On turning to the adjacent longer wall, opposite the banks of lift pods, the first restaurant appeared to Mike to be a very expensive place that even now that he was quite well off he would probably not consider using. Next up was a second café, one that offered a choice of two, three or four chaired tables, again self-service and beyond that an establishment serving oriental cuisine and advertising dishes from China, Japan, Thailand and Indonesia. Mike wondered which dishes someone from Korea or Malaysia would choose before noting a sub-text offering patrons the opportunity to ask for any dish not advertised on the menu and in any case at least one couple sitting near the window were eating fish and chips, English-style.

The next wall was occupied by a large window overlooking an extensive swath of western London's urban landscape. He stopped briefly, looking out before deciding that the view deserved a closer look, not now but later and moved on to the bar that occupied the left-hand end of the wall that was mainly taken up with the lifts. Noisier than any of the other venues, noisier even than the open fronted café, this bar was characterised by a mêlée of people – some coming, some going, a few seated alone, quietly and others seated in groups that were gossiping noisily or exchanging banter. Some individuals were busy texting or consulting tablets and in a quiet corner, tucked away from the intrusion of a large wall-mounted television screen, one lady was reading today's copy of the National Guardian.

'I guessed it would be the bar where I'd find Mike Cannon!'

Mike hadn't heard Frazer approach but recognising the voice he turned, grinned and put out his hand. They shook hands warmly. Hardly, Mike thought, the welcome of someone who could have betrayed him even if it was all those years ago.

In physical appearance Frazer had changed more than any other former member of ESA that Mike had seen again since leaving prison. He was certain that he could have walked past him in a crowded street, even brushed against him, and not recognised him. It was not just aging that had altered his looks. Mike was the younger of the pair by twelve years yet Frazer with his tall slim build, dark hair and boyish looks had never seemed that much older. Now, however he had totally white hair, had put on weight and looked muscular whereas before his appearance had been wiry. Now he presented a general air of fitness rather than the former impression that he might topple over if you knocked into him by accident. And his clothes. The Frazer he remembered had never worried too much about looking smart but now he sported the type of outfit popularly known as 'demi-mode'. Not as extreme as current high fashion but not as ordinary as standard chain-store attire. The lapels on his jacket were not quite as narrow as fashion trends demanded but were cut a little sharper than tradition expected. His trousers were slim legged but not tapered to the degree a younger man would have thought trendy. His whole appearance told people that Frazer Oak was successful. He had made his way in the world and he wasn't afraid to let people know that he was his own man and he certainly wasn't going to be a slave to the latest whims of fashion's top brass. Mike felt that his own wardrobe was, perhaps, a little too casual for the occasion.

'Come on. We'll eat over here,' Frazer said, leading Mike to the unexcitedly named *'Thames Restaurant'*, the one he had previously dismissed as being too expensive.

'I'm OK with a snack if that's all you want,' suggested Mike.

'Nonsense, Mike. Catching up on all those years is going to need more time than it takes to eat a sandwich or a grill with chips! Anyhow, I can afford it. It's my treat.'

The table had been booked in anticipation of this meeting and clearly it was not the first time the waiter had shown Frazer to his 'usual table'. Frazer wasn't showing off with a special guest but Mike had the impression that Frazer had spent enough money here to earn the prompt and careful attention of the staff. Menus perused, orders for starter and main course placed, they sat back and looked at each other. Frazer smiled. He had a history to tell that linked the Frazer of ESA with the prosperous, confident Frazer of today. Mike was intrigued and prompted Frazer to tell his tale.

'So what happened to you after I fled Westhead all that time ago?'

'I fled as well. As soon as I heard that you had gone and Buckhurst was dead. I knew the army would be coming for us so I simply upped and went back home to Leiston. I realised I wouldn't be safe there long term and reckoned I had a day, two days at the most in which to disappear. I went to stay with an uncle in Saxmundham, took on a new name – Frazer King, taken at random from the *King's Head*, a pub I passed one day, and took on odd jobs in computer maintenance. But I knew I was heading nowhere in particular. Frazer King didn't have an ID card and I couldn't see a future in what I was doing. So I tried for a post with a company based up near Norwich, giving them my real name. They seemed keen. I told them I was applying for a new National Identity card, that I had lost mine in a fire. They asked for references and I gave them the names of two firms where I had recently worked on short-term contracts, freelance. I also had to tell them that my previous employers knew me by the name of King. I told them that it was my mother's family name. Anyway they employed me and everything was OK for a week. Then on the next Monday morning the police were waiting for me when I turned up for work. They had records and DNA information collected during their ESA raids. It was no good. I just held my hands up. The result was that I ended up in Gressenhall Rehab Centre in Norfolk for a two year stint.'

Their starters arrived. After a few mouthfuls and genuinely appreciative comments Mike asked Frazer what happened next. So far, but on a much smaller scale, his story had echoes of his own flight and prison experience.

'At Gressenhall I met up with James Court and Simon Upton. By the way I was really sorry to miss Simon's send off but as you know I was abroad, working. Of course the two lads were serving five years and were in a different wing so I didn't see too much of them.

'So you were given two years and served two years.'

'Too true! There was no remission in those days. Anyway I was working in the engineering technology workshop. I reckon I did more teaching than the teachers. One person I spent a lot of time with was a guy called Earl Town. He was a huge dark-skinned bloke, strong as anything. But he was also very funny. When a new intern arrived he would scare them to hell with his appearance and piercing looks. They would creep around him trying to keep in his good books. And then he would choose his moment to burst out in gales of laughter and slap them on the back. It was just his way of saying, 'Hello.' Anyway, we became mates and exchanged stories about how we came to be in rehab. His was a very different story. He came from here, Fulham.

'So he must have been with one of those copycat urban brigades.'

'Yes and no,' Frazer explained, enigmatically. 'This part of London was changing fast in those days. Flood protection work was being undertaken all along the lower Thames so some people in some places, including parts of Fulham were being moved out. As a result there was a breakdown in neighbourhood communities, schools, clubs, religious groups and so on. As time went on more and more people chose to move out; in some ways it wasn't too different from what happened in coastal areas like ours. At least in East Suffolk the government provided some support for those who chose to leave. Here in Fulham the opportunities for employment quickly deteriorated and the demographic became heavily biased towards the young and the old. Many young people, unemployed, had time on their hands and with traditional social links having been lost the way was clear for gangs to move in and fill the vacuum.'

Frazer paused to eat.

'I imagine these gangs financed themselves through illegal trading,' suggested Mike.

'Yes. Most did and the top gangs broadcast their status by parading with expensive clothes and high-powered cars but there were also co-operative groups that acted within the law. My buddy Earl was part of one of these. They ran a communications and mail service and charged reasonable rates so they became popular, particularly with the elderly residents when they decided to deliver local mail free. Then a young man joined them who, after a while, took over their operations and added other money-making schemes, including protection. One gang in particular didn't take kindly to this newcomer muscling in on their territory so sporadic warfare erupted. Anyway, Earl stayed on in the mail business but was also required to deliver demands and collect payments for the extortion business. He never used his fists and he never carried a gun – his physique generally helped him avoided the need for violence.'

'Was this before *Martial Law* came in?'

'Yes, just before the army came along and things were generally OK for Earl. He worked hard, collected his wages and all seemed fine until the warfare escalated. One weekend the police, with army backup, had a blitz in this area and arrested random gang members. One of these was the second i/c in Earl's lot who tried to save himself by naming others and inventing damning rôles for them. He claimed that Earl was a ringleader in the extortion business and used the mail service as a cover. Earl was given five years, three in the prison wing and two in the rehab wing where we met.'

'This isn't just a history lesson, though.'

'No, but its background to what came after.'

Frazer paused whilst their main course was served. Mike noticed that the restaurant was filling up quickly now with a queue of people waiting to be seated. Clearly the choice of noon for their meal had been a wise one.

'No,' Frazer repeated but with less emphasis than the first time. 'We were released within three weeks of each other. Earl went first. We exchanged contact details but I didn't expect ever to meet up with him again. Greetings at Christmas, OK; you know the sort of thing. We were from such different backgrounds and we only had rehab at Gressinghall in common. Anyway, to my surprise about three weeks after getting back to Leiston there he was, standing at our doorstep one morning at about ten-thirty. With a broad grin and a hearty handshake he announced that he had come to offer me a job!'

'He was lucky to come out and already have a job himself after rehab. Many boys and girls found it difficult. During martial law the economy had taken a bashing,' Mike commented.

'Sure. But where Earl lived, here in Fulham, there was a pocket of opportunity. After I had invited him in and after we'd had a beer he reeled off a whole range of available openings – skills and crafts needed in the regeneration of the area. I said I would have a think about it. He invited me down to see him and we fixed a date for the Tuesday after the next weekend.'

'Had you been actively looking for work?'

Frazer stopped eating, looked at Mike and smiled. 'Sort of. Not very seriously. Being inside changes you.

You either plan to climb up or you don't plan anything and you stay down. Earl had chosen the former path, I was drifting down the other. I'd kidded myself that I was waiting for the right job to come along and as Earl was just a labourer I didn't expect much to come out of this visit. When I got down here I found the place was a dump. Half the buildings were unoccupied and some of them damaged or partly demolished. There was fire damage that I assumed could have been the result of gang warfare. And there had been looting. Anything worthwhile had been removed – trees, plants, railings, whole windows, roofing materials, carpets and household equipment. The roads were in a very poor state with great holes where, Earl explained, material had been dug up by the gangs to make barricades or provide missiles. One small area centred on a school, a church and a church hall had been repaired but it was a fraction of what was needed to be done. Then as we continued our tour we turned a corner and Earl stopped in front of a huge pair of gates cutting off the road. On our side, derelict housing and on the other a complete clearance. It had been flattened but the area was crossed by new roadways cutting through the area and dividing it into plots – gently undulating earthen areas with patches of grass and weeds beginning to colonise them. This was a regeneration area. Next to the gate was a Starcabin marked with a simple sign designating it as the 'Office' but attached to its wall, beside the door, its purpose was explained in a number of notices. The office was the centre for an organisation named as the

WEST FULHAM REGENERATION SCHEME,

the area involved being shown on a map. A separate notice

listed trades and skills required by the contractors and another invited tenders from suppliers. There and then, on the spot, Earl and I formed our own supply company. My brains and his brawn, It was a perfect combination. We started with building materials sourced from all over London and the south-east. At first we worked all hours and made very little profit but as the redevelopment progressed we were able to provide anything that was required and soon profits began to roll in. When companies started to move into the development I saw a new opportunity. I sold my share of our business to Earl, who still owns and runs it, and moved into recruitment. After a couple of years I sold that business to one of my employees and joined one of the firms I had helped with personnel in the early days. But my reputation must have been noted further afield as Air London came knocking and I jumped ship so to speak. And that's it. OK. Let's order sweet and you can tell me how you came to be an author.'

Mike gave a brief résumé of his life in prison and his life since then. He really wanted to continue and bring up the subject of his betrayal but Frazer had other ideas.

'You did well, Mike. Somebody had to tell the story. Now let's skip coffee; we'll have some later. There's something I want to show you.'

They walked out of the restaurant. Frazer had a brief, friendly, animated conversation with the front of house guy but didn't pay for their meal. Perhaps, Mike thought, he had some sort of credit arrangement with the proprietors. Re-entering the foyer Frazer gestured towards the lifts. Pod B was empty and waiting and when Frazer gave a touch to button 33 they were headed for the top of the tower. Reading Mike's thoughts Frazer explained, 'No need to pay. It was complimentary. It always is at the Thames; I've got free meals for life there. The owner was one of the first people I placed through my recruitment business. He started as a waiter but he had ambition. There's quite a club of us now – started at the bottom and made the climb. There's now a competition to see who will be the first to make enough money to move east and live somewhere inside The Box.'

'Is Earl a member of the club?'

Frazer smiled briefly and then his eyes focused somewhere far away. Returning his gaze to look at Mike he said, 'No. Earl only made it to the first rung of the ladder but he's perfectly happy there.' Frazer's smile returned. 'I count him as an honorary member anyway.'

They stepped out of the lift and onto the Tower's viewing platform. Walking over to the continuous circular glass window Mike was a little un-nerved by the feeling that he could simply step over the barrier rail and out into the sky. London was spread out below them. They were facing N.81degrees E. according to the display attached to the bar in front of them. A complete panoramic view of the capital was available as the platform rotated slowly in an anti-clockwise direction. They were looking downstream along the river Thames. The narrow, embanked course and famous historic buildings had been retained and would be recognisable by any time traveller from the previous three centuries. The Parliament buildings at Westminster, Big Ben's clock tower, the Royal Hospital at Chelsea and Lambeth Palace and Southwark Cathedral to the south were all visible sitting behind heightened and reinforced flood defences. Also identifiable using the rotating map in front of them were Buckingham Palace, the abandoned and as yet un-redeveloped Victoria rail station and the desirable residences in Belgravia and Kensington, each of them brought into view as the platform moved to their left. Then, after crossing the western arm of The Box, Fulham lay below them.

'Here we are Mike. Look at this!'

The Thames to the west looked totally different from the view downstream. Whereas the river at the Chelsea Embankment was perhaps somewhere between two and three hundred metres wide Mike saw that from Battersea Reach and up past Hurlingham and on towards Hammersmith (names again courtesy of the map in front of him) the river spread in places up to one kilometre between its banks. Frazer was giving a commentary on the territory he now regarded as home.

'Under Martial Law the government was able to call upon the military to keep law and order but they also gained other wide ranging powers and made funds available for a radical development of flood defences. Today London's river is a necklace of long lakes linked by highly embanked protected areas. The wider areas have the ability to absorb local groundwater and added floodwater from upstream without causing catastrophic rises in the surface water level.'

There had of course been some sacrifices. A number of previously riverside properties were now hidden below the inundation. In particular the map pointed out the watery location of Hurlingham Park (formerly a centre for sporting activities) and the Fulham Football Club's former home at Craven Cottage. Between them lay Fulham Palace. Once surrounded by the extensive grounds of the Bishop's Park, the Palace now occupied a small island preserved by a protective wall and connected to the river bank by a causeway, rather like a cherry at the end of its stalk.

But it was Fulham itself that Frazer had brought Mike to see. By walking leisurely to their right they could spend time taking in the new developments before the view slipped away from them.

'Here it is. Fulham Village. A phoenix arisen from the wasteland.' There was pride in Frazer's voice. 'Fulham is in the vanguard. It's not a blueprint for other developments in London, rather an inspiration for those that follow. And those aren't my words; they were spoken by the Minister for London himself at the opening ceremony for this tower.'

The two men were silent whilst Mike took in the scene. A waterside parkland strip was dissected by a maze of pathways and punctuated by playgrounds, kiosks selling refreshments and buildings housing amusements. At one point small boats were pulled up on a small sandy strand. The road that backed the park contained a tramway and beyond that lay a residential zone of tiered apartments, each block looking out over the top of the lower block in front. Behind these homes an arterial road, originating at the Chelsea Interchange on The Box, disappeared beneath a large complex of commercial buildings.

'Shops, offices and leisure provision,' stated Frazer, anticipating the question forming in Mike's mind. Beyond the complex the road reappeared to head off through an industrial area, past Fulham Football Club's New Cottage football ground and on towards Hammersmith.

'Impressive.'

'Certainly is! Well, there you are. It's our gleaming brave new world. But it's not what this visit is about, is it? Let's have coffee and you can tell me why you've come all this way to see me.'

They turned and Frazer led Mike off the revolving viewing platform and through the coffee shop entrance, ignoring the staircase to the upper level where patrons could take in the view and relax as they took refreshment, preferring to choose a table on the lower deck where their discussion would not be hindered by the distractions of London's landscape. It was Mike's turn to lead the conversation.

As he had done with Kassim and Simon and Cassie he took out his 'hit list' and handed it across to Frazer without preamble. Mike sat back and waited for a reaction and he didn't have long to wait. Frazer looked up over the paper held in his left hand as he slowly lowered it onto the table.

'This is a nonsense. Half these names should go immediately. Gods sake mate! Cassie? And you can't be serious about Kassim. Come on Mike; Vandra was one of the best operatives ESA had.'

Frazer picked up the list and read it again. His expression suggested that he was hoping to find that he had been mistaken by what he had read the first time. When the paper was again returned to the table he gave a rather more measured appraisal of its contents.

'I know why those names are there. Blind belief or

unqualified hope won't give you the answer. You've got to get the proof and of course all those names except one are the names of innocent people.'

'So is my list a fiction? Have I missed anyone off or am I just imagining that we were betrayed? '

Frazer was quiet for a while, thinking back to the fateful day in question.

'You know, Mike, on paper I must be your prime suspect. I was part of the operation. I knew more about your actual movements than anyone apart from Anna; more even than Simon. For a couple of hours and more no other ESA member saw me. True Simon, God rest him, phoned me about every half hour but I could have been anywhere, doing anything during that time. I must be top of the list on knowledge and probably pretty near the top on opportunity. But you know what? I didn't have the *desire*. You need to complete that third list and find out who had the strongest motive and who had the desire to act. Who had the desire to achieve something that was more important to them than protecting and preserving the cause that was ESA.

'Do you mean a desire for payment? Like a Judas?'

'Could be. If it was a mole planted by the military or the authorities they would certainly have expected payment.'

'And if it was a betrayal? If it had been one of our own members?'

'Could also be for money. ESA paid us; not a lot but they paid us. Most of our members didn't have families. We were single or, like Simon, married to a strong supporter of our cause. But you'd be hard put to make ends meet if you had children and your only income was what

ESA provided. Of course it may not have been for money. One of our colleagues may have had a change of heart and decided to jump ship because they genuinely believed that ESA was rapidly heading up a cul-de-sac or at least a side street. I can't really imagine any of our members doing that but in theory it's possible.'

They talked about Frazer's part in the operation that had ended so suddenly with the ambush. Nothing that Frazer said could prove beyond doubt that he hadn't betrayed Mike and Anna but he did reinforce the view in Mike's mind that Simon was blameless.

'When I saw the increased military activity on the road I contacted Simon. He instructed me to get back to the safe house immediately. Then I got your message. When I got back the amount of construction completed suggested that Simon had been busy working most of the time. Always provided a creditable cover story and always made it work did our Simon. In theory he could have been the source of information but in practice he would have had little opportunity to go off and meet anyone or use some other form of contact.'

Frazer took out and looked at the time on his PERC despite the presence of a large digital wall clock on the wall facing them.

'Time to go. Hope I've been useful. Now we've found each other we must keep in touch. You must come along one day and meet Earl.'

They shook hands and briefly embraced and then Frazer took his leave, waving farewell from the coffee house door and leaving Mike with two empty coffee cups and the bill.

It was early evening when Mike drove his Cantabrian onto the hard-standing beside his house but still light enough and warm enough for him to collect a glass of wine and sit out at his garden table. At first he looked across the garden and mulled over his long-term plans for the area but as the light gently faded his thoughts turned to his investigation. The newly poured second glass of wine remained untouched on the table before him.

Triggered by the lack of natural illumination the subtly placed garden lights behind him began to glow, at first softly and then more brightly. The air was losing its warmth but Mike knew his next task would not take long. From a pocket in his jacket, now placed on the back of his chair, he took the crumpled list of suspects and smoothed it out on the table. In another pocket he found a pen and then crossed out the heading to the third column: The title was altered from MOTIVE to DESIRE. In the top row that related to Kassim he put a cross and then scored out the whole of that row with a bold stroke. Similarly for Simon and again for Cassie. He hesitated over the space relating to Frazer. He wanted to put a cross. He couldn't put a tick or even a query mark. He left the space blank thus leaving his lunchtime companion on the list for the present. After all, Frazer had made the point himself – on paper he was the prime suspect having both knowledge and opportunity. Continuing down the list he deleted Anna believing that during her arrest by Buckhurst she had not been play-acting but he left both Reuben and Beth Stamford with blanks – he still needed to build up information about them. Then there was Heron. No-one he had so far questioned had given the slightest hint that they thought she had entertained any desires apart from seeing the continuing success of ESA. He put a cross in the last column but somehow he couldn't bring himself to cross her off the list. The problem was that apart from the one brief conversation at Simon's funeral nobody he had talked to had seen, let alone had words with her since ESA days.

He thought for a moment and then turned the paper over and started another list. Each of the people with whom he had discussed the list had given him some clue as to the character of the traitor.

First on his list was *Body Language*.

Marissa had pointed out Simon's openness. She had believed in Simon's version of events during that eventful Friday back in October 2201 not just because he was her partner but also from her reading of the way he presented himself – his eyes, his voice, his movements. Mike had seen the same honesty during his talk with Cassie and also with Anna although he had not questioned her specifically about the events. He was fairly certain also that Frazer had told him the truth although some of his detail may have been prone to a little exaggeration and that Reuben, when spoken with after the funeral also showed no signs of there being any form of gulf between them. He turned over the paper and crossed Reuben off the list but after a moment's hesitation decided that Frazer should stay for the present.

Next he added the heading *Reward*.

If they had been betrayed by a mole planted by the military or some government agency the infiltrator would have been working for a reward. Mike surmised that such a person may have been imprisoned or sent to a rehabilitation centre for a short while and then quietly moved on the pretext of a transfer before being released and rewarded, possibly also being given a new identity. Mike decided to investigate further the history of the ESA members who had been sent to detention centres.

The third heading was *Motive*.

Who at ESA had a motive for shopping their compatriots to the army? Who had the desire strong enough to cancel out, to replace their long held loyalty to their organisation?

He still needed to talk with Beth Stamford and Vandra Mornington. And also Heron. His meeting with her in the churchyard hadn't provided him with information either way. So the answer seemed to lie with one of these three ladies. And he knew just the person to set him off on the next stage of his investigation. He didn't know how to get in touch with either one of his three remaining suspects but he felt sure that Anna's aunt, Claire Bois, could point him in the right direction. He had suggested as much to Kassim and Kassim hadn't disagreed.

He checked his list. There were now lines deleting the names of Kassim, Anna, Cassie, Reuben and Simon. Frazer remained but on reflection he decided that he was close to deleting him as well. So that just left the three for which he had little information: Heron, only there for lack of hard information plus Beth and Vandra. He picked up his PERC and dialled Anna's number to ask her to give him her Aunt Claire's contact details.

CHAPTER TWENTY TWO
CLAIRE & ANNA

Thursday 13th May 2224, Chillesford.

'Christ almighty, Mike,' exclaimed Claire. 'You can't be serious.'

Most people who knew Claire Bois had never heard her swear or use bad language. Mike could recall only one other occasion. He had been the driver on a school bus run and Claire had been his attendant. When a deer jumped out of a roadside hedge near the village of Snape he had braked hard to avoid a collision. Whilst not exactly an emergency stop the sudden deceleration gave his passengers a jolt but the children, restrained by regulation harnesses, were little more than slightly shaken. Claire, standing at the time with her back to Mike was catapulted towards the front of the bus her backside being firmly plonked on the floor.

'Arseholes,' Claire had exclaimed. One boy near the front had sniggered but that had probably been in response to the unedifying sight of the bus attendant lying on her back, legs temporarily in the air displaying her underwear rather than the single word expletive used to express her surprise and annoyance.

On this present occasion it was her response to reading

the list of names Mike had placed before her.

'Come on, now,' she continued. 'You don't really believe that my Anna and your Cassie were capable of betraying all of us at ESA?'

'She's not my Cassie. Not any more.'

'No. Sorry. But you know what I mean.'

'Yes. And that's why I've altered the list. That was my starting point. I first ran the names past Kassim. He insisted that his name and Heron's and Simon and Cassie stayed there until I had clear proof that they *hadn't* been responsible.'

Mike took out his revised list and passed it across. Claire read it and thought about it for a while before commenting.

'That's better,' she announced. 'So it's down to these three ladies. I can't speak for Heron as I didn't have much to do with her but I got to know Vandra and Beth quite well when Anna and I were in rehab at Beeston. Let's have another coffee and I'll tell you all about it.'

Claire, now noticeably less mobile than Mike remembered, eased herself out of her chair and headed to the small kitchen that opened off the sitting room. It was the first time he had been to this house and until about half an hour ago he didn't even know that she had moved here. Anna had only provided him with a telephone number and e-post address. He had spoken to Claire on the phone, arranged the date and time for his visit and not thought that she may have moved from the home he had visited a few times about twenty-five years earlier. On reaching Chillesford along the new road built across the former but now abandoned Bentwaters military base he had gone to the old house only to be told that Mrs Bois had been moved for some years now. She had a bungalow in Kiln Place a little further along the road, on the left. It was, his informant thought, the second house on the left of the small development. And so it had proved to be.

Claire returned with the refilled mugs.

'Now, where shall I begin? I think with Vandra since you appear to think she had it in for you from the start.'

'Good,' interjected Mike, 'but I need to ask you something first. Why were you four sentenced anyway? You were nothing to do with Heron's *armed gang*.'

'I can quite understand your question. We shouldn't have been there at all! Of course at first when the army came we were all under suspicion. You know – guilty until proved innocent – a little like your list. Even poor Michael was pulled in for questioning. Anyway the reason they took things further was because we were a nuisance. We were 'bolshy'. Instead of quietly helping the military with their investigation we did everything we could to hinder it. We hid computers, refused to answer questions or gave wrong answers so as to slow down their progress. That's how we came to be labelled as *active members* of an illegal group. In court we couldn't deny that we had actively tried to mislead the investigation.'

'Good for you! Two years rehabilitation seems a bit harsh though. Anyway Vandra made it quite clear from the start that she didn't like me.'

'Not a very strong motive for betraying you and putting Anna's life at risk and in my view you're quite wrong. Yes, at first she was suspicious of your reason for joining ESA. I can remember her saying, 'once a journalist, always a journalist' and that however well intentioned you were you wouldn't be able to resist sniffing around, finding some real or imaginary scandal and publishing it. But in the end she came to admire you.'

'What changed her view?'

'You'd better ask Anna. She got to know her quite well in Beeston. It may have been through her friendship with Heron. I think Vandra may have been the only true friend Heron had in ESA. Everyone else was just a colleague, apart from Beth Stamford of course who she'd known since her schooldays.'

'What was Vandra really like?'

'Hard working. Very hard working and outspoken and loyal. She never gave up her support for ESA. Even in rehab she gave the staff a hard time. They were really trying to help us back into what they thought of as a 'normal' life but Vee took delight in her game of one-upmanship. On one occasion she feigned illness. She collapsed when waiting to go out with a farm working party. The centre's medical staff were worried so they called up the paramedics. When they arrived Vandra jumped up, grinning, claiming that she was suddenly, miraculously much better. And there were other incidents, each one punished with an extra month added to her sentence. She had another six months to serve after Anna and I were released.'

'So you don't think Vandra would have betrayed us?'

'No. Even if she reckoned that you personally were expendable she wouldn't have put Anna's life in danger.'

'Do you know what happened to her after rehab? She's one of the few ESA people I've not been able to track down.'

'After the six months she came back to Leiston. She stayed with her twin sister Dalanya and husband Graham Stonebridge. Dalanya got her some sort of work and Vandra got herself a little place of her own. Then about ten years ago they all moved away and I lost touch with her.'

'And Beth Stramford?' asked Mike.

Beth also originally came from Leiston but she had stayed outside mainstream ESA operations. She always worked in the Saxmundham office. I know she volunteered to stay there with Michael following the reorganisation when things were centralised at Westhead.'

'Wasn't she originally Kassim's link to the people at Bentwaters?'

'Yes. As you know Kassim believed that the key to our continuing existence was to be on good terms with Buckhurst and co. It was Beth who kept routine communication going.'

'Did she have anything to do with Bentwaters after Kassim moved over to Westhead?'

'I don't think so. We were busy with normal operations and all our work came through Westhead so I never had further contact with her, never even went to Saxmundham after the change. She didn't say much about her time with Michael and I didn't think to ask. Of course Michael would have known what went on but he's in a poor way now and lives in a private hospital. I hear that he doesn't have any memories of those ESA days. Poor old Michael. Last time I saw him he was a very sad looking figure.'

They sat quietly for a time, Mike thinking of the Michael Warren who had first welcomed him to the unit's cabin across Westwood Broad. Breaking the silence Claire added, 'She was very quiet at Beeston, Beth was. Pleasant enough but quiet. Kept her head below the parapet as they say. She was quite the opposite of Vandra.'

'Did she leave with you and Anna?'

'No. There's a strange thing there. After about a year she was transferred somewhere else. There one day, gone the next.'

'But she served her full two years?'

'I don't know. She was sentenced to two years but after Beeston I lost track. I don't know where she went. In fact considering the four of us I don't really know why she was there at all. She didn't lead an active operation like I did. She didn't have anything to do with guns like Anna and she wasn't disruptive like Vandra. Really she had just been a clerk. A very good clerk but as far as I know, just that.'

'Do you think her sentence was a cover, a smoke screen to protect her, and after a year she was released with some sort of reward for pointing the finger at ESA? Do you think she could have been a mole planted by the military?'

'All I know is that she came to ESA before the military were brought into the area. Before Martial Law. She joined when Kassim expanded the old Aldringham Seven and needed staff at his new Saxmundham office.'

'So you've no idea what happened to her after rehab?'

'I don't think she came back to East Suffolk. Anyway no one I've talked with has said anything about her.'

'A new identity, I think.'

'Possibly. Even without much further information you seem to have made out a case for her complicity in a plot. Be careful, Mike. Don't jump to conclusions.'

'No. I won't do that. However much it may appear that she's the person I'm looking for I'll have to look further for the full story. Somehow I need to track her down. So Vandra's off the list but Beth stays on.'

There seemed nothing else that could be usefully said on the subject. Mike wasn't inclined to rush off the moment he had finished with the matter and in any case Claire, ever the good host, had prepared a light lunch and seemed genuinely pleased to chat to an old friend and catch up on news of mutual acquaintances.

'I'm sorry you had to go to the old house. It never entered my head to tell you I'd moved. I've been here seven years and grown quite attached to the place. At first I found it a little small but now I'm less active it's just right. The old house belongs to the past.'

'So when you left rehab did you come straight back here? 04 or 05 was it?'

'Yes, September 2204. I came straight back to my home in the village. I knew things would be a little strained between Ranji and myself as after a few months he'd stopped visiting me in Beeston; said that he didn't like the place, found it intimidating. He came and collected me when I was released and welcomed me home but within a week we both knew we couldn't go back to the way things used to be. He admitted he had met a lady whilst I was away saying at first it was companionship but later it was sex as well. He was sorry, he said, but we had grown apart and he needed to be with her. There was nothing I could do. If I had persuaded him to stay we wouldn't have been happy so two days later he mover over to Sudbourne and I was left alone in the house. We owned the house between us but at least he let me stay on. But I couldn't afford the upkeep and I needed the money so I sold up, he only took thirty percent of the sale and I moved in here. It could have been different if I'd been able to find a full-time, well paid job but ex-prisoners – even those only remanded for rehabilitation – were often not well regarded by employers. Casual or seasonable work was plentiful though but I didn't have a car so only Woodbridge was easily accessible. I did shop-work mostly but became depressed and with time even that sort of job was beyond me.'

'You seem OK now. I wouldn't have guessed you'd have suffered from depression. You've always been one of the most positive people I've known.'

'Anyone can hit hard times Mike. The journey back to full health came when I moved in here. Setting up this little home gave me a purpose and I began to think about doing something along the lines of my work with ESA; something that had a purpose and offered companionship and something I could do from home. So I set up my *Suffolk Friends* business. It's an on-line register of organisations; anything from trades-people and leisure clubs to literary clubs and childminders. Basically its non-profitmaking. It operates as a co-operative and I just get paid like an employee.'

'That's fantastic! You certainly look good on it and it's great to see you settled. On reflection do you think ESA was a good thing, bearing in mind what followed its demise?'

'Of course,' Claire replied, without hesitation.

'But when you look back don't you see Buckhurst's death, your marriage and a couple of others I know about ending in a split and people imprisoned. After all I lost twenty-one years of my life.'

'No Mike. ESA wasn't a failure at all. Of course those things happened and that's regrettable but more importantly I see communities served and in some cases even saved from disintegration. I see friendships and I see courage. I know you believe this as well because that's the message that comes out from your book. ESA had an important part to play in forming our thriving East Suffolk as it is today.'

Friday 14th May 2224, Westleton

On leaving Claire's the previous day Mike had returned along the new road across the old military base to join the A1152 road and turn north-eastwards towards Snape Church End and Leiston before travelling along the long familiar and hardly changed route to Westleton. He was on his way to stay with Marissa but before reaching his overnight stop he had made a small detour through Middleton. Simon had not been buried there – he had been cremated in Ipswich and his ashes had been scattered over heathland near Westhead but Mike had taken some comfort from standing in the churchyard at the spot where he had seen his friend's mortal remains depart from his view for the last time, just two weeks before. For a while he had thought about those years he now termed 'BB' – before Buckhurst. He had not stayed long.

It would be wrong to say that Marissa had moved on following her loss of Simon. Yet she had not stayed rooted in her past either. After a week of tidying up Simon's affairs she had begun to get to grips with her future. She and Simon had made a pact that on the loss of their partner the one that remained would seek to forge a new life and that would mean continuing to be involved with whatever community they were a part of, not withdrawing from it.

'Early days,' she had said to Mike, 'but I can't live in the past forever; I can't waste whatever future I'm blessed with.'

Her first positive action had been to renew her registration with the General Teaching Council and with that necessary step taken she had contacted all schools within about fifty minutes travel. Next she had forwarded her details to Claire's *Suffolk Friends* netsite thereby advertising her availability for tutoring. In each case she had limited her availability to midweek offering just three days – Tuesday, Wednesday and Thursday. So far she had been offered a few weeks covering maternity leave in a primary school in Leiston, starting after the summer break and two hours a week tutoring a child living in her own village who had missed months of schooling through ill-health.

As far as Mike could see the house showed few signs of change. He probably wouldn't have been too surprised if Simon had walked in from the garden suggesting that Marissa put the kettle on to make a drink. Books and equipment that were more likely to have been his than hers were still in place although, in passing their bedroom, door open, he noticed that the picture of Marissa and Simon that stood on her bedside table had been replaced. Now just Simon appeared in the frame dressed in his 'ESA cares' T-shirt, looking out over the bed.

Marissa's home that evening had been a stopover on his route to visit and talk with Anna in Walberswick. His post-funeral visit with Cassie seemed a long time ago now and he felt that Cassie might just as well have been in Australia or Argentina now that she was back in Scotland. On that occasion he had not had a chance to quiz Anna about his list of suspects and following Claire's information about their time together at Beeston he now had some specific items to discuss with her.

So on to Walberswick. As usual he received a warm welcome and ample refreshments and with James away at work in Saxmundham they had plenty of time to ponder over the identity of their betrayer. As he expected Anna was able to corroborate everything her aunt had said. But she was also able to add some new detail. Yes, Vandra had been a firebrand during their stay in rehab. Anna had illustrated her statement with a different story. Demoted to cloakroom-cleaning duties following her 'miraculous recovery' prank Vandra had removed a toilet seat from the staff restroom. With the missing item nowhere to be seen and Vee not owning up the seat had been promptly replaced. A few days later she had paraded around the camp with the missing item draped around her neck. At least it proved she was a good cleaner; Vandra had been quite fussy about personal hygiene. Mike asked Anna what Vandra had thought about his own rôle within ESA. She thought for a while and then told him that Vandra had respected his handling of the Buckhurst affair. She had said that anyone not fully devoted to ESA could well have left her, Anna, to whatever fate was to be handed out to her. Vandra seemed to have overcome her suspicion that as a journalist Mike would have taken up any chance of sending information about ESA to some media organisation, probably in return for payment.

Beth, on the other hand, was portrayed by Anna as a very different character, a paragon of virtue as far as the authorities were concerned. In prison parlance she had kept her head down, her nose clean. She was quiet, neat and tidy, hardworking and very serious. Yet she had been a good friend to Anna during their internment. Anna felt that she was biding her time and upon release would step out into a new world, the whole ESA episode being put behind her and forgotten. Mike asked why Beth had been arrested in the first place. Anna replied that when questioned routinely by the army she had refused to answer their questions. Her refusal was regarded as contempt and was punished by arrest and a spell in rehab. It had seemed strange that she acted in that way; there seemed to be no reason why she should have remained silent. Anyway, Anna continued by saying that one morning the two girls had been sitting in the canteen with their regulation, no choice, take it or leave it mugs of coffee together with the apple and plain biscuit allocated to each of them. After a brief spell of gossip – possibly Beth's only vice – she had suddenly told Anna that she was leaving camp that evening. No! Not escaping. Certainly not, she had stated. She was being transferred. No-one to Anna's knowledge had ever been transferred before except for Tanzi Northwick who had spent her last three months in an ordinary prison near Birmingham. She needed to attend a specialist hospital for regular treatment of an unusual medical condition. What Anna added next made Mike sit up and concentrate.

'I don't think Beth ever went back into rehab and she may not even have spent her last year in detention. The info network between the centres was pretty good but we never heard another word about Beth. She simply seemed to have disappeared off the face of the earth,' she said and added, 'I thought about her for a while after leaving rehab but I've never voiced these thoughts before.'

That had been the last conversation that Beth and Anna had ever had except that as she was leaving the canteen to walk over to the uniformed warder who had called her name Beth had turned, smiled and said one word, just the name of her daughter, Carolina. Then she had gone. Mike asked whether Anna had tried to locate Beth after her own release. She had, starting by talking to Michael Warren but he hadn't seen or heard anything regarding Beth since she had been sent to Beeston. He was, however, able to give Anna Beth's last known address in Saxmundham. Former neighbours unfortunately had no information about her whereabouts. Her husband and small daughter Carolina had moved away soon after Beth was committed to rehab. It had apparently been a sudden move and no-one knew where they had gone. The only other point of contact would have been Heron as they had been to school together but since Heron had also disappeared both possible leads ended there. Anna hadn't pursued the matter and hadn't even thought about Beth for many years now.

At that point in their conversation young Ailsa Court, now aged thirteen, came in, delivered by the school bus, and the conversation changed. As Anna was attending to her daughter's immediate needs and Mike was left to make small talk with the youngster he was struck by how much Ailsa looked like her mother. Like Anna, that was, when Mike had first known her. When she had first arrived at Hut 2 Anna had been eighteen and Ailsa was only five years shy of that age now.

Half an hour Mike decided was a decent enough time to stay on and talk so after thirty minutes or so he took his leave after promising to stay in touch and keep Anna and James up to date with his investigation. From Walberswick he drove back past Westhead and down to Westleton; Marissa had persuaded him to stay overnight again and make his return to Fordham in the morning. They ate out at the pub that evening where Mike was sufficiently well-known for his appearance with Marissa to be accepted without comment. They had sat and relaxed quietly, eaten in the bar, taken their drinks out into the garden and then, as dusk began to fall, had left. By the time they arrived back at Marissa's the warm velvet sky had enveloped their visual world, lights were appearing in cottage windows and the low level solar garden lamps that marked the path between the road and her front door were shining brightly like giant glow-worms.

It may have been the warm weather – the spare room under the eaves at Marissa's had always been a little airless in summer or it may have been Beth Stamford's story being played over and over again in his head but for one reason or another Mike found sleep hard to come by. He needed to find out what had happened to Beth otherwise he would just end up with two dilemmas and no final result. Two dead ends, Heron and Beth. At least he knew Heron was alive or had been up until two weeks ago but apart from that her whereabouts were as equally unknown as Beth's. Heron's dedication to ESA had never been questioned but Beth on the other hand had just done her job and done it well but apart from that she had not shown any great enthusiasm for the cause. And if Anna's information was correct she may well have been let off half the tariff attached to her sentence. Possibly she shouldn't have even been arrested let alone sentenced in the first place. Mystery. Mike drifted into sleep, woke, thought about Beth Stamford again and with no further insight forthcoming sleep closed over him for a second time.

Some time later he became aware of movement. Light and movement. Marissa, he assumed, had gone to the bathroom. The small patch of light visible through the slightly open bedroom door suddenly grew brighter and equally rapidly was extinguished. Marissa's soft footfall moved along the corridor but passed her own door and reached the entrance to the spare room. For a moment Mike could hear only her gentle breathing then she pushed the door further ajar and stepped inside.

'Are you awake, Mike?' she asked in a whisper.

'Yes. I'm just dozing, waking and dozing again. It's hot.'

'OK if I come in for a few minutes?'

'Fine.'

She walked over pushed the cover back a little and sat on the edge of the bed. She spoke about Simon and the everyday things she missed. Mike said little. Just now and again he gave the odd murmur of sympathy or agreement. She ended by saying, 'It's quiet here now. If he ever came back I'd even forgive him his snoring!'

There followed a short period of silence then Marissa stood up and asked, 'Do you mind if I stay here? I'll just lie on the top of the bed. I think I could sleep better here.'

'That's fine but I can go and sleep downstairs.'

By way of an answer Marissa pulled the top cover back over the side of the bed next to her and lay down on it close to the edge and facing outwards. Mike wriggled carefully under the light cover to the far edge and turned on his side leaving a neutral area between them. They lay still and silent for a while.

'Good night,' she whispered.

'night Marissa.'

Saturday 15th May 2224

Mike stirred when a ray of sunlight fell across his face. He opened his eyes, blinked and gradually became aware that Marissa was still lying beside him. He resisted the urge to stretch out his limbs to relieve them of any overnight stiffness and to prompt the blood supply to return fully to the furthest reaches of his body. Instead he lay still on his back, breathing as quietly as possible, waiting for her to provide signs of her own wakening. It was no more than a few minutes later that she gave a little snort, turned onto her back, lay for a while, gave a yawn and then stretched out her legs. Suddenly she turned onto her side and smiled.

'Good morning,' he said, almost in a whisper.

She did not reply but sat up, lifted the hem of her plain white T-shirt, pulled it up over her head taking with it the band that held her blond hair in place and let the items drop to the floor. Turning, she pulled the cover back and moved to sit astride him, pushing herself upright to display her small, well separated breasts that terminated in seemingly identical dark nipples. Then leaning forward, supported by her hands she lowered each nipple in turn to brush against Mike's lips before sitting upright again and looking for some sign of approval. When he gave her a smile of encouragement she lowered herself again allowing him to take her right breast into his slightly open mouth where he gently kissed it until she withdrew and replaced it with her left one. Then feeling him stiffen beneath her she raised her bottom and supported by one hand used the other to take hold of his erection, now no longer just stiff but hard and, nudging aside her scantily brief knickers, she took him inside herself.

At first gently, whilst moving her body slightly to a more comfortable position, and then more firmly she initiated movement until he responded and they moved together but only briefly before Mike climaxed, pushed hard into her a couple of times and relaxed with a satisfied sigh. She remained above him for a few moments until her breathing returned to near normal then, smiling, she ran her hand briefly through his hair before clambering back across him to sit briefly on the edge of the bed. Then after retrieving her T-shirt and hair band she set off towards the bathroom.

Mike lay where he was. He needed to use the toilet but decided he could wait until Marissa had finished rather than go downstairs. He closed his eyes. The sound of the shower temporarily invaded his consciousness until his mind pushed that into the background and provided a re-run of the morning's surprising development. Rather disturbingly, though, when his mind looped through the events for a second time it was not Marissa but Cassie who was initiating sex – brunette as opposed to blonde, her larger breasts moving mesmerizingly up and down dominating the picture before he opened his eyes and quickly pushed himself up into a sitting position. Then, as quickly as those disturbing thoughts had appeared they were gone to be replaced by a new awareness. He and Marissa were, he realised, good friends comforting each other after a loss – for him Cassie, for her Simon. They were not and never would be true lovers. The clue had been that during the daydream he and Cassie had kissed passionately; in reality he and Marissa had not.

Mike raised his left arm, looked at the tattoo, brought it up across his lips and gave it a gentle lingering kiss.

CHAPTER TWENTY THREE
BETH

Thursday 27th May 2224, Fordham

Mike left Marissa's after the weekend, staying one extra day, Monday, and returning to Fordham on the Tuesday. As the kilometres passed by along the A12 and then the E14 his thoughts had returned from the unexpected delights of the past few days to deal with the unresolved problem of who had betrayed ESA. How had the Mercians been able to entrap Anna and himself so easily? The question had been an almost common element of his waking hours for weeks now, repeating itself in a seemingly never ending circle rather like a mantra. During his stay with Marissa they had briefly talked about the possibility of sharing the same house, either Fordham or more reasonably in Westleton. For the future it was a possibility, even a likelihood but for the moment Mike was obsessed with the betrayal and he needed to deal with that little problem before making any life-changing decisions.

On the previous day, Wednesday he had travelled to London – car to Cambridge and rail to Stratford. He had been summonsed to meet his brother-in-law Rupert Church to discuss the next step to be taken towards the possible filming of *The Outlaw*. An interested film producer had engaged the services of a scriptwriter. They wanted to sign a contract soon but Rupert, behaving rather reasonably for once, had demanded that any changes to the storyline were first passed by Mike whereas the film company wanted the freedom to make changes (for artistic reasons, they explained) as and when they were needed. The film, they said, was to be 'based on' the book. Rupert was concerned about maintaining the integrity of the story. Mike wasn't really concerned at all but progress was somehow made and it was expected that the contract would be drawn up and ready for signing in the near future. Mike returned home, rail to Cambridge and car to Fordham, a little depressed. It wasn't a result of the meeting in particular but more the fact that he had lost a whole day's investigation. Then Thursday dawned with a blank space on the calendar and he was free again. And it was raining so he wouldn't be tempted to undertake more work out in his garden.

He looked down at his list.

Seven down, two to go now that Vandra had been elevated to sainthood and removed from the list.

The two remaining were Heron and Beth. Or should that be Beth and Heron?

As usual when he was faced with a difficult choice or decision or, as in this case, a seemingly dead end – a situation where careful thought was required – he made himself a mug of black coffee and brought out his latest must-have comfort food. Today it was the rather tasty oatie biscuits, all too readily available from the local village shop. He sat down, took a bite and a sip, pulled the computer monitor over towards him and looked at his original list of suspects for inspiration.

Beth or Heron?

He reviewed his current state of information about them. He worked systematically through the list of indicators he had drawn up after his visit to Frazer.

Body language was basically a non starter. He hadn't seen Beth since before Buckhurst was killed and he had only seen Heron for a couple of minutes at Simon's funeral.

Could either of them have been *rewarded* for the betrayal? For Heron it seemed that keeping ESA operations going would have been sufficient reward in itself; for Beth, if Anna's ideas were correct, there could have been a reduction in sentence and possibly even more benefits upon release.

As far as any *motive* was concerned he could think of no reason why Heron should swap her loyalty to ESA over to an alternative authority for which she clearly had little regard and he didn't know enough about Beth to decide how she would have responded to a monetary bribe.

Not much to go on. But on balance, since no-one seemed to have thought that Heron could possibly have turned against an ideal for which she had spent so much time and energy, it had to be Beth who was moved to number one suspect. But that elevation was made purely on the basis of a rather weak theory based on extremely tenuous information. Her position at the Saxmundham office both before and after the reorganisation of ESA and her withdrawal from rehab at Beeston each needed further investigation. Heron, he guessed, had systematically covered up any trail that she had left following her departure from Suffolk. Perhaps Beth would have done the same. There were obviously records of the inmates housed at the rehabilitation centres such as Beeston but they were covered by the government's fifty year ban on publication and he wasn't going to wait until 2253 or 2254 to continue his quest. So what about former neighbours in Saxmundham? Anna had tried that line of enquiry many years before so there was no chance that a foot-slog around her former home in that town would bring any better result. Michael Warren was old now and suffering from memory loss. Mike could possibly tease some facts out of him but he didn't wish to cause his friend any distress. Someone had told him that Beth had originally come from Leiston but at present he decided that any investigation there was also likely to be a waste of time and he was hopeful that some more helpful line of enquiry could be found.

Frustration. Another biscuit removed from the packet and another sip of, by this time, lukewarm coffee.

As he raised the biscuit to his lips his PERC chimed, indicating a caller.

'Hello, Mike.'

'Hi, Marissa.'

Mike didn't feel it was yet time to use a term of endearment but suspected that given time their friendship may move up to that level.

'Mike, you remember we were talking about tracing Heron or Beth? Well, I've had an idea. How about the netsite for the National Registry? They have records of marriages, partnerships, births, deaths and other things. There could be a lead there. Just a thought.'

'Marissa, you're a marvel! Thanks. It's a great idea and you've just saved me from finishing off a whole packet of biscuits whilst I fished around for a lead.'

They talked about other things including Marissa's relief that Charlie the cat, who hadn't appeared at all during Mike's recent visit, had turned up on Tuesday evening as though nothing unusual had happened.

Mike clicked off. He had another oatie to celebrate Marissa's brainwave although he was a little miffed that he had not thought of the idea himself. And then he took a further biscuit to celebrate Charlie's safe return.

The National Registry had been established to bring together population statistics for the whole of Great Britain, enabling government departments to make meaningful plans for the future but much of this information was freely available to the general public. When he opened the netsite Mike was faced with a three-way selection. The menu consisted of a blue box labelled *Births and Deaths* with a green box for *Marriages and Partnerships* whilst *Current Occupancy* was backed with gold.

Mike paused. He knew Beth Stamford had been married and that she had a child, a daughter. He could start looking up details for her marriage but he would have to make some assumptions and use a little guesswork.

He tapped the green Marriages and Partnerships box on the screen in front of him and followed through a series of sub-menus selecting first *Suffolk* from the Areas menu and then the *East Suffolk* division to cover Leiston where he assumed, had tradition been followed, the marriage would have taken place. So far so good. Next he was asked for the year of registration. Mike reached across for a pen and paper and resisted the temptation to take another biscuit. When Beth was with ESA in 2201 she would have been in her late twenties, possibly early thirties. If she had been at school with Heron she would be of a similar age but that fact didn't help to narrow it down since Heron had never given away her own age. Mike had remembered seeing Beth in the office with a girl aged about six or seven. It had probably been a school holiday. So her marriage could well have been in about 2194, possibly earlier.

Mike started with East Suffolk marriages in 2194. No-one named Stamford had been married in the area that year. Back to 2193. There was one Stamford recorded but that lady had married a Mark New and taken his family name. 2192 – again nothing but 2191 brought a result. On the 17th August that year Bethany Sandon Woodford had married Aldane James Stamford in Leiston. Bingo! Of course! It was then that Mike remembered that Michael Warren had sometimes referred to Beth and Al although he would never have guessed that the full version of the name Al was Aldane. He had assumed that Beth's full name could have been Elizabeth or even just Beth but he had never thought of her actual name as Bethany. He briefly flirted with the idea of telling Marissa about his discovery but his mind was racing ahead; he didn't want to stop at this point now that he was on a roll so he quickly jotted down his findings and returned to the main menu.

Mike was interested in the origins of Aldane James Stamford since he and Beth could well have returned to his home area. Mike tapped on the blue box, the gateway to information on Births and Deaths and on to Births from the sub-menu. An amazing selection of alternatives now confronted him. He could examine the records starting with any one of eight pieces of information: Family name, obviously, also year of birth or actual day of birth then place of birth starting with Suffolk through ever increasing refinement via sub divisions of the county down to individual towns and villages. If that didn't help you could look under mother's name or father's name. Unfortunately his knowledge of Aldane James Stamford was just that: His name. He could have guessed Lincolnshire as the area. A long buried memory suggested that someone may have told Mike that he came from there but he had little choice other than to search under the family name – Stamford. He tapped on Family Name and then on to 'S' before a box appeared with a request that he type in the family name to be researched or if possible the full name of the person under investigation.

Mike typed ALDANE JAMES STAMFORD.

Fortunately there had been few Aldane James Stamfords born in Britain over the years. Had his first name been Alan or Alex or Alastair or even Alwyn the list could have been fairly long so Mike was pleased that a tap of the 'GO' button brought up just three entries.

Aldane James Stamford b.Welby, Lincs 20.10 2053. *d. Pinner, Gtr London 01.01.2153.*

Aldane James Stamford b. Grantham, Lincs 30.11.2165

Aldane James Stamford b. Pershore, Worcs 09.05.2200

OK. It had to be number two, then. Number one could have been a grandfather or great-grandfather and the last entry could have been a nephew but such speculation had to wait for a further investigation some time in the future. Mike brought himself back from the realms of fantasy and scribbled down Aldane's details at the foot of the note he had made about the marriage.

There was a buzz on his PERC. A text had arrived from Rupert. The contract with the film company had arrived and he was pleased with it. Mike needed to sign off three sections and then it would be all systems go. The meeting to complete this would be at 1200, next Thursday (June 03) at the Kettering office.

There had been a time when Rupert would have phoned, discussed the matter in hand and then chatted casually but now he arranged things by ultimatum. The message that Mike had read out in his head was a full version of the extremely abbreviated text his eyes read on the screen. Anyway as long as Rupert adored sister Gayle and Gayle adored Rupert that was OK. Having had his train of thought interrupted Mike decided to phone Marissa with news of his morning's work.

'You were spot-on about the National Registry,' he told her and then proceeded to outline his findings.

'Are you sure that it really is Beth's husband you've found?'

'Not completely certain, no. But this Aldane seems to fit and at least it gives me a lead to follow.'

'What will you do next then?' she asked.

'Go on to the *Current Occupancy* section. Start with Grantham, the place where Aldane was born, in the hope that he's returned there. If that doesn't locate Beth we broaden our search around the town and if that doesn't work we'll have to think again.'

'What's this '*we*' business then Mike? I thought it was your quest,' she commented in a serious tone. As she spoke Mike could hear the very slight clicking noise that she made when she gave a quiet laugh, one that was little more than a smile.

'Bye, Ma,' he responded and hurriedly ended the connection. He knew she didn't like that abbreviation for her name but he reckoned she'd forgive him. She was more likely to have been smiling than scowling as she put her phone down. He ate the last oatie biscuit.

Friday 28th May 2224, Fordham

Daily tasks interrupted his investigation until the afternoon. His recent absence from home had led to a run-down of food in particular, a thin layer of dust covered furniture that had been unused since his return and the strong winds that had buffeted the eastern counties a few days earlier had left the need for some essential remedial work to plants in the garden. During lunch his mind again covered the planned next step in his pursuit of Beth Stamford. Realising that the midday news broadcast, switched on by habit, was now redundant he zapped it off, pushed his plate, cutlery and empty mug to one side and settled once again in front of his monitor.

'OK,' he said to himself, 'Current Occupancy.'

This section listed every property in the country and its present owner. It was updated daily. As before a tap on the screen gave him a new menu listing the various ways to access the available information. Mike chose 'Area' and from the list provided he selected Lincolnshire. The sub-area list caused him to pause. Mike didn't know Lincolnshire at all well and he couldn't specifically place

Grantham within any of the divisions presented to him. Rather than bring up a netsite such as '*Mapdit*' or '*Place-Finder*' and work through even more menus he turned, leaned out of his chair and pulled a Great Britain Atlas from the bookcase. A quick flick through brought up the relevant page and Grantham, he found out was in the Kesteven division of Linconshire. He dropped the atlas onto the floor beside him in readiness for further use if required and turned back to the monitor screen.

The list read Holland, Kesteven, Lincoln City, Lindsey, South Humberside.

OK. Kesteven for starters. And it turned out to be a good place to start for although there were no recorded Aldane J Stamfords living in the area there was surprisingly one Beth S. Stamford and two Bethany S Stamfords listed. Unfortunately second and subsequent forenames were only given as initial letters but, Mike thought, it shouldn't be too difficult to find out whether any of these ladies were his quarry. He studied the list for clues.

Beth S. Stamford & Jackson Stamford occupied an address in Great Ponton.

Bethany S. Stamford lived in Grantham, and the other

Bethany S. Stamford & Byron J.R. Albert lived in Welbourn.

Could any of these ladies be his Beth? Well, not his exactly as he had hardly known the girl but the one in which he was interested. It could be so if Aldane had died or divorced or separated or moved away. Beth could have re-married or just moved in with Byron or less likely Jackson. It would seem unlikely that she would have married another person with the same family name as her first husband so that left an apparently single lady or someone who may have taken a new partner. Mike sat back and rubbed his eyes. This would need a bit more investigation or some inspired guesswork. There seemed no reason to select one or the other for initial investigation so he called for a second opinion; he phoned Marissa.

'Calling to apologise?' she asked. Again to his relief he heard the sound that suggested there was a gentle laugh behind her serious-sounding enquiry.

'No, well yes, I mean. Anyway I'm going to patch through to you the list I've got from the NR that's up on my screen. Are you ready for it?'

'Go ahead.'

Mike sent the list containing the three B.S. Stamfords to Marissa's PERC.

'Got it,' she confirmed after a few seconds. Then, 'Hold on,' she continued, 'I'll patch it to my monitor so that I can see it clearly.' Mike nearly made a gently rude comment about her eyesight but decided not to take the risk of a second attempt at humour so soon after the first.

'OK. Got it. Where's Aldane then?'

'He's not there. Not recorded so there's a good chance he's no longer on the scene. If he is still around with Beth they must be living somewhere else and we've got the wrong ladies on this list. Got any gut feeling about those three?

There were a few moments silence followed by an 'Umm'.

'No info on children?' she asked. 'What about Carolina, the little girl?'

'Not so little now. She'd be about thirty and probably

long gone and in any case the list only contains names of the property owners or lessees. So, Marissa, take a stab at the list and give me an idea where to start.'

Again a few moments for thought followed by a gentle, reflective sigh and then her reply.

'Formally she's known as Bethany and this is a formal record so I don't think number one, Beth, is our lady. That leaves number two who appears to be a single lady or number three who, if it's our Beth, must have got herself a new partner. What do you reckon she'd do, Mike? Would she take on someone new rather than live on her own? I never met her so I can't decide that one.'

'I didn't know her well enough to even guess on that one. But we've got two Bethany S. Stamfords and two postal addresses. I think we need to contact them and find out what the middle 'S' stands for. We're looking for Sandon. Not very common I guess. If neither of them claim that as a second name we're almost back to square one I reckon.'

'So do we write to them?'

'I think that's best. Straightforward surface mail. No need to muck around trying to find phone numbers or e-post addresses. I'll get onto that straight away and go down to Newmarket to get them in the post today.'

'What approach will you take? Do you need to mention ESA at this time?'

'I'll simply ask if we have the correct address for Bethany Sandon Stamford. They can reply by e-post, text, phone, surface mail or even come and knock on my door.'

'It looks like we could be getting somewhere now. Well done, Micky.'

Marissa was getting her own back but despite the use

of a name-form he hated he knew the congratulations were heart-felt.

Later that evening he rang Marissa again.

'Christ, Michael! All this attention! Is it me you're sweet on or are you still hankering after B. S. Stamford?'

'Just saying thanks and Good night.'

'I reckon you deserve one more chance to charm me,' she said followed by her smiley click. 'Try again tomorrow. Good night.'

Monday 31ˢᵗ May 2224, Fordham

An e-post message had arrived from Bethany S. Stamford of Grantham on the Saturday, the day after Mike had been to Newmarket to post the letter to her. She was not the Bethany Stamford he was looking for. Her second name was Samantha. Her family had lived in the area for generations and as far as she knew she was the only Bethany and no-one among her relatives had a middle name of Sandon. The only possibility she could think of was a family of Stamfords who, she seemed to remember, had lived in the newer part of town, Barrowby, across the E11 road. But that was a long time ago. She hadn't heard anything about them for years. 'All the best for your search,' she had finished. She repeated her e-post address after her name at the foot of the message.

'What a nice lady,' Mike had said to himself as he had jotted down Barrowby at the end of his lengthening list of items headed 'New Leads'. Then he had sent a message to Ms Bethany not Sandon Stamford thanking her for her prompt reply and her suggestion about Barrowby. Within two minutes the chime indicating incoming mail had sounded and she had replied asking him to let her know how his investigation progressed. But then worried that an apparently single lady was striking up a correspondence with him he had promptly erased her details from his address book and gone into the kitchen to seek out and open a new packet of biscuits.

But early on this Monday morning a letter arrived from Lincolnshire. Fortunately it was Max on the post round, not Grainger who rarely made it to Mike's before midday. And fortunately Cambridgeshire, the county that contained Fordham, was not included in Royal Mail's latest attempts at efficiency whereby all mail had to be collected from a nearby postal sorting office; home deliveries were suspended in those areas being used to trial this scheme. Just four kilometres down the Ely to Newmarket road from his village the Suffolk area had been selected to test the plan. For years Cambridgeshire had attempted to annex the little enclave of Suffolk containing Newmarket claiming that it could cut the cost of services supplied by the local authority to this area. But Newmarket had a population that was fiercely loyal to Suffolk and which had on one occasion even declared independence for a couple of weeks rather than agree to the Boundary Commission's proposal to transfer them to their easterly neighbour. The Boundary Commission, not for the first time, had relented and returned to the status quo but now, mail-wise at least, the people were suffering for their conservatism. If Mike had been forced to travel four kilometres up to Soham and the same distance back home many letters would still be sitting in the Post Office until their thirty day rule come into force and they would have been destroyed. Mike thought that if ever he was in need of ready cash he could do worse than to set up a doorstep delivery service.

The letter. As he opened the envelope Mike hardly dared admit to raised hopes about this, his last remaining positive leads. As it was he had to read it twice before allowing his mouth to move into a broad smile.

Dear Sir, it began formally, despite the fact that his original letter had contained his full name and contact details.

Your enquiry has reached the home of Mrs Bethany Sandon Stamford. I am unable to say that I am the same Bethany Stamford you are hoping to contact and therefore you may wish to send me some details about the lady in question and perhaps some information about yourself.

The letter was signed *B. S. Stamford* under the assurance of *yours sincerely.* No alternative contact details were provided. Mike had never seen Beth's signature so that didn't help confirm the identity of this contact. He felt both excited and wary about this reply. There seemed to be a real chance that he had located Beth but he was unsure how to proceed. What should he write in reply? Mike being uncertain about the use of the English language was an unusual if not a unique situation in his life but for once he felt in need of assistance.

'Marissa. Hi! Ring me back ASAP.'

Frustratingly he was unable to make contact with her but it was less than an hour later when his PERC rang and they were talking.

'It's unusual for you not to answer at the first ring. Didn't you have your phone with you?'

'Sorry, Mike. I'm up in Dunwich. My phone was switched off. Anna and I are working on the ESA display for the Coast Heritage Centre's *Martial Law* room. We've some really good ideas for showing how things were at the time. We'd like a signed copy of your book as a centre-piece, please. Anyway, what were you calling about?'

Mike outlined the new development.

'That's great,' Marissa enthused. 'I quite see your problem. A poorly worded letter could slam the door shut on this one for good. Come on over to Walberswick. Anna and I will help you sort out a reply. We'll be back by lunchtime, back by 12.30 I should think.'

'I was hoping to have you all to myself.'

'Are you sure this letter isn't just an excuse.'

'No, really!'

'Only kidding. Now are you coming up or not? You're welcome to stay over at Westleton on the return.'

'In that case I'm on my way.'

The by now familiar journey to the east coast went smoothly. Mike was in no mood to let a slower than usual last section between the A12 and Walberswick, held up by a large removal van on the narrow lanes, interfere with his buoyant mood. The only slight concern was a feeling that his good mood was more to do with completing his quest than his seeing Marissa face-to-face for the first time in a week. When he arrived at Anna's house he was welcomed by the site of a table set for lunch. And James was there. Back at Westhead in ESA days no-one would have considered Anna a good cook. She had been content with ready prepared fast food but since then her skills had developed. Perhaps it was James' influence. James was a gannet.

Lunch was eaten in the conservatory as the unseasonably cool north-easterly wind would have made alfresco dining uncomfortable. Afterwards there followed conversation and the inevitable banter, only ended by James' disappearance back to work. The girls cleared away, brushing aside Mike's half-hearted offer of help and returned, chore completed in a more serious mood, ready to plan the next step of the investigation.

'Play it cool, Mike,' Anna suggested. 'Explain briefly why you want to find Beth – catching up with an old ESA colleague – and give the barest details about yourself. Do just as she asks. If she is our Beth you don't want to frighten her off. She may have thought that she had made a complete break with those days. She may not wish to talk about them.'

'Yes. Keep it short, keep it simple,' counselled Marissa. 'Shall we start on a draft now?'

They agreed to make it a formal letter again and worked on Anna's little notepad, drafting, correcting and paring until they were satisfied. Mike read through the latest draft. They agreed it would be the version that he would print out, sign and post. He checked through one last time.

Dear Bethany Stamford.
The Beth Stamford I am hoping to meet worked with the East Suffolk Association between 2198 and

2201 at their head office in Saxmundham. As you
may know I have written a book recording my time
with ESA. I am hoping to catch up with, and meet
informally, those ESA members who I haven't seen
for many years. I have no intention of publishing
further information relating to ESA or the Martial
Law period in general.

> *Yours sincerely, Mike Cannon.*

'*Yours sincerely*, Mike. When did you last end a letter
or a message with that?'

'Back in school, probably. But I think it's the appropriate
wording in this case. Formal and low key.'

They agreed. Anna printed the letter and Mike signed
it, placing it in a handwritten addressed envelope. Marissa
and Mike took their leave and returned to Westleton via a
circuitous route through Yoxford so as to make sure that
their letter would catch the evening collection from the
main road post box. Mike stayed overnight at Westleton.

Thursday 3rd June 2224

There was no hurry to set off for Kettering. His lunch
date for meeting Rupert had been set at 1200 midday so an
arrival about 1130, 1145 would be OK. Just about an hour's
journey. If he left by 1030 he could take it easy, probably
stop off for a drink midway along his route. Somewhere
near Huntingdon would do fine. He had made this journey
several times since moving to Fordham and not once had
he fallen foul of any of the dreaded three Cs – congestion,
construction or cops.

Mike cleared away breakfast, tidied around a bit and then thought about clothes for the visit. Rupert liked formal; neat and tidy, but nothing flamboyant. Was it a time to smooth things along with Rupert, not make waves and agree to anything his publisher suggested? If so then neat and tidy it would need to be. Or was it an occasion where he needed to stand firm on principle and force Rupert to support his own point of view? Probably a traditional business outfit would be best if this was the case but Mike really wasn't bothered either way. The book had been published; Rupert could do what he liked with the film. Mind you, he still resented Rupert changing the book's title and he did like winding him up when he became pompous. So he decided it had to be casual dress – not smart casual, just slightly scruffy casual.

The letterbox snapped shut loudly but not quickly enough to trap the letter pushed right through by mailman Max. His colleague Grainger by comparison was adept at trapping his delivery under the flap and at times mangling the envelopes and their contents in the process. Mike had decided to get an outside mailbox but it wasn't a priority and he hadn't got around to doing it yet. Half dressed he scuttled downstairs hoping for a reply from Lincolnshire and to his pleasure, surprise and with just a little excitement he saw that the sole item lying on the hallway floor was addressed to him in the now easily recognised round handwriting.

Dear Michael, it stated, a little less formally this time.

I had thought to refuse your request but since

you know my address and could turn up here uninvited I have decided to suggest that you come up here so that we can talk. As you may suspect we came here to start a new life, to distance ourselves in time and space from those events. I'm not keen to delve too far into old memories but I may be able to answer some of your questions. I shall be free from 1400 hours tomorrow, Thursday 3rd June or Friday at the same time. After that I shall be unavailable and there will be no point in your trying to contact me further. If you decide to visit on one of these two dates just turn up. We shall be expecting you.

Regards, Bethany.

The tone of the letter confused Mike. It seemed as though Beth was reluctantly allowing him back into her life, offering a very narrow window of opportunity but with a slight thawing of her opposition to his request as indicated by her use of the word 'Regards'. For Beth, having been trained as a clerk and receptionist it was probable that writing formally had become second nature. However, whatever the tone of the letter it definitely contained an invitation and that was what really mattered.

Today Thursday he was busy but tomorrow he was free. Logically it was Kettering today and Lincolnshire tomorrow. But what the heck? Rupert's contract could wait. He would be a little pissed-off about it but he'd grudgingly set a new date. And Mike would make an effort by wearing more acceptable apparel. Seeing Beth Stamford couldn't wait another day; a sleepless night wondering about the outcome of the meeting followed by a long expressway journey just couldn't be part of any sensible plan.

Mike sent Rupert a short text and then one to Marissa that was even briefer. Then he turned off his phone to avoid the temptation to access the inevitable awkward replies. He knew that Marissa would ask to go along with him. A trip anywhere with Marissa would have been great but Beth's invitation had been to him alone and he didn't want to put any obstacle in the way of completing a successful mission. Muck this visit up and the chance of resolving the truth about ESA's demise could be gone for ever. Then he made some sandwiches, found a bottle of water and added an apple in case he didn't find anywhere convenient to stop or if he was held up. Arranging such a snack inevitably reminded him of the time when he was on the run and lunch choices were limited.

Heavy overnight rain had given way to a grey but dry morning. However as he travelled first westwards on the E14 and then northwards on the E11 a gentle brightness filtered through the thin layer of overcast cloud and as he relaxed into his diving his mood also brightened, buoyed by the excitement of potentially gaining the result he had worked towards for over two months now. First Cambridge, then Peterborough and a little later Stamford were put behind him. Non-stop. But by the time Grantham came into view in the distance he was in need of a comfort stop. He glanced at the dashboard clock and was pleased to see that he had made enough progress to take a short stop for lunch before leaving the E11 for the last leg of his journey. As if by request, a couple of minutes later a sign indicating the Gonerby Services, 7km ahead, passed overhead on its gantry with the WC, knife and fork and petrol pump symbols impressing themselves on his mind in a way that a worded menu would have failed to do. At the stated distance he pulled off to the right on to a slip road, skimmed past the lorry park and the hotel exits and parked at the back of the service area car park. Mike hated parking near to those people who needed to place their cars right close to the building's entrance. He had visions of large families with young children carrying all sorts of bags and eating sticky takeaway food as they brushed past his Cantabrian or, even worse, opened up their multi-doored family transporters to knock or scratch his paintwork. The extra walk to the services was no problem.

Gonerby Services met Mike's needs. Not especially outstanding in terms of cleanliness, catering and comfort but not particularly poor either. After the thirty minutes needed for toilet and refreshments he returned to his car and set the Routesafe Navigator by entering Beth's address code. He hadn't needed anyone annoyingly twittering directions and warnings to him on the Expressway but from now on he would find the directions a comfort whilst following a route over previously un-travelled roads. As he turned his car to exit the Service Area he became aware that Marissa, had she been sitting beside him, would have been a great comforter on this leg of the journey.

Avoiding the return to the expressway Mike exited directly onto the A607 road that arced around to the east as a dual carriageway, crossing the main East Coast rail line and a river before reaching a roundabout and deteriorating into the type of rural route that snaked across the countryside like a slalom course neatly by-passing the small towns and villages it was originally created to serve. With Barkston left behind at the roundabout Mike headed for Honington, Carlton Scroop, Caythorpe and Fulbeck with a broad vale to his left and an escarpment fronted ridge to his right. From his schooldays he remembered that the chalk uplands of the Lincolnshire Wolds lay seawards, to the east, so these hills had to be the limestone ones but their name escaped him, buried in a mass of rarely needed information stashed somewhere at the back of his mind. Fulbeck village gave way to a small town named Leadenham and then ahead of him, again occupying a spring-line position below the escarpment lay Welbourn, the settlement referred to in Beth's address.

'800 metres, turn right,'

The Routesafe lady instructed him to turn away from the village that lay to the left of the road and take a country lane that lead directly up the face of the escarpment. Towards the top a 'Stop: Give Way' sign was visible as the only indication that there was a road along the ridge hidden behind the laneside hedges until that visual statement was supported by his on-board navigator.

'100 metres, stop and give way. Cross Pottergate Road and continue ahead'.

Having stopped, looked and waited for a car travelling at some speed along the straight, level, ridge-top road Mike pulled across to the flatter land that lay beyond the top of the scarp.

'500 metres, destination on left.'

Routesafe had the co-ordinates for every single address in the country providing that you were not heading for a location added since the last monthly update. Today he had been advised absolutely accurately all the way along the route since leaving Gonerby, which in Mike's view was almost always the case although on one route approaching his home in Fordham he had been unable to get the navigator to advise him of the route that he regarded from experience as the most appropriate. Today, though it was full marks and a gold star for the system.

Approaching a building that gave the impression that it was or may have been part of a farm he swung his Cantabrian through a pair of open gates and turned right onto a driveway to park beside two other cars that already occupied part of a large yard. Ahead was a house and to his left lay an open sided, empty barn.

Brake on, ignition off. There was a tap on the front passenger door glass. Mike looked up and seeing a figure standing beside the car he lowered the window.

'Hello, sir.'

'Hi,' Mike responded, less formally.

'Mike, I assume. You're expected. Leave your car here and I'll show you where to find her.'

Mike formed the impression that this isolated house welcomed few visitors and that those who came here were usually invited. The casual, uninvited visitor would most likely be greeted by closed gates and an unrelieved oppressive silence. He had half expected that the middle-aged gentleman who walked around the car to meet him as he climbed out would ask to see his National Identity card but he simply held out his hand, shook Mike's and turned to indicate where Beth was to be found.

'Take the path along the right side of that plantation, turn left in front of the great barn and you'll find a door when you turn again past the end of the building. She'll be in there.'

Mike thanked him, turned and locked his car and set off on foot in the direction of the barn. Past the trees, left past the end of the huge metal-framed and walled barn and then to the right, around the end. To his left then, separated from his path by a hedge, was a broad, closely cut grass area that traversed the plateau in a broad swath towards the horizon. In appearance it was rather like the straight section of a horse-race course or a golf course fairway. To his right the long panelled wall of the barn was broken half way along by a light-green painted door standing out in contrast to the grey metallic expanse that it punctuated.

Mile pushed the door open with his right hand, stepped down and took a few steps inside.

The interior appeared dark compared with the bright summer sunlight outside apart from the light streaming in at the far end to his left through a large opening that occupied much of the end wall up to roof level. As his eyes grew accustomed to the reduced level of illumination Mike was able to make out the shape of first one and then a second small aircraft inside and by squinting to his left at the rectangle of light he saw a third standing outside on the concrete apron. Mike knew little about aircraft types. Large commercial airliners and famous fighting planes OK but small planes used for leisure, sport or short journeys were beyond his interest or experience. The plane in front of him was a low-winged, single-engine, propeller craft painted totally in white apart from the registration letters marked out in red. The plane outside was larger. It was possibly capable of carrying a pilot and three or four passengers and appeared to be powered by two small jet engines placed at the rear. The third aircraft, lying to his right by the end wall, was just a shell – a blue coloured, engineless body that had been raised up to shoulder height and rested on a stout supporting cradle. Two similarly coloured wings stood leaning against the wall behind the fuselage and nearer to him an aero-engine stood on a pallet on the floor beneath what appeared to be a hoist suspended from a roof beam. Tools tidily occupied racks on the wall ahead of him and less tidily on a work bench and scattered on the floor around the dismembered craft.

Mike turned to move towards the light to see if he could find Beth outside but was abruptly stopped in his tracks. A circular metal cylinder had been pushed into his back, between his shoulder blades, and a hand placed lightly on his right shoulder. Within two seconds a kaleidoscope of impressions invaded his mind. The metal felt like the end of a gun barrel, the person holding it was almost certainly left-handed and a scent of perfume was fairly subtle but quite unmistakable.

'Heron,' he said.

'Who were you expecting, Mike?'

He remained silent and still until the hand was removed and the gun dropped. He turned round slowly to face her. Yes. It was Heron, dressed in army style combats, just as he remembered her. And the Piata in her hand was aimed towards him, pointing towards his chest. Heron. Always in control. In any situation.

'We'll sit over there.'

She indicated two old, dirt-stained lounge chairs that

possibly once belonged to a suite but were now placed against the wall near to the hanger entrance. Mike walked across and sat down facing the door. When he was seated Heron moved across to the other chair, turned it around to face Mike and sat down with the pistol still trained on his body.

'Do we really need the gun?'

In answer she got up and walked to the far side of the entrance where she could still keep an eye on him, looked out briefly and then raised the Piata, knocked off the safety catch and fired a single shot outside. Returning to the chair she sat down and placed the gun on the floor beside her. If a situation arose where a firearm was needed she would easily be able to retrieve it.

Heron was still in control.

Mike's mind was empty apart from the scene in front of him; he had no agenda for pushing the meeting forward. However for the first time in ages his mind had slipped into its reporter mode. He was taking in everything that impinged on his senses and became certain that Heron wanted to, even needed, to talk but that whatever she needed to say would be delivered according to her rules, without interruption. Yet he needed first to ask just one simple question.

'Where's Beth Stamford?'

'Dead.'

That briefest of answers had a finality about it that told Mike he had asked his last question for the moment. Now it was Heron's turn. She paused, looked down briefly then raised her eyes and began to speak.

'Beth died about fifteen years ago. She was living in Barrowby near Grantham. Following her death her husband Aldane soon sold up and moved away. As far as I know he now lives near their daughter Carolina. Somewhere in the South-west.

She paused, looked away again as though trying to look into the past and then returned her gaze, looking directly at Mike.

'I left Westhead the evening of the ambush. We all knew that you had gone. For a while I scurried around between one place and another trying to keep ahead of the authorities. First night I chanced using my own place in Darsham then next day moved on to a safe house we had set up in Yoxford. After that it was my cousin's home in a village near Beccles . About four nights there, I think. The police did call once. That scared me and I was all ready to flee but they were investigating a different matter entirely. Anyway we hatched a strategy and it was cousin Macey's idea that I came up here. Remote. I hiked to near Bungay then hitched my way in stages always avoiding the coasts where I could wander into a Military Restricted Area. Most of the truckers were great – no questions and the occasional free meal. One asked for ID but that was only to avoid picking up an illegal immigrant. After Peterborough I picked up a ride heading towards Bourne, the A15 road and Lincoln. Just short of Bourne this trucker pulled into a lay-by and demanded sex as payment for the ride. I left him with sore genitals but without the compensation that he had arrived at that situation after having enjoyed sex. But that got me thinking. There were things I would happily provide sex to obtain. Things like companionship, protection, a roof over my head and three good meals a day. That would be a reasonable trade-off. So I wandered around Lincolnshire for several months picking up men in pubs. The first two didn't work out. One was in a little place called Toft, the other place I don't even remember, but after five months I met a guy named Byron Albert in a pub called The Greyhound in the village of Folkingham east of Grantham. Ron, a widower, was and still is a gentleman. We lived in his house for a while, enjoyed each others company, then moved in up here.'

Heron sat back and gave a slight smile.

'So that's it?'

'More or less, yes.'

'And that was Byron Albert I saw back at the house?'

'Yes.'

'But how do you make a living?'

'Here,' replied Heron, raising her arm and pointing around the aircraft hanger.

'Here,' she repeated. 'We rent this out to our neighbour who owns the grass airstrip out there. He keeps and maintains his planes in here. Ron does a little restoration like that old Cessna lying in bits over there although I reckon its more like building a replica the length of time he's taken over it. We're not rich, we're not poor. We make out OK.'

'So what about ID? When I was on the run it caused me no end of problems.'

'Yes, I know. I've read your book,' said Heron, sourly, apparently annoyed at Mike's interjection with a detail about his own life. 'That's what the men were for, what Ron is for. OK, the sex and companionship are good. I don't love Ron but I wouldn't leave him. We started off with a plan. If ID was needed we'd either use Ron's, which was usually OK or we'd abandon the plan entirely.

'But you're Beth Stamford now, not Jane Heron or so the National Registry believes.'

'Yes. I changed my name. Not officially, at first, but bit by bit we left information that Ron Albert's partner was Bethany Stamford. I was Beth in the village shop and in the pub. The mail came here addressed to Beth Stamford. People who know you don't ask for ID.'

'But you are actually recorded as Beth Stamford by the National Registry. If no ID card had been issued to you in that name you wouldn't be given at this address in their archive,' Mike reasoned.

'Ever the journalist, Mike. Always investigating, always niggling away for the final detail and of course you're right. Eighteen months ago I handed myself in. This wasn't noticed by anyone, it was no longer news so the fact was never recorded in the papers. I went to the police as I reckoned that following the amnesty the Martial Law investigation was now history. No-one would wish to be bothered with a 'wanted' lady from way back who was long thought to be lost to the system. After all I would have been given five years at most before the amnesty. I hadn't killed any one. I hadn't been the leader of an illegal group. As far as the authorities were concerned I was at most just a humble foot-soldier. And I was right. At a brief formal hearing they stamped my record as 'closed' and thanks to the amnesty I walked away completely free. Then I was able to officially become Beth Stamford. I changed my name by appeal to the Magister's bench in Lincoln and with the official documents to hand applied for and received my ID card. So you are actually speaking to Bethany Sandon Stamford.'

'Why Beth?'

'Do you really need to know all the details? It's history now.'

'But to me it's an unfinished story. I'm sure you know why I'm here, Heron and we haven't touched on that yet.'

'OK.' She nodded her agreement. 'It's a long story. Beth and I go back a long way. We met at Leiston High School. She came from Brick Kiln School in the town, I came from Coldfair Green Village School. We were put together on the first day and stayed friends from there on. She was Beth Woodford in those days and I was Jane Wood so we were often grouped together. During that first year I had about six months off school, mainly in hospital. When I got back Beth helped me to catch up. She was the clever one; I just wanted to flirt with the lads. Anyway after school we drifted apart. She went on to college in Ipswich, learnt communications skills and landed a job as a receptionist with a firm of land agents in the town. That's where she met Aldane – he was a trainee negotiator with the same firm. Later they both found positions with another firm, relocated to Saxmundham and when their daughter was born Beth left to be a full-time mother. Later she felt able to look for something part-time. That's how she fetched up at ESA. When she went into rehab Aldane took their daughter and moved back to Grantham to be near his parents. Anyway, after school I took up shooting as a hobby. Became quite good actually. If I'd stuck at it I could probably have made Olympic standard. At the gun club I met Franc Heron who was a marine engineer. He was Australian by birth and so handsome and when we married we started a new life over there. It was great at first but things between us went sour – you don't need the details – we separated and I came home. Lived in Darsham. Then Beth and I joined up again when I also joined ESA.'

She paused for a few seconds and then stood up abruptly.

'I need a drink,' she explained and moved over towards the doorway where her bag and a bottle of water stood on the ground by the wall. Mike looked down towards the gun. He could have grabbed it but that would have ended their conversation. And in any case there really may only have been one bullet, just for show. Heron came back with the water, took a drink and placed the bottle down by the gun. She didn't offer any to Mike.

'I met Beth again by chance. Ron and I moved quite frequently before we came up here and we lived for a short time in Grantham in a little terraced house near the centre. I met Beth in a supermarket and with Ron away trucking for days at a time I used to visit her in Barrowby now and again. One day, quite out of the blue, I feinted and fell over in the street. Luckily Ron wasn't on the road that day and he was at home at the time. He took me to be checked over at the Minor Injury Unit at the hospital. When asked for my ID card I told them that in our hurry to get there I'd left it at home. They quite understood, it was a common occurrence but they needed to record my visit. I could only think to give them Beth's name and address. Date of birth was easy as we were born on consecutive days, I was the older, but the problem came when they asked me for my GP's name. I told them that I'd seen several doctors, I didn't stick to one but I'd attended the Barrowby Medical

Centre. They looked it up and luckily Beth had been registered there. When I was discharged I was given a letter with Beth's name and address together with medical centre details along with her NHS number and National ID number. I told Beth and we had a laugh about it but when she died suddenly about eighteen months later I began actively taking over her identity. A little later we moved here when Ron gave up the trucks and as far as the locals were concerned we were Byron Albert and Bethany Stamford, no questions asked.

'Did Beth talk about her time in rehab?'

'It was mentioned when we were catching up on gossip. Why?'

'Claire and Anna who were also at Beeston think she only did one year of her sentence.'

'They're wrong. She did two. For the second year she was transferred to the authority of Cranwell Rehab to be nearer Barrowby. Carolina, the daughter, was seriously ill and at one time they feared she wouldn't survive. During her second year Beth was paroled to live at home or in hospital accommodation and had to report to a police station at least twice a week. She certainly completed two full years.'

'Do you think Beth would have sabotaged our operation?'

'No, Mike. She didn't. I know that for a fact. There was a mole but it wasn't Beth. Buckhurst had a lackey working in our Saxmundham office. She was called Jasmine something or other. White or Black or Brown I seem to remember. She passed over details of our personnel, how we were organised and what we did. No more than anyone off the road could have found out had they asked. She was harmless but we got rid of her at the reorganisation. She didn't know about the guns or the training.'

You're certain?'

'Yes, Mike. Definitely. Neither Beth nor Jasmine thingy betrayed you. I know because I'm the traitor you're looking for.'

Heron raised her eyes and look directly at him. At that moment he knew that she was speaking the truth. He had never seriously considered Heron as the culprit. True she was still on the list but only because of a lack of evidence to prove her innocence.

'Christ's sake, Heron! Why?'

Then all the bitterness behind her action came out. Heron stood up, walked briskly towards the entrance where she first kicked and then thumped hard a few times on the great metal door causing its runners to vibrate in their tracks and a couple of booming reverberations to sound across the void under the hanger's roof. She turned, walked back slowly and regaining something like normal breathing stood in front of Mike for a few seconds before giving the explanation.

'Because, Mike, I hated that viscous, fucking bastard Buckhurst. I wanted her dead. I let the Mercian's know where you were going to be, what you were doing and more to the point the fact that you were carrying a gun. I knew they'd be there and I knew Buckhurst couldn't leave such an opportunity to some junior officer. I picked up their unit on the main road and stalked them until they set up their trap. I was hidden a little distance from their ambush point so that I could assassinate her and escape undetected. Unfortunately

Buckhurst positioned herself so that I wouldn't have been able to hit her without also injuring or killing Anna. But you were in a perfect position. You got your shot in and the gun fell out of her hand. But as she fell I was able to shoot her. Through the head. I killed Buckhurst. After that I knew you were better off following our contingency plan so I didn't intervene. But I saw it all.'

'But, Heron. We all disliked the Mercians. Many of us may well have hated Buckhurst in particular but we would never have jeopardised ESA just to get back at her. Why was your anger and hatred so much greater than ours?'

Heron turned, took a couple of slow steps and sat down in the chair.

'Haven't you guessed, Mike? You're the investigative journalist here and I know Carlos told you about Kassim's story. Didn't you realise that it was my mother who was killed by the army when they forced her car off a bridge; that I was twelve and badly injured? No, it wasn't Buckhurst's fault that I grew up without a mother and missed half a year of schooling. She just took on the mantle of the killer. She became the focus of my hate. You can't hate a whole army, not even a division of that force but I assure you, Mike, you can easily hate one person.'

In Mike's mind it all fell into place.

'You're Kassim's daughter!'

'Yes, Mike. I'm Jane Wood. I'm Kassim Wood's daughter.

There was nothing more to say. He got up and looked at Heron uncharacteristically slumped in her chair, head down, apparently exhausted.

'Do you hate me, Mike?' she whispered without looking up.

'No, Heron. I should but the time for hate has passed.'

'I'm sorry,' she said, briefly raising her eyes to look at him.

He nodded, walked over, touched her lightly on the shoulder, turned and left the building through the door by which he had entered then turned left along side the hanger wall. There were still unanswered questions swimming around in his mind regarding Heron's work with ESA. There may have been a greater purpose in arming a few of her ESA colleagues, there may have been a plan for armed resistance but all of that was of little importance now. He doubted that Heron had planned to set up resistance to the authorities and fight until the last man fell and he preferred to believe Cassie's explanation for the firearms training. Mike would have liked to ask her why Kassim had never publicly acknowledged their relationship but that was a minor detail now the main question had been answered. As he turned away from the building and started walking alongside the plantation he was startled by a noise, a sharp crack that he guessed could have been a gun shot. A large flock of crows that had been strutting on the grass runway took noisily to the air and wheeled around before finding a roosting place in a clump of trees nearby. Then the silence returned. Mike was tempted to turn back to the barn but the shot may have been, after all, just the airstrip owner clearing the birds away for an expected incoming aircraft. With his final chapter now complete he continued walking down the path, back to where his car had been parked.

EPILOGUE
JULY 2224

The New Times
Wednesday 7th July 2224
Film adaptation of The Outlaw.

*It was announced yesterday that the American media group
Metro Universal has purchased the film rights to the best
selling book* The Outlaw. *Mike Cannon's record of his time
spent with the East Suffolk Association during the Martial
Law period is to be made into a cinema film with an
expected release date of spring 2225.*

*Midland Publishing's Rupert Church said that he was
satisfied that Metro Universal's screenplay would remain true
to the original narrative although there would inevitably be
some simplification of the book's complex storyline. The film
will present the story as a series of flashbacks by the author
as he is preparing his manuscript. It is expected that the
film will be shot mainly in East Suffolk with exact locations
being used where possible although it is likely that scenes
representing areas away from Suffolk will not be afforded
the same authenticity.*

*The lead parts of Mike Cannon and Alana Buckhurst
are to be played by Miles Hillingdon, recently seen in the
box-office hit* Cause and Effect 3, *and Hollie Royal from the*

TV series Elizabeth the Second. *The part of Cassie Vale will be taken by the previously unknown Rathina Redbridge.*

Mr Cannon himself has turned down the offer to act as a consultant on the production and also the opportunity to take on a cameo rôle as his own father. Half of the fees Mr Cannon receives from the film adaptation will be donated to The East Anglian Coast Protection Fund and to the establishment of a Young Journalist's Bursary.

The Daily Record
Wednesday 7th July 2224
Martial Law Memorabilia

A new exhibition was opened yesterday in the Martial Law room at the Dunwich Coast Heritage Centre. The ceremony was attended by Karene Chalfont, the Minister for Coasts and best selling author Mike Cannon. **The Record** *is proud to have been a contributor to the fund set up to establish this record of an important time in our nation's history.*

'The cheek of it!' exclaimed Anna, turning her notepad so that James could see the article. 'They are at it again. Making out they were a major player after the event. As far as I can remember their Register Foundation made a minimal donation and they didn't even take up the invitation to attend the event.'

The Six Parishes Magazine
July 2224
Churches' Register for June

Funerals

Tuesday June 8 Spencer Newbury, 94 at Wellingore
Friday June 11 Miles House, 77 at Coleby
Thursday June 17 Bethany Stamford, 54 at Welbourn
Tuesday June 22 Galicia Brompton, 22 at Coleby